The
Freeholder

The Freeholder

By Joe David Brown

WILLIAM MORROW AND COMPANY, NEW YORK

FOR

FRANCES

WHO KEPT

DAVID AND TEDD

QUIET

THE WAIF FROM

YARMOUTH GAOL

CHAPTER I

IN THE year of our Lord 1800, there were some grateful souls in Yarmouth who accounted Dr. Percolus Phillips as near sainthood as the godless times and the practice of medicine would allow. Perhaps they were right. However, since mostly they were the ragged, hunger- and disease-haunted flotsam from the docks and quays of stinking Yarmouth harbor, with ne'er a shilling to pay an honest doctor, their opinions weren't important.

The really substantial element of Yarmouth considered Dr. Phillips a fool—no, even more than that—a dangerous fool. And more than one purple-faced shipowner or prosperous merchant had been heard to say that the doctor was a rank anarchist for teaching the scum of the waterfront that they, as well as the gentry, had livers, gizzards, and bowels. Such knowledge, these gentlemen muttered, was bound to cause dissension in an England where every man was expected to do his duty.

Ordinarily, Dr. Phillips dismissed such criticism with a wave of his big hand or a shrug of his bony shoulders. But there were times, for he was human, when his bones ached and his feet dragged after a day of ministering to his seldom-bathing, never-paying patients, and he wondered seriously if he shouldn't limit his practice to persons with more money and fewer ailments.

Tonight was such a time. While other doctors were snug at home having a quiet glass of Madeira, or discussing Admiral Nelson's latest exploits over a mug of bitters at the inn of the Blue Dragoon, Dr. Phillips was plodding his weary way toward Yar-

mouth gaol. A chilling March wind was blustering in from the
sea. Every strong blast brought an emphatic, sometimes profane,
exclamation from the good doctor. He was a tall, skinny man, with
big bony hands and feet. He had a loose-jointed, loping stride, and
because he was trying to snuggle deeper into his cloak against the
wind, his customary stoop was almost a crouch. His age was hard
to determine. He had the blond, almost gingery coloring that seems
to embrace age early, but then, like a maiden after an unpleasant
experience, decides to live out life in unapproachable serenity. His
features were large and his nose slightly uptilted. It was now quite
red from the wind. The doctor paused a moment and, drawing a
cotton handkerchief, blew his nose vigorously.

"Damme," he said, standing with one shoulder hunched against
the wind, "I'll have the wheezes for a fortnight." He wiped his nose
carefully, sighed deeply, and hurried on.

A scant half-hour before, the doctor had been preparing to sit
down to his supper of hot mutton and porter when the call to
Yarmouth gaol had come. It was brought by the son of the chief
gaoler, a runny-nosed, stammering lout, who could tell nothing
except that one of the women prisoners was preparing to deliver
a child.

Dr. Phillips' first impulse was to ignore the call. Twenty years of
practicing medicine had taught him, among other things, that
while a physician could sometimes turn the course of death or
disease, he could really do nothing at most births except watch and
look wise. However, because he was a good man and because he
knew that while death was commonplace in Yarmouth gaol, birth
was fairly rare—and could be more frightening to the gaolers—
he bolted his supper and went.

Now, like all men of charity, he was cursing his own weakness
rather than the call which had turned him out on such a night. And
by the time he had taken the last turning and saw Yarmouth gaol
looming up at him in the darkness, he was glad he had come. He
crossed the stone-laid courtyard quickly, produced his handkerchief, and gave his nose another lusty honk, and kicked impatiently
at the iron-bound gaol door.

He didn't have long to wait. There was the sound of a heavy
bolt being thrown, and in the flickering light of a horn lantern, he
saw that Chief Gaoler John Sykes himself had opened the door

for him. When Sykes saw the doctor, his fat face split into a grin. "Lor', Hi'm glad it's ye so soon, yer honor!"

Dr. Phillips stepped in. "I came as quickly as I could."

Sykes beamed. "An' it's a Christian gentleman ye are, yer honor. It's a foul night, an' that's strite, an' it's goodness and mercy wot ye got in yer soul, yer honor." He was a short, hairy man with an enormous paunch, a pig-brute of a man, with narrow reddish eyes and heavy jowls. He looked like a cruel man. He was. But it was a stupid cruelty. He could lay on the lash or hang a man, but left to himself, he never would have thought of either of these things. Chief Gaoler Sykes did as he was told. If he was king among the helpless souls thrown in his stone and iron castle, he was an ingratiating bootlicker to anyone above the rank of assistant gaoler.

He clanged shut the prison door and shot the bolt. When he turned, his voice was troubled. "It's a birth wot we're havin', yer honor. One of the prisoners is givin' birth to a child—she's a woman."

Dr. Phillips slung off his heavy cloak and grunted. "A bit odd, I suppose."

Such subtlety was wasted on Sykes. "That it is, yer honor. She was tooken with the cramps this noon, an' she's bin wytin' till now." He showed his yellow teeth in a grin. "She ain't makin' much progress as Hi can see, an' the Lor' loves me as the father of five."

Dr. Phillips waved his hand impatiently. "Well, let's see this woman."

"Aye, yer honor. Right this way, yer honor." Sykes turned and, holding his lantern high, waddled off down the stone corridor. The doctor had followed him only a short distance, his nose still wrinkling to the sour stench of the prison, when somewhere in the interior of the gloomy building he heard the faint mewling of a newborn baby.

Dr. Phillips sighed and then grinned good-naturedly. He thought of his half-chewed supper and the chilly walk and how it had all been a waste of time.

Sykes heard the sound too. He paused and looked back apologetically. "Hi'm sorry, yer honor. It's a fack Hi didn't have no way of knowin'."

The doctor waved aside the protest. "It makes no difference, man. I'm here now—so go ahead. Go ahead!" The child's cries sounded strangely muffled, and he wondered if some stupid gaoler had placed it on its face.

The doctor was at Sykes' heels when they reached a cell at the far end of the corridor. He brushed the gaoler aside and entered first. It was a small cell and completely bare of furnishing. A tallow candle end was making a faint yellowish glow in one corner. In another corner there was a pile of straw. The muffled cries were coming from that direction. Two brutish, hulking assistant gaolers were standing in the center of the cell, staring stupidly. Dr. Phillips hesitated only a moment. He crossed to the straw pallet and leaned over.

The first things he saw were the dark, pleading eyes of the pale-faced girl who lay there biting her lips in agony. She was small-boned and frail, almost child-like. He gave her an encouraging smile and reached for the child. Then he recoiled from surprise. There was no child on the straw bed. The birth cry was coming from the body of the mother. The child was still unborn. It was crying in its mother's womb.

Because he was a good doctor, Percolus Phillips gave his amazement free rein for only a moment. He opened the bag he carried, praying that he would find the weird French instrument he needed. His hand closed on it in satisfaction. He turned to one of the wide-eyed assistant gaolers. "Here—you, man—get me water! Quickly!" he snapped as the man hesitated.

"You!—" he pointed to Gaoler Sykes—"bring that lantern closer and roll up your sleeves and do as I tell you." Sykes approached slack-jawed with surprise, and stared stupidly.

For a moment the doctor had forgotten the mother. He turned to her and his voice was low and gentle. "Now, m'dear, we're going to need all your help. You must do as I tell you. Do you understand?" The woman's eyes were fixed on his face. Her teeth remained clenched in her lips, but Dr. Phillips thought he saw a shadow of understanding cross her face. "That's right, m'dear," he said. He put a big hand soothingly on her cold face and brushed back a strand of matted hair.

In after years, Dr. Phillips was to tell his colleagues of that delivery many times. He could remember—or he thought he did—

every detail. Perhaps he did. If so, he was an amazing man. For he worked swiftly, his hands grasping and pulling brutally at times, gently and tenderly at others. The muffled cries of the child goaded him, forced him to work frantically. In fact, that screaming, slippery red mite was his sole thought.

Somehow the frail body of the woman meant nothing. She was only a vessel. She was there, but she was forgotten. If she had screamed or moaned or writhed, perhaps it would have been different. Perhaps she would have been uppermost in the doctor's mind. But she lay passive with pain. She accepted her fate. Not the child. He—for soon it was apparent that it was a male—not only screamed for life, he fought for life. He demanded life. And he won.

Miraculously, it was all over. The child lay at his mother's side, his breathing as strong and regular as hers was weak and labored. From time to time she moaned softly, but the strain was gone from her face.

Dr. Phillips felt her cold forehead. "He's a fine son, isn't he?" he asked kindly.

Her childish face pinched into a weak smile. "Oh, 'e's a dandy —a reg'lar dandy."

"What is your name, m'dear?" Dr. Phillips asked.

"Tench, sir," she said. "Maud Tench."

"And the boy's father?"

" 'Is father wos a sailor, sir. 'Is father wos a sailor with Lud Nelson. Oh, 'is father wos a reg'lar 'ero, sir." Her breath was growing shallow.

Dr. Phillips smiled. "And did his father have flaming hair like this?" He gently ran his fingertips over the bright orange down that covered the infant's head.

The girl's eyes were bewildered. "Hi—Hi couldn't sye fer certain, sir."

Sykes' laugh was as loud as an iron-wheeled dray passing over cobblestones. "Haw! Haw! Aye, Hi guess the blighter didn't tyke off 'is 'at!"

Dr. Phillips looked up sternly. The laughter gurgled away as Sykes lowered his eyes.

The girl didn't seem to have heard. Again her wan features pinched into a smile. "Hi don't know 'oo 'e wos, sir—but Hi knew

'e wos a sailor with Lud Nelson becos all us girls didn't have t'do
with no others when 'is Ludship's fleet wos in."

Dr Phillips nodded. He had seen so many Maud Tenches that
he could almost have told her story: spawn of the docks, serving
girl at eleven, prostitute or near-about at fourteen. He didn't
know why she was in prison, but probably for theft—in prison
for stealing when her condition forced her to stop her regular
trade.

As Dr. Phillips stood watching her, he didn't need his physician's
eye to see that she was dying. She had lost too much blood. Her
breath was coming in gasps. Even a healthy woman would have
had difficulty in withstanding her ordeal. Her frail body, weakened
by a diet of prison slops, was exhausted. Death was near and the
defenses were down.

Suddenly, her breath stopped, flickered, and then started again
—slowly. Dr. Phillips began to chafe her cold hands and arms.
Maud Tench opened her eyes slowly. "Thank ye, sir." A long moment, then: "Can—can Hi nime my . . . my son, sir?"

"Certainly," Dr. Phillips said.

"Hi want to call 'im 'Oratio—after 'Oratio Nelson, the grand
'ero, sir."

Dr. Phillips nodded. "It shall be, m'dear. His name shall be
Horatio Tench."

Maud Tench lay quietly a moment, then gave a sudden panic-
stricken start. She opened her eyes wide and stared about her in
terror. Her glance fastened on the bars of the cell. She shrank back.
"Will . . . will my baby be free?" she gasped.

"Yes, m'dear," said Dr. Phillips. "Your baby will be free."

Maud Tench relaxed with a deep sigh. Her bloodless lips
stretched in a smile. She died.

For a long minute there was silence in the cell, broken only by
the spluttering of the tallow candle. Percolus Phillips sighed and
straightened up. "She's dead," he said.

Gaoler Sykes let his heavy face sag. "God rest 'er soul," he said
piously.

Dr. Phillips placed Maud Tench's hands across her breast and
closed her wide eyes with his forefinger. He lifted the baby from
the pallet. "Now it's you we have to worry about, eh, m'lad?" The
infant brought his small arms up jerkily and yawned. Then feeling

the warmth of Dr. Phillips' body, he puckered his lips and began a smacking, sucking sound.

The doctor smiled. "Eh? It's food you want—and so soon. You fought a hard battle and now you want to eat?"

The infant made a low, grunting sound.

" 'pon m'word, I almost believe you know what I mean," said Dr. Phillips. He turned to Sykes. "Do you have a woman prisoner who can . . . ?"

Gaoler Sykes shook his head quickly. "No, yer honor, we ain't." Now that the frightening crisis had passed, Sykes was anxious to get the corpse of Maud Tench in a sailcloth and the baby in the nearby Waifs' Home and forget them both. "We ain't had no woman wot could serve in such matters in months, yer honor."

One of the assistant gaolers cleared his throat. "Wot about the barmy 'un?" he asked.

Sykes turned on his assistant with ruffled dignity. "Yer barmy yerself. That wild woman'd eat this tyke 'fore mornin'."

"What is this?" asked Dr. Phillips.

Sykes shot his assistant a dirty look and turned to the doctor. "It's a wild woman wot we've got, yer honor. She's a black woman wot the ship *Annie* brung in from the coast of Africa." He tapped his head knowingly and smirked at the doctor. "Captain Fletcher, a fine man, yer honor, as a personal favor was bringin' back a few slaves fer some noble friends of 'is."

Dr. Phillips let this lie pass. He knew, even though the Court of King's Bench had outlawed slavery, that an occasional slave ship still docked at Yarmouth. "Does this woman have a baby?" he asked.

Goaler Sykes shook his head. "No, yer honor. She gave birth to an infant whilst the ship wos still three days off shore. An' she flung it overboard, yer honor. Aye, she throwed 'er own child over the side."

"But why?" asked Dr. Phillips.

"She's a Coromantee, yer honor. She's a barmy 'un. She's wild."

Dr. Phillips looked at Sykes while his mind tried to separate the truth from the lies. The child in his arms grunted again and began smacking his lips.

"Where is this woman?" Dr .Phillips asked.

"She's below in the dungeon, yer honor." Sykes shuffled his feet uneasily. "We have to keep 'er chained fer fear she'll do murder in 'er dangerous state."

"I'll see her," said Dr. Phillips.

"Aye, yer honor," Sykes said. He gave his assistant another dirty look. "Aye, foller me."

Still holding Maud Tench's son in his arms, Dr. Phillips followed Sykes through a series of dank stone corridors. Each one seemed more depressing and stinking than the one before. Occasionally the doctor caught a glimpse of a pale face and wild eyes as one of the prisoners came whimpering or cursing to the door of a cell. Once a gaunt, mad creature spat at them. Sykes laughed while the doctor drew back, moved with disgust and pity. Dr. Phillips had no idea that Yarmouth gaol extended so deeply into the earth, or that sections of it could be so foul. He held the infant close and tried to stay in the circle of light cast by the horn lantern held by the waddling Sykes.

Finally, at the very end of that maze of foul corridors, Sykes paused before a heavy iron door. "Be on yer guard, yer honor," he whispered.

The doctor nodded.

The door swung inward with a screaming of hinges. Almost instantly Dr. Phillips heard the rattling of chains and a frightened whimper. The stench from the cell struck him with the force of a wave of heat. Although the practice of medicine had given him a stomach of iron, he felt sick. Instinctively, he placed his hand over the face of the child. Sykes seemed to be immune to the odor. He stepped into the cell and the whimpering became louder. Dr. Phillips followed, prepared to see some fearful apparition which would make his blood run cold. Instead he gasped. In the yellowish light a huge black woman was squatting on her heels. She was entirely naked and her body was strong and well-proportioned. She was fastened to one wall by heavy iron chains which encircled both wrists and one leg. When Dr. Phillips' shadow fell in the circle of light, the woman cowered closer to the floor. Her eyes were turned so far upward that only the whites showed.

"Why, this woman is frightened half to death," Dr. Phillips said.

Sykes swung the lantern uneasily. "She's a tricky 'un, yer honor. Don't get close."

The doctor snorted. "Nonsense." He stepped closer to the

woman and kept his voice low. "We're your friends," he said kindly. "Friends. Friends to you." He put out one hand slowly, holding the infant with the other, and placed it on the woman's bare shoulders. She shrank back and began moaning and swaying from side to side in an ecstasy of fright.

Dr. Phillips turned to Sykes. "Take those chains off."

Sykes licked his thick lips. "Now, yer honor . . ."

"Take them off!"

Sykes seemed about to protest again, but after a fearful glance at the doctor, he placed his lantern on the stone floor and fumbled for a ring of keys at his wrist. Finally he found one and, holding it at arm's length and after much nervous groping, he managed to unlock the chains. The woman didn't seem to notice when the chains clattered to the floor. When Dr. Phillips began to inspect her galled wrists, she fell back against the wall and trembled.

Dr. Phillips saw, with some surprise, that her body was clean. The odor in the cell seemed to come from a mass of rotten, foul straw which littered the floor. He saw that the woman's breasts were large and pendulous and virtually bursting with milk.

When he turned to Gaoler Sykes, his voice was cold. "I want this wretched woman removed from this hole!"

Sykes gulped. "Aye, yer honor."

"And I want you to feed her well. D'you hear, man?"

"Aye, yer honor."

Dr. Phillips motioned impatiently. "Well? Go get those louts of yours and fix up a clean cell. I want to inspect it before I leave. When it's ready, come back and tell me."

"Aye, yer honor."

Dr. Phillips turned to the woman again, but when he saw that Sykes was lingering, he looked up sharply. "Well?"

Sykes stammered. "The light, yer honor . . . it's the only . . ."

"Go without a light!" Dr. Phillips roared. "You can find your way!"

Sykes licked his lips. "Aye, yer honor." He fled.

Dr. Phillips sat down opposite the woman and began to speak soothingly. His words were without meaning, but he kept them soft until the woman stopped trembling. After a few minutes she looked at him, and though she still shrank back against the wall, her eyes were now watchful. Gently Dr. Phillips placed Maud Tench's infant at her feet. At first she didn't look at the bundle, but suddenly the child gave a whimper and began his sucking insistence for food.

The woman froze to attention. Dr. Phillips held his breath while she put out one hand. She stared wide-eyed at the baby and then looked back to Dr. Phillips. He smiled and motioned to the child and made soothing sounds. With a sudden movement that frightened the doctor, the woman grabbed the child and pulled him to her breast.

When Gaoler Sykes returned to the cell fifteen minutes later, the black woman was squatting in the center of the cell, swaying gently from side to side and crooning. And Horatio Tench was having his first meal on this earth.

It was early morning before Dr. Percolus Phillips returned to his home. The woman and the child were in a clean, straw-filled cell. As he sat down for a snack of cheese and ale, the doctor wondered briefly what would be the destiny of a child born in prison and suckled by a black savage. But then, because he was a weary man and a busy one, Dr. Phillips soon put the matter out of his mind.

CHAPTER II

HORATIO TENCH knew nothing of his birth. His earliest memories were of the bare walls and battered furnishings in Yarmouth's bleak Waifs' Home. He never knew that he was born in a prison cell or that he stole his mother's life for his own. Neither did he know that he fed at the breast of a black woman until he was four months old and that she screamed and fought when they wrested him away.

But Horatio Tench knew other things. He knew how the dawn mist from the moors could cling like spider webs and leave a taste of ashes on your lips. He knew how to clean a herring with one deft slash of a sharp blade. And he knew how to repair rotted fishing nets, working swiftly until the coarse, salty strands left his tiny hands a mass of blisters and ulcerating pain. Horatio knew how to do a dozen menial tasks by the time he could walk steadily. For he was an orphan and orphans had to work to earn their gruel and tea.

He knew other things, too—things that weren't taught; things that were distilled from the shrewdness of his nature. He knew how to wheedle an extra slice of bread with ingratiating good humor when he was hungry. He learned to work cheerfully and quickly so the overseers would notice such a good lad and give him easier tasks, or maybe that rarest reward of all for an orphan—a kindly smile.

But most of all, red-haired Horatio knew his strength. For as long as he could remember, he towered over his fellows. His legs were straight and sturdy, his back broad, and his hips slim. He had none of the chubbiness of childhood. When he stretched his powerful little frame, unborn muscles shadowed his calves and thighs and arms. Unlike some orphans, Horatio was never beaten. He never went hungry. On the other hand, neither did he know the feel of a tender caress nor had he ever been allowed to eat all he could. He had never heard music nor had he seen a picture. He didn't know beauty. He failed to recognize ugliness.

In all, he was a good child. He learned his lessons and by the time he was seven he could read and write after a fashion. But he didn't thirst for knowledge nor was he a blockhead. His disposition was even because of instinct rather than self-control. There was no real cruelty in his nature nor bitterness. But he did have a capacity for anger that was awesome. It lay deep within him, black and sluggish. It was difficult to tap but impossible to dam. His anger was not thunder and lightning. It was hissing, consuming lava from a volcano which, once erupted, left him helpless and powerless.

Horatio showed this anger for the first time when he was seven. Those who saw it never forgot.

Somehow, in a manner known only to boys, he acquired a tiny basket carved from a cherry stone. It was an inconsequential trifle, scarcely worth a ha'penny. But because it was his sole possession, and just owning it answered some need, Horatio valued it more than any Indian potentate cherished his jewels. He fastened the basket to a worn fishline and wore it around his neck as a pendant. He slept with it under his hard pillow at night. When he awakened, it was the first thing he reached for. When he had time, he would slip it from under his yellow, faded workhouse smock and finger it lovingly. It was more than a toy. It was the first thing he had ever had which was completely his own.

One cold, midwinter afternoon, the fishermen of Yarmouth sent bait nets up to the Waifs' Home to be repaired. The job was too big for the fifteen orphans so the town's charity boys came along to help. There were eight of them, stumbling, clumsy, half-grown brats. One was Sid Purvis, a weasel-faced, shifty-eyed son of an impoverished tailor. He was fourteen and large for his age, with the heavy paws of a mastiff and a sneering laugh.

He sat next to Horatio with a portion of the fine mesh net in his lap, but his hands dawdled over his work. Occasionally he would stop altogether and smirk knowingly in the direction of the overseer, a palsied old fisherman named Bains. "Coo! 'E can't see the end of 'is nose. Hi tyke me time."

Horatio instinctively disliked this leering fellow, but he had a small boy's natural awe of someone older than himself, so he smiled and tried to be agreeable. Purvis was too much of a bully to miss this opportunity. Before the day was over, he was driving Horatio in his best imitation of a first mate. "Belay that!" he shouted, or " 'Urry up, ye snotty-nosed bilge scum. Tauten it hup, Hi sye. Tauten it hup!"

Since it was the older boy's game, Horatio played it, but he was glad when darkness put an end to their work.

It wasn't until he prepared for bed that Horatio discovered his cherry stone basket was missing. For a moment he stood with his hands to his throat in stunned incredulity. Then he shouted and his voice was tinged with a sob. "Me baskit! Me baskit! I've lost me baskit!"

The other pinch-faced little orphans came running. They were as stunned as Horatio. Just knowing that one of them had owned something had pleased them. They raised their voices in a frenzy of suggestions: "Look in yer bed." "Did ye shyke yer clothes?" "Myebe it's on the floor." They helped him shake the hard, narrow bed. They got down on their hands and searched the floor. But finally even the most persistent went away and left Horatio empty-handed and empty-hearted.

That night he lay on his bed for hours, staring into the darkness. It was the first time he ever prayed with fervor, the first time that a prayer meant more than a memorized lesson. Like all people who had prayed before or since, his prayer was movingly intense because he wanted something. After a long time he fell asleep.

He was up in the harsh dawn. After slipping on his smock, he again searched everywhere for his treasure. He marched into the drafty dietary with feet as heavy as his heart and ate his watery porridge. At morning prayers his lips moved in the parroted responses, but his heart said over and over again: " 'Elp me find me baskit! 'Elp me find me baskit!"

When the orphans marched out into the misty morning, close to the moors where the nets were stretched, the charity boys already were there. Horatio took his place next to Sid Purvis. He glanced up and his heart leaped for joy. There was his basket, around Sid Purvis' scrawny neck. There was a knot in the string, and Horatio knew it must have broken and fallen to the ground where Sid found it.

Instinctively Horatio put out his hand. His face was flushed with a smile. "Ye found me baskit," he said. "Ye found me baskit!" The other orphans heard and they crowded around, smiling delightedly. Old Bains, the overseer, was fifty yards away unrolling a new supply of nets.

Sid Purvis looked at the smiling faces and raised his eyebrows in mock surprise. He pushed aside Horatio's outstretched hand. "Wot baskit, ye ratty scum?"

The smiles flickered out. The color drained from Horatio's face. "The baskit ye have 'round yer neck. It belongs to me. I lost it yesterday."

Sid Purvis sneered. "Now, Hi sye, ain't that a one, though?—" mimickingly—" 'Me baskit. Hi lost it. Hi lost it!' " He twisted his evil sharp little features into a scowl. "Look 'ere, me bucko, wot a man finds, 'e keeps. That's the lor. Hi ain't syin' ye lost this and Hi ain't syin' ye didn't. Wot Hi'm syin' is seein' as 'ow Hi got it, Hi'm goin' ter keep it, or me nime ain't Sid."

Horatio's face was white. He was choked with anger and he could feel the blood pounding in his throat and temples. He took two short, stiff-legged steps toward Sid. His voice was cold. "I want me baskit!"

Sid Purvis looked down at the lad, a good head shorter than himself. He tightened his lips and darted his small eyes around. Then a look of craftiness replaced his scowl. "G'wan!" he said. He pushed Horatio in the chest and sent him sprawling.

For a moment Horatio lay on the ground. The surprised gasps of the other orphans sounded far away. He could feel a coldness sweep his body, and he began trembling. He got to his feet slowly, deliberately. He even brushed the damp soil from his hands. His face was set and white. There was an oaken splicing pin on the edge of the net where he had worked the day before. It was a murderous weapon, heavy and worn to the hardness of stone. He picked it up and, charging forward, aimed it with all his strength at Sid Purvis' sneering face.

There was the sickening, solid sound of heavy wood meeting flesh. Sid Purvis fell as if struck by lightning. Luckily, he had ducked just as the pin struck him in the center of the forehead. It probably saved his life. As it was, the pin had dealt him a numbing, stunning blow which left him half-conscious.

He looked up bleary-eyed, just in time to see Horatio moving forward again, stiff-legged, white-faced, the pin held high. Sid Purvis threw up his hands in a protective gesture and tried to find his voice. *Smack!* The pin descended across both his wrists with such force that his arms were numbed from elbow to fingertips. Sid screamed and scrabbled blindly to regain his feet. He was too late. Horatio held the pin poised and took deliberate aim. Sid saw the blow coming and managed to scream again. Then the pin crashed downward on the top of his head. He remembered no more.

But his wild scream had saved his life. Old Bains had heard it and came running. He had stood frozen with shock while Horatio had knocked Sid unconscious. Luckily, he recovered in time to catch Horatio's upraised hand as he aimed another blow at Sid's unprotected head.

"Belay, lad," Old Bains said. "Belay that pin!" His voice was trembling. He had seen a hundred bloody waterfront brawls but nothing to rival this red-haired, white-faced youngster's display of cold violence. Horatio's childish face was contorted into the fury of a grown man, his lips compressed into a thin, cruel line. His eyes, ringed with a child's curling lashes, were set and flecked with red.

Old Bains looked at the circle of numbed, frightened faces about him, at the unconscious Sid on the ground, and then back to Horatio. His voice was ragged. "Ye might 'ave kilt 'im, lad," he said, breathlessly.

Horatio looked up. His lips curled. His body was still stiff with fury. "I meant to kill 'im," he said. "I meant to smash 'is 'ead in the ground. 'E stole me baskit."

There was no remorse in his voice. And he was deadly calm, the only calm one in the crowd. Before old Bains could put out a restraining hand, he stepped forward and straddled the prostrate body of Sid Purvis. He flipped him over roughly and found the tiny carved basket dangling from his neck. With a vicious yank

Horatio broke the string, and calmly, with sure fingers, retied it and slipped it around his own neck. Then, still straddling the unconscious Sid, he raised his head for one proud, triumphant moment and looked at the horrified faces around him. His voice was coldly challenging. "Nobody takes nothing that b'longs t'me." Then he turned to the nets and, seemingly oblivious to the crowd's fascinated stare, he began to work where he had left off the day before, deftly, swiftly.

He didn't even look up when old Bains revived Sid Purvis five minutes later and sent him home sniveling. He showed the same unconcern that night when Mrs. Basset, the matron of the Waifs' Home, made him copy a latin verb one hundred times as punishment. That was his only punishment. Mrs. Basset was the daughter of one departed vicar and the widow of another. Her circumspect background, coupled with a complete bewilderment, had left her wholly incapable of imagining violence. She had always found Horatio a good lad and she thought old Bains' account of the incident was merely an old man's distortion of a childish brawl. And, mercy knows, Mrs. Basset often said, it was enough to fair make your blood run cold to watch two lads run screeching at each other.

Only those who had seen Horatio's anger never forgot it. From that day on, he was a marked man among his fellows. His cowardly playmates rushed to please him, the timid left him alone, and the bold paid him respect.

Old Bains never forgot the cold, murderous look on Horatio's face. Once he remarked that such a lad was destined to become either a hero or bait for the gallows. Since he was a simple man, it never occurred to him that a man could be both.

As for Horatio, he was not aware that he stood apart. For all his violent entrance into the world, for all the force inside him, he could as profitably have delayed his birth for ten years. The first ten years of his life were lost. He was never to recall consciously any of the thousands of drab memories he stored up in the years he lived in the Waifs' Home. They were buried deeply in his mind. There they stayed, coming to the surface only occasionally, always unbidden. Whenever he heard the boom of a cannon, he remembered how a small boy in a thin nightshirt sat on the edge of his bed and shivered while the guns of Yarmouth fired a victory salute over the Corsican Bonaparte. Sometimes when he saw gulls wheel screechingly in the sky, he remembered how a flame-haired lad stood on the edge of the moors and watched thunderheads roll in from the sea. There were a thousand sounds and smells that sent fragments of memories rushing through his mind: the scrape of feet against a wooden floor; the sour, heavy stench of wood smoke on a rainy day. But they were all colorless, commonplace memories.

He was ten before he was born into a world that was neither drab nor colorless. For then he was adopted by Samuel Tompkins, the one-legged ropemaker. Forever after he could not smell new rope without a shiver.

CHAPTER III

IT WAS no charitable impulse that led Samuel Tompkins to adopt an orphan. He had no measure of sentiment in his heart or soul. He was a short, powerful man, a bull of a man, with an enormous neck and a square, brutal face. His eyes were as hard and as lusterless as the pewter buttons on a navy jacket. But it was his hands that set him apart and told people of his strength. They were square and sinewy and gloved with thick calluses—hard as stone. They could twist the toughest fiber of hemp. Or they could batter a man's face and break his neck. They had done all these things, and God only knows what else.

During his youth, Tompkins had been a gay, roistering sailor. He could climb to the top of the highest mast or hold up his end in a catch-as-catch-can brawl in any waterfront dive from Mandalay to Suez. But it was as a gunner that he excelled. He had a feel for the roll of a frigate, a sort of delicate balance that anticipated rather than followed the rhythmic sway of a deck. He could brace his stout legs, absorb that motion, narrow his eyes, and blast to bits the smallest target in the heaviest seas.

He was a good sailor, and his officers were truly sorry when his right leg was blown half off during the battle of Abukir Bay. It was during the heat of battle. A young ship's surgeon, bloodstained and groggy from overwork, had found Tompkins as he lay on the deck, mad with pain and drenched in his own blood. It took only forty seconds and a dozen strokes of a scalpel to remove Tompkins' leg and, because time was precious, little more than twice that time to suture the severed vessels. That haste changed Samuel Tompkins' nature.

He was returned to England and, after a time, was discharged with honor and a small pension. His leg was a mass of pain, but His Majesty's doctors told him that the pain would go away in a matter of months. They were wrong, or careless. It took five years for that stump to heal—five agonizing years. Samuel Tompkins never knew that the overworked ship's surgeon had left a bone chip in the stump. Tompkins only knew that the leg was the source of a horrible, driving pain which set him trembling with a panting, exquisite torture. It seemed to heal, and then suddenly it would erupt as a foul, suppurating mass, a stinking, horrifying mass which drove him from his companions and, at times, caused him to beat his head against the wall.

Finally he undertook to drown his pain with rum. It had not helped. When sober, his pain made him ill-tempered. He became a raving maniac when drunk, an actual maniac with foam-flecked lips and red-rimmed eyes. No one dared approach him when he was drinking. Apprentices in his ropemaking shop shuddered at the sight of him. Most ran away after a few weeks. Others who were more stupid or more conscientious were half-killed by Tompkins when his torment was on him.

Eventually the ordeal was over. The pain in his stump stopped, miraculously, almost overnight. But Tompkins was never the same. He had learned to love scalding rum. And he had discovered that a man with a hard, quick fist could always have his way. The pain had left, but the madness it brewed had remained.

Horatio was barefooted and carrying a worn, patched pair of boots when Samuel Tompkins called at the Waifs' Home to claim him for a son. The boots and the yellow smock he wore were his only possessions. It was a sharp, drizzly day, and, as Tompkins' cloak was dripping small puddles on her parlor floor, Mrs. Basset made her farewells brief. "Now be a good lad, Horatio, and give satisfaction to your new father," she said.

Horatio nodded. "Aye, mum."

Tompkins, fortified with a pint of rum, laughed loudly. " 'E'll give satisfaction, mum."

The road to town had been washed into a quagmire. Before

he and Horatio had gone halfway, Tompkins was in an ugly, cursing mood. His peg leg kept sinking into the soft mud. A half-dozen times he recovered his balance just in time to keep from pitching forward on his face. Finally, tiring of cursing the road and the weather, he looked down and saw that Horatio was shoeless.

"Why ain't ye wearin' yer boots?" he snarled.

Horatio managed a weak smile. "They don't fit no more, sir. They're too small."

Tompkins stopped short, weaving because of the rum and his unsure footing. "Ye ain't got no boots?"

Horatio looked apologetic. "Only these, sir." He smiled uneasily. "They say I grow too fast to keep me in boots."

Tompkins cursed the Waifs' Home bitterly before scowling at Horatio. "Well, put them boots on. Hi ain't goin' to have a sick brat on me hands."

"They pinch, sir."

Tompkins' face flushed with rage. "Put 'em on, Hi told ye!"

Horatio looked up at the swaying, cursing man. For a moment surprise flickered across his face, then alarm. Then he clenched his teeth tightly and stuck out his bottom lip.

Tompkins' grimace was fiendish. "Ye gonna put them boots on?"

Horatio clenched his teeth tighter and shook his head.

Tompkins' heavy hand shot out so suddenly and so unexpectedly that Horatio didn't have a chance to duck. He stood a startled moment in slack-jawed surprise. Tears welled in his eyes. *Smack!* The hard, quick hand slashed across his face again, with such force this time that Horatio was knocked sprawling on the muddy road. The blow was so crushing that he lay there a moment before he realized where he was. His face was smeared with cold, sticky mire and he could feel the dampness of the road through his thin smock. He turned slowly, half in caution and half because of the pain in his head. He sank back with a gasp. Tompkins stood directly above him, swaying on his good leg. His peg was poised above the small of Horatio's back. Horatio looked into the man's face and for the first time in his life he felt fear. He pressed back against the ground.

"Git up," said Tompkins. His voice was a whisper. "Git up or, by God, Hi'll drive this 'ere peg clean throo ye."

Horatio had no doubt but that Tompkins meant it. He kept his eyes pinned on the man's face while he regained his feet slowly. Without once removing his eyes from Tompkins' face, he fumbled in the thick mud until he found his boots. He sat down slowly and began to put them on. He had fastened one before the spell was broken. Sobs of rage and frustration began to swell his chest. He lowered his head and wept bitterly while he fastened the second boot. Then he clenched his teeth and raised his eyes.

Samuel Tompkins had not moved from the center of the road. He sucked at his teeth and something intended for a smile twisted his thick lips. "Now stan' up," he said, softly, "an' come along like a good lad."

Horatio hobbled across the muddy road in his too tight boots. Samuel Tompkins' hand closed about one of his wrists. "Now we'll go," he said, "an' if Hi ketch ye trying t'limp, Hi'll smash yer head fer ye."

It was twenty minutes later when they turned down a narrow, cobblestoned street hard by the cathedral and reached a doorway marked by a weather-beaten sign: "Sam'l Tompkins—Cordage." Tompkins stood in the entrance, shaking the rain from his cloak and swearing fluently at the weather, before he opened the door and pushed Horatio ahead of him into the dark interior.

Horatio was to know that shop as well as the palm of his hand. He learned every corner and crevice, every loose brick in the huge fireplace that stood against the wall. He discovered every mouse hole, the squeak in every floorboard, every knothole. But he never lost the wonder that filled him the first time he stepped across the threshold. From birth, Horatio had been used to emptiness and bareness. The room he saw now was filled high with rope, huge stacks and coils of rope that spread their sinuous length along each wall. And the smell of these ropes, the acrid, biting smell of fresh fiber and pitch and resin filled the air. That was not all. Intermingled with it was the smell of wood smoke, and the still lingering aroma of basted joints of meat, and the smell of sweat—a heavy odor of toil. It was a good room. It had the dim, half-light of a fo'castle. It reflected good eating and honest toil, and, despite its cluttered look, it was neat. It had the neatness of a taut ship. At first sight, the room seemed to Horatio to be an enchanted place, perhaps because it was so much better than he had expected.

Momentarily, he was glad to be part of such a place. Then he remembered the hated presence of the man behind him and he stiffened and clenched his teeth.

Samuel Tompkins took no notice of Horatio. He flung off his cloak and hung it on a ram's horn near the door and bellowed: "Cheezum! Where are ye, Cheezum!"

Somewhere in the rear of the shop, a high-pitched voice answered "Aye, Aye," and Horatio heard the approach of shuffling footsteps. The events of the day had prepared him for much, but his mouth went dry with fright and he gasped when he saw the creature who was approaching.

At first Horatio thought it was only the torso of a man waddling toward him—the broad-shouldered, long-bodied, heavy-bellied trunk of a man without arms or legs. Then, as this creature moved closer, he saw that he did have arms and legs, but they were short and frail, scarcely larger than his own. The man—for it was a man—stood slightly more than four feet tall. As he walked, he swung his heavy body from side to side, as if to help his frail legs propel his weight. It was several seconds before Horatio summoned up enough courage to look up at the man's face. He was prepared to see some mockery of features. Instead, the head surmounting that half-formed body was well-formed and pleasant. The face might have been handsome if the nose had not been so sharply upturned and so broad at the base. The man's chin was firm with the suggestion of a cleft. His brow was high and wide, and his eyes were dark and deep-set.

He stood facing Horatio Tench and Tompkins before he spoke. His voice was vibrant and soft but slightly shrilled. It was not a child's voice, but neither did it match that powerful body.

"Ah, you're back, and you've brought our new helper," he said.

Samuel Tompkins snorted. "This 'ere is the Tench waif." He turned to Horatio and made a motion toward the misshapen man. "This 'ere is Aber Cheezum, second in command around 'ere. Ye'll do wot 'e tells ye. An' don't go takin' no liberties 'cos 'e's a bloody dwarf."

Aber Cheezum didn't seem to hear Samuel Tompkins. He held out his small hand and smiled. "I'm happy to make your acquaintance, Master Tench." Horatio hesitated, then put out his hand slowly. When he felt Aber Cheezum's warm clasp, he knew instantly that he had found a friend.

Still holding Horatio's hand, Aber stepped back and surveyed him from head to foot. There was a bubble of laughter in his voice. "God bless me," he said, "you're a sight. You fair look as if you swam here."

Horatio looked down at his mud-covered smock and managed a small smile. It died on his lips when Samuel Tompkins growled a short, humorless laugh and slapped a heavy hand on his shoulder. "We 'ad a little trouble gettin' acquainted, but now we understan' each other, don't we, lad?"

Horatio stiffened and his face flushed. He clenched his teeth. Samuel Tompkins tightened his hand. "Don't we, lad?" It was a command.

Aber Cheezum spoke quickly. His voice was light. "Of course. Of course. Don't you, Master Tench?"

Horatio looked at his new friend. Their eyes met, and Cheezum's handclasp grew a little tighter in encouragement. Horatio sighed and his jaw relaxed.

"Aye," he said, very low.

They dined at seven o'clock. When Horatio saw the regular fare in Samuel Tompkins' shop, once again he felt that momentary gladness that he was part of such an establishment. Aber Cheezum was the cook. As he brought pan after pan, dish after dish, to set on a long oaken table in the center of the shop, Horatio's wonder grew. There was a great spitted ham, still cracking and popping in its brown, crisp skin. A Robinson stove near the fireplace gave up a mutton pie, bubbling under a flaky crust, and a cottage loaf, brown and crunchy and smelling as only fresh bread can. A half-dozen potatoes, swollen with their own goodness, were dug out of the ashes in the fireplace and placed around the ham. Aber paused to wipe his streaming forehead and caught Horatio's wonder-struck eyes.

He chuckled. "We have a good galley, Master Tench."

Horatio nodded dumbly. The sight of so much food had started dozens of small geysers in his mouth. He swallowed hard. "It's . . . it's a lot."

Aber Cheezum smiled. "Now we'll see how it tastes." He placed his hand beside his mouth and gave a low, shrill whistle.

Samuel Tompkins grunted an answer from his room in the rear of the shop. He had been there all afternoon, dozing and taking large draughts from a bottle of rum. He had removed his peg and he hopped to the table on his one leg. His shirt was unbuttoned, exposing his hairy chest and belly. At the sight of the full table, his face brightened. He wiped his mouth with the back of his hand and sat down. His lips twisted as he looked at Horatio. "Ye'll eat well 'ere, laddie, but ye'll earn yer keep." Then he fell to.

For a few minutes, Horatio almost forgot his own appetite in fascination at Tompkins' gluttony. The big man ate as if he had been starved for weeks. His fingers tore and fumbled and crammed. No sooner had he poked one tidbit in his mouth than he was reaching for another. The veins began to rise in his neck. His eyes bulged in exertion. His face was purplish. Grease began to trickle down his chin. His gurgles and grunts and chomping reminded Horatio of the pigs at the Waifs' Home.

He ate his own food slowly, savoring every drop of goodness. But a lifetime of eating anemic gruels and porridges had left his taste buds unprepared for such a rich variety. Finally they gave up in bewilderment. Horatio tried to tempt back his appetite with another morsel of crunchy rind from the ham, with a choice bit of mutton from the stew. It was no use. Regretfully he pushed back his plate with a sigh.

Samuel Tompkins saw the gesture. He turned his strained face in amazement. He looked so ludicrous, big mouth bulging with food, eyes distended, and grease dripping from his chin onto his hairy chest, that Horatio smiled in spite of himself. He lowered his eyes. "I've had enough," he said.

Samuel Tompkins took a couple of tentative chews and gulped down the food in his mouth. He belched noisily. " 'Pon me word," he said, and turned to Aber Cheezum to bear witness to this strange performance, "the lad eats like a bloomin' canary." Then he guffawed. "A bloomin' bird, a bloomin' bird. Hah! Myebe Hi got a bargain at that. 'Pon me word, myebe Hi did."

Aber Cheezum seemed to understand. He was smiling, but his eyes were solemn. "Maybe you'd like some lentil soup, Master Tench? I have some left from noon."

Horatio lowered his eyes in embarrassment. He started to refuse, but the mention of soup had started his mouth watering again. "Thank you," he said.

Samuel Tompkins guffawed again. "Soup? Soup! Hah!" He looked at Horatio closely and suspicion replaced his amusement.

"Ye ain't sick, are ye?" he asked sharply. "Ye ain't got no blasted sickness?"

Aber Cheezum returned from the hearth with a steaming mug of thick soup. He spoke quietly. "The lad's got a shipboard appetite. Remember how hard it is to get used to shore cookery after a diet of salt pork and bread?"

Samuel Tompkins looked at Horatio speculatively, then belched again, shrugged his shoulders, and went on stuffing food in his mouth.

Horatio ate the soup slowly. It tasted wonderful. Once he looked up and Aber Cheezum smiled at him. He lowered his eyes, but not before he had smiled back.

Samuel Tompkins ate until his eyes were glazed. He thrust back his chair and filled the room with great rumbling belly belches. He sucked at his teeth, wiped his greasy mouth with the back of his hand, and nodded to Aber. The little man arose and went to the back of the shop. He returned in a few minutes with a pitcher of amber liquid and three mugs. One of these he filled and handed to Samuel Tompkins, who threw off in a gulp and held out his mug to be refilled again.

Aber put a mug before Horatio. "Would you care to try this, Master Tench?"

"What is it?" Horatio asked.

Aber smiled. "Ah, it's mead, Master Tench—the nectar of the gods. It's fine old mead, made with my own two hands and the finest honey England can produce." He filled the mug and handed it to Horatio. "Try it," he said.

Horatio sipped the liquid carefully. It had a bitter, nutty taste. He took another sip and nodded. "I like it."

Aber Cheezum smiled and Samuel Tompkins roared with laughter. " 'E likes it, 'e does. 'Pon my word, 'e likes it."

Horatio drank the mead slowly, rolling it on his tongue. After he had finished his mug, Aber smiled at him. "It's been a wearying day," he said, "and I think you'd best go to bed."

Horatio nodded. He stood up and started to walk away, but hesitated.

"Yes, Master Tench?" Aber asked.

Horatio flushed with embarrassment. "I ain't got a nightshirt," he said.

Samuel Tompkins' eyes widened in disbelief. His bellow of laughter filled the room. " 'E ain't got a nightshift. Hah, hah! 'E ain't got a nightshift. 'Pon me word." The laugh ended in a snarl and he twisted his face into a sneer. "A nightshift. What are ye, a blasted female? A nightshift. Hah!" His little red-rimmed eyes glowered. "Come 'ere. Come 'ere. Hi'll teach ye about nightshifts."

Horatio hesitated and in that instant Aber Cheezum was on his short legs. He came around the table and laid a hand on Horatio's shoulder. He smiled at Samuel Tompkins and his voice was light. "I'll set the lad right. Aye, I'll take care of the lad." Tompkins looked at them with darkened brow, then shrugged and turned to the table and poured himself another mug of mead. Aber nudged Horatio ahead of him toward the rear of the shop.

In the half-darkness of the room they shared, Aber faced Horatio and his voice was soft. "Lad, sometimes rough sailormen forget. Now, let's see what we'll find here." He turned to a heavy wooden chest and, opening it, began to rummage around. "Ah!" he said after a while, "here's the very thing!"

Horatio took the garment Aber handed him and examined it with surprise. It was a man's silk shirt with ruffles and pleats, a beautiful handmade garment. Horatio's mouth was an oval of surprise. "This . . . this is so fine," he said.

Aber Cheezum's voice was soft. "Take it and sleep in it, Master Tench. I'll try to make you comfortable as I can."

CHAPTER IV

ABER CHEEZUM was a man of his word. During the weeks that followed, Horatio felt first gratitude, then deep affection for this grotesque, kindly little man. Aber could not always shield Horatio against Samuel Tompkins' anger. But whenever possible he was there, a calm and soothing buffer against kicks and curses and blows. Only his presence made Horatio's life in the ropewalk bearable. Gradually, because he had a friend to turn to, he began to accept his ill treatment with a stoicism which, by its very coldness, angered Samuel Tompkins all the more.

Had Horatio cringed or begged for mercy, perhaps he would have fared better. Since he did neither, Tompkins, with his natural bullying brutality, set out systematically to break Horatio's spirit. Without warning and for no apparent reason, he would slap Horatio across the face or rap him on the head with his hard knuckles. Sometimes these blows brought tears to Horatio's eyes. But he refused to duck or seek to escape. He would clench his teeth and stand rigid while the infuriated Tompkins rained blows on his unprotected head. Aber watched closely for these outbursts and when they came he was there, a calm, deft figure, speaking quietly. "Now, hold . . . now, hold. We have work to do. Now, hold . . ." Quickly, but without seeming to push, he would plant his short body between Horatio and Tompkins. "Now, now—" soothingly—"I'll find work for the lad to do."

For some reason, this never failed to stop Tompkins. He would step back, chest heaving, red-rimmed eyes glowering, but he never tried to push Aber away. Nor did he ever fail to heed him. Horatio could not understand the relationship between this good-natured dwarf and the hulking, brutish Samuel Tompkins. At first he thought Tompkins was afraid to antagonize such a valued worker. The little man had a prodigious capacity for work. He did all the marketing, all the cooking. He kept Samuel Tompkins' shop in perfect order, and every day he did a man's work at ropemaking. Despite the frailness of his hands, he could twist rope almost as quickly as Tompkins. He had a special marlin spike, and, as he sat cross-legged on the floor wielding it, hemp strands seemed to pop and crackle with life and merge into a continuous coil of rope.

Since Tompkins was unlettered, Aber also did all the bookkeeping and wrote the infrequent letters which were necessary to the business. There was no doubt that Tompkins would have found it difficult—probably impossible—to have replaced the little man had he walked out in anger. Yet even a mind as young as Horatio's could see that mere expediency could never have dammed the flood tide of Tompkins' anger.

One thing was certain: Aber was not afraid of his heavy-handed employer. He was neither surly nor subservient—but always even-tempered and placid. At times this calmness bordered on indifference, particularly when Tompkins bellowed orders. Then the little man's face would become set, without a flicker of emotion. He kept his voice flat, literal. "Aye, aye," he said, or, if the occasion demanded, he said "No" in a voice without embellishments. If Aber felt either affection or dislike for Tompkins, he never showed it. The nearest he came to an expression of feeling was one day after Tompkins had swung out in a drunken rage and struck Horatio across the mouth. Horatio sat with cold eyes while Aber ministered to his cut lip. Finally he patted Horatio on the shoulder. His voice was low. "Sometimes, lad, we have to sail under harsh masters."

Horatio and Aber worked silently while Tompkins was in the shop. But in the evenings, while he caroused in town or lay in a drunken stupor in the rear of the shop, they talked for hours. Since there was always work to be done, they were never idle on these occasions. Sometimes they were busy carding or pulling hemp. At other times they tarred rope. It was years before Horatio realized that it was during these talks that he received all his formal education. Aber, half-humorously, corrected his grammar and his speech. He spoke of ancient times and of foreign lands. He told Horatio of poets and poems, of books and men. Aber seemed to know everything, and, as with everything else, he shared his knowledge with Horatio.

These evening talks were the delight of Horatio's life. He would sit graven-faced, pulling hemp or coiling rope, feeling warm and comfortable while the little man droned on and on.

Aber was from the midlands. "Ah, Master Tench, I was born in Lichfield, the same dirty, warped, mellow, beautiful little Lichfield that sheltered that filthy, sloppy glutton Samuel Johnson." He would pause in his work and his eyes would brighten. "Ah, but he was a genius, Master Tench—a pure genius, the greatest thinker in England. And I—*I*—" he slapped one frail hand against his barrel chest—"this worthless morsel of clay—why, *I* had the pleasure of walking those same streets. I walked the same streets that hulking, nasty—ah, but brilliant—Dr. Sam-u-el Johnson walked." His fine mouth twisted into a wry smile. "And the dogs barked just as loudly at me as they did at him. And the people? Why, bless me, Master Tench, it was difficult to tell whether *I* was walking along there or whether the shade of the great Dr. Johnson had returned!" He lifted his eyebrows in mock wonder. "Do you know why, Master Tench? Do you know the wonderful reception those honest, wonderful, thoughtful people gave that genius Samuel Johnson and me? Bless me, Master Tench, 'pon my word—they laughed."

He smiled grimly. "Ah, how they did laugh, those fine people. They giggled, tittered, snickered, crowed, chirped, chuckled. How the tears did run down their merry cheeks!" He snorted. "They were fine people, Master Tench—beautiful, wonderful, kind people. They set their dogs on me. They threw rotten turnips at me—and when I scrabbled along, I thought they would stew in their glee."

Only once did Aber mention his family. In a conversation he casually spoke of his father, then suddenly he paused, and for the first time Horatio saw anger darken his eyes. "Ah, my father," he said slowly, "and what of him? A wonderful man, Master Tench—a strong, big-bellied man—one of nature's noblemen."

His mouth twisted. "He had a name for me, Master Tench, this wonderful father of mine. The worm! The worm, he called me! I slithered and crawled along the floor until I was eleven—and my father, my blessed, sainted father called me a worm!"

Aber never dwelt on these boyhood memories, and only through a chance remark did Horatio know that he left home when he was eighteen. For a while he had been a clown with a wagon circus.

"I was a good clown, Master Tench. Nature equipped me admirably. The very sight of me would cause an audience to howl. I wore a big red, grinning mouth." He sketched the outline of his mammoth mouth with his small fingers. "I came out and stood there and the laughter rose like a gale from the sea. I couldn't dance. I couldn't tumble. I couldn't sing. But it was all right. 'Pon my word, it was all right! They doted on me. Just the sight of me was enough for their tuppence." He smiled and shook his head. "But I was young and their laughter hurt my pride. I wasn't satisfied to make my way on my—". a wry smile—"God-given qualities.

"No, Master Tench, I decided that the sight of me wasn't worth a tuppence. I decided to be a performer. Nothing would do but that I should learn handsprings. Ah, it took hours. It took hours because I, Master Tench, am not built for acrobatics. I practiced hour after hour, day after day, week after week—and, finally, I learned to turn cartwheels." Aber continued to smile, but his eyes were somber.

"It was to be a surprise. I hadn't revealed my great accomplishment. Then, one night at St. Ives, I decided to let the world know my secret. It was a good time. We had a big audience that night. All the townspeople were there, and the fat farmers, and even some refined gentry. How excited I was. My heart was pounding! When my turn came, I went bounding on the stage. They laughed—aye, they laughed—but their laughter pleased me. 'I'll show them,' I said. 'I'll show them that I'm a performer.' I began to turn cartwheels. There wasn't a pause in their laughter. They didn't applaud. They laughed. They bellowed!" Aber shook with mirthless glee. "I turned cartwheels until my breath was wheezing, until I was blinded in my own salty sweat. I turned and

I twirled until I was so addled that I couldn't stand. Then I collapsed and crawled away.

"They laughed! They laughed! Aye, and the tears were streaming down my cheeks. Suddenly I saw it all as it should have been. My pitiful stupidity was revealed by the light of reflection." His eyes had a faraway look and he was silent for a long time.

When he spoke again, his voice was low. "You see, Master Tench, I realized a great truth. I had been deluding myself. I had tried to make the world in my image. Learning to turn heel over head had been to me a wondrous thing. It took all my strength, all my effort, all my perseverance. Ah! I had expected those good people to acclaim me. But I was so wrong. They saw nothing difficult in my feat. Their prattling children could have done better. They couldn't know my agony of effort, the tears of frustration, the long practice." He shook his head slowly. "If I had been a handsome big man with normal limbs and had swum the Hellespont, I would have been a hero. I would have won their plaudits. They had no way of knowing that turning heels over head was to me a Hellespont."

He smiled. "Aye, that's a lesson for you to ponder, lad. If you were to spread your arms and soar into the sky, you might confound people—but the birds would only think you had poor wings. Nothing seems miraculous that we can do ourselves, though sometimes such things are the greatest miracles."

He sat silently a moment, staring into the fireplace. Then he raised his eyes and saw the look of sadness on Horatio's face. He laughed and sprang to his short legs. "Here! Here! Look! I can still turn cartwheels." He flipped his squat body over and over again with such speed that Horatio was doubled with laughter.

Marketing day was the high spot in Horatio's life. Every Saturday he and Aber left the shop before dawn. They hurried through the deserted, silent streets to reach the market while the greens and fruits were still crisp and fresh, and before blow flies had been at meats which hung exposed and still dripping blood before the butcher stalls. They carried two big baskets and a heavy purse with them on these dawn expeditions. They bought only the best and choicest foods. Samuel Tompkins ate with the speed and manners of a pig, but he boasted, and truthfully, that none except the finest food was served on his table. It was an odd contradiction in the brutal man's make-up. Aber made the most of it.

Aber went from stall to stall, picking only the biggest and reddest apples, the crispest and waxest beans, the tenderest tiny radishes and onions, the heaviest and soundest potatoes. He inspected everything carefully. Every purchase called for a thoughtful decision. He thumped the melons, pinched the fruits. He placed the fresh-milled flour on his tongue and ran it about in his mouth in a search for the slightest bit of grit or chaff. All the hucksters and green merchants knew Aber. They called to him right and left as he walked through the marketplace. Sometimes one had held back a choice bit of produce for him. They brought it forth with the air of a jeweler uncovering his finest work. Many of the merchants were farmers and had raised their wares themselves. They stood by in their leather smocks and broad-brimmed hats and rubbed their hands as Aber made unerringly for their best offerings. Usually, when Aber bought heavily at their stalls, they pressed apples and carrots and slices of melons on Horatio.

Horatio knew little about history, but his instincts were strong. On these early morning visits to the marketplace, he gulped hungrily at every sight and sound. Without realizing it, in this noisy, smelly street he was being allowed to look backward into the centuries. He was seeing the last, fading pictures of an old world, a world vastly different from the one in which he was to live out his life.

One morning he and Aber were caught in a milling, festive throng which had attended a dawn hanging before Yarmouth gaol. It seemed to Horatio that the crowd was composed mostly of women. As they clawed the vegetables and meats in the stalls, dirty, runny-nosed children clutching at their long skirts, they gleefully recounted every tense moment of the event.

One big farm woman Horatio never forgot. She was immense, with watery, dull eyes, a loud bellowing laugh, and had enormous breasts. She had disengaged one swollen, melon-like pap from her dingy gown and supported it in a pudgy hand to nurse a frail, pinch-faced boy of about three. The child had wrapped his skinny legs around his mother's waist and he nursed while she lumbered and waddled from stall to stall. There was something so repulsive about the woman, something so evil about her voice and laugh, that Horatio stared in fascination.

Her voice carried above the hum of the crowd. "Aye, it wos a good 'un. Bless me, God, it wos a good 'un!" Her fat body shook with mirth. "Aye, an' did ye see 'is legs quiver? One time Hi thot 'e wouldn't be able t'stan' whilst they got the rope round 'is neck. Hi tell ye they do these things right now, though. Whin 'e dropped Hi heard 'is neck pop clear and fine as could be." She slapped her fat hands together and the nursing child looked up in alarm. "It wos over like that," she said. "It wos just a short snap an' 'twere all over.

"Aye, indeed, Hi wos right hup clos," she whinnied shrilly in answer to a question. "Ain't no use tryin' ter keep Violet Shorter away whin there's a 'anging. Hi just pushed an' shoved till, bless me, God, ye would 'ave thot Hi wos t'one wot wos 'avin' me neck stretched." A group of farm slatterns who were her audience giggled and tittered.

"Cos," Violet continued, with a thoughtful pluck at her chin, "it was nothin' as good as some 'angin's Hi've seen." She cast her eyes slyly at her attentive audience. "But then ye must remember there's one man at a 'angin' who's never satisfied on no account." The women whooped with pleasure. Violet Shorter's bellow over-shadowed them all. Her fat body shook with bubbly laughs. " 'Im wot gets it," she said gasping. " 'Im wot gets it!"

Aber had been standing nearby. He turned, frozen-faced and tense, and looked at the woman. His voice was heavy with contempt. "I wonder why you didn't bring back the rope."

Violet Shorter whooped with delight. "Hi did," she said. "Bless me, God, Hi did—as much as they would give me." She plunged her hand into her market basket and triumphantly flourished a short piece of execution rope which had been cut into sections and thrown to the crowd. Then, because it was impossible to miss the look of disgust on Aber's face, she quit laughing. A crafty, malicious grin twisted her lips. She looked at the rope and back at Aber. She bubbled with laughter again. "This 'ere rope is near big enough ter 'ang a little man, the likes of you. Bless me, God, if they 'as ter 'ang you, it won't tike much rope." The crowd roared.

Aber, his face white, walked away. Horatio followed, and the laughter of the crowd brought tears to his eyes. Horatio never mentioned the incident, but the picture never left his memory.

Almost always, when they had completed their shopping, they walked down to the waterfront to see the ships. Aber had spent fifteen years at sea as a cook and galley hand. His eyes glowed as he pointed out various ships to Horatio. "Look, Master Tench, look—there's a three-masted. Ah, that's a rare bird, that one is. See how she rides like a gull on the crest of a wave. And over there— no, to the right—see that frigate—that's the hawk of the sea, Master Tench. That's a fighting ship if ever I saw one. Seventeen guns, at least—aye, maybe more."

The harbor was a delightful, exciting place and Horatio began to love it. When he was sent on errands, he always ran quickly so that he could spend a few minutes on the docks. On Sunday afternoons, his only free time from the shop, he would sit for hours gazing out at ships riding at anchor and sniffing the winy, salty breath of the sea.

He was sitting thus one bright, sunny afternoon when he met the stranger. It was during the summer of 1812. The harbor was filled with trim, fighting ships. The man came on the pier quietly. He had been there several minutes, gazing out to sea, when Horatio first noticed him. He was a tall thin man, sharp of jowl and shin. At first glance, Horatio took him to be a shipowner. Then he noticed that the man's brown suit was worn and shabby. Horatio decided that he must be a clerk or custom inspector. Yet there was something about the man's bearing, something about the tilt of his head, that gave him an air of authority.

The man sensed Horatio's searching stare, and he looked down and smiled. "'Tis a beautiful sight, isn't it, lad?" His voice was soft but slightly nasal. Like all seaport youths, Horatio was used to a variety of accents and dialects. This voice was different from any he knew.

Horatio nodded toward the harbor and parroted the words he had heard sailors use. "Aye, they're the best, sir, and they're off to sink the long-nosed Yankees."

The man lifted his eyebrows and laughed softly. "And, pray, what are the long-nosed Yankees going to do about this?"

"Why, they can't do anything, sir," Horatio said. "England is Queen of the Seas. Aye, sir, no one can stand against England on water."

The man's face lighted with a musing smile. "Ah, but suppose —for argument, mind you—that Providence willed otherwise? Suppose England were to lose to the long-nosed Yankees. What then?"

Horatio's vague knowledge of the war, his meager store of catch-phrases, had left him unprepared to cope with such heresy. It was inconceivable. He looked at the stranger closely to see if he were joking. "England can't lose, sir," he said firmly. "England has never lost!"

The man nodded solemnly, but there was a twinkle in his eyes. "Ay-eh, I see. England has never lost so England will never lose. Is that it?"

"Aye, sir," Horatio said.

The stranger took out a snuffbox. After tapping it thoughtfully, to Horatio's amazement he placed a pinch of the brown powder under his lower lip instead of sniffing it. He looked out to sea a minute before he again turned to Horatio with a smile. "You've heard a lot about America, I suppose, my lad?"

Horatio shook his head. "No, sir—nothing except that they want to make the English slaves."

A small smile tugged at the corners of the stranger's thin mouth. "Ay-eh? I had never heard that. And why do they want the English to be slaves?"

"Why . . . why, I don't know, sir," Horatio said. He groped in his memory to try to recall what Aber had told him about America. It surprised him to find this calm man questioning statements he had heard from every sailor in Yarmouth. His eyes were wide. "Don't you know about America?" he asked.

The man nodded slowly. "Ay-eh, lad, I know America." He looked toward the horizon and his voice was soft. "I know America and I'm learning more every day. Once I thought I knew all there was to know. But I didn't, lad. I thought America was rock and dirt and clay. I thought America was people and ships and houses. I thought America was a place." He smiled and sighed. "Ay-eh, lad, I'm a seafaring man and I'm not soft, but I know now that America is a dream. It's a poem, lad, a song, a hymn, a prayer. It's a woman's voice and a child's laugh. It's good food, lad, and it's good friends. Ay-eh, America isn't a land. It's a state of mind. It's a fire crackling on the hearth. It's hard cider in brown jugs—and it's a loved one who is far away." That tiny smile tugged the corners of his mouth again. "It's more than all these, lad. It's everything. It's home!"

Horatio had listened in stunned silence. Finally he found his voice. "You . . . you are an American."

The man's laugh was low. "Ay-eh, lad—a long-nosed Yankee."

Horatio flushed. "But how . . . why . . . ?"

The man sat down on the dock by Horatio. "I was a ship-master, lad, out of Salem, bound for Le Havre." A shadow flickered across his face. "One of your capital ships captured me. Now I'm a prisoner, lad, bound for London this evening—paroled on my word for a last look toward the sea and homeward."

Horatio stared in awe, but the man smiled at him so kindly that he flushed again and lowered his head. The man laughed at his embarrassment and placed his hand lightly on Horatio's shoulder. "Now, heed me, lad," he said, "and I'll tell you about America. I want to tell you—because I want to repeat the things to myself."

There, while the breeze blew fresh and salty from the sea, while the waves sparkled in the sunlight, the man spoke of America. His voice was low and soft. He didn't speak of history, of government, or of war. He spoke of the people he knew, of hunting in the autumn woods, of fishing in the broad, slow streams. He told how corn grew taller than a man's head, how fresh cider tasted when it came from the presses, how the church bells rang in Salem. And, finally, he told how a man could be free, despite his birth or his poverty.

Horatio sat entranced. "And how does a man have an equal chance, sir?" he asked.

The man's face was solemn. "It's a written guarantee, lad. It's there for everyone. Our President is chosen by the people. Our Congress is composed of farmers, and fishermen, and merchants and tinsmiths."

The wind was dying and the sky was darkening. Far off across the water, Horatio heard the creaking of riggings of the ships at anchor. The man's low voice rolled on and on. Suddenly he stopped talking and began to recite a poem which an American had written. It was a strangely written work and Horatio could not understand all the words. But he understood the thought and the meaning, and as he sat facing the sea, he felt a curious elation. He had no words to express the emotion that came rising from his whole being like deep organ notes and left him with bright eyes and tightened muscles and with such a keen awareness of the world about him that it seemed not a sight, not a sound could escape his hungry senses.

After a while the man was quiet. He sat looking at the sea silently, then he arose with a sigh and held out his hand. Horatio clasped it a moment and they smiled and the man walked away.

He was at the end of the pier before Horatio recovered from his reverie. "Sir!" he called. "Sir! What was the name of that poem?"

The man paused. His voice was soft. "They call it the Preamble to the Constitution." He walked away quickly. Horatio never mentioned his meeting with the American to anyone, not even Aber. And sometimes when he and Aber had completed their shopping and were going home, Horatio would pause for such lingering looks at the sea that the little man would chuckle. " 'Pon my word, I believe the lad has salt water in his veins. 'Pon my word, I believe he does." Horatio would smile. He never told Aber that his eyes were directed beyond the sea—beyond the sea to a land where men were free.

CHAPTER V

I N HIS sixteenth year, Horatio stood six feet tall and was as slim and hard as an oaken foremast. Too slim. He could almost span his waist with his long-fingered, strong hands, but his shoulders were so broad that he had to turn sideways to enter narrow doorways. These massive shoulders made him look awkward, almost clumsy. Their width made his neck appear to be scrawny, his limbs too slim. He carried his shoulders thrown well back, and he seemed to be top-heavy, slightly off balance. His appearance was deceptive. Horatio had the balance and agility of a cat. Long hours of twisting rope and pulling hemp had given him forearms and biceps of iron. In a fashion, he was handsome. Not spectacularly so, for his cheeks and jawline still had a boyish fullness. But his features were well-formed and pleasant—and, what was unusual for the times, his teeth were straight and even and sound.

He had luckily escaped the periodic epidemics of small pox, so his complexion was clear and unmarked. As might be expected, this set him apart in an age when both men and women were pockmarked from the cradle—this and his hair and eyes. Horatio's hair was golden-orange, unbelievably bright. People stared at Horatio's hair, and this attention embarrassed him. He kept his flaming mop hacked short and it covered his head in a mass of ringlets. His eyes were a deep blue tinged with green, the color of a stormy sea. There was something unnaturally speculative about his eyes. They were almost too calculating. Men sometimes had an unconscious urge to double their fists when they met Horatio's gaze for the first time.

The eyes were not challenging. But they were watchful. It was the watchfulness that some men and some races carry in their eyes when they try to look in all directions at the same time to escape the next blow or the next curse. As Horatio grew older, his caution against Samuel Tompkins' unpredictable temper had increased.

He had ample cause, although Tompkins had not struck Horatio with his fists for three years. When Horatio was thirteen, Tompkins' sadistic treatment of him reached a dangerous, sickening climax. The ropemaker, reeling and stumbling after a hard night of drinking at a public house, had returned to his darkened shop and stumbled over a coil of rope which Horatio had forgotten to put away. He went sprawling with such a bellow of rage that Horatio was awakened and lay cold with nervousness and fear. Before he knew it, Tompkins was in his room raining blows on his face and head. They were not open-handed cuffs but great, crushing blows, delivered with drunken insanity. The attack was so murderous that, for the first time in his life, Horatio was opening his mouth to cry out when one hard fist caught him on the side of the head and he lost consciousness.

Aber Cheezum finally stopped the raging, cursing man. It took Aber ten minutes to revive Horatio. For a week afterward his eyes were blackened and his face swollen and bruised. Samuel Tompkins gave no sign that he regretted his attack. The truth was, however, when he had finally stopped pounding the boy and saw him lying so white and still in his own blood, he had been frightened sober.

The next day he carefully tarred a short length of heavy rope and hung it on a peg in the shop. Thereafter, when his anger reached the stage of violence, he used the rope as a lash, laying it on with his full strength.

Even these beatings were becoming more infrequent. It was not because Tompkins was afraid of the growing boy. Fear was as alien to him as compassion. Rather it was because, as he had grown older, Horatio had developed a soft-footed wariness when Tompkins was around. Also his capacity for work was so great that Tompkins secretly realized that he was doing the work of two men. Sometimes he did the work of three, for Aber's frail legs were failing rapidly. Some days they were so bad that it caused him unbearable agony just to walk.

On these days Horatio took over. He cooked the meals, making frequent trips to the back room to get instructions from Aber about how to prepare a gravy or learn the cooking time for a roast or stew. In the evenings Horatio sat with the little man or rubbed his swollen, twisted legs with goose grease and applied hot cloths to try to lessen the pain.

One night he had completed ministering to Aber's legs when the little man looked up and smiled. "Ah, Master Tench, they look hopeless, do they not? I suppose they have given up after carrying this weight around for so many years."

"They're fine," Horatio said. "They look much better than they did yesterday. You'll be well within the week."

Aber shook his head slowly. "No, lad, I fear they're finished." He sighed and sank back on his narrow bunk. "I suppose I should be thankful that they've given me service all these years." His face was thoughtful. " 'Tis odd, isn't it, that a man's spirit is often at cross purposes with his body. When I was a youth, I thought that Providence had played me a foul turn by giving me this twisted body to house my heart. As I grew older, I sometimes fancied that it had a purpose. I looked at my poor arms and my poor legs and I had a strange feeling that somehow I was made as I am for a deeper reason than I could discern. I could feel the soul within me, straight and strong. I said to myself, 'That is the true Aber Cheezum. My spirit is strong and clean-limbed! I am whole. It is my body that is twisted and weak. I will live by my soul. I will forget my body.' "

Aber looked at Horatio with a small smile. "Ah, but I couldn't forget my body, Master Tench. I couldn't forget it and the world would not let me. I thought I had beautiful, fine things stored away here in my breast. I thought that somehow Heaven might have marked me for its own." He shook his head slowly. "Now I know that isn't so, lad. I'm past forty, and I'm tired and I want to sleep. And now I'm learning a strange truth. My body and my soul do belong together. They are linked together. My soul wants to sleep, lad, and my body is going to let it. Now I've learned that a man can no better live entirely by his soul than he can live entirely by his body." He looked down at his misshapen limbs again and smiled ruefully. "How eagerly, though, I would sacrifice this twisted husk if I could make it give up my soul straight and strong."

Horatio had stood silently while Aber spoke. Now he looked down at the kindly man and covered his frail hand with his own. "You'll be all right tomorrow," he said. "Tonight you're just weary."

Aber nodded and smiled. "Aye, Master Tench, I'm just tired. I'm sorry I let you hear my stupid thoughts." He clasped Horatio's hand tightly. "Tell me, lad, what are you going to do in your life? What dreams do you have?"

Horatio shook his head. "I don't know. B'fair, I don't know." He paused a moment, and when he spoke his voice was hesitant. "Do . . . do you know about America?"

Aber looked at him closely. "Aye, lad, I know."

"Do you know," Horatio's voice was earnest, "that there all men are equals? Do you know there are no noblemen, no gentry, no classes? Do you know that a man can make his way without explaining his birth, or despite his poverty?"

Aber nodded. "Aye, I've heard those stories, lad. I know them all. But I know people, too. I know that black men are slaves in America. What of their birth and poverty? I know poor people sweat and slave in America. Such talk is a dream. I know all the tales of beauty and equality, all the high-sounding words and flowing phrases. But I know, too, that Benjamin Kramer, the broker on High Street, recruits men to send to America. He pays their way and they work as lackeys to repay him. Are these men free, lad?"

Horatio flushed. "They are after a while. Some men work a lifetime and are never free."

Aber smiled. He had been studying Horatio's face. "Aye, I think that is a good point," he said. Quickly—"Do you want to go to America, Master Tench?"

Horatio was unprepared for the question. America had been a cherished dream but, as is the case with most dreams, he had treasured it as something unattainable. He hesitated a long time. "I . . . I think I do."

Aber spoke quietly. "Then go, Master Tench. Go when the time is ripe. America may not be perfect, but any land is good when a man takes with him two willing hands and the determination to work for a dream." He smiled. "When the time is ripe you will go to America, Master Tench." He cut his eyes slyly. "Ah, you will go to America—and not as a bonded servant sent by Benjamin Kramer. You'll go first-class, Master Tench, on a speedy ship. You'll be a gentleman, Master Tench. Yes, a colonial gentleman!"

The conversation rested there. Horatio put Aber's joking plans out of mind, but something else the little man had said remained to haunt him. Thereafter, when he passed the dingy shop of Benjamin Kramer, he looked at it with a new interest. Once when five men, laden with seabags, emerged from the shop and walked toward the docks, Horatio followed them for a distance with quickened pulse.

He began to spend every precious moment of free time in the vicinity of Kramer's shop instead of on the docks. He became familiar with every worn cobblestone in that street. He knew every waterstain and patch of peeled paint on the sign above the dark doorway which creaked in the breeze and said: "Benj. Kramer, Importer & Broker." Several times he saw Benjamin Kramer come from the shop. He was a tall man with a fierce beak of a nose and dark, shrewd eyes. Once Horatio was on the verge of approaching him, but he lost his courage and turned away quickly.

Twice he actually summoned up enough nerve to put his hand on the fly-specked door of the shop. His courage failed before he pushed. This went on for weeks until one day, disgusted at his cowardice, he walked boldly up to the door, pushed it open, and strode inside.

He could not have told what he expected. Whatever it was, he was disappointed. The interior of the shop was dark and sketchily furnished. A small spring bell hanging above the door rang furiously. Benjamin Kramer was seated at a desk in the rear of the shop, writing with an old-fashioned pen by the light of cruzie. He lifted his head at the sound of the bell. When he saw Horatio he smiled slightly.

"Ye finally got up courage t'come in, did ye, lad?"

Horatio's cheeks were flushed, but he walked to the desk and stood erect, almost belligerently.

"I want to learn the details of making a voyage to America."

Benjamin Kramer put down his quill and sighed. He leaned

back in his chair and folded his long waxen fingers across his stomach. He looked amused.

"Who are ye, lad?"

"I only want . . ." Horatio stopped when Benjamin Kramer shook his head and waved a finger.

"I know, lad," he said, softly, "but gentlemen can't transact business until they have become acquainted. Who are ye?"

Horatio stood stiffly. "My name is Horatio Tench."

Kramer smiled and inclined his head. "I'm honored, sir." He lowered his head and looked at Horatio craftily. "D'ye know, sir, there's a penalty for 'prentices who run away. And for those who help them."

"I'm not a 'prentice," said Horatio.

Benjamin Kramer raised his brows and leaned forward. "Ah? 'Tis home ye don't like, is it, lad?"

Horatio's voice was firm. "I have no home. I'm an orphan, without parents or kin." He had no compunction in disowning his foster father.

Benjamin Kramer was showing a new interest. "What can ye do, lad?" he asked. "Are ye learning a trade?"

"I've been working at the cordage shop of Samuel Tompkins."

Kramer nodded with sudden understanding. His lips twisted in an amused grimace. "Ay, yes," he said, softly, "I know the gentleman." He leaned back and studied Horatio. "When d'ye want to go to America?"

The question was so unexpected that Horatio stammered. "I . . . I don't know. . . . I—I wanted to learn the details. . . and . . . the cost."

Benjamin Kramer smiled and threw apart his graceful hands. "There's no cost, lad. Old Uncle Ben takes care of that. When ye reach America ye sign up for a period of work to repay him." He lowered his voice. "D'ye have money, lad?"

"Well, I . . . I . . ."

Benjamin Kramer waved his hand. "It makes no difference, lad. Ye can work." He looked at the papers on his desk. "I can book ye passage almost any day from now until October."

Horatio's heart was pounding. "I'll—I'll be back when I'm ready," he said.

Benjamin Kramer inclined his head and smiled. Horatio was almost to the door when he heard the man speak. He turned. "Eh?"

Benjamin Kramer had risen. His shrewd, dark eyes were studying Horatio. "You'll be back," he repeated.

Horatio hesitated. "Aye. I'll be back."

For a week Horatio cuddled to himself his dream of going to America. He did his work as usual, but there was something so mechanical about his actions, such a faraway look in his eyes, that Samuel Tompkins watched him uneasily and accused him of inattention and laziness. He kept his length of tarred rope handy, and he used it so often that Horatio's back was crisscrossed with ugly welts. Horatio's almost absent-minded acceptance of this ill treatment goaded Tompkins to greater lengths of brutality. The shop rang with his curses and snarls and the sharp smack of the rope across Horatio's shoulders.

Aber's protection was missing. The little man's legs were swollen to twice their normal size now and he was forced to stay in bed. The parish physician had bled him twice within the week. Each time it seemed to Horatio that Aber had weakened and his condition had grown worse. Even Samuel Tompkins had been forced to give grudging acknowledgment to the small man's illness. Occasionally he would come to his bedside and ask how he felt, and leave after growling some advice.

After he had left the room one morning, Aber turned to Horatio, who had brought him a cup of tea. "I think he's upset because of my illness, Master Tench."

Horatio's face was a cold mask. "I hate him," he said. There was no emotion in his voice, no anger, no bitterness. It was a flat, calm declaration. Aber spoke quickly.

"Ah, Master Tench, you shouldn't worry. You have dreams."

Horatio smiled. "Drink your tea. I've sweetened it with honey."

Horatio and Tompkins worked alone in the shop and that morning passed with its usual quota of snarls and curses. Shortly after noon two ship captains entered the shop and bought a sizable supply of rope for sheets and hawsers. Then, as he always did after making a good sale, Samuel Tompkins broke out a jug of rum and passed it around. The captains were both squat, hard-drinking men, and they lingered until the jug was empty. When Tompkins saw them out the door, Horatio noticed nervously that he was drunk.

Horatio was huckling hemp by pulling it straight over a large board studded with sharp iron teeth. When Samuel Tompkins walked back into the shop, he bent over his work and dared not raise his eyes. The ropemaker approached to within a few feet of him and stood glaring and swaying a little. He stood there until he sensed the growing uneasiness in Horatio, then he growled a low laugh and started toward his room. As he passed Horatio, he flipped his big hand out quickly and caught him a stinging blow on the cheek. For a split instant red fury boiled in Horatio and his hands tensed and trembled. He clenched his jaw and continued huckling the hemp.

Tompkins remained in his room the rest of the afternoon and Horatio knew he had embarked on one of his frequent drunks. He worked quickly with an uneasy dread until it was time to prepare the evening meal. He spitted a half-dozen mutton chops and placed them over the glowing coals in the fireplace. He then prepared a cup of tea and took it in to Aber. They chatted for a few minutes and Horatio returned to the shop.

When he walked through the door his stomach tightened. In his absence, Samuel Tompkins had come in and was seated at the still bare table. He was shirtless and the hair on his great chest and belly was matted with spilled rum. When he saw Horatio his little red eyes gleamed and he leered and waved a half-empty rum bottle.

Horatio paused a moment and he could feel the blood drain from his face. Tompkins did not miss this reaction. It seemed to amuse him. He hiccuped and took another smacking swig from his bottle and laughed loudly. His voice was thick. "Whash the food! Whash the cookth!" He swayed unsteadily in his chair and shook with loud belly laughs.

Horatio walked quietly. He had seen Tompkins in these jovial drunken moods before. He knew his glut of exuberance could change in a moment to dangerous ill-humor. He turned his eyes from the table.

"I'll have the food ready in a few minutes."

Tompkins went into another gale of laughter. He beat the table in his glee. He laughed until he was choked by a rush of bubbly phlegm, and then sat coughing and spitting and struggling to catch his breath. He straightened up and drunkenly focused his red eyes on Horatio. "Food! Food!" he shouted. The sound pleased him. He made a chant of the word, and he punctuated his roars by thumping the bottle against the table. "Food! Food!" *thump* "Food! Food!" *thump* "Food! Food!"

Horatio stood stone-faced through this. His stomach was cold with fear and anger and disgust.

"The food isn't cooked," he said.

Samuel Tompkins lurched back drunkenly and leered. "Bring food!" he said and hiccuped.

"It isn't cooked," Horatio said.

Samuel Tompkins twisted his mouth. This time his piggish eyes had a malicious gleam.

"Bring food!" he shouted.

Horatio stood uncertain for a moment. Then he got a plate and went to the fireplace. He took two of the half-raw chops off their spits and placed them on the plate. His hands were trembling and he was filled with disgust at his own nervousness. He walked slowly to the table and placed the plate before Tompkins.

Tompkins looked down at the food and twisted his mouth and cut his eyes with a sly, drunken cunning at Horatio. "Raw!" he said. "Raw!"

Horatio tried to keep his voice flat. "Aye."

Tompkins pushed the plate back with a sweep of his arms. It clattered to the floor. He swayed back in his chair and looked up at Horatio and bellowed with laughter. "Hah-Hah! Raw! Hah-Hah!" He reached out a hairy hand and grabbed Horatio's wrist in an iron grip. "Like raw meat!" he roared. "Like bloody meat!" Before Horatio could pull away, he took his hand and bit it viciously.

The feel of that greasy, wet mouth against his hand filled Horatio with disgust. His arm trembled. His knees began to shake. "Stop it!" he shouted. "Stop it!" His voice was shrill.

Samuel Tompkins roared with laughter. "Like raw meat," he gasped. He pulled Horatio's hand to his mouth again.

Without thinking, Horatio swung out his free arm at Tompkins' head. The blow caught him slightly above the right ear. He was knocked sprawling to the floor.

For a horrified moment Horatio felt that his heart had stopped with shock. Then he felt a fierce elation. He stood with heaving chest and fists clenched, looking down at Tompkins.

The big man seemed to be stunned. He turned slowly on the floor and looked up. At first incredulity flickered across his face. Then his anger came rising in like a flood. His face turned purplish. The veins rose on his neck. He scrambled up with a bellow and charged.

Horatio was waiting. He took dead aim and drove his fist with all his strength into that hated face. The blow caught Tompkins on the left cheek and laid the bone open. He toppled backwards and landed with a crash, but almost immediately arose again, slowly this time. He waited for his head to clear, then advanced with cautious cunning. Horatio stepped back, but Tompkins sprang with lightning movement and caught him around the waist in a crushing embrace. Horatio wheezed as the wind was forced from his body. He could feel his ribs bending in that powerful hug. He felt a moment of panic. He remembered his free arms. He clasped them high above his head and brought them down with all his strength on the back of Samuel Tompkins' thick neck. Tompkins grunted and fell to the floor with a thud.

Horatio raised his foot to smash it against Tompkins' head. Before it descended, he was pushed backward and he heard Aber Cheezum's voice. "Now . . . now . . . that's a good lad." Horatio's breath was coming in quick gasps. He was trembling from head to foot, but he allowed Aber to push him back against the table.

Tompkins was on his feet again. Blood was streaming from the cut on his cheek and dripping from his chin onto his hairy chest. He was swaying drunkenly and his eyes were glazed. He shook his head slowly from side to side until it cleared, and he saw Horatio again. He snarled and took a half-step forward, but stopped short when he saw the huckling board where Horatio had left it. Quickly he snatched it up and advanced slowly, the board poised, his eyes glued on Horatio.

Both he and Horatio seemed to have forgotten Aber. Now, however, the little man sprang between them. Tompkins' eyes never left Horatio's face. He advanced closer . . . closer. Horatio stood tensely, legs spread apart, right fist cocked. Suddenly, with a snarl, Tompkins sprang and swung the board. Aber leaped for his arm.

There was a sickening thud. The spike-filled board hit Aber squarely in the face. He was impaled for one horrible instant before Tompkins jerked back the board and withdrew the sharp spikes. Aber crumbled to the floor.

There was a stunned silence. Horatio dropped to one knee beside Aber and turned him over. He recoiled with a gasp. Aber's white face was covered with blue, evenly spaced deep holes. They were beginning to fill with blood. "Aber!" Horatio said hoarsely. "Aber!" He cuddled Aber's bloody head to his chest and stared unbelievingly. "He's dead," he whispered. "He's dead."

He never knew how long he knelt there, but suddenly he remembered Samuel Tompkins. Tompkins was standing shock-still in white-faced horror. He looked down at the board in his hands. At that moment he saw Horatio staring at him with cold hate, and the horror in his eyes was replaced with fright. He scrambled to recover the board. It was too late. Horatio was on him like a cat.

"Stop! Stop!" Tompkins cried. "It wos a mistake! It wos a mistake!"

Horatio's mouth was a cruel slit. "I'm going to kill ye," he said hoarsely. "I'm going to kill ye!"

The battle was one-sided. Ten men could not have stopped Horatio. He smashed the reeling Tompkins in the face and belly and drove him, gasping and croaking, from one end of the shop to the other. Finally Horatio's hands fell on the huckling board. He used it to complete the job.

Only then did he return to sanity. He paused to wipe the blood from his face, and knelt beside Aber Cheezum and folded the little man's hands across his chest.

He left the darkened shop and walked the empty street for an hour before he went to Benjamin Kramer. He was aboard the American merchantman, *Salamander,* at midnight. They sailed on the morning tide for Charleston.

CHAPTER VI

THE brig *Salamander,* a taut, trim vessel of 310 tons burden, was a fast sailer. She caught a pleasant breeze from the south'd which continued to carry her clear of the English Channel and on her course for Madeira, where she intended to stop briefly to tender bills of exchange for a cargo of wine.

She anchored safely in Funchal Roads, and five days later, her holds bulging with pipes of the island's finest wine, she again set sail on a course that carried her fifty to sixty leagues westward of Palma and Ferro. Eighteen days out of Madeira, she skipped across the equator with a steady breeze, met the southeast trades, and bore a straight course homeward.

These were the basic facts of Horatio's first and only ocean voyage—almost all that he could recall clearly. For two days after he left England he was in a state of shock. He answered when he was spoken to. He moved when asked. He even ate food when it was served, but afterward he had no clear memory of his thoughts or actions. He had no way of knowing it, but he passed into that vague, shadowy world which nature has provided for soldiers fresh from the battlefield, and for others who have wrestled with horror and terror and grief. Finally, the fog began to lift and he groped his way 'tween decks, threw himself on his hard bunk, and slept the clock around. He awakened with a feeling of intolerable grief, but he soon put it from him. His mind was not yet prepared for grief.

But he was young and strong, so finally, bit by bit, fragment by fragment, he began to piece together the events of that last frightful night in Samuel Tompkins' rope shop. He recalled with a shudder how Aber's face had looked after it was pierced and ripped by the huckling board. The memory brought tears to his eyes. He lay for hours in his bunk with clenched teeth, or stared blankly out to sea.

He never felt a moment's remorse for having killed Samuel Tompkins. His hate for the man was still so active, so fierce that sometimes in the night he dreamed that Tompkins was cuffing him or lashing him with a length of tarred rope. These dreams were so real that he would awaken with a start and lie tense and sweaty until the lapping of water against the ship's hull, the hum of the breeze through the rigging reassured him that Tompkins was dead. He would smile grimly in the darkness and rejoice that he had killed the man. His hate was so great that he would have done it again—gladly. A thousand times.

He shared his cramped, poorly ventilated quarters with two other men who were going to America through the offices of Uncle Ben Kramer. One was a slow, heavy-footed tinsmith from Aylesbury. He had left his wife and four children to seek his fortune in the New World because he had heard that diamonds the size of hen's eggs could be picked up in the fields. His name was John Addleston and the sailors called him Sir Addle. The other man was a pleasant, open-faced, apple-cheeked German named Hans Zwieger who spoke English with great difficulty. He said his parents had died and he wanted to go to America because of an uncle who had gone there twenty years before as a bonded servant and was now a substantial innkeeper in Pennsylvania. How he had ever reached Benjamin Kramer's shop was a mystery which his halting English or reticence failed to reveal. "Ach, it vas no goot . . . no goot," he said with a shake of his head.

During the voyage Horatio spoke to his companions only when they addressed him directly, and then he kept his answer brief. Once or twice they grumbled over the food, but he was indifferent. Ordinarily he may have been given duties aboard ship, but the *Salamander* was well-manned, so he was left alone to brood and plan.

So the time passed. The days turned to nights, the nights to days —and the weeks passed . . . and a month—another week and days.

He was lying in his bunk the morning he heard the cry. There were cheers from the crew and the soft swish of their heavy-callused bare feet as they ran to and fro on the deck. Horatio ran on deck and found a place at the rail. The sea was calm and dazzling in the early morning sun. Far on the horizon, lying like a purple shadow, he saw it—land! He stood there, feet braced apart, squinting his eyes against the sun, the wind whipping his face—and somewhere, deep within him, he felt that curious, tense exultation which he had experienced when first he heard of America. Then, high in the rigging, one happy sailor let out a squeal of pure animal joy. He squealed again and again, and threw back his head and began to sing. One by one, the grinning men on the decks below joined in. Horatio's lips didn't move but his heart sang with them. He felt that he could leap in the air and soar with the screaming gulls. He felt free. But, suddenly, tears came unbidden to his eyes. His throat was tight. His lips formed one word. "Aber!"

There was no ceremony on the dock. A half-dozen men were waiting in a barn-like shack. From their clothing and bearing, Horatio knew five of them to be gentlemen. The other man was a fat, egg-bald clerk who sat behind a battered desk littered with papers and ledgers. The gentlemen turned slowly and looked Horatio up and down when he entered. One testy-looking, tiny man in a long black waistcoat and beaver hat left his seat to prod him speculatively in the ribs. Horatio felt his neck and ears turn crimson. The tiny man sucked thoughtfully at his teeth, snorted, and resumed his seat.

Grunting with effort, the fat clerk opened a heavy ledger, picked up a pen, and pointed it at Horatio.

"Name?"

Horatio's heart was pounding. "Horatio Tench, sir."

The fat man slapped his square hands on the desk and reared back in exaggerated surprise. He blinked his owlish eyes.

"Wal, bless mah ole bones," he said with mock awe, "this heah lad has got manners."

The gentlemen laughed, and the fat man joined in with a low, throaty rumble. Horatio's palms were damp. He knew his face was beet-red. He felt angry, but the anger died when the fat man flashed him a grin of real friendliness, so he smiled back.

The fat man turned to the ledger. "Yo're off'n the *Salamandah* out thar, ain't yo', boy?"

Horatio nodded. "Aye, sir."

The clerk ran a pudgy finger down a row in his ledger. "Now les' see, les' see. Tench! Whar is ole Tench?" His finger paused. "Right heah yo' are, boy. It says heah . . . ummmm . . . it says heah that yo're shippin' out from Yarmouth. Is that right, boy?"

"Aye, sir."

The fat man looked up. "Don't say how old yo' are, though, boy . . . an' it don't say wha'cha do." He smiled at Horatio. "Square 'round thar now an' tell these gennelmen how old yo' are an' wha'cha kin do to earn yo' keep. Wouldn't be su'prised if one'r these gennelmen might be innerested in buyin' yo' bond. Yes, suh, might save yo' a long trip back home!" His throat filled with another rumbling laugh.

Horatio turned slowly. The sight of all these well-dressed men left him almost numb with embarrassment. He wet his lips. "I'm ten and six or nearabouts," he said. "I never knew my birth date. I . . . I am an orphan. I worked—I was learning the ropemaking trade at a shop in Yarmouth."

The little man who had inspected him so closely spoke up. "Can you read, boy?"

"Aye, sir," Horatio said.

The man narrowed his eyes. "Write?"

"Aye, sir."

The little man had his lips framed for another question when a new voice broke in. "Young man . . ." Horatio shifted his eyes to face a gentleman he had not noticed before. He was by far the most elegantly dressed man there. He wore a light gray coat, dark pantaloons, and a fawn-colored high hat. His chin was resting on his long, tapering hands which were curled around a gold-handled cane. He was of medium height and slim to the point of wiriness. His handsome face was unlined but his long sideburns were gray. His dark eyes were fixed on Horatio searchingly. His voice was soft.

"Do you know anything about cotton, young man?"

Horatio liked the man instinctively. Everything about him seemed to express breeding and wealth and kindness. He nodded eagerly. "Aye, sir. It's too dear . . . and . . . and it's no good!"

The gentlemen roared with laughter. The elegantly dressed man raised his eyebrows ruefully but smiled.

"You mean, I suppose, that cotton is no good for rope?"

The laughter had bewildered Horatio. "Well, sir," he stammered. "I . . . I shouldn't have said it's no good. It's too dear."

The gentleman looked at his chuckling companions archly. "I know what you mean, young man. But would you believe it, some people think it's too dear for any purpose?" He smiled. "They begrudge an honest man a living." He looked thoughtful. "Do you know anything about raising cotton, or ginning it—or—" he let his smile broaden—"*picking* it?"

Horatio shook his head. "No, sir."

The man stood up. "Well, you will, young man. You will." He nodded to the fat clerk. "I'll take this young man, Billy. Draw up the papers and we'll sign them before we leave town. I have some shopping to do before I return to Fair Haven."

There was an immediate chorus of protest from the other men, but it was so vehement that Horatio knew it was false. "Now, hold on there. . . ." "Why, of all the highhanded . . ." "You'll place your bid, you robber. . . ."

The man threw back his head and laughed. He waved his cane grandly as if to make passage through the protesting men. "Fix up the papers, Billy, and if any of these town robbers boosts the price, just keep making mine a little higher."

The fat clerk was shaking with laughter. "Yes, suh, Gen'rul Jameson. Yes, suh!"

The man motioned to Horatio. "Come along, young man." He tipped his hat to the other men. "Good day, gentlemen."

He was still smiling when they emerged from the building. He looked at Horatio thoughtfully. "Are you hungry, young man?"

The swift turn of events had left Horatio dazed. "Well, I—"

"I thought so," the man said. He reached in his pocket and brought out a coin. He held it a moment and looked at Horatio searchingly. "You're not unhappy, are you?"

"No, sir," Horatio said.

"You're not planning on running away, are you?" the man asked smiling.

Horatio flushed. "No, sir!"

The man laughed. "I didn't think so." He handed Horatio the coin. "Now here's a dime—ten cents in silver. Go to that inn yonder—" he pointed to a nearby inn with his cane— "and get you something to eat. After you've finished, come back here and wait for me. If anyone asks who you are, tell them you work for General Jameson."

Horatio nodded. "Aye, sir . . . er, General Jameson."

The man smiled and walked off toward the town, swinging his stick jauntily.

It was several hours before General Jameson returned in a shiny black carriage driven by a Negro in livery. A woman was riding with the General, but Horatio had no chance to see her because the General alighted quickly and approached smiling. "Well, young fellow," he said, "I see you didn't run away."

Horatio smiled. "No, sir."

The General motioned toward the wharf shanty. "Well, come let's see what Billy has for us to sign."

The fat clerk was still radiating good humor. "Yo' had 'em beat hands down!"

General Jameson nodded. "No competition, Billy?"

Billy's rumbling laugh filled the room. "Nary a bit, Gen'rul. Nary a bit." He hitched his chair closer to the desk. "Reg'lar five-year contract." He picked up a sheet of paper perforated down the center and turned to Horatio. "Yo' want me t' read this heah foolishment?"

Horatio looked blank. "Why, I . . ."

Billy laughed. "Don't make no difference. Yo' gotta listen. The law says yo' gotta listen." He started reading from the paper so rapidly and in such a rumbling monotone that Horatio grasped nothing except his name and the words "five years." Billy paused and cleared his throat. "Now, I'll tell yo' what this thing says, boy. It says that yo've bound yo'self to wuk well an' faithfully for Gen'-rul Jameson heah for five years. In return he pays yo' passage money to this country an' he promises to keep meat on yo' bones an' clothes on yo' back. Any time befo' the five years is finished, if yo' has the money an' Gen'rul Jameson is willing, yo' can buy yo'-self free. If yo' stays out the term of yo' indenture, the Gen'rul has to send yo' away happy with new clothes, fifty dollahs in cash, a gun, an' he has t'give yo' forty acres of land or the equivalent in sound money. That's all."

Horatio brightened and nodded.

Billy slapped the contract on the desk. "Now yo' sign heah in two places." After they had signed, Billy tore the paper in half along the perforated lines and handed Horatio one half and General Jameson the other. He leaned back and chuckled. "Now I pronounces yo' man an' wife."

General Jameson folded his half of the indenture carefully and placed it in a black leather wallet. "You'll make the exchange for this out of my account, Billy?"

Billy nodded absently. He was studying Horatio carefully. "Yo're sure a big 'un," he said finally. He turned to the General. "Yo' ain't gonna let those niggers of yours smash up this heah boy, is yo', Gen'rul?"

The General's laugh was light. "Silence, Billy, you'll frighten the young man."

Horatio was still wondering at this humor when he and General Jameson reached the carriage. The General motioned to the vacant seat next to the Negro driver and Horatio raised one foot to climb aboard when the General stopped him in casual afterthought and nodded toward the rear of the carriage. "Oh, yes, Tench, this is my daughter—Miss Clover." Painfully aware of his awkward position, Horatio flushed and tried to execute a small bow. The effect, he knew, was far short of graceful. He could have saved his worry. Clover Jameson hardly looked his way. But in his brief glimpse Horatio saw that she was as pretty as her father was handsome. Her skin was fair, almost too pale, but her eyes were big and dark and ringed by incredibly black lashes. Her hair was jet black. She was so small, so fragile that if it had not been for her frilly yellow gown, Horatio might have taken her for a child. She also had a child's pretty, soft mouth, but there was nothing child-like about the glance she gave him. It was at once bored and haughty. She made no acknowledgment of his bow. Horatio stood a moment in indecision, then clambered to his seat. The Negro clucked to the bays. In the instant before the carriage started, Horatio heard Clover Jameson's voice, low and petulant, "Just who is that person, Daddy?" The General's reply was lost in the sound of creaking harness and turning wheels.

Horatio had never ridden behind horses before. He was torn between fascinated contemplation of the great, shiny rumps jogging before him and the sights and sounds and smells of the town about him. Even this waterfront was different. On the warehouse platforms were great bales of skins and furs, bags of rice and hogsheads of tobacco, barrels of turpentine and racks of dried fish. It was just the sort of wharfage he had expected to find in this raw, new country.

Perhaps that is why Charleston proper came as a surprise. He expected to see rude, temporary-looking houses. Maybe even Indians. Instead, he sat open-mouthed in wonder. These streets seemed as aged and much more splendid than the finest sections of Yarmouth. He was too wonder-struck and excited to see it clearly. He had a confused and vague impression of huge houses nestled in the cool shade of tremendous old trees, big stores and fine churches, secluded streets lined with stuccoed houses, multicolored tiles, hipped roofs, wrought-iron grilles and piazzas which had two and three decks, braces of fine horses and women dressed finer than queens. It seemed that there were flowers everywhere. There was something sleepy and yet urgently awake about this town, something exhilaratingly new yet nobly old.

And, when at last they left Charleston's cobbled streets and struck a broad, clay turnpike, the spaciousness and largeness of everything overwhelmed him. Giant live oaks, gnarled with age and bearded with Spanish moss, were everywhere. He contrasted them with the scraggly, wind-twisted trees which grew near Yarmouth. He thought of the reeking, twisting, narrow streets of Yarmouth and then looked with wonder at the broad, flat acres stretching on either side of the road as far as the eye could see. This was truly a new world. And that endless canopy of sky? Surely this was not the same sky that domed England. This sky was blue, calm, filled with slow-moving white clouds. The sky he knew had been greenish-gray, and the clouds had seemed dark and somehow threatening on the calmest day. Everything was wonderful. He smiled with a secret delight.

After an hour's travel they mounted a slight rise and General Jameson's cane tapped him on the shoulder. He turned and the General smiled and pointed with his cane. "Over there, Tench. That's where we're bound. That's Fair Haven."

Horatio squinted against the setting sun. In the distance a cluster of gleaming white buildings rose out of an island of green in the brown fields. There were a half-dozen buildings of all sizes. Towering majestically and protectively over them all was a huge manor house, fronted with immense white columns. The central part of the house was two-storied and made of brick, but it was flanked with two rambling wooden wings which were one-storied. A broad veranda swept the entire length of the house. It was the biggest, most pretentious dwelling that Horatio had ever seen. He sat lost in admiration as with each turn of the carriage wheels it seemed to loom larger and grander. But it wasn't until the carriage left the road, entered a massive wrought-iron gate, and wheeled up a drive lined with cedars that Horatio saw Fair Haven in all its glory. He had never dreamed of such grandeur.

It was not surprising that Horatio was dazzled. For nearly a century, far worldlier and more expert eyes had been proclaiming Fair Haven as one of the loveliest homes in America. It had the rare quality of being both ambitious and comfortable, both pretentious and livable. Its long wings gave it spaciousness, but its central brick portion lent it age and dignity. Time and weather had faded these bricks to a soft russet, that unmistakable shade of age that could not be duplicated in any kiln. It was the sign that for all its sumptuousness, money alone had not created Fair Haven. One knew that this house had seen birth and death, love and long living.

The manor sat on a slight rise and looked down a rolling, velvet-smooth lawn to the river a quarter-mile away. This lawn was dotted with great towering oaks and crisscrossed with small, well-kept paths. Horatio could not detect an extra long blade of grass or a single fallen leaf on its incredibly green expanse. As he looked down toward the river, which had caught the sunset and seemed to flow golden before his eyes, Horatio shook his head wonderingly. "B'fair," he said, "it's a palace. It's a palace."

The carriage pulled up before the house. It had hardly stopped before an old Negro man came from the veranda and shuffled splay-footedly down a path flanked by boxwood high as his head. He caught the bridle of the lead horse, all the time grinning and bobbing his head. "Yes, suh! Yes, suh!" he said. "Yes, suh!"

The General alighted and helped his daughter down. She walked into the house quickly. General Jameson was talking to the old Negro. "Everything go well in our absence, Jerusalem?"

The old man continued smiling and bowing. "Yes, suh, Marse. Yes, suh." He started to gather up the bundles on the floor of the carriage, but the General stopped him. "Leave them there until later," he said. He nodded toward Horatio. "First I want you to take this young man to the quarters above the stable. He'll be staying with us awhile."

The Negro nodded eagerly. "Yes, suh."

The General smiled at Horatio. "I think you'll be comfortable there, Tench. Jerusalem will show you where to eat. I'll see you tomorrow and we'll have a chat."

Old Jerusalem was grinning broadly at Horatio. "Yo' got baggage?" he asked. Horatio shook his head. Jerusalem inclined his head. "Foller me, please. Foller me."

When they were out of earshot of the front of the house, the old Negro's whole manner changed. His face was stern and sullen. He looked at Horatio closely. "Yo' 'dentured?"

Horatio nodded. "Aye."

Jerusalem snorted. The sound was sharp and contemptuous. He didn't speak again until he had showed Horatio to a whitewashed, severely furnished room above the carriage house. He grunted. "Yo' eats in de kitchen wif de house help, 'dentured mans." He gave Horatio another long, searching look and laughed. There was no humor in the sound. It was cold and malicious. "Ah wonders how long yo' gonna stay heah after King gits done wif yo'," he said. He snorted again and shuffled from the room.

Horatio took a deep breath and looked about the walls of his new home. He lay back on the bed slowly and looked up at the ceiling.

CHAPTER VII

H E WAS awakened at dawn. "Rise up, 'dentured mans! Rise up!"

Horatio sat bolt upright in bed and for a startled moment had difficulty in remembering where he was. Then he saw old Jerusalem's scowling face. He rubbed his eyes and grinned sheepishly, "B'fair, I didn't know where I was."

Jerusalem snorted and tossed some clothes on the bed. "Marse Randolph want ter see yo' soon's yo' had yo' breakfast. He say ter put on dese clothes an' yo' gonna git fitted fer some boots sometime terday. Hustle yo' bones naow! Hustle yo' bones!" He shuffled from the room.

Horatio sprang from bed. Filling an earthenware bowl with water from a matching pitcher, he doused his face and head. The clothing delighted him. The waistcoat and baggy pantaloons were made of a grayish-white unbleached cotton, but the shirt was of finer material, which he later learned was cotton broadcloth. It had a limp stock attached. After he dressed, he stood in the center of the room, smiling and running his hands over his new clothes and wishing he had a mirror to examine himself. His waistcoat felt snug when he squared his big shoulders, but he was still smiling and feeling every inch the gentleman when he walked out into the misty, half-light of the morning.

He breakfasted on fried pork sidemeat and tender lye hominy covered with syrup at a wooden table in the center of Fair Haven's mammoth, stone-floored kitchen. The fat Negro woman who served him scowled ferociously at first, but when he asked for a second helping of everything, she smiled. "Yo' likes ter eat."

Horatio grinned. "Yes, mum."

The woman studied Horatio closely, then her broad face became wreathed in smiles. "Ah don't keer wut they says, me'n yo' gonna git erlong all right," she said.

They were laughing and chatting and Horatio was finishing the last of his breakfast when Jerusalem entered. He looked at the cook severely and scowled at Horatio. "Marse Randolph want ter see yo' naow, 'dentured mans."

As Horatio followed Jerusalem into the house and through a long hallway, he felt first surprise and then awe at the fittings of Fair Haven. He had never seen such luxury. They passed room after room filled with delicate, highly polished furniture and carpeted with thick, beautifully colored rugs. Horatio began to feel uncomfortable in the midst of such finery. It seemed to him that his feet clattered with unnatural loudness on the polished floors. He was walking almost on tiptoe when they reached a door at the end of the hall and Jerusalem knocked softly.

Horatio heard General Jameson's voice. "Come in."

Jerusalem opened the door, motioned Horatio inside, then shut the door again softly. General Jameson's study was in keeping with the rest of the manor. It was a large, slightly oval room and the walls were covered with books. That alone was enough to make Horatio bug-eyed. He had never seen more than a half-dozen books in his life, and he had no idea that so many had been printed. The floor of the study was covered with a thick, grayish-green carpet, and it seemed to Horatio that he sank in it to his boot tops. General Jameson was seated at a low writing table. Horatio stood hesitantly at the door until he looked up and flashed him a smile.

"Ah, Tench—" he motioned to a leather-backed chair—"be seated here. I'll have this completed in a moment." Horatio sat uncomfortably.

After several minutes General Jameson finished writing with a flourish, sanded the paper well, and sat back with a sigh. "Well, young man," he said in his pleasant voice, "I trust you slept well on your first night at Fair Haven?"

Horatio nodded and smiled. "Aye, sir."

The General looked at Horatio carefully. "And the clothing?"

Horatio ran his hand over the front of his new waistcoat. "B'fair, it's wonderful, sir."

The General smiled. "I'm pleased. Everything you have on was grown here, woven here, and tailored here." He pointed a slim finger. "That very waistcoat was once growing in my fields."

He sat smiling a moment, then settled deeper in his chair. "Now, young man, I think we should discuss your work here. Old Doctor Franklin, up in Philadelphia, used to say that early to bed and early to rise makes a man healthy, wealthy, and wise." He smiled. "As you no doubt see, we try to follow that formula around here." He paused, pulled reflectively at his bottom lip, and his whole manner changed. He leaned forward and his face was serious. "You are a young man, Tench, but you're big and husky—can you fight?"

The question surprised Horatio, even frightened him a little. Instantly his mind leaped back to that last night in Samuel Tompkins' shop and he could feel the blood rushing to his face. He swallowed and looked at the floor. Finally he looked up. The General was watching him closely. "Well, can you, Tench?"

Horatio took a deep breath and looked full in General Jameson's questioning face. "Aye, sir. I can fight if I have to—but . . . but I don't like to."

The General's expression didn't change. "But what if you are forced to fight, Tench? Would you do it then?"

Horatio nodded slowly. "Aye, sir, I would fight then."

The General settled back, his face still serious. "Well, then, Tench, I'll explain the situation at Fair Haven. I feel that I should apprise you of the facts at the beginning, so that you'll be prepared for any—er . . . ah—difficulties that you may encounter." He took a deep breath. "I have more than a hundred hands, Tench. All of them work unless they are too old or are still in the cradle. Most of them have been with me a long time. Some of them came during my father's day. Others were born here. By and large, they are well-trained and reasonably civilized and they appear to be loyal and happy. But I can't be sure. Old Jerusalem out there—" he motioned toward the rest of the house—"held me when I took my first steps. He was my father's body servant, but I still don't understand what goes on in that black head of his and I never will. I dress my black people and I feed them, and sometimes when I walk among them I feel that they are nothing but happy, overgrown children." He shook his head and his face was serious. "They're not children, Tench, and I'm not sure that they are really happy. I shan't dwell too much on the manner of people they are. I could talk all day and still not teach you as much about them as you'll learn in one hour by observing them in the fields or at the warehouses."

He leaned forward. "What I do want to tell you, Tench, is that you're in danger here. You may have to fight! I expect that you will!"

Horatio had been listening with growing bewilderment. "But . . . but why, sir?"

The General dropped the corners of his mouth in a wry grimace. "It isn't a pretty tale, Tench, and it doesn't add luster to Fair Haven. However, I suppose it must be repeated." He settled back with a sigh. "In my father's day, the overseer of this plantation was a bonded servant—a big, hairy lout of a brute named Lampley. He was English, Tench, and I think originally from the northern part of your country. I hated the man when I was a child and the memory of him sickens me now. Many's the time I've seen him club some poor field hand to the ground and whip him until my blood ran cold. My father was—er, shall we say a . . . a severe man, Tench—and he never interfered with Lampley. The man ran the place with an iron hand. He carried a bull whip with him wherever he went, and he delighted in using it. The hands hated him, naturally—and they still hate the memory of him, though—" the General paused and his voice thickened with disgust—"though, some of them are Lampley's children and grandchildren. It's a circumstance, I might add, which pleases them no more than it did their mothers."

The General's voice was sharp. "Lampley was a swine—a completely worthless pig. He worked for my father until his indenture expired, then he was made overseer officially and his cruelties and filthiness increased with each year. I had long before made up my mind what I would do when I became master of Fair Haven, and on the day after my father's funeral I went to Lampley's quarters to tell him to pack his belongings and get off the place. He was not there, and though we looked for him all that day, we didn't find him until the next morning."

The General's voice was flat. "He was dead, Tench, and he had died horribly. We found him in the hog pens—or what was left of his worthless carcass after the hogs had done chewing at him. What amazed us was that he apparently had been trampled to death by the hogs. Finally we surmised that he had fallen in the pens in a drunken stupor and the hogs had become panicky and trampled him. There wasn't an inch of his body which didn't bear a hoof mark."

The General stood up and walked to a nearby cabinet. "We held to that theory for a long time, Tench, until one day I found several of these in a gully near the creek." He reached in the cabinet and brought out a stout oaken club and handed it to Horatio. Horatio examined the heavy stick curiously. An animal's hoof was fastened to one end with a tough thong of leather. He raised his eyes. "This is a pig's hoof?"

The General nodded and took the weapon. "Yes, it's a pig's hoof and it's razor sharp." He thumped the heavy end of the club on the floor. "A man could be pinned down and killed slowly with a weapon like this." He replaced the club in the cabinet and resumed his seat. His face was somber.

"I'm not sorry that Lampley was killed. I'm not even sorry about the manner of his death. I think it only fitting that a pig's hoof was used to do the work." He leaned forward again. "I am sorry and disturbed by a series of events that have followed Lampley's demise. I found long ago that I couldn't use a paid overseer at Fair Haven. Most men who take jobs of that type are naturally coarse and low and brutal. I tried several of them, and despite my implicit orders, they beat and abused my people. I ran them off the place. Then, five years ago, I bought the bond of a German named Sturm and decided to train him for the job. I felt that, at least, a bonded servant would follow my orders. He didn't stay on the place four months. He was beaten unmercifully one night by a group of workers—men and women—who waylaid him by the stables. He recovered and I gave him permission to carry a whip and a blade for protection." General Jameson shook his head. "It did no good. He was attacked a second time and beaten so badly that I feared for his life. He was in such a fright that I sold his indenture to a merchant in town.

"The second incident occurred a year ago. I bought the bond of an Englishman named Hardcastle. He was a big, strong man with a rare sense of humor, and I thought that either his strength or his humor might save him. The results were much the same, though no stealth was employed this time. The workers at the warehouse deliberately slowed their work, and when Hardcastle remonstrated with them, they laughed in his face." He cleared his throat. "Hardcastle made the mistake of slapping one of them. Then King cut him to ribbons in a fight."

Horatio remembered the name. "Who is King, sir?"

The General smiled slightly. "King is the best worker on this plantation. He was born here and—" he paused an instant—"if I were to ask him to lay down his life tomorrow, I believe he would do so. He's a huge black man and you'll realize what the other hands think of him when I tell you that he was named Alfred at birth. The hands gave him the name of King when he was twenty. They picked him through some ceremony of their own. Maybe you'll understand why when you see King."

The General shook his head slowly. "I was so furious, so upset when I saw Hardcastle's battered face that I did something which I had done only twice before in my life. I ordered a man—King—whipped. I picked the men to do it and I supervised the laying on. King took that lashing without a whimper, without flinching. When they cut him down, he turned politely and bowed to me and walked away. Alas, Hardcastle wasn't made of such stern stuff. He refused to go near the warehouse, and I didn't press him because I felt contempt for his cowardice. I sold his bond."

General Jameson slapped the table, and for the first time Horatio saw anger sparkle in his dark eyes. "Now I've had enough! The laws of this state do not allow me to teach a black man to read or write. And I must have a man who can help me with my accounts. I must! I've put King in charge of the workers in the fields, but I must have a man in the warehouse who can keep records. If need be, I'll bring in drivers with whips, but, by God!—" he slapped the table again—"I'm going to fight this thing."

He sat a moment, eyes flashing, then spread his hands and smiled. "You see, young man, you have a job. I'm going to try you at the warehouse. You're young and the hands may accept you. If not—" he paused and shrugged—"you may have to fight. I've never tried a young man before, but neither have I tried a man with shoulders as broad as yours." He looked directly in Horatio's eyes. "I want you to understand one thing. If you are forced to fight, I am prepared to back you to the limit. I want you to hesitate at nothing." His eyes darkened. "If necessary, I'm willing to sacrifice a man or two. As for yourself, I don't think you'll have to worry about getting killed. You may be beaten, but the penalty for murder is quick and certain and the hands know it." He smiled wryly. "I do think that you should be warned that the men are adept at a test of strength they call pop-skull. In it, one man smashes his head against the head of another. They duel in this manner until one of them is battered senseless."

The General sat silently for a long time, apparently lost in thought. He looked up suddenly. "Are you willing to help me in this fight, Tench?"

Horatio hesitated. He remembered the pleasant, beaming cook in the kitchen. "Well . . . well, maybe I won't have to fight, sir."

Something almost like annoyance shadowed the General's fine brow, but his voice was pleasant. "Ah, Tench, you're young and new to this country. I'm merely asking for your allegiance. I'll give you a good home and keep you well clothed—and all I ask in return is your loyalty." He shrugged. "I had hoped for some measure of gratitude."

Horatio hesitated for the barest second. He tightened his jaw and nodded. "I'll do what you say, sir."

The General stood up and thrust out his hand. "Thank you, Tench. You'll have cause to see that a victory will be well worth the battle. There are many things here waiting for a man who has determination and willing hands."

Horatio clasped the General's hand and smiled. General Jameson raised his eyebrows in mock surprise. "Can it be that you are amused?"

Horatio shook his head. "No, sir. I was thinking of what you said. A dear friend once told me that nothing could stop a man with willing hands and determination. He . . . he even mentioned a plantation."

After lunch General Jameson and Horatio left the house for a tour of Fair Haven. It was a bright, sunny afternoon, and as they walked along, the General smiled and chatted but made no reference to their earlier conversation. He took especial pride in pointing out the arrangement of the huge formal garden behind the manor. It was made up of six separate gardens, which were divided by trim hedges and walks in intricate patterns. The General motioned with his cane. "Yonder is the herb garden, Tench, and next to it is the bowling green. Over there is the fruit garden. The others are planted in flowers."

Horatio nodded. "It must take a lot of work, sir."

The General smiled. "Indeed it does, but you should see it in the spring. I think you'll agree . . ." He stopped and was looking toward the manor. Horatio followed his gaze. A tall woman in a purple dressing gown stood on a balcony outside one of the upstairs rooms, leaning heavily on a Negro maid and looking down on the garden. At the distance Horatio could not make out her features, but he could tell that she was thin to the point of gauntness. Her face was dead white in the bright sunlight. The General waved his cane and she raised a white hand in a weak reply. The General turned away and there was a little furrow of worry between his brows. "That's Mrs. Jameson, Tench," he said quietly. He poked at the ground with his cane. "She's been ill for sometime but we hope . . ." He broke off and looked up with a quick smile and spoke briskly. "But come, I have to show you around."

There were a half-dozen outbuildings near the manor and they visited them all. Horatio was fascinated. The hands were still at dinner and it was like roaming through a small village that was uninhabited.

One of the buildings was a cobbler's shop, and when Horatio saw that the shelves which covered it from floor to ceiling were filled with shoes, he stood open-mouthed in amazement. The General chuckled. "It isn't usually this full, Tench. Almost none of the hands except house servants wear shoes during the summer. In the spring they leave their shoes here to be repaired. They'll be calling for them when the first frost falls."

The harness shop was nearby and various articles of leather were hanging from wooden pegs on the wall. The General smiled with pride as he took them down for Horatio to examine. He showed him a finely tooled martingale set with brass rivets and a pair of new saddlebags which were being stamped with an intricate floral design. Horatio nodded with appreciation. "This is fine work, sir."

The General smiled. "Indeed it is, Tench. The man who did

this is almost eighty now and he's nearly blind. His name is Ep and he's a rare character. He's been here every since my grandfather's day, and he works when he pleases and does what he pleases." He chuckled and motioned Horatio over to a sidesaddle which sat on a block near the window. It was covered with dust and he rubbed it off and showed Horatio a half-finished design. "Ep started working on this three years ago for Miss Clover. He's never finished it because she came in one day and threw a tantrum and insisted that he rush the work on it." He shook his head. "Well, there it sits. It doesn't appear that Ep will ever finish it."

One long building was completely filled with spinning wheels and looms. "This is where your clothing was made, Tench," the General said. He fingered the piece of cloth on a table in the center of the room and smiled with pleasure. "I'll put up my broadcloth against anyone's, Tench."

They passed to the blacksmith shop, the laundry, a wagon shop, and lastly they visited the smokehouse whose rafters were covered with hanging hams and sides of bacon and turkeys. Horatio was dazzled. He shook his head. "You have everything here, sir."

The General nodded. "Yes, Tench, we're self-contained. But you haven't seen it all yet. We won't visit the stables until you get ready for a horse, and, of course, we've got hogs and milch cows— and over yonder—" he pointed to a row of buildings in the distance —"are our tobacco houses. Tobacco used to be the principal crop at Fair Haven but now we raise only enough for our own use. We have a grist-mill down by the creek, and directly, when we reach the quarters, I'll show you our cabinet-making shop."

Horatio looked at him with amazement. "You mean the furniture in your house was made here?"

The General laughed delightedly. "Bless me, no. Old Uncle Gus is an excellent workman, but hardly that good. Most of the manor furniture was made by your own countrymen, though we do have several excellent pieces made by French and Italian artisans. Uncle Gus is kept busy making beds and cradles and chests for the quarters."

They walked on and Horatio's wonder grew. There was a slaughter house, turkey and chicken houses, and a dairy. Horatio shook his head. "B'fair, it is a real town," he said.

The General seemed pleased. "Indeed it is." He pointed down the road. "And here come some of the inhabitants."

Approaching was a long line of Negroes, their bare feet raising clouds of dust on the dirt road. As they drew nearer, Horatio could hear them chattering and laughing like a group of children turned out of school. Women were leading the procession, and to Horatio's inexperienced eyes they all looked strangely alike in long shapeless dresses flopping about their ankles and tightly tied kerchiefs covering their heads. Behind them were the men, and although they were of all ages and sizes, they, too, seemed to Horatio to have a startling resemblance to each other. They wore coarse cotton shirts, darkened by sweat at the armpits and neckline, and tight breeches which scarcely covered their shins. The children brought up the rear and they were darting in and out of the line, yelling shrilly. Suddenly they must have seen the General and Horatio because the line became more orderly and the laughing and chattering stopped.

As the line drew nearer, Horatio remembered his conversation with the General and his curiosity was tinged with uneasiness. Then he saw that every black face in the group carried a broad smile. He and the General stepped to the side of the road, and as each woman drew abreast, she flashed a wider smile and bowed. The men swept off their great floppy hats and their teeth showed startlingly white against their broad, black faces. The General had removed his own hat and he returned the greetings, smiling and nodding. When the little pickaninnies passed, they lowered their heads embarrassedly and cut their eyes at the General and giggled. He reached out his hand several times to run it across a small woolly head.

Horatio had never seen so many black people before. As the group drew abreast, he had been smiling, but now his face was thoughtful. Somewhere deep within him he had felt a sudden nudge of memory. It was a memory which eluded him and could not be fully drawn, but it left him with the odd feeling that somehow, somewhere, he had seen these dark faces before, he had smelled the odor of their bodies and . . . and . . . the feeling was so acute, so obviously unreasonable that he shook his head in bewilderment.

He turned to watch the group with a thoughtful frown. They

were laughing and giggling once more now, and two tiny boys were running in and out of line, leaping up and down and squealing delightedly.

Horatio turned slowly to the General. "There are a lot of them, sir."

The General smiled. "Why, that's the merest part of them, Tench. The merest part. The men in that group work in the stables and around the grounds. Directly I'll show you my husky men at the warehouse. But come—first you must see the quarters."

Horatio already had begun to expect miraculous things of General Jameson and his beloved Fair Haven, so he was not surprised to find that the slaves' quarters were in reality a small village. There were row after row of single-roomed, weather-beaten cabins encircling a square in which were located two wells. There was a monotonous similarity to all the cabins, but yet it was a pleasant place. The small porches had been scrubbed until the pine plankings were faded and fuzzy and this cleanliness seemed to extend to the very ground itself. Countless thousands of hard, bare feet had worn the black soil bare of grass and had packed it hard and smooth. And over the whole area there hung the pungent fragrance of wood smoke, the unmistakable, not unpleasant odor of sweaty bodies and strong lye soap, of long-eaten corn-bread and cabbage, and dozens of stronger stenches that age and human habitation put on a place.

An old woman, stooped and shriveled with age, sat on one of the porches picking at a mass of what appeared to be dirty wool. General Jameson saw her and his face brightened. He swept off his hat. "Good morning, Aunt Margaret. I see you're hard at work." The old woman raised her head and peered at the General. Horatio was astonished that anyone could be so old. She seemed to be made of brown wood ash and cobwebs and her eyes had faded until they seemed to be blank. She bared her toothless gums in a smile. "Marse James," she cackled. "Marse James."

General Jameson smiled. "She thinks I'm my grandfather," he said quietly. He raised his voice again. "I hope you are in the best of health, Auntie Margaret?"

The old woman picked up a double handful of the dirty fiber and thrust it out at him. "Ise gittin' mah buryin' dress ready, Marse James. Ise gittin' mah buryin' dress ready."

The General nodded. "I see, Auntie, I see." He took a pinch of the fiber and handed it to Horatio. "Have you seen this?"

Horatio turned the fiber in his fingers. He nodded. "It's cotton, but it's stained."

General Jameson shook his head. "No, it isn't stained, Tench. It grows that way. It's nankeen—what we call slave cotton. Every full-grown hand at Fair Haven is allowed an acre of land to plant what he wants. Most of them plant nankeen."

"Why don't they grow ordinary cotton, sir?" Horatio asked.

General Jameon laughed. "Because it's much cheaper for me if they grow nankeen, young man. There's no danger that by accident—" he lifted his brows—"or worse—that my cotton will get mixed with the workers' cotton. This way there's no danger that I lose any."

He replaced the cotton in the old woman's lap and lifted his hat again. "Good day, Auntie." Aunt Margaret gave no sign that she heard. She was again busy at work pulling at the cotton in her lap and muttering to herself.

The General's face was thoughtful as they walked away. "Aunt Margaret," he said, "was a house servant during my grandfather's day. I used to slip down here when I was a youngster and listen to her stories. She was an old woman even then, but she claimed she remembered being captured as a child and being out on the block at Charleston." He smiled. "The house was so overrun with servants when she was a girl that her only duty was to put the chairs at the table before each meal and pull them back again when it was finished."

"How long do the . . . the hands work each day, sir?" Horatio asked.

"Twelve hours generally," the General said. "I put that rule in effect when I took over the management of Fair Haven. Until that time they had worked from can to can't."

"Can to can't, sir?"

The General smiled. "Ah, Tench, I forget you are a stranger to our shores. 'Can to can't' means from the time you can see in the morning until you can't see at night." He shook his head slowly. "During the height of our summers that can be a long, long time." He tilted his head and paused. "Listen!"

Horatio stopped. Far off in the distance he could hear men's

voices raised in a slow, rhythmical chant. He looked questioningly
at the General.

"You hear the hands at the warehouse."

"They sound happy, sir."

The General smiled and shook his head thoughtfully. "I hope
they are happy, Tench, but I very much doubt if a song is any in-
dication. All oppressed peoples seem to sing, and 'tis an odd thing,
there is something similar about their songs—something earthy,
strangely moving. When I was a lad, not as old as you, I sailed
aboard one of my father's ships for Odessa. I've never forgotten the
Russian serfs I saw there on the docks, big, blank-faced men, looking for all the world like clumsy bears in their heavy fur coats.
And they chanted while they worked. The songs seemed to come
deep from within them and the sadness of them told more than
anything of their years of oppression under cruel czars. Indeed,
'tis strange when we think of song as reflecting joy and happiness.
In truth, our greatest music was born from unhappineess. During
the war, I hear men singing around the camp fires at night. They
sang of home and their dear ones, and their voices differed little
from the voices of British prisoners in a nearby stockade. They all
had the same somber, tragic note in their voices. 'Tis an odd fact,
for fair."

They walked in silence.

There were three warehouses, barny, oblong buildings, sitting
high off the ground on pillars of mortared stone. A chest-high platform, about eight feet wide, reached by steps at either end, ran
across the front of each building. The platforms were thronged
with sweating black men loading bales of cotton into huge wagons
drawn by patient mules. As Horatio approached, he saw that the
song the men sang was really a chanting cadence by which they
loaded the wagons. He watched as a tall thin Negro emerged from
the wide doorway of one warehouse, pulling a low, iron-wheeled
cart on which rested a bale of cotton. As he approached the edge
of the platform, the Negro sang out:

> *"Ise got er big-g-g-g 'un heah,*
> *Oh, Lawd, Ise got er*
> *Big-g-g-g 'n heah!"*

The waiting workers converged on the bale, one at the rear, and took up the chant:

>*"Git dis big-g-g-g 'un,*
> *Huff-f-ff!*
> *Git dis big-g-g-g 'un,*
> *Huff-f-ff!"*

At the third explosive huff, they strained their muscular shoulders and sent the bale tumbling into the bed of the wagon. The Negro with the now empty cart threw back his head:

>*"Dat makes two-o-o-o*
> *An' two-o-o-o ter go!*
> *Oh, Lawd, dat makes two-o-o-o*
> *An' two-o-o-o ter go!"*

The entire performance was so well timed and done with such zest that Horatio smiled with delight. They were on the platform before the largest warehouse before one of the Negro loaders saw them. His white teeth flashed in a wide grin and he threw back his head and yelled. "Get ter wuk, yo' no-'count loafers, 'cause heah comes Marse Randolph bigger'n life!' His throat swelled with a high, rollicking laugh which died on a shrill falsetto.

General Jameson smiled and bowed right and left. The Negroes bowed and grinned back, but Horatio saw that they were examining him closely from the corners of their eyes. Not a single man turned to face him directly. Horatio made every effort to be casual. His palms were damp.

The Negro loader raised his voice again in a bantering tone. "Yo' come down heah ter whup dese no-'count niggers, Marse?'"

General Jameson joined the laughter. "Not today, Rufe, not today. Is King inside?"

"Yes, suh, yes, suh. He's inside," the men nodded. Horatio was aware that although their faces were split in wide grins, their amber eyes were cool when they shot him glances of wary appraisal. He felt the blood rising to his face and he fought to keep it down.

There were a dozen men in the warehouse, but Horatio spotted King immediately. He would not have failed to see him in a crowd ten times as large. It was not his size, for King was not unusually tall; he was perhaps even a shade shorter than Horatio. Neither was it his build, though he was beautifully proportioned with broad shoulders, long, hard-muscled arms and legs, slim hips, and a flat belly. There was just an air of unmistakable command about the man. He was talking to one of the loaders, and apparently he was giving an order, for the man stood at rapt, obedient attention, nodding respectfully.

General Jameson called, "King, oh, King!"

King turned quickly. When he saw the General he smiled and dismissed the loader with a wave of his hand. Horatio noticed that his smile was one of real friendliness and dignity. As he approached, Horatio saw that he walked gracefully, bouncing slightly on the balls of his feet. There was a lazy grace about the way he carried his body, and Horatio thought of a cat. Then he realized that was not true. There was nothing slinking about King. If he had the gait of a cat, it was the gait of the biggest of them all —a lion perhaps.

King was black, coal-black. His features were broad and generous. As he drew nearer, Horatio was surprised to see that his crisp, woolly hair was sprinkled with gray. His voice was low and soft, and he didn't make it servile when he spoke to General Jameson.

"Good day, suh."

General Jameson returned the greeting. "How is the work progressing, King?" he asked.

King shrugged his shoulders. "Might be good an' might be bad, Marse Randolph. Ah figger we got nigh on to ten hundert bales moved."

The General grunted with approval. "You always do a good job, King." He gestured toward Horatio. "You'll be in a better position to handle things from now on, though. This young man—Mister Tench—will be down tomorrow to start a list."

King had kept his face averted from Horatio. Even now it seemed that he faced him against his will. It was something felt rather than seen because there was not a flicker of emotion on his face. He made no acknowledgment of the General's half-introduction, but turned and looked at Horatio silently. Their eyes met and hung for a moment, then King turned back to the General. His voice was flat. "Ah'll be 'spectin' Mistah Tench."

The General's face was watchful, but his voice was cheery. "Fine! Fine! I know that things will move more smoothly with him here. Come, Tench, I'll explain your duties—I'll see you before I leave, King."

King's voice was still flat. "Yes, suh, Marse Randolph."

General Jameson's face was thoughtful as they walked to a rude chest-high desk in one corner of the warehouse, but he made no comment. He picked up some forms from the desk. "Now, Tench, I want you to make a list . . ." He paused when he realized Horatio was looking over his shoulder. He looked up and followed Horatio's gaze to two ugly bull whips hanging from pegs above the desk. "Relics of a bygone age," the General said softly. He turned to the papers briskly.

"Now, Tench, I want you to fill out one of . . ."

CHAPTER VIII

HORATIO was at his desk at sunup. His duties were simple. All the Negroes had been put to work in one warehouse, and as they wheeled the bales of cotton out to the waiting wagons, they paused at Horatio's desk while he examined the ginner's tag and entered the number, weight, and grade of each bale in a large ledger. For the first few hours he stood tense and keyed for trouble, but as the monotonous morning wore on, he began to relax.

The workers seemed neither to notice him nor pointedly to ignore him. They pushed their heavy burdens up and stood wooden-faced while he made his notations. King had joined the other men. He showed the same passiveness. There was not a shade of emotion on his flat, handsome face. Once he pushed up a tremendous bale which scaled more than six hundred pounds. Horatio smiled as he put the figures down. "B'fair, that's a weighty one. I didn't know they ever came that big." King neither answered nor turned his head. They were the only words Horatio spoke all day. They were the only words he heard. There was not a sound in the warehouse except for the scuffle of the men's feet on the floor, the rattle of their iron-wheeled carts, or an occasional grunt as they loaded a bale.

It was mid-afternoon before Horatio became aware of this unnatural silence. He recalled that not a single voice had been raised in the loading chant. No one had laughed. He had been prepared for whispering or sly laughs, perhaps mischief or outright rebellion.

He had, in fact, some half-formed ideas of how he would meet signs of insurgency, but against the silence of these sweaty black men he was powerless. The silence gave him a feeling of uneasiness and inadequacy, and this soon fused into shame, then into anger. Before the day was over, he began to resent the black, unemotional faces which passed before him in a constant flow. His motion was brusque and sullen as he waved them on.

He was exhausted and still resentful when he stood before General Jameson in his study and handed him the ledger. The General turned the pages with his long, slim forefinger, counting as he went. Finally he looked up with a thoughtful frown. "Nine hundred and sixty-nine bales, Tench. Not a very good day's work for sixty men, is it?"

Horatio felt a rush of anger, but he kept his voice calm. "I don't suppose it is, sir."

General Jameson leaned back and pursed his lips thoughtfully. After a moment's silence he sighed and spoke. " 'Tis up to you, Tench. We'll have to get those bales moved more quickly or our new crop will be sitting in the weather." He smiled. "Get your supper now. I know you must be tired."

Horatio took the ledger and tucked it under his arm. "I'll see that they go speedier tomorrow, sir."

The General nodded. "Good night, Tench."

Horatio had his hand on the door when General Jameson's voice stopped him. "Ah, Tench . . ."

"Yes, sir?"

The General's voice was thoughtful. "I . . . I wouldn't do anything just yet," he said slowly. "Let us wait and see what happens tomorrow."

Before noon of the next day it was apparent that the men were working even more slowly. Horatio could tell it only by the row of figures in his ledger. He looked around closely from time to time but could detect no signs of dawdling or idleness. It seemed that every man was working with the same efficient, unhurried dispatch which he had seen on his first visit to the warehouse. They pushed their trucks across the uneven floor without pausing. They lifted the bales with a minimum of motion. He singled out individual men and watched them closely. They didn't appear to be lagging. Once he decided that the delay must be on the loading platform.

He left his desk and stood there, but saw nothing to arouse his suspicion. He realized that he, himself, seemed to be working as quickly as he had the day before. No sooner had he checked one bale than another worker stood before him, waiting with bored indifference. Again and again he looked at his figures. There was no disputing it. Scarcely two-thirds of the work was being done that had been done the day before. It was years before Horatio learned the secret of the maddening riddle. He was the victim of a passive resistance which had puzzled overlords since ancient Egypt. Every man had slowed his work so slightly, with such perfect timing, that the over-all tempo appeared natural. If one man had worked at normal speed, the secret would have been revealed. If one man had slowed too much, perhaps that would have given a clue. But the men geared their pace to King's—and he led them well. Every man was working unnaturally, so the unnatural appeared to be normal. Even Horatio had unconsciously geared his movements to accommodate them. He had been looking for isolated incidents of idleness. Consequently he couldn't see the forest for the trees.

That night General Jameson perused the ledger with a frown. His voice was edged with annoyance. "Six hundred and two bales, Tench! Why, 'tis not even a good half-day's work!" He looked up sharply into Horatio's set face. "Couldn't you see they were using you for a fool, Tench?"

Horatio flushed. "I looked for signs of idleness and I couldn't find any, sir."

The General scowled at the ledger. "You had sixty men—the same as yesterday?"

"Yes, sir."

The General pulled thoughtfully at his lower lip. "Tench," he said finally, "I think that every man should be able to load four bales an hour. Perhaps that's too high for an average. Let's settle definitely on three bales an hour. It is useless for you to try to watch every man. So tomorrow I want you to pick one man and keep an account of his movements. The instant—" he slapped the desk— "the very instant!—that man lags behind three bales an hour, I want you to speed him up." His face was dark. "I want it done!"

Horatio's jaw was clenched. "Yes, sir."

General Jameson paused a moment, and when he spoke again,

his voice was low. "I think you know, Tench, that King will hold you accountable for anything that happens. I want you to watch him, and I want you to be careful." He looked at Horatio steadily and pulled his big gold watch from his pocket and handed it to him. "Use this to keep time. Three bales an hour."

Horatio took the watch silently and walked from the room.

He was waiting with blank face and set jaw when the workmen came filing into the warehouse the next morning. He stood quietly until the last man had entered. Before they scattered to their duties, he rapped his desk with his knuckles. The men turned slowly, their faces indiscernible in the gloomy dawn's light. Horatio's voice was shorn of the mannered English he had learned from Aber. "Ye have not bin working hard enough," he said. "Ye'll work harder and faster today." He was tempted to say that General Jameson was dissatisfied with their work, but he decided against it. "I'll hold ye responsible," he said. He turned to his desk with a calmness he didn't feel.

For several long moments there was dead silence in the warehouse. He fought against a desire to look up. Then he heard the shuffle of feet as the men moved to their work. Within a short time there was the rumble of a truck being pulled across the uneven floor. He waited until it stopped behind him. He turned slowly. King was waiting.

King stood relaxed, almost slouching, one long muscled arm held against the bale of cotton on his truck. His flat face was expressionless. Horatio made his notations from the ginner's tag quickly, then, because he could not fight down an inner compulsion, he looked up. King was watching him closely. In the instant their eyes caught, Horatio seemed to detect a shadow of amusement on his black face. It didn't last long. King bent his heavy shoulders and began hauling his burden toward the warehouse door. Horatio turned with set face and looked at General Jameson's watch. It was exactly 5:05 A.M. He made a small check mark opposite the bale number.

The morning dragged. At 6:05 A.M., King had moved four bales. Three hours later, at 9:05, he had moved fourteen. The other men seemed to be working with the same speed. Horatio looked at the steadily lengthening list of figures with satisfaction.

It wasn't until 11:30 that he remembered to check King's work again. He saw that in the last hour and twenty-five minutes King had moved only two bales. Fearful that he had made a mistake, Horatio ran his eye down the figures again. There was no mistake. There were only two check marks to indicate King's appearance at his desk. He looked about the warehouse. King was nowhere to be seen.

Horatio turned back to his work but kept a watchful eye on the warehouse door. Fifteen minutes later King still had not appeared. He checked a few more bales, then put down his pen slowly and strode to the warehouse door. There was a low chuckle. He turned quickly. Every man in the warehouse had stopped working. He could not tell who had laughed, but about the whole group there was an air of sly mischievousness, as if they were children and one of them had thrown a snowball. His face was flushed with anger when he turned and walked out the door into the sunlight.

He saw King immediately. He was stretched lazily on a bale of cotton on the platform and laughing and jesting with the loaders. Horatio stood a moment taking in the scene and the loaders saw him. The laughter died on their lips, and they turned quickly to their work but watched him closely out of the corners of their eyes. King glanced at the doorway quickly. When he saw Horatio, he half rose, then smiled and lolled back. Horatio walked across the platform and stood above him before he spoke. His voice was tight. "Why aren't ye working?"

King smiled and stretched elaborately before he spoke. There was a hint of laughter in his tone, but his eyes were dark and watchful. "Ah's tired," he said.

Horatio's voice sounded strange to his own ears. "Get up and go to work!"

King stretched again exaggeratedly and stood up slowly. His smile was mocking. The loaders on the platform had stopped work entirely. Horatio heard the shuffle of feet behind him and he knew the warehouse door was crowded with black, watchful faces. He spoke again, measuring every word. "I want ye to work."

King's smile was thin. His voice was lazy and low. "Ah don't think Ah wants to, 'dentured mans. Yo' do mah wuk fer me. Yo' de one wut wants it done."

The low, uneasy laugh of the watching crowd had hardly started when Horatio threw back his hand and slapped King full across the face. The laugh broke on a gasp, then became a shout of surprised joy.

King stood stiffly, the marks of Horatio's fingers outlined clearly across his face. His big chest heaved with one deep breath of anger. He crouched at the knees and threw out his hands in a waving motion. "Give us room. Stan' back," he said. His eyes were pinned on Horatio's set face. With a sound halfway between a laugh and a snarl, he sprang.

Horatio was waiting. He cocked his fist with such force that he could feel the seams split in his too tight coat. He held the blow a moment, then let it fly at King's head. King jerked his head to one side and the blow bounced off his shoulder. Quick as thought, he caught Horatio in a bear hug and drew back his head and brought it forward with a quick snap. It seemed to Horatio that the world had exploded in his face. The blow caught him in the center of the forehead and he was the vortex of a thousand swirling, multicolored lights. His jaw was unhinged and he felt sick. King released him and his knees buckled. He staggered backward until his shoulders struck the wall of the warehouse. He slumped there, shaking his head dazedly.

The Negroes were wild with excitement and glee. "Git him, King!" "Bust his haid!" "Pop his ole haid, King!" Laughing, giggling, jumping up and down. White teeth flashing. Dark eyes bulging.

King stood unmoved by their shouts, smiling faintly, knees slight bent, arms outstretched and waiting. He stood poised until Horatio began to shake the fog from his head, then he sprang again. Horatio thrust out his arms instinctively. His hands caught both of King's arms just above the elbow and he hung on grimly. He was not an instant too soon. King's head shot forward with the speed of a viper, but the battering blow was short.

Again and again, he drew back his head and tried to crash it into Horatio's face. Horatio hung on frantically, muscles straining, mouth twisted in a grimace of effort. His head was clearing, but hot, needle-sharp pains were stabbing at the back of his eyes. They stood locked, straining and grunting, neither man giving an inch. Suddenly King feinted forward, then stepped back and, with an eye-bulging effort, swung Horatio off balance and sent him flying

off the platform. Horatio hit on his hands and knees with a bone-
jarring jolt. He had scrambled halfway to his feet when King
came hurtling off the platform in a flat, headlong dive. He grappled for Horatio and his fingers caught the collar of his coat. Horatio lunged forward and the coat was stripped from his back as
easily as a shuck is pulled from an ear of corn.

Both men were on their feet, circling warily. The shouting,
gesticulating slaves had come tumbling off the platform. Now they
scrambled and stumbled in their eagernes to clear an arena. King
and Horatio had their eyes glued on each other. King's cat-like
crouch was deeper, his lips no longer smiling, sweat beading his
forehead. Horatio stood erect, a dull red smear on his forehead
where he had received King's first blow. His fists were doubled
and cocked, his face set. His coat was hanging in shreds.

King lunged. There was no mistake this time. Horatio held his
blow until that black face was almost in his own. The blow was
short but it had all the strength of his shoulders behind it. Horatio
felt a sharp pain as King's teeth pierced his knuckles. King's eyes
went soft and he staggered. He took a half-step backward, waver-
ing slightly, and spat out a froth of blood and fragments of a
broken tooth.

Horatio stepped forward and lashed out with his other fist. King
drew his head back and Horatio missed. The force of the blow
threw him off balance, and before he could recover, King had
him in an iron grip. Horatio saw the black head move forward
in a blur. He tried to dodge. It was too late. He felt the sickening
crunch of bone as his nose was smashed at the base. Once more the
world was filled with those whirling, popping lights. His head fell
to one side. Not a moment too soon. King's skull caught him a
glancing blow above the right eye. He felt the skin tear apart like
dry parchment. He felt the warm, sticky flood of blood down his
face. He threw out his hands. Just in time they caught King in the
face and halted another thrust from his battering head.

They stood a moment, straining, chest to chest, then fell to the
ground. They tumbled over and over. The thick red dust rose in
clouds. It filled Horatio's mouth and eyes. His nose was useless and
every gasping breath filled his throat with dust, thick, gritty, chok-
ing. Horatio clung desperately to the twisting, straining black man
who once again was trying to crash his hard skull into his battered

face. Suddenly he felt panicky. It was an obscene, bowel-gripping fear. It filled him with self-loathing. And it was a fortunate thing. It succeeded, where pain and anger had failed, in erupting his awesome volcano of murderous anger. His limbs began to tremble. His heavy breathing became a snarl. He kicked and turned and twisted like a cornered beast. He had been fighting for survival. Now he fought to kill. He lashed and twisted and flailed and snarled insanely. It was impossible to hold him. He wrenched from King's grasp and sprang to his feet.

Now he was cold. His eyes were set. In his battered, bloody face his mouth was a thin, cruel line. He moved in a haze of red, trembling rage, no longer fighting with reason—fighting with a primitive deadliness. He lowered his head and charged with a snarl of hate. His right fist struck King in the chest. He brought it back in a sweeping backhand and slapped him deafeningly on the right ear.

King was unprepared for such a change in tactics. He had no desire to murder. He wanted merely to beat this tall young man and frighten him away. He knew that he had been succeeding. By all rights, a few more blows should have put an end to it. Now he was startled to see this battered youth take the initiative, to see his dulling eyes burn with murder. Had he fought a purely defensive battle, perhaps his experience and coolness would have won. But he met Horatio's next charge head-on and tried to gain the offense.

They grappled, chest to chest, belly to belly. King dug his fingers into the back of Horatio's neck and strained to pull his head closer for another blow with his skull. Horatio placed his hands against King's chest and pushed with all his might. King dug his fingers in tighter and hung on. It did no good. Neither pain nor strength could combat Horatio's pure animal anger. He could feel King's fingers slipping slowly, slowly from behind his neck and around the sides of his face. He could feel the sharp nails digging bloody grooves—but he felt no pain. One more mighty shove and the fingers lost their hold altogether. King stumbled backward, off balance. Horatio sprang and they fell to the ground. Horatio reached up a hand to gouge at King's eyes. King arched his neck and Horatio's hand slid slowly down his face and the forefinger caught in his lips. King shook his head wildly, but that forefinger hooked in the corner of his mouth. Horatio pulled with all his strength, a wrenching tearing motion. King's cheek parted in a jagged line from mouth to ear. For one horror-struck, gasping moment, he fell back. Horatio was on his feet like a cat. He sent the heel of one boot smashing into King's face. The crowd caught its breath as one man.

King tried to rise. His eyes were blank in his torn face. He never reached his feet. Horatio's face was a mask of cruelty as he stepped forward and smashed him in the face with all his strength. Horatio picked him up by his cotton shirt and pounded him again and again. It was sickening. He pounded him until the crowd was protesting in horror, but no man was brave enough to try to stop him. He pounded him until it seemed the life had gone from him. Then he tossed him aside.

But the madness was not gone from him yet. He turned slowly to face the frightened, wide-eyed crowd. He stood for a moment, clothes ripped to shreds, blood-drenched, face battered, chest heaving. He sprang among the crowd, flailing right and left.

"Git to work," he half-sobbed through clenched teeth. "Git to work, damn ye, git to work!" They scattered like leaves before the terrible gale of his anger.

He never knew how he reached his room. He was lying on his bed, his swollen, feverish face turned upward, when General Jameson came in. His voice was solemn. "I've just come from King's cabin," he said.

Horatio didn't move.

The General sighed. "He will live, I think, but he'll be abed for a long, long time."

Horatio lay motionless, his eyes fixed on the ceiling.

General Jameson waited, but when it became apparent that Horatio was not going to speak, he cleared his throat uncomfortably. "I . . . I want you to know that . . . that I . . . I think that it was necessary that something like this happen. I'm sorry that you were injured. You are not to go back to work until you have recovered completely."

If Horatio heard, he gave no sign. The General waited until the silence grew heavy. He looked at Horatio's grotesquely swollen face and bit his bottom lip. He sighed again and leaned forward and patted Horatio's shoulder. "Remember you are to stay abed until you feel fit to return to work. I'll sent Jerusalem over again to bathe your face."

At the door he paused. He tried to make his voice casual. "Oh, yes, I've told Jerusalem to bring some house servants over and fix up your room more comfortably. I want it fixed as . . . as—er, befits the new overseer of Fair Haven."

Horatio continued to stare at the ceiling.

BOSS OF

FAIR HAVEN

CHAPTER IX

THEY called him Boss Tench, this high-booted, hard-working overseer, whose cold blue eyes were smoky with brooding. He stood six feet, four inches tall and had the leanness of a foxhound in the spring, but his shoulders were broad enough to carry a bale of cotton.

In his four years at Fair Haven he had become a legend, and since legends beget legends, no one was quite sure where fact left off and fiction began. His mere presence in a cotton field was enough to make the laziest hand work himself into a lather. They told it gleefully. "It's lak dat cotton done turn ter popcawn when ole Boss Tench come ridin' in der field. Ain't nuthin' dere, 'cept a leetle bit—den, bam! bam! bam!—fust thing yo' knows, dem bags done bustin' full jes' lak puttin' popcawn on er hot stove."

The hands feared him, but in their fear they took a fierce pride. When they spoke his name, their eyes widened with mock apprehension and genuine awe. Stories of his strength were numerous. Some were obviously false. Others had the seed of truth but had flowered wildly in their fertile imaginations. Many were undoubtedly true. A dozen stable hands had been watching the day he became infuriated at a balky mule. They told the story around a hundred hearths while their white meat and turnip greens simmered over the coals, while their sharp-shinned, scrawny little pickaninnies sat open-mouthed.

"He hit dat mule right smack 'tween de eyes. Yes, suh! His face wuz all kinda scrooched up 'cause he wuz so mad. He hawl off

an' bam!—man 'o man!—it soun' lak he done smack dat ole
mule wif a sledgehammer. Dat ole mule jes' kinda look su'prised.
Den its eyes git all kinda white an' its legs buckle an' it jes' fall
kerplop on de groun'. Boss Tench he jes' stan' dere a minnit an'
his eyes shinin' lak a cat's eyes 'cause he's so mad. Den he reach
down an' grab de halter an' pull dat ole mule right back on its feet.
De mule kinda fidget a minnit, but Boss Tench lay his hand on
its neck an' it git quiet as er mouse and jes' shiver an' shake. Den
Boss Tench turn an' his voice cole as ice. 'Dis heah mule ain't
gonna give yo' no more trouble,' he say. Den he walk away. Dat
mule still a good mule, too. Ebertime Boss Tench come near it
still shake. Yo' don't neber haf ter whup dat mule no more. When
Boss Tench hits 'em, dey stay hit. Yes, suh!''

His name was mentioned in more elegant places. The planters,
in their fine clothes, spoke his name above the rims of their iced
drinks when they gathered at the oak-paneled clubs on Church
Street. "Two thousand bales? And why shouldn't he, man? Jameson should make twice that many. Look at that overseer he has. He
can look at a nigger and make him work harder than that shiftless
lout I have could if I gave him ten bull whips. Two thousand
bales? The devil take it! If I had Tench, I could make six thousand
bales. I vow I could!''

Or, indignantly: "It was the most insolent thing Ah've evah
seen, suh! Mah niggers were strugglin' with those bundles and Ah
turned to this Tench fella and tole him to give them a hand. He
jes' looked at me! He jes' looked at me and turned his back and
walked away. Ah was so surprised Ah didn't do a thing. Ah should
have caned the insolent fella. Insolent! Insolent! That's what he
is, suh—insolent!''

And his fellows took his measure—the Goodies and the Jere-
miahs, the indentured servants and the day laborers, the freed
Negroes and the pimply apprentices who got drunk and caroused
at the cheap ordinaries on the waterfront. "Leave him alone,"
they warned. "Leave him alone whilst he's drinking." He had the
money so they sold him scalding rotgut and they gave him distance.

They feared him. And because fear was the only yardstick of
success they knew, they admired him. When he entered their
smelly little dives dressed in his town clothes of velvet pantaloons,

striped vest, brown coat, looking like a gentleman, they cleared a path for him. They kept their eyes carefully averted while he got stone drunk. Never once did he laugh or join their revelry. They had tried to make him one of them until they learned that liquor touched over some deep-seated, explosive hoard of bitterness and hate. Snarls and backhanded slaps had discouraged most, but there were some, big, swaggering men, who demanded the full measure. He gave it to them. He broke noses and battered heads in a dozen places before there was no one left to stand against him.

The cheap women, with their deep bosoms and slack mouths, fared no better. Some of them had been bold enough, or stupid enough, to try to melt this big handsome man. If they persisted in annoying him, he slapped them across their startled faces and sent them packing.

If there was any saving grace to this ill nature, it was that he was no bully. Man or woman, rich or poor, he did not cull them.

So Horatio walked alone. No man knew him. Only two men were close enough to have the opportunity to try. One was King. The other was General Jameson.

It was inevitable that he and King should be friends, or else that they would fight again—and this time until one died. Both men knew that. When King had recovered and reported back to work, a red livid scar marring his black cheek from mouth to ear, Horatio had put the choice up to him with characteristic bluntness. "I'm glad you have recovered," he said. "I want to be friends—but I must be master."

Half a hundred black men paused in their work, eyes wide and breaths held, while King made his decision. He stood silently a long time before a half-smile flickered over his lips which were still flecked with scar tissue from the beating he had taken. "Ah reckons yo's boss," he said. Horatio thrust out his hand. King hesitated, whether from awkwardness or indecision no one ever knew, then he gripped the hand firmly. Fifty black men let out their pent-up breath with a grateful sigh. The rest of that day, and afterwards, they sang as they worked.

King thought that he had abdicated, but he soon discovered that he had lost neither his tribe nor its respect. By merely daring to stand up to Boss Tench, he had gained more stature than he would had he beaten ten ordinary men. If anything, his fight and, later, his friendship with Horatio had established him more securely as the true leader of the hands at Fair Haven. There was no pretense in Horatio's make-up. He had a ready fist to enforce his orders; he demanded a full day's work from every man, but he realized that he did not understand these black people, so he made no effort to meddle in their affairs. He had to grant permission for their marriages, arrange for their funerals, and punish their crimes. All this he did through King. At first he gave King authority only after discussing every matter with General Jameson. But, as time went on, he made the final decisions himself. Eventually he began to let King use his own excellent judgment. General Jameson was approached on only the most serious or important matters.

It was a more than satisfactory arrangement, and the respect between the overseer and the straw boss overflowed the bounds of mere friendship and became genuine affection. They were a powerful pair. Fair Haven flowered and prospered. Never before had there been so much laughter and music in the quarters. Never before had the black, crumbly soil given up such abundant crops.

King, more than anyone, felt the reckless desperation in Horatio. Many nights he sat alone in Horatio's room, waiting for him to return home after a night's drinking in town. He would slip off Horatio's boots and ease him gently into bed, and when, as frequently happened, his hands and knuckles were torn and bruised because of a brawl, he would wash and bandage them.

On other nights King kept vigil at the stables, waiting patiently to unsaddle and rub down Horatio's bay after the horse and his master had made a swift, wild excursion into the night. God only knew where Horatio went on these nighttime journeys. He rode until his horse was heaving and trembling with exhaustion and his own joints were stiff with fatigue. Only then would he return to the stables, toss his sweat-covered reins to King, and fall on his bed to sleep a long, dreamless sleep.

Others, too, knew about these night rides. Field hands sat bolt upright in bed until the thunder of Boss Tench's horse's hoofs died away in the distance. They would lie back, quiet and thoughtful and frightened. Young, giggling plowboys, walking the road with their sweethearts, sometimes heard the thunder of hoofs approaching hell-bent. They would dive into the bushes and stare wild-eyed and listen to their pounding hearts while Boss Tench sped by like a demon of the darkness. Then they crept from the bushes, all thoughts of romance gone for the night.

The hands had their own explanation for the breakneck dashes through the darkness. "Boss Tench wuz out chasin' de Debbil las' night," they said. "Whoo-sh! He come by mah place goin' so fast, dat old hoss's feets kickin' up so many sparks, it done look lak dey on fire. Boss Tench reely chasin' de ole Debbil las' night."

It was a good explanation, better than their superstitious souls could know. There was only a slight mistake. Boss Tench wasn't chasing the Devil. The Devil was chasing Boss Tench.

Only General Jameson, the ruler of Fair Haven, could have told them about that. He alone knew that his young slavemaster, the man who seemed to fear neither man nor beast, was, in truth, the most frightened of all men.

Theirs was an odd relationship. If it was poor in affection, it was rich in gratitude. It had not always been so. Horatio left his bed after his fight with King with a chill in his blue eyes. The look made General Jameson uncomfortable. Despite his gentle manners and his quiet speech, he was not a soft man, but he had felt qualms of conscience when he saw Horatio's puffy, smashed face and during the long days when King's life hung by a thread. He was realistic enough to know that the bloody battle was a small price for the results he wanted. And he had no regrets. Still he did wince inwardly every time he looked in Horatio's eyes, and he read in them accusation and bitterness. He tried to show his gratitude. Horatio's room above the carriage house was furnished with a fine rug and shiny furniture. He kept Horatio supplied with pocket money and after working hours he was free to come and go as he wished.

Horatio accepted these favors quietly, without comment. And he never gave General Jameson cause for complaint about his work. He was up with the sun and he worked harder than the lowliest hand. General Jameson had only to give an order and it was carried out to the letter. There were never protests or sly arguments or countersuggestions. Horatio was addicted to hard work as other men are addicted to pleasure. Within four months General Jameson knew he had the best overseer in the country. He was pleased, but it hurt his vanity that he could not penetrate the shell of this servant who had turned overnight from a willing, eager youth to a hard-eyed man. General Jameson felt responsible, and he wished desperately that there was something he could do.

He had no way of knowing that he was only partially right when he interpreted the light in Horatio's eyes as accusation. The resentment Horatio felt toward General Jameson actually was only a small part of the resentment he felt toward life itself. Horatio had been convinced that life was cruel and unkind because of Samuel Tompkins. Now Tompkins was dead and he had fled half around the world only to discover that a man still had to use force and brutality to make his way. His beautiful dreams of peace and equality were shattered. He was given long hours to examine those dreams as he lay in bed after his fight with King. Out of the shattered, smashed fragments he could find only one piece that was intact. That was opportunity. Horatio left his bed fiercely resolved to make the most of opportunity. Keeping General Jameson pleased was part of his duties. That he did; but he nursed the same vague contempt for the owner of Fair Haven that a soldier feels for an officer who directs but does not join a battle.

It was General Jameson's custom to invite Horatio to dine with him on Tuesday nights. Outwardly, these quiet dinners were arranged to give the General a chance to discuss the management of Fair Haven with his overseer. Actually, however, the General had two other reasons which he probably did not examine too closely himself. One was that it gave him an opportunity to use all his considerable charm in an effort to establish some bond with Horatio which was not based on courtesy and obedience. It was the human gesture of a very human man. So was the third reason. The plain truth was that General Jameson was lonely. His invalid wife was confined to her bed now and his daughter had been enrolled at a young ladies' school in Philadelphia. Never before had the General had so much free time on his hands. These dinners with Horatio were a pleasant break in the monotony of the week. He began to look forward to them.

Horatio dreaded them. It meant that he had to ride in early from the fields and bathe in haste and put on his town clothes. He was awkward and confused amid all the shining silver and spotless linen on the General's table. He was bored by endless talk of minor problems which he knew that he and King could settle in five minutes. But courteous forbearance of the General's whims was part of his job, so he sat at graven-faced attention once a week and ate the General's fine food and listened to his conversation.

He never forgot one balmy night in April. Horatio had been at Fair Haven a year. Darkness had just begun to fall and through the ceiling-high windows to the dining room he could hear the soft chirping of the tree frogs and katydids. General Jameson was carving a joint of lamb and he looked up casually.

"That Hans Zwieger, Tench. . . . Do you remember him?"

Horatio shook his head. "No, sir, I don't believe I do."

The General cut a slice of meat with graceful precision. "Bonded man," he said. "Thought I heard he came over on the same ship with you."

Horatio thought a moment. "Oh, yes," he said, "I do remember him." It was the first time since his voyage that he had thought of the pleasant, apple-cheeked German who had shared his quarters on the *Salamander*. "Is he well?"

The General served Horatio's plate and smiled. "He is now, but I daresay it won't be for long. The man's evidently a scoundrel, Tench. His bond was bought by Captain Hollyday, and yesterday a Bow Street runner showed up and placed him under arrest for murder."

"Bow Street? Murder, sir?" Horatio's voice was stiff with incredulity.

The General nodded. "Yes, never heard of the Bow Street tribe myself, but it seems they are a very talented breed of human bloodhounds the English use to track down criminals. Followed this man all around the world before they finally caught up with him." He took a bite of lamb. "Ah, this is delicious, Tench. I think the lambs this year . . ."

"But Zwieger, sir?"

"Oh, seems that he's the very devil of a murderous scoundrel. He murdered his employer in London. Very brutal affair."

Horatio's hands were icy. "What will happen to him, sir?"

General Jameson shrugged. "Oh, he'll go to the gallows, I imagine. Poor Hollyday is furious. He'll never get back a penny of his money and he had already begun to fancy the man's services, too."

Horatio was numb with shock. He took a bite of his lamb but his mouth was dry and he had difficulty chewing. He fought to keep his voice steady.

"I . . . Do the English usually pursue a man for mur—for killing someone, sir?"

General Jameson was tackling his dinner with great relish. "Yes. I think that we have some sort of treaty with them on matters of that sort. Good thing it is, too." He chewed meditatively, then his face brightened. "Oh, yes, Tench, what are you going to do about the milch cows that need freshening in the south pasture?"

Somehow Horatio managed to struggle through that evening. He spoke of milch cows and seeds and planting, but he was in a chill of anxiety. He was afraid that his uneasiness would show in his face and in his speech. He forced himself to be talkative, almost gay. He was altogether such a different person that General Jameson stood at the door a moment watching him after he had said good night. He congratulated himself on having at last broken through Horatio's cool reserve.

Horatio was aware of the General's eyes on him as he left the house. He was worn with worry. In his tortured mind he could see the General smiling grimly. "He knows," he thought. "He knows." He walked stiffly to his room, expecting any moment to have someone step out of the shadows and clap a heavy hand on his shoulder. What had the General said about pursuit of a murderer? "Good thing it is, too!" The General had been toying with him all evening and he had fallen into the trap. The General was clever. What to do? What to do?

In his room he tore off his clothes and threw himself in bed and tried to sleep. It was no use. He turned and tossed for hours. He was painfully aware of every sound in the bright night, the creak of every board. Finally, he must have dozed because suddenly he found himself in the warehouse. King was standing at his side chuckling, and General Jameson was tugging a truck across the floor. A tiny, monkey-like little man was riding the truck. A large ginner's tag fluttered from his waistcoat. The General halted the truck before Horatio and stood there panting and wiping the sweat from his forehead. Horatio put out his hand and read the tag on the little man's coat. "Bow Street Runner," it said. "Bow Street Runner!" he exclaimed. The little man stood up with an evil gleam in his eye and grabbed Horatio by the arm. "Aye, Bow Street Runner," he said. "Bow Street Runner!" His voice echoed and echoed in the warehouse. Horatio began to run and the little man started after him. King and General Jameson fell into a spasm of laughter. Horatio ran toward the door but it seemed that the floor stretched and stretched under his feet. Sweat was beading his forehead. He was gasping for breath. He wanted to rest, but he dared not because he could hear the little man's feet sounding hollowly on the floor behind him. He looked back over his shoulder. He gasped. It was not the little Bow Street Runner at all. It was Samuel Tompkins pursuing him. His face was twisted evilly and his wooden peg thumped loudly. *Thump! Thump! Thump!*

Horatio awoke with a start. He was wet with sweat. He shook off the dream and lay in straining panic until he realized the thumping he heard was a horse kicking the side of a stall in the stables. He lay a moment, then sprang from bed and dressed with shaking fingers. He ran out to the stables and saddled his bay and went plunging into the night. Five minutes later he was tearing past the slave quarters. It had been that night that the black people heard Boss Tench "chasin' de Debbil" for the first time.

In the weeks that followed, he was dumbly miserable. He threw himself into his work with a desperate frenzy. His temper flared so unpredictably that hands approached him with eye-rolling fright. His body was crying with exhaustion when he went to his room at night but he could not sleep. His whole being was taut with the agony of worry. He heard footsteps in the rustling of the wind through the trees. A mouse's scurrying across the floor became the soft swish of a tiptoeing man's coattails.

One night he dreamed he was back in the marketplace at Yarmouth. He heard a bellowing laugh and he looked up to see the suety, flat face of Violet Shorter. She waddled toward him, her monkey-like little son clutching tightly to her dress while he suckled at one of her enormous breasts. She stuck her face close to his. "'im wot gits it!" she said. "'im wot gits it!" She raised a short rope and thrust it at him and he recoiled in horror. The suckling child began to whinny with glee and he saw that the child had the face of Samuel Tompkins. "No!" he shouted. "No!" he wakened to find that he was standing by the bed, tense and breathless. He had no idea how long he stood there, but finally he broke the spell and rummaged through his drawers and found a flask of rum. He uncapped it with trembling fingers and drank it down in a long, throat-searing gulp. He tumbled back in bed and lay tense until the rum began to flow through his veins with a slow, spreading warmth. He slept.

His eyes were bloodshot and his hands trembled as he dressed at dawn. His head ached and he could still taste the cloying sweetness of the rum. The rising sun dazzled his eyes and the motion of his horse sent sharp pains into the base of his skull as he rode into the south fields where hands were breaking ground. Two thin workers had paused to relink a trace to their plow. He watched them fumble a moment, then dismounted and shouldered them rudely aside. He had barely slipped the links together when the mule lurched forward. The chain tightened and caught his finger between the links. He cried out with the pain, and turning suddenly in his fierce anger, he aimed a blow at one of the men. "Damn ye!" he shouted. "Damn ye!" The man cowered with sudden fright, head bowed and eyes shut tightly. The blow never fell. He looked up with surprise. Boss Tench stood there as if transfixed. His eyes were staring and his lips slightly parted. In the instant he had started to strike the man, he had seen a picture of himself about to receive one of Samuel Tompkins' blows. His angry shrill had even sounded like Tompkins. Horatio lowered his hand. "I'm sorry," he said. The men stood wide-eyed while he remounted his horse and rode toward Fair Haven.

General Jameson was in his study. Horatio wasted no time on preliminaries. "I have something to tell you, sir," he said. There was no expression on his face and his voice was flat as he told of his adoption by Samuel Tompkins, of Aber, and of that last night in the rope shop. He was not a glib man, not even a particularly articulate one, but as his story rolled out he relived those frightened years and General Jameson could not fail but relive them with him.

He sat quietly, without a change of expression, until Horatio had finished. He turned and looked thoughtfully out the window for a long time. When he spoke, his voice was gentle. "What do you want me to do, Tench?"

Horatio took a deep breath. "I don't know, sir. I wanted you to know if they send after me."

There was another long silence as the General stared thoughtfully at his desk. Finally he smiled. "Well, they haven't sent for you, Tench. I don't see why they should have much difficulty in tracing you." He pursed his lips slowly. "I have connections in England. I'll post an inquiry today. Maybe they can tell me something of the situation. I'll make my inquiries discreet. We'll wait until we hear. I'm glad you told me of this, Tench. We'll carry on just as if nothing had happened. I want you to know that I will do everything in my power to protect you if worse comes to worst."

Horatio's voice was heavy with gratitude. "Thank you, sir."

It helped some. Horatio left the General with the quiet feeling of absolution that confession brings. But there was not much help for the agony of the waiting. The days were not so bad. Once again he plunged into his work as if singlehanded he had to plow and harrow and plant every one of Fair Haven's black, rolling acres. He was everywhere, giving an order here, springing to help with a heavy task there, thin, tight as a wound watch spring, seeming devoid of all interest except for the job at hand. He drove himself with such fury that his clothes rustled with the crusted salt from his own sweat. He drove himself but he made no more attempts to drive the hands. All he asked was that they be busy. But, unconsciously, they began to step up their own slow tempo to match his own. They dragged home to their cabins exhausted and toil-worn but there was pride in their eyes. "Done plowed de whole fiel'," they said. "Ain't nebber done it so fast befo'." And they laughed. "Boss Tench'll sho' be happy 'bout dis. Yes, suh, Boss Tench'll sho' be happy." They laughed happily at their own prowess, and they shook their heads in wonder at Horatio's own Herculean labors.

But the nights were long. More and more Horatio lulled himself to sleep with alcohol. He drank for forgetfulness and when his stomach rebelled, he "chased de Debbil."

General Jameson was a pillar of comfort. Never once did he make reference to the message which they both were awaiting so anxiously. Even this seemingly complete disregard of news from England cheered Horatio. It seemed to make it unimportant. Despite this, he was always waiting tensely when General Jameson came from town after picking up the post. The General played the game well. "Well, Tench," he would say casually, "there doesn't seem to be any news in the world that concerns us too much." The General was kind.

Horatio had no way of knowing that he, too, was worried. Already his indolent, fox-hunting cronies had begun to make half-jesting, half-serious protests about the new fertility of Fair Haven. "You're goin' to send the market price down unless yo' let up, yo' scannel." They envied him and he gloated in their envy. He was fiercely resolved not to let the English snatch away his prize of an overseer. If necessary, he planned to go to see the President himself. He intended keeping Horatio at all costs. He didn't hesitate when that cost involved compromising his principles.

The word came in a lengthy communication from his British agents. He took it to a quiet corner of his club on Church Street, broke the seals, and read it through slowly. When he had finished, his face was sober. He sat there for a long time, deep in thought, and finally arose and walked over to the fireplace where a small fire was laid. After the barest pause, he threw the papers on the hot coals and stood there thoughtfully until they were charred.

Back at Fair Haven he shut his study door softly and turned to face Horatio. His face was still sober. " 'Tis a serious matter, Tench," he said. " 'Tis a very serious matter." Horatio stood stiffly, waiting. The General took his seat with a sigh. "I received the whole report this morning and burned it after I had read it through. Both Tompkins and—er, ah,—Cheezum are dead." He sat looking at the polished surface of his desk until he could no longer hesitate before Horatio's set, waiting face, then spoke quickly. "You are being sought, Tench, about that I shan't try to deceive you. However, I feel that you will be safe as long as you remain at Fair Haven and do not move about and attract attention to yourself. I think you must reconcile yourself to that. I believe that with, er—with the proper pressure brought to bear in the proper places, I can stop any pursuit."

"I'll do anything you ask, sir."

The General looked at Horatio's serious face a moment. "Thank you, Tench. I know I can depend on you, but just so there be no misunderstanding, I think I should state what it may be necessary for you to do to protect me in case I take certain, ah—risks. Naturally, first I have to demand—" he smiled—"that you obey my orders in regard to our mutual welfare. It could be most embarrassing to me if certain arrangements I am undertaking were revealed."

"I understand that, sir."

"Good." The General nodded. "We won't belabor that point. I think we understand each other. Secondly, I think I must warn you that, once accepting my protection, you will have to keep it until I think the time is safe to do otherwise. That's of utmost importance. For instance, it may be necessary for you to remain on here at Fair Haven even after your bond has expired. Naturally, in such a case, your status will be altered considerably. Those details can be worked out later." He smiled again. "All I want to be sure of, Tench, is that if we are fellow-conspirators, I won't be found out."

Horatio was overwhelmed with gratitude. "You know I'll do anything you ask, sir."

The General arose quickly and thrust out his hand. "It's a deal then, Tench. I'll send word to my English agents today to get busy. I'll do all in my power to protect you."

Horatio could feel the tightness drain from him. "I . . . I can't tell you how grateful I am, sir. I'll see that you never have cause for complaint."

The General looked at him fondly. "Nonsense, Tench, I'm gaining more than I'm risking. Now take the day off and come dine with me tonight."

Horatio's throat was full. "Thank you, sir." He turned quickly and left the room.

The General watched him go silently. He sat down and for a moment a tiny shadow crossed his fine brow. Then he shrugged and pulled paper toward him and dipped his pen in the inkwell.

As Horatio walked back to his room, for the first time since Aber had become a quiet memory, he felt like weeping. He clenched his jaw and swore silently that he would forever remain faithful to the kind General Jameson.

CHAPTER X

GENERAL JAMESON'S wife died in the spring. Her suffering had endured so long and been so acute that efforts at grief seemed forced and false. Even the hands, always eager to squeeze the last bitter drops of pathos from a situation, were hard put to make a convincing show of sorrow. They sang dirges with self-conscious solemnity while the body of their tall, regal mistress, whom almost none of them knew, was lowered in the ground. Only the General's grief was genuine. His fine face was etched deeply and he moved as if in a daze. He had fashioned a wreath of honeysuckle and bramble roses with his own hands. He kissed it and dropped it in his wife's open grave.

But even he realized that death had been a blessing and within a week Fair Haven returned to normal—almost to normal. Clover Jameson had taken her place as mistress of the big house. Almost immediately she began to make changes. Clumsy, barefoot plowboys were put to work rearranging furniture. House servants busily polished furniture and floors. Half-grown little black boys scurried about beating rugs and shining door knobs. Singing laundresses bent over sudsy tubs in the courtyard.

Horatio tried to ignore this activity, but when it left him shorthanded with the spring plowing, he protested to General Jameson. The General shrugged wearily. "I'm sorry, Tench. My daughter says she needs more help."

"But she's upsetting the whole schedule, sir."

Again the General gave his tired little shrug. "I know, Tench.

Even I have been dispossessed—but I suppose her happiness is more important than the crops."

Horatio let the matter drop, but it did give him another reason for deciding that he disliked Clover Jameson. He had heard numerous stories of her temper tantrums as a child and the house servants still rolled their eyes and shook their heads when her name was mentioned. Also he had never forgotten her haughty dismissal of him on the dock in Charleston. In the more than four years since then, he had not seen her except at a distance. She had been away at school most of the time, only returning to Fair Haven in the summer months when he was busiest in the fields. On the few occasions he had seen her out riding or walking on the grounds, he had managed to pass her at a distance.

He stood directly behind her at her mother's funeral, but since she was veiled and swathed in heavy mourning black and had not looked in his direction, it was not a meeting. Since her return to Fair Haven, he studiously had avoided getting within her range.

This was not resentment altogether. Horatio's automatic recoil from women bordered on timidity. Except for the colorless drudges he met in waterfront dives and the flabby slatterns Samuel Tompkins periodically dragged into his shop, Horatio had never known any women. In his twenty years he had never held a woman in his arms. Morality had nothing to do with it. It was pride. The trulls and greasy barmaids of the docks disgusted him. But he did have all the desires and hopes of a healthy male. He hoped devoutly to find a woman of his heart. Finding her was a task for him alone. Once when General Jameson half-seriously offered to buy him the bond of a woman for a wife, Horatio refused so vehemently that the General passed the matter off as a joke. Horatio never gave it a thought, but Clover Jameson was the only woman of respectability who even obliquely had approached his life since he left the Waifs' Home.

He met her first near the gate to the south pasture. He had found a hole in the fence and had dismounted to patch it. He was so intent on the task that he did not know she had ridden up until she spoke.

"Good morning, Boss Tench."

He looked up quickly to find her smiling down at him. She was riding sidesaddle on a small, brown mare and had discarded her heavy mourning gown for a plum-colored velvet riding habit. Her smile was friendly.

He was both surprised and embarrassed. He had never expected her to address him as the workers did. In fact, he was surprised that she spoke to him at all. A slow blush warmed his ears and this embarrassed him all the more. He barely glanced at her, but nodded and turned back to the fence.

She made no move to ride on. "It's a beautiful day, isn't it?"

Horatio checked a grunt just in time. He was painfully aware that his greeting had been boorish. He twisted the last strand of wire in place and wiped his hands on his breeches. "Aye, it is," he said. He tried to manage a pleasant smile.

She was gazing out over the fields and for the first time he had a chance to look at her closely. He had forgotten she was so pretty. She had her father's broad, fine brow, but her face fell down to a small pointed chin, so that it was heart-shaped. Her eyes were deep blue, almost violet, and they were fringed by incredibly long, coal-black lashes. Her mouth was full and soft, and she was so fair that her skin seemed slightly transparent in the sun. He could see a tracery of fine blue veins across her cheek.

She was small, almost fragile, but her erect little figure was mature. Horatio thought she was fascinatingly beautiful. She took a deep breath and let it escape with a sigh before she turned. He lowered his eyes.

"Where are you riding now, Boss Tench?"

The repetition of his title made Horatio's blush deepen. "Why . . . I . . . I was checking the fences," he said.

"May I ride with you?"

Horatio's small laugh was flustered. "Why, . . . of course!"

As he mounted, his big bay nuzzled the ear of her mare and whinnied softly. Horatio jerked the reins roughly. Too roughly, he realized, and this made him feel all the more of a fool.

Clover Jameson didn't seem to notice. Her red mouth opened in a smile, showing the even whiteness of her teeth. "I've been wanting to see you for ever so long. Poor Daddy is certain you hate me for interfering with the planting."

Horatio sat stiffly and stared straight ahead. He groped desperately for an answer.

"I hope you don't hate me, Boss Tench?"

He had to look at her now. She was still smiling and watching him closely. "Of course not . . ." He caught himself just in time to keep from adding "mum." It gave his reply a half-finished lilt. He flushed again and added a little lamely, "Everything turned out all right."

"Oh, I'm so glad. I couldn't bear to think I was being a nuisance."

Her voice was sincere, but Horatio could not check his sideways look of suspicion. She saw it and thrust out her little chin and looked at him almost defiantly. "I know that's hard to believe, Boss Tench, but it's the truth." She raised a tiny, gloved hand in an earnest gesture. "I know everyone thought I was a bother, but I simply had to do something for poor Daddy in his grief. You see, Boss Tench, he and mother arranged Fair Haven together shortly after they were married. After she . . . well, after she passed away, Daddy was cut to the heart every time he looked around. I've tried to make a new place . . . a place where—" She left the sentence hanging. Her chin quivered slightly.

Horatio didn't know what to say. Clover Jameson was so utterly different from his mental image of her that he was bewildered. He cleared his throat embarrassedly and muttered, "I'm sorry."

She looked up quickly and flashed him a grateful smile. "Oh, I'm so glad you understand. I knew you would if I explained, Boss Tench."

Horatio made a grimace of protest. Her constant use of his title embarrassed him. "Please don't call me Boss Tench. That's what the hands call me . . . and it doesn't seem right coming from you."

She smiled slightly and her mouth made an oval of surprise. "Oh? And what should I call you?"

Horatio made a flustered gesture. "Well, call me Horatio or just Tench as your father does."

She looked at him so fixedly that he flushed and cursed himself for a fool. How could he forget himself so far as to ask General Jameson's daughter to call him by his first name? He stared ahead, rigid with mortification.

He was relieved when she finally spoke and her voice sounded pleased. "What do your friends call you?"

He swallowed hard "Well . . . I . . . I . . . I don't have any friends."

Her slight smile was reproving. "You're teasing me," she said.

For some reason he felt strangely pleased by her disbelief. It made it seem that he was friendless because of choice. He relaxed a little and smiled at her. "It's true. You must believe me."

She continued regarding him so long and thoughtfully that he shifted uneasily in the saddle and another blush warmed his ears. "I hope we can be friends, Boss Tench," she said. Then, realizing what she had called him, she slapped her small, gloved hands over her mouth, widened her eyes in mock horror, threw back her head, and laughed so delightedly that Horatio joined in.

He felt more at ease after that. When they came to places in the fence which needed repairs, he dismounted and worked quickly, pleasantly aware that she was watching him and that he worked well.

Once when he mounted lightly, scarcely touching the stirrup, she looked at him with admiration. "You ride so well."

He flushed with pleasure. "Thank you."

She lowered her long lashes and smiled. "You know, I've watched you ride many times. I can stand at my window and look out over the fields and when the sun's shining, your hair looks like . . . well, like gold."

She saw his flush and spoke quickly. "Oh, I like your hair."

She smiled. "Once I said to Dovey— 'Dovey, why is hair like that going to waste on a man?' And she said, 'Missy, eff'n yo' went wifout a hat lak dat man do, yo' hair'd turn de same color.' " She mimicked her maid so perfectly that Horatio laughed and forgot that comments on his hair usually embarrassed him.

They rode for another half-hour after that, laughing and chatting, and when she told him good-by, she looked around and then smiled and held out her hand. There was something almost conspiratorial about the gesture, and when Horatio took her small warm hand, he felt a strange thrill of pleasure.

Early the next morning Horatio saw General Jameson in his study and gave a report on the progress of the planting. The General listened quietly, nodding with pleasure. " 'Tis an amazing thing you've done, Tench. It will be another big year for Fair Haven."

"I hope so, sir."

The General's smile was musing. "I've missed our weekly dinners, Tench."

Horatio hoped his voice sounded convincing. "So have I, sir."

The General smiled. "Do you suppose that we could resume them this Tuesday?"

"Why, yes, sir, but I thought now that Miss . . ."

The General interrupted, "My daughter joins me in the invitation."

Horatio smiled with real pleasure. "Thank you very much, sir." Once again he felt a twinge of conscience for having misjudged Clover Jameson.

Somehow this dinner wasn't the same. There were the same bewildering array of silver, the same tureens, and the same dazzling expanse of tablecloth; but Clover Jameson's presence made all the difference in the world. It seemed incredible that such a small, child-like person could have so much charm and rippling humor. Horatio watched fascinated as she parried a jest from the General one moment, mimicked one of the hands another, and was so altogether delightful and full of fun that he forgot to notice how fragile the General's silverware looked in his calloused hands.

And she showed an astounding knowledge and interest in Fair Haven. She wanted to know about the crops, about the repairs on the warehouses, about the prospects of bird hunting and beagling. With the General, Horatio had always found himself politely abrupt or painfully inarticulate, but now it seemed that he had suddenly been handed his tongue. He answered all her questions fully. He even found pleasure in doing it.

After dinner they adjourned to the high-ceilinged drawing room and Clover consented to play the harp. Old Jerusalem, snorting and grunting, brought it in from the music room and when Clover sat at it, her tiny, fluttering hands pulling the strings, Horatio thought his heart would burst with pleasure. First she played a rollicking, gay little tune, and the General tapped his foot approvingly. She played another tune, a little less gay. Then her small face became solemn and she began a slow, touching melody which was as soft as the sound of falling tears. Horatio sat stone-still. He watched those soft, tiny fluttering hands as if in a trance. He forgot the room and its fine furniture. He forgot General Jameson and Fair Haven. He was alone with those tiny hands, and they seemed to be plucking at his own heart. Suddenly the music stopped with a sharp twang of a string. Clover stood up quickly and put her handkerchief to her face and ran sobbing from the room. Tears were glistening in General Jameson's eyes. "She's the fairest angel in the world," he said softly, "and she is so lonely, I shall be glad when our period of mourning is up, Tench. She needs young people around her and laughter."

That night Horatio lay for hours, staring into the heavy darkness. Clover Jameson's tiny, fluttering hands still seemed to be plucking at his heart strings. And in his dreams he held her tiny figure in his arms and stroked her hair lovingly.

He saw her almost every day in the weeks that followed. He wore only clean, fresh cottons to the fields and he blacked his boots and kept himself clean-shaven. No matter how hard he worked, she never rode by without his seeing her. Sometimes he found an excuse to ride with her. When that was impossible, he always managed to talk to her for a few minutes. Once or twice she didn't appear at all and his day was spoiled. Just the sight of her choked him with pleasure. He began to treasure a thousand little things about her—the way she cocked her head when she spoke, the way her curls fell from under her hat, the way her velvet skirt fell in folds from her rounded knee, the way her mouth looked as soft and red as a rose petal. She was the first woman he had ever wanted—and because she was, he had no clear realization of how badly he did want her.

He looked forward to dinners in the big house. He left the fields early on Tuesdays and bathed slowly and shaved carefully. The General's table had no terrors. He scarcely noticed it or paid attention to what he ate. His food was at the head of the table and he devoured it hungrily with eyes and ears. He loved to hear her shriek with laughter or suppress her mirth in a napkin as if she were a naughty child. Clover Jameson was the most wonderful person he had ever known. He tried to remember strange, quaint expressions of field hands to repeat, just to see her face light up. And it hurt him unbearably, almost physically, when he had to turn his attention from her to answer a question or engage in conversation with the General.

One night early in June she embarrassed him. Somehow she

had heard of his night rides and what the Negroes called "chasin' de Debbil."

"Tell me, Tench," she asked, cocking her head prettily, "do you really know the ole Debbil?"

Horatio's ears burned. He had not ridden out his misery in months, just as he had not drunk himself unconscious in town. He hated to think of how miserable he had been. His fears of English justice seemed faraway and remote.

"Well, do you, Tench?" She was waiting. Even the General was looking at him expectantly. He, too, had heard of these dashes in the darkness.

Horatio floundered. "I just . . . well, I just like to ride at night. I . . . I find that I sleep better that way."

"And you really don't chase the Devil?" Her voice was mockingly disappointed.

"Not any more than some people," he said. Their laughter was sufficient reward for his embarrassment.

She showed him to the door after he said his good nights. As he walked through the long, darkened hallway, he was tinglingly conscious of her footsteps behind him, of the rustle of her gown. As he reached the door, she leaned close and her breath hissed deliciously in his ear. "Is it a good night for chasing the Devil?"

For a moment, he didn't know what to say. He caught his breath. "I—"

Her voice was low and soft. "I'll meet you at the stables at midnight." She was gone with a swift rustle of skirts and her low laugh trailed back. He quite completely lost his breath.

He was waiting, as impatiently as the two saddled horses, when her trim figure came running out of the shadows on the stroke of twelve. She giggled and whispered delightedly when he helped her mount. "Oh, this is going to be fun! This is going to be fun!" Her whispers lent a clandestine air to their meeting. He was trembling when he mounted his bay and they galloped off into the night.

Once out of earshot of the house, she chattered gaily and exclaimed over the view under the bright moon. But he was struck dumb. There were a thousand things he wanted to say, but he could only nod and laugh at her remarks. Even his laugh sounded strange.

"And where do you go?"

He fought to keep his voice casual. "Nowhere usually—if you like we'll ride to the footlog across Mills' branch."

"Let's!" she said. "Let's! I'll race you there." She dug her small foot into the mare's side and it was off in a flurry of hoofbeats. He could have caught her easily, but he trailed a length behind, the sweet night air whipping his face and ruffling his hair. He was deliriously happy.

Her mare slowed when it reached the heavy shadows under the massive oaks bordering Mills' branch. He reined his bay to a walk and, side by side, they moved slowly under the huge boughs that cast eerie patterns from the bright moon. At the branch's edge she dismounted and ran to the center of the narrow bridge which was made from a single elm tree. He tethered the horses and joined her. She leaned against the handrail and thrust her small white face upward. "Oh, it's lovely," she whispered. "It's lovely."

His heart seemed to be pounding in his throat. He fought to keep his breath in check. He could smell her perfume and her hair.

She turned slowly and faced him. Her face was a white blur in the moonlight and her eyes were wide and luminous. "I don't see any ole Debbil," she said. Again softly, "I don't see any ole Debbil."

He clenched his hands at his sides. She parted her lips slightly and half-closed her eyes. "Maybe you're the Devil." She put out her small hand slowly and ran it across his cheek. Her fingers burned his face. There was a catch in her voice. "What a beautiful, pretty Devil you are."

In an instant she was in his arms. "My darling. My darling!" Then he found her hungry lips, and he felt that he was drowning in warm floods of joy.

CHAPTER XI

NOW he felt he had discovered the world. He explored it happily, cautiously at first, then with reckless abandon. No longer did he swoop down on the fields in cold-eyed wrath. He was a happy man and he laughed and joked with the hands. They shifted uneasily and rolled their eyes nervously. His good humor was too new to be infectious. But they would smile and chuckle when they saw him approaching, the sun seeming to strike sparks from his flaming hair. "Umm-ugh!" they grunted. "Dat man sho' done got religion. He sho' gittin' jolly." They were right.

There was misery too. She yielded only so far. In an instant she could turn from his darling into the cold mistress and make him the servant. "Stop it! Stop it, I say!" She grew rigid and tore from his embrace.

He would be miserable. "Darling, I . . ."

"Don't touch me! Don't you dare. Who do you think I am!" She let him dangle on the hook of her indignation for hours.

It was weeks before he realized this was a little game in which she delighted. She drove him half-mad with her fluttering hands and willing lips, then withdrew behind a barrage of withering scorn. It was her game and it was cruel, but he indulged her in it, took a warm pride in it. He loved her desperately. The fact that she could walk the shaky tightrope of passion and never lose her balance made her all the more desirable and heavenly. Retreat was more precious than surrender.

It was surprising how much time they found for each other. She slipped out to meet him almost every night. Sometimes they rode in the moonlight, but their favorite rendezvous was a bench under the drooping branches of an Iris yew near the boxwood maze behind the manor. Once or twice he was deliciously awakened when she slipped into his room in the middle of the night and threw herself at his side and covered his face with kisses. She would stay with him until the sky began to turn purple, then slip away, leaving him heavy-eyed but light-hearted.

The Tuesday night dinners were agonizing. He was almost afraid to look at her directly because his love would shine in his eyes and General Jameson would discover their secret. Yet she seemed to be a magnet that drew all his senses, and the struggle within him was so great that he felt he was all thumbs and elbows. She played the game better than he did. Her manner was coolly polite and apparently bordering on boredom. Eventually this constraint served to do the thing against which she was guarding. The General became suspicious, but not in the way they had feared.

She told Horatio about it one night after she had slipped to his room and they lay in each other's arms. She giggled. "Daddy got after me after you left tonight. He said I wasn't nice enough to you."

He laughed. "You aren't."

She snuggled closer. "He said I should show you more courtesy because he is so grateful to you."

The General's interest warmed Horatio. He sighed and hugged her tightly. "If there was only something we could do, darling. If only we could tell him about us."

She pulled away. Her voice was sharp. "You aren't to think of such things. You promised me you'd never say anything. You must promise me!"

"My darling, I have promised."

She sat up. "Promise me again!"

"Of course I promise, darling. I do!"

She relaxed and again cuddled close. "Everything will straighten itself—when . . . when the time comes."

"We'll be married when my bond is out."

"Oh, yes, my darling."

"You'll always love me?"

"Oh, yes! Yes! Yes!" She held him close and sighed with her lips near his ear. "We'll always be together. Always! I'll be loving you like this when you're eighty-five and I'm eighty-three. I'll love you always. I'll meet you at the door with long, sweet kisses and we'll walk along holding hands."

He was overwhelmed with tenderness. He held her close. "I've never done anything to deserve someone as wonderful as you."

He began to accept matters as they were—the secret meetings, the ever-changing moods. He begrudged every moment that he was away from her, though most of the time he went about his work half-groggy for lack of sleep. She slept most of the day in the darkened coolness of her room. He had never known such happiness—nor so much misery. He felt ashamed that he had to slip about in the shadows, but at the same time he dreaded meeting the time when he had to face General Jameson and tell him that he loved his daughter. In his mind he already had lived through that encounter half a dozen times. Sometimes when she had just left him, her kisses still fresh on his lips, it seemed that he had nothing to fear. Everything, then, was wonderful. He saw himself standing before General Jameson in the study at Fair Haven. He would stand proud and erect and his voice would be firm.

"I love your daughter, sir," he would say, "and she loves me."

General Jameson would raise his fine brows in surprise. He would sit silently for a moment, then his face would light with a small smile. "Can it be possible, Tench?"

He would disdain to reply, but simply would walk to the door where Clover was waiting. He would offer her his arm and she would take it proudly and walk in to face her father.

"Yes, Father," she would say calmly, "it is possible. I love Horatio and nothing can ever separate us."

General Jameson would get to his feet and smile broadly. "Separate you, my dear? Separate you? Why, my dear, I'm delighted. I'm overjoyed and I give you both my blessing." Then he would kiss her and clasp Horatio's hand tightly and shout for old Jerusalem to bring a bottle of choice wine for the betrothal toast.

That was one dream. He had others. They weren't so wonderful. In them he could see the General's face flushed with rage. "Marry my daughter, Tench? Are you out of your mind, man?

Marry my daughter? Why, I'll have you whipped and put to work picking cotton in the fields. Marry my daughter, indeed! You're a murderer, Tench. I'll have you sent back to England and you'll hang from the gallows before Yarmouth gaol. Marry a Jameson! You're mad, man. You have neither mother nor father. For all I know you grew from the mold on the dock pilings. Marry a Jameson? If you marry, Tench, I'll buy you a greasy serving maid. Marry my daughter, indeed! You're nothing, Tench!"

Those were his dreams. Of the two he took his choice, depending on his mood. But at all times he was haunted by the fear that General Jameson would learn of their meetings before they had an opportunity to face him. If that happened—but then he dared not think of that. At the very best, he knew that the General would think of him as a scoundrel and ingrate. At the very worst, he would be thrown into the hold of a stinking ship and be sent back to England and the gallows.

Apparently he had no cause for worry. The General gave no sign that he knew their secret. If anyone at Fair Haven did know, it was King. That was not surprising. Nothing seemed to escape his calm eyes. But Horatio could not even be sure that he knew. It was simply a vague and annoying feeling that he had when King approached him in the fields one sweltering summer afternoon.

King's face was solemn. "Big Ep done ast fer permission to marry up wif Dovey," he said.

For a moment Horatio thought King was joking. When he saw that he wasn't, he threw back his head and laughed. Horatio could not have imagined a more improbable match. Big Ep was a rollicking, ebony-black field hand who stood six and a half feet tall and weighed nearly three hundred pounds. He was an excellent plowman, but built along such Herculean lines that he seemed to dwarf the biggest mules. The sight of him plowing would send the other workers into gales of laughter. "Why don't yo' carry dat mule, Big Ep? He gonna git in yo' way eff'n yo' don't," or "Why don't yo' pull de plow an' let dat leetle-bitty mule hold it, Ep?" Big Ep would laugh mightily. He enjoyed jokes about his size. "Dis ole mule bettah git outta de way, 'cause heah Ah come!" he would shout.

Dovey was the direct opposite of Big Ep in color, size, and disposition. She was a house servant, a tiny, scrawny little creature barely more than four feet tall. She was a yellowish-copper color and her sharp little face was sullen and petulant. The thought of the two mating was too much for Horatio. He laughed again.

King's face was impassive. "Dey don't think it's funny," he said.

Horatio stopped laughing. "Of course not," he said. He shook his head and shrugged. "Well, I don't see any reason why they shouldn't get married, King." He couldn't suppress another laugh. "I'll give a pretty pence to see their children, though."

There was still no amusement on King's face. "Ah don't think dey ought ter be 'lowed ter git married," he said.

Horatio was puzzled. "But why, King?"

King shrugged. "Dovey's a house servant."

"That makes no difference."

King didn't change expression. "Not ter me er yo', it don't," he said, "but it'll make a whole heap er difference ter Big Ep an' Dovey."

Horatio was surprised and a little annoyed. "Why should it?"

King looked at the ground, then sighed and looked Horatio in the face. His gaze was level. "Dovey was brought up in de house. She's ust ter eatin' house vittles. She gits Missy Clover's ole dresses ter wear. She ain't ust ter smellin' sweat an' eatin' hoecake. She ought ter stay in de house an' leave Big Ep alone."

"You don't think Dovey will be a good wife?"

King shook his head. "No, sir—not ter Big Ep she won't be." He looked at Horatio steadily. "Ah ain't got nuthin' against Dovey an' Ah ain't tryin' ter bother wif Big Ep's life. But Ah jes' don't wanta see somethin' happen dat gonna be all wrong. No man gotta right ter get messed up wif some woman who thinks she's better'n him. If Big Ep wukked in de house an' Dovey wukked in de fields, den it would be differunt. Den if Big Ep wanted ter git married up wif Dovey, it would be 'cause he really wanted her fer a wife. Lak it is now, he's so proud of hisself fer gittin' a house servant fer a wife dat he don't even think how leetle an' dried-up she is. Big Ep jes' thinks he's got somethin'."

Horatio flushed. "Don't you think a man can pick a wife who's better than he is?"

For the first time there was a flicker of amusement on King's face. "Ah ain't said dat couldn't happen at all. Ah think a man oughta try ter git woman better'n him. De important thing is dat she hadn't oughta *think* she's bettah than her man. A man ain't got no business thinkin' he bettah than his woman neither. Yo' can't put a stuck-up mean mule in double harness wifout trouble."

"What if a woman sometimes . . . well, just *knows* that she's better than a man and marries him anyway?"

King looked at Horatio steadily. "Gittin' a good woman is one of the most important things a man does, Boss Tench. It's more important than his land er his house. Yo' gonna pick yo' a woman someday, Ah reckon, an' when yo' do, jes' remember dat yo' ain't marryin' no woman 'cause whar she come from as much as yo're marryin' her 'cause whar she's goin'."

Horatio managed a wry smile. "I'll take the matter of Big Ep and Dovey up with General Jameson."

He was delighted when General Jameson gave his assent quickly. He didn't even mention that Big Ep was a field hand and Dovey worked in the house.

CHAPTER XII

HE LEARNED of the ball quite by accident at one of the weekly dinners. They had been talking about the cotton yield and General Jameson sighed and shot Clover an amused glance. "Ah, Tench, it's been a profitable year, a quiet, restful year, but now I suppose we should brace ourselves for the onslaught since my daughter is throwing open the gates to Fair Haven."

Clover colored and looked down at her plate. "Now, Daddy—"

The General laughed and looked at her fondly. "You know I'm only jesting, my dear. I know you've been lonely this last year—and you know I will do everything possible to make your precious ball a success."

Horatio stiffened. His evening was spoiled. They passed on to other subjects, but he was seething and scarcely listened. Several times he tried to catch Clover's eye. She studiously avoided his glances.

He excused himself early and went to his room. He was still fuming when she came to him several hours later. She laughed at his anger.

"Oh, my darling, don't get upset about that silly ball."

"Why do you have to have a ball?"

She laid her hand against his chest and hugged him. "Oh, darling," she protested, "I'm not giving the ball because I want it. Heavens! I'll be bored to tears. I'm thinking of poor Daddy and how lonely he is. The period of mourning is up. You must give a ball to let your neighbors know that they can come calling."

"So all the Church Street dandies can come too, I guess."

She giggled and stroked his face. Her voice was patient as if she were soothing a child. "What do I care about men? I have you. It's Daddy I'm worrying about. He's been so lonely this past year." Her voice was soft. "The poor dear. He's happy as a child about our plans. Can't you see that?"

His voice lost its sharpness. "He says he doesn't want it."

She made a grimace of disbelief. "Oh, pooh! If you could only see his face light up when we talk about it, you'd know better. He's always loved to have people around him. I'm doing it all for him." She pressed closer. "You know that you're all I want—all I care about."

Now there was a new activity at Fair Haven. Black people swarmed in and out of the manor and over the broad lawns like so many industrious ants. The house was polished and scoured until it glistened inside and out. The lawns were mowed to a velvety sheen. The box was cut, the shrubs trimmed. And there was laughter and excitement. He alone was glum and unaffected by all the preparations. At first she tried to soothe him and laugh away his dark mood, but finally gave up in exasperation. Then he was shamed and felt like a fool and tried to put the best face on his misery. At times her gaiety was even infectious. She was everywhere, giving an order here, pleading there, dashing off to Charleston for fittings of her party gown, shopping for favors—being altogether so happy and excited that he was torn between pleasure and jealousy. He saw much less of her, but he told himself that this was temporary and unavoidable. She had so much to do.

She stayed with him only a few minutes the night before the ball. She was bubbling with excitement over her gown. She gestured wildly. "Oh, it's lovely—by far the nicest thing I've ever had made. It's . . . it's so stylish and soft . . . and . . ."

He squeezed her so tightly that she stopped talking with a little grunt.

"Now, now!" she said with annoyance.

"Will I get to see you in your beautiful gown?"

She sighed. "Of course, of course."

"When?"

She was definitely annoyed. "Oh! You know you'll get to see me. I'll . . . I'll wear it any time you say."

He shook his head. "I want to see you the first time you wear it."

She looked at him in alarm. "But you can't! You know you can't!"

"You could slip out for a few minutes."

"No!"

"Why not?"

"Why, I can't leave a house filled with guests."

"Just for a few minutes," he asked softly.

She bit her lips and frowned. "Oh, all right," she said finally. "I'll meet you under the yew—but, mind you, just for a few minutes."

The ball was a notable success. Of all the people at Fair Haven, black and white, Horatio was the only one who found it otherwise. His troubles began at dawn. He saddled up and rode to the fields to find them deserted. It was the same at the warehouses and at the stock pens. He was stern-faced when he reined up at King's cabin. "Where are the hands?" he demanded.

King looked surprised. "Dey don't wuk 'cause of de ball."

Horatio frowned. "Why?"

King made an effort to hide his smile. "Dey have ter welcome guests."

Horatio flushed. "On whose orders?"

King shook his head. "Why, Ah don't know, Boss. It's jes' sumpin' dat everybody knows. Nobody wuks in de fields when dey's a party at de big house."

Horatio realized he wasn't getting anywhere. He wheeled his horse. "We'll see about that!" he said.

General Jameson was as surprised as King. "Why, of course, Tench," he said, "the hands don't go to the fields when we have a party here at Fair Haven." He smiled. "We need them to help welcome the guests."

Horatio tried not to show his anger.

Lunch was particularly unsatisfactory. The kitchen was hot and steamy and filled with servants and dainty, frilly tidbits. He was forced to take a platter of warmed left-overs to his room because the kitchen table was stacked high with absurd little bonbon baskets made of carefully peeled orange halves dipped in a glaze of syrup and sugar.

It was late afternoon before he found out how the field hands helped welcome guests. He was stretched across his bed, half-dozing, when he heard a hundred voices raised in a low moan. He sat up with a start, then strode to the window. He could see only a part of the long drive leading to the main house, but that portion was lined on both sides by grinning, waving field hands dressed in their Sunday finery. An open carriage was coming slowly up the long drive. In it were an elderly man and two young girls, who were dressed within an inch of their lives and giggling and preening with pleasure. The low moaning Horatio heard was the oh-ing and ah-ing of the hands as the carriage passed and they caught a glimpse of its occupants.

Horatio snorted with disgust, but then he had to laugh. In the face of such vocal admiration he knew the dowdiest, most over-stuffed frump would ascend the steps to Fair Haven feeling every inch a queen.

The sound of admiration from the front lawn increased as the afternoon wore on. By nightfall it was an almost constant moan. The hands lighted flambeaus and the grounds were bright as day. The courtyard below Horatio's window was filled with barouches, carryalls, and carriages. Dozens of little black boys scampered around, wiping them clean of dust inside and out, while older stable hands unhitched the horses and led them off to be fed. General Jameson's hospitality extended to his guests' horses and conveyances.

Every window in Fair Haven shone with light. Horatio knew that the huge, tiered chandeliers in the downstairs rooms had been filled with candles. For the first time he felt a little envious. Aye, that was a sight he would like to see. Some of the chandeliers held a hundred and fifty candles.

Envious then—and when the music started. It was a lovely, lilting tune, a waltz, although Horatio didn't know that. He stood by his window, staring into the night, and he clenched his jaw at the beauty of it. Music had a strange effect on him, although he had heard it so infrequently that he could recall every time.

When the music stopped, he could hear the faint sound of laughter, and it seemed that one faint shriek, a little louder than the rest, might belong to Clover. He thought of her dancing and laughing gaily with dozens of thin-nosed dandies, and he burned with anger. The music started again, low and soft, and altogether so delightful that he wondered, feeling a little foolish all the while, if he could learn to dance. He tried to manage a shuffling step in time to the tune, but stopped in disgust.

All the same, he felt pleasantly happy when he began to dress for his rendezvous with Clover. Since she would be wearing her new gown, he decided to wear his new waistcoat with velvet facings. He also wore his fawn-colored trousers, which had been a gift from General Jameson, and a pair of light, ankle-length boots. Over this he threw his heavy cloak, partly because he had no idea how long he would have to wait in the night air for Clover and partly because it was black and would hide him in the shadows.

It was a sensible precaution. The boxwood maze behind the manor was filled with strolling couples, and although he skirted it, he had to stop several times and stand in the shadows when a laughing couple passed along the outside path where the box was trimmed short. As he had expected, the nook under the yew was deserted. He sat down on the bench and waited and listened to the music. He waited for a long time. After an hour he was impatient. But when she finally came, it was so silently that she was almost at his elbow before he saw her. She also had thrown a dark cloak over her party gown. He arose with a little laugh and made an effort to take her in his arms. She drew back. "Don't," she said nervously. "I've brought you a cup of punch. Here—drink it!" She thrust a small cup into his hands. Her thoughtfulness warmed him. "I want to see your gown," he said.

She was fidgety with impatience. "Oh, all right!" She slipped her cloak off and made a quick turn. In the half-darkness he could tell nothing of the gown except that it was white and frilly, but he made the correct comment. "B'fair, it's beautiful," he said. He reached out a hand for her. "B'fair, you're beautiful!"

She drew back. Her half-whisper was almost a hiss. "Stop now! Hurry and drink your punch. I must get back." She looked back over her shoulder toward the lights of Fair Haven.

He took a sip of the punch. "Ah, this is good."

"Hurry!"

He took another sip and smacked his lips.

"Drink it all down at once," she said.

"It won't hurt if you stay a few minutes," he said. "Sit down."

"No! No!" she said impatiently. "I have guests. I must get back!"

He laughed and reached out his free hand and pulled her toward him. "The guests can wait."

He was not at all prepared for what happened. She jerked back furiously. Either her hand or his slapped against the half-full cup in his left hand. It was knocked from his grasp and fell against the front of her gown. She gasped and looked down quickly. Even in the darkness a stain big as a man's hand could be seen near the hem.

There was a moment of silence, then her voice cracked full of anger. "Oh, you fool! You beastly, damnable fool!" She was almost beside herself with rage. She gathered up the front of her dress in both hands and shook it vigorously.

He stood dumbly a moment, then leaned forward. "Here, let me . . ."

"Oh, you fool! You beastly, stupid fool!"

Her hand shot out quickly and struck him stingingly across the face. He stepped back in surprise. Before he recovered, she was running back across the lawn. He watched her until she disappeared in the shadows around the house. His chest was heaving with anger.

Naturally they made up. But this time it was Clover's doing. She had decided to let him dangle a week, but when that time passed and he still had not come near her, she took matters in her own hands. She slipped into his room one night and smothered him with kisses and apologies. He forgot his anger in the delicious shock of being awakened in such a manner, and, if anything, the separation had made him love her all the more.

But the quarrel had been prophetic. Things were never quite the same for the remainder of the summer. Scarcely a day passed without visitors, mostly haughty-eyed young blades and coquettish, highly dressed girls of Clover's age. They gathered on the cool veranda, and while Horatio rode in the fields under a blazing sun, he could hear their languid voices and laughter.

One afternoon Clover and two friends who were overnight guests passed him in the fields, poised and elegant in their riding costumes. Clover gave him the barest nod, but one of the girls, a slender brunette, gave him a bold, searching look and fluttered her eyelashes. When they were a few yards away, he heard her say something in a low tone. A burst of laughter made his cheeks burn, especially when he heard Clover's careless remark, "Is he? I've never noticed."

The next time they were alone, he demanded to know what had been said. Clover scowled. "She said you were handsome—the black-eyed flirt!"

"Ah? And you said you hadn't noticed?"

"Of course! What should I have said? Should I have agreed with her and had every idle tongue in Charleston say that I was taken with the looks of . . . of . . ." She hesitated.

"A servant?" he asked levelly.

She shrugged impatiently. "Oh, you always want to twist what I say. Can't I do anything without your making an issue of it?"

He realized he was unfair, and, anyway, secretly he was pleased with what the black-eyed girl had said, so he pacified her.

Some quarrels did not end so happily. When men came calling he was furious, especially when Lieutenant Beauveau Carter, a slim, young dandy with long yellow hair, began to turn up regularly. Horatio had heard of Lieutenant Carter often. He was the son of the owner of Charleston's Carter Shipyards, and his wild horsemanship and drinking escapades were topics of conversation even in the ordinaries. After the Lieutenant's first visit, Horatio had been in a rage. "You're not to see that man," he said. "He's no good!"

Clover looked at him reproachfully for a moment, then giggled. "What are you laughing at?"

"Why, he's as meek as can be."

"Well, he isn't to come back again!"

She looked hurt. "What would you have me do—drive him away?"

"Yes."

She sighed and hugged him close. "Oh, my big darling, don't be upset about that silly man. Let him come—maybe the rest of them will stay away. You know no one can ever take your place, darling.

No one! Ever! You mustn't make things difficult for me. I'm just playing a game until we can be together—forever."

He tried to be understanding, but as the weeks wore on, their bickering and quarreling increased. Sometimes for a week at a time she would be soft and tender and he had no doubt that she loved him dearly. At other times she ignored him completely for days. Later he was to realize that the time she spent with him was in direct ratio to the emptiness of her social calendar. But he was blind because he was in love for the first time in his life—terribly in love.

CHAPTER XIII

HORATIO'S indenture expired in the fall.

It seemed impossible that he should forget so important an anniversary. But it slipped his mind completely. He arose at sunup and spent the whole day supervising the second picking of the cotton. When he returned to his room at dusk, he was so saddle-weary that he threw himself face down on his bed. He had been lying there a half-hour, sleepily debating whether to bathe and eat or let nature take its course, when old Jerusalem puffed up the stairs and said General Jameson wanted to see him immediately.

Horatio swung his feet off the bed irritably. "All right, tell him I'll be there directly."

Jerusalem lingered and grinned craftily. "Reckon yo' bettah put on yore town cloes 'fore yo' go."

"What the devil for?"

Jerusalem cackled with merriment. "Nobody 'round heah tells me no secrets. Marse wants it—dat's all Ah knows."

Horatio was too utterly tired to be curious. He dressed quickly, without particular care but with a great deal of muttering.

It wasn't until he entered the General's study that he realized why he had been summoned. The General was smiling expectantly. On the desk before him he had placed his carefully preserved half of Horatio's indenture.

Horatio paused. "B'fair, sir," he said. "I'd clean forgot that today was the day."

The General laughed merrily and took his hand warmly. "I take it, then, Tench, that you won't be leaving Fair Haven tonight."

Horatio shook his head. "You know better, sir."

"And you know, Tench, that we would be quite lost without you," the General said fondly. "Now, be seated, and let's complete our business so we can dine and celebrate."

"Aye, sir."

The General studied the ledger thoughtfully. "Under our agreement," he said, "you will recall that, in addition to your upkeep, I pledged myself to make, er—certain other payments upon the expiration of your bond." He looked at Horatio with a smile. "Do you recall what they were, Tench?"

Horatio grinned. "Just one, sir—forty acres of land. I remember at the time that I found it hard to believe that anyone had that much land to give away."

They laughed and the General nodded. "Ah, you would remember the land. We'll come to that in a minute. First, let me discharge my other obligations. We'll take them in order." He paused. "Number one is my promise to give you a suit of clothes of good quality." Smiling, he picked up a sheet of paper from his desk and handed it to Horatio. "Here's an order to my tailor to cut you a suit from any piece of cloth you choose."

Horatio flushed with pleasure, but he felt that he must protest. He knew that, legally, the General could present him with a shapeless suit of Osnaburg and nothing more. Besides, thanks to the General he already had three suits of better than average cut in his wardrobe. "Really, sir, I don't . . ." he began.

The General paid no attention to his half-protest. "Number two," he said, rising and walking over to the cabinet in the corner of the study, "I promised to give you a suitable firearm." The General selected a gun from the cabinet and held it out to Horatio. There was a touch of laughter in his voice. "I hope this answers the purpose."

Horatio looked at the gun and was overwhelmed. He knew the gun well, a perfectly balanced, double-barreled fowling piece that bore the hallmark of Wilson, the famous London gunsmith. Horatio had coveted the gun ever since the first day he had seen the General using it on a partridge hunt. And to think the General was giving it to him! It was . . . it was . . . He couldn't find words to express his gratitude. He took the weapon and ran his hand along its beautifully chased barrel and shook his head with wonder. "I can't think of anything to say, sir," he said finally.

The General smiled. "You don't have to say anything, Tench." He looked at Horatio thoughtfully. "There's also a detail of fifty dollars which I owe you, but if I may, I'd like to discuss that a little later. Right now I think we should get to the matter of the land." He sat down and made a steeple with the tips of his fingers. "Under our contract, as you've mentioned, I agreed to give you forty acres of land or the equivalent in money. Naturally I want to make whichever payment you desire. I hope you understand that."

"Aye, sir." Horatio nodded and rubbed his hand along the stock of his gun.

"Since, however, we are to assume that you will be remaining at Fair Haven," the General continued, "I really see no advantage to you in having to bother with your own crop on some distant forty acres. It seems to me that the wisest thing would be for you to accept a cash payment in lieu of land."

The protest came out before Horatio thought. He had looked forward to owning land too long to accept a substitute. "But, sir, it wouldn't interfere with my duties to raise my own crop."

The General smiled pleasantly. "I'm sure that's true, Tench, but I have your own welfare in mind as much as I do your duties. Who would you get to break your land? Who would plant it? Where would you get your mules?"

Horatio colored. "Why, I thought . . . I thought that I could use some hands from Fair Haven. Naturally, I . . . I would see that I made you some sort of payment for their services."

"That wouldn't do, Tench. No, that wouldn't do at all." The General shook his head firmly. "Raising cotton, even forty acres of it, is a job that requires constant management. You can work a thousand acres in one piece, but you can't work a thousand acres and a forty-acre splinter."

Horatio's voice was earnest. "I could work at night and the hands could . . ."

The General's wave was almost impatient. "Surely, Tench, you're not suggesting that I work my hands at night! And look at you, man. You crawl home half-dead most of the time. Do you think I want to destroy your health?"

Horatio looked glum while he tried to marshal more arguments. After a short silence the General laughed. "Come, come, now, Tench—let's look at this thing sensibly." He spread his fine hands on the desk in front of him. "I assure you that it will be impossible to tend to your land and mine too. Don't misunderstand," he added hastily. "My concern is not over your duties here. I'm thinking of the added work. Your happiness is of the greatest concern to me, Tench. You do realize that, don't you?"

Horatio nodded. "Aye, sir."

"Then," said General Jameson, "listen to my proposition. I'll give you four hundred dollars in lieu of your forty acres—ten dollars an acre." He smiled. "I believe you'll agree that's an equitable price. There's another fifty dollars due you under the terms of our original contract. I prefer to deal in round figures, so I have here five hundred dollars." He opened a drawer and took out a clinking purse and threw it on the desk casually. "Take it and let's square our account."

Horatio looked at the purse and felt quite breathless. He had never seen so much money in one lump before and he was impressed. Yet . . . he ran his hand across his flushed brow and tried to organize his thoughts.

The General smiled at his indecision. He leaned forward. "And that's not all, Tench. You're working for wages now. I'll give you thirty hard dollars a month to add to that sum there—thirty dollars and your keep."

Horatio hardly knew what to say. He knew that the General's offer was lavish. But he had dreamed of land of his own for a long time. He looked at the General and squirmed a little uneasily. He thought he saw a shadow of anger on his handsome face. He was mistaken. When the General spoke again his voice was hurt, tinged with reproach.

"I'm not a bargaining man, Tench. I assure you that I have your best interests at heart."

Horatio spoke quickly. "Oh, I know that, sir. It's . . . it's just . . ."

Again that shadow crossed the General's brow, but only for an instant. Suddenly he leaned back and laughed loudly. "Ah, Tench! Tench!" he said, shaking his head, "you're hungry for land and that's a fact."

Horatio smiled embarrassedly.

The General's mood changed. His smile died and he looked at Horatio sadly. He spoke gently, almost reluctantly. "I see how you feel, Tench, and I must say that I don't blame you." He paused and looked down at his desk. "I seem to have been trapped in my own subtlety. I was . . . I was trying to persuade you, sell you, as it were. I should have spoken frankly. What I should have said . . . well, the fact of the matter is that I think it would be extremely unwise of you to . . . to separate yourself from Fair Haven in any respect. You've not forgotten our talk a long time ago, have you, Tench? You must remember that you're still sought in England. I . . . I don't think enough time has elapsed for you to . . ."

He didn't have to continue. Horatio flushed and interrupted quickly. "I'll do what you say, sir." He didn't see the General's point, didn't try to analyze it. He knew full well that the General was looking after his interest.

The General looked grateful for being spared further explanation. "Thank you, Tench," he said quietly. He studied Horatio's face and moved his chair forward briskly. He made his voice jovial. "Here, let's not be glum. I'll tell you what I'll do. When the time comes I'll sell you land. Bless you, I'll sell you all the land you want. After all, you're a young man, Tench. You'll be wanting to get married one of these days and raise a family." He paused for a chuckle. "If I'm any judge, forty acres probably won't be near enough to accommodate your brood. In that case, we'll have to arrange to get you more land.

Horatio sighed and nodded glumly.

The General arose quickly and thrust out his hand. "Let's seal a fine agreement, Tench."

Horatio's smile was forced, but the warm clasp he gave the General's hand was sincere.

At dinner he received his second blow of the evening. Clover wasn't home to share his first meal as a free man. The General made some vague reference to a social engagement in Charleston. "But she asked me to be remembered to you, Tench," he said. "She asked me to convey her heartiest congratulations." It was little comfort, but it helped some. So did the General's fine port.

All in all, he was in a fairly happy frame of mind when he returned to his room. He lay awake a long time, staring into the dark. It was true he wasn't *completely* free but . . . He smiled. Aye, life wasn't too bad. No, not half-bad. His full purse made a reassuring lump under his pillow . . . his new suit would be as fine as any in Charleston—and his gun, his beautiful gun, leaned in a corner of the room. He sighed . . . yes, life could be good. He fell asleep feeling warm and comfortable.

It was the next afternoon when Horatio met the bearded stranger.

King was with him, handling the reins in a light, fast gig which had been built for General Jameson's wife at the outset of her illness. The gig was almost never used. Horatio had taken it this day partly because he wanted King's company and partly because he had to make some purchases in Charleston which would be too bulky for his saddlebags. It was a clear day and the sun shone hot, but it seemed to Horatio that he could feel a hint of autumn crispness in the air. For the tenth time since they had left Fair Haven, he lifted his head and breathed deeply with relish.

King looked at him and chuckled. "Ever' time yo' does dat, Ah specs ter hear yo' whinny."

Horatio grinned. "B'fair, I feel like it."

King nodded slowly. "Ah reckon yo' does. Ah reckon yo' does at dat." He flicked the reins and his voice was thoughtful. "Ah reckon it mus' be a mighty good feelin' ter know yo's yo' own boss an' ain't hitched up ter nobody."

There was no sadness in his voice, no self-pity, but Horatio suddenly felt embarrassed. He felt as if he had been flouting his newfound freedom. He flushed and looked at King quickly.

King didn't turn from his driving but he sensed the glance. He smiled. "Ah ain't hurtin' none, Boss."

Horatio reflected that, indeed, that did seem to be the truth. It was something that had always puzzled him. Like most of the better planters, General Jameson boasted that he had never sold a Negro but that any one of his hands was free to buy his freedom at any time. Yet Horatio had never heard a Negro at Fair Haven mention buying his liberty. He knew it wouldn't be easy for a Negro to accumulate enough money to buy himself, but it was by no means impossible. Some of the hands gathered as much as a bale of nankeen from their single acre each year. In addition, it was General Jameson's custom to give each hand a five-dollar gold piece when the crops were in. Most of them spent their money for trinkets and geegaws and Sunday finery, but King was never in the groups that swarmed around peddlers' wagons which came to Fair Haven. It was strange. He studied King's handsome, intelligent face for a while.

"Why haven't you bought your freedom, King?"

King's smile vanished. He sat silent for so long that Horatio flushed and felt like a meddling fool. "I'm sorry, I shouldn't have . . ."

King shook his head quickly. "No, Boss, dat ain't it . . . Ah . . . Ah was jes' tryin' ter think how ter answer yo' so yo' would unnerstan'." His face was thoughtful. " 'Most de furst thing Ah kin 'member—even when Ah was a leetle biddy boy, Ah uster think Ah wanted ter be free more'n anythin'. Ah reckons dat's de furst thing any nigger thinks after he fines out he ain't free." He paused a moment, then shrugged and smiled. "But, den, atter yo' gits a leetle older, Ah reckon yo' knows dat it takes more'n a sack full er money ter be free. Yo' kin gits a piece er paper wif yo' money sayin' yo' is free—but dat paper don't change de color er yo' skin. Ah reckon dat's a mighty sad feelin' when yo' fines out yo' jes' ain't got no chancet ter really be free."

"You could work for yourself," Horatio said.

King smiled. "Ah could wuk all right. Ah could wuk, dat's a fack—but Ah'd be doin' de same kinda wuk Ah'm doin' now, an' Ah reckon Ah wouldn't git erlong near so well. Hard wuk jes' ain't enough eff'n yo' ain't in de right place." He turned to his driving and remained silent so long that Horatio thought he had dropped the subject, then he spoke slowly. "Long time ergo, when Ah was 'bout half-high, ole Marse Justin went over the sea somewhar an' brung back a leetle ole mule. Ah forgits wut dey calls it, but it warn't no bigger'n a Jack colt. But it war stout—Man, it war stout! —it could tote near 'bout as much as any mule we had on de place. Ole Marse war awful set-up 'bout dat mule, but right erway it gib us all sorts er trouble. The odder mules wouldn't have nuthin' ter do wif it. Dey war always kickin' it an' chasin' it away from its feed so fin'lly Marse had ter sell it. He was awful mad 'bout dat 'cause he say dat leetle mule war the bes' of its kind in dis place whar he foun' it."

King wrinkled his brow. "Ah uster think 'bout dat leetle ole mule er lot. Ah liked it purty good. It wukked hard an' it could tote a lot more'n some of the big ole lazy mules dat war always a-pickin' on it. But Ah reckon it jes' didn't belong 'cause it war differunt. Ah uster wonder if we took one er dose big ole mules ober de sea if maybe de leetle mules would er treated it the same way." He clucked to the horse and drove awhile before he spoke again. "Reckon hard wuk's not enough eff'n yo's differunt."

Horatio nodded. "I know what you mean."

King looked surprised. "What Ah means? Ah don't mean nuthin'." But there was humor in his eyes.

Horatio sat thoughtfully for a few moments. "But wouldn't you *like* to be free, King?"

King smiled slightly. He pointed to the small polished brass lamp fastened to the frontboard of the gig. "Feel dat, Boss." Horatio touched the lamp, then drew his hand back quickly. The sun had heated it blisteringly hot. King chuckled. "Hot, ain't it? It burned me when Ah touched it, too. Reckon we feel a lot erlike."

Horatio flushed. He was saved a reply because just then they saw the bearded stranger.

He was a tall, shaggy bear of a man wearing butternut home-spun and a coonskin cap. He stood on the side of the road, staring dejectedly at the rear wheel of an enormous, dilapidated wagon. A woman and a little girl, also dressed in homespun and wearing shovel bonnets, sat on the board seat of the wagon. Behind them, and stacked to an incredible height, was a mass of household goods —a feather mattress, a battered old chest, dozens of pots and pans, a cane-bottomed rocking chair, and other odds and ends.

King reined up and Horatio saw at a glance what had happened. The overloaded wagon had come down a nearby rise too fast, and when the driver applied the brake, it had skidded sideways on the road and the right rear wheel had crunched into the shallow ditch beside the road, splintering the spokes.

Horatio leaned from the gig. "Can we be of help?"

The bearded man gave him a rueful grin and kicked at the broken wheel. "Reckon not, friend, less'n yo' got a extry wheel handy." His voice was deep and melodious and for some reason there was something about him that seemed strangely familiar to Horatio. He climbed down from the gig and went over to survey the damaged wheel. One glance told him that it could not be repaired. He turned to the man and was a little shocked to discover that his bearded face was on a level with his own. Horatio was so accustomed to towering above people that it always surprised him when he found someone who could look him in the eye without throwing back his head.

"Going far?" Horatio asked.

The stranger spat in the dust and gave him another rueful smile. "Too fur t'swing a pole under the rear axle if'n that's wut yo' got in mind."

Horatio shrugged. "Well, James Talbot's shop on the edge of Charleston is the nearest place to get a wheel. We're going in that direction if you want to ride along."

The stranger digested this offer slowly. Finally he turned to the woman, who had been staring at her hands in her lap ever since Horatio appeared. "Wife," the bearded man asked, "would yo' weary too much eff'n Ah left yo' a spell t'git a wheel in Charleston?"

The woman didn't lift her head but smiled placidly. "Lawsy, no, we'uns can make out jes' fine."

The stranger grinned at Horatio. "Much obleeged, friend. Mah name be Lafe Mitchell."

Horatio had scarcely given his own name when the little girl seemed to realize what was going on. "Pa! Pa! Yo' can't leave me, Pa! Leave me go, Pa!"

Her mother rebuked her mildly, "Ada Mitchell, mind yo' . . ."

Lafe Mitchell laughed. "Reckon she could?" he asked Horatio.

Horatio was saved an answer. The little girl came sliding down from the wagon in a flurry of homespun and long blond curls. As Horatio lifted her into the gig, he marveled at how frail she was. She was the first child he had ever lifted. She sat between him and King and folded her hands composedly. "Ah ain't aimin' t' sit in no wagon all day while mah Pa goes traipsin' off," she said.

Lafe Mitchell grinned. He had climbed on the narrow back-board of the gig and he squatted there with his bearded chin resting on the seat at his daughter's back. There was pride in his voice. "She looks after her Pa, this girl do."

They had ridden a quarter-mile before it occurred to Horatio why Lafe Mitchell seemed familiar. His drawl, the homespun, the coonskin cap—they all reminded him of the flatboaters he used to see in the ordinaries in Charleston. He turned.

"You're a Kaintuck?"

Lafe Mitchell smiled and shook his head. "Alabamy," he said. "Leastways they call it Alabama now." He paused. Then, as if deciding he owed some explanation as to why he and his family and worldly goods were on a Carolina road, he spoke slowly. "Ah fit fer Andy Jackson agin the Redsticks an' war late gittin' started. Seems like all the good lan'—leastways, all Ah had a hankerin' fer—war took up 'fore Ah came erlong. Las' five y'ars Ah been holpin' mah uncle wuk his farm up near Beaufort, but las' spring some Guvermint warrants come through an' Ah lef' mah family an' went back to Alabamy t' git me some lan'. Wal, Ah foun' it, an' Ah come back t' git mah wife an' daughter. We'uns war movin' erlong toward our lan' when that dadburn wheel broke."

He sighed. "Can't hardly wait t' git thar. Got me near 'bout two hundred acres of the richest, reddiest lan' yo' ever seen."

Horatio couldn't believe his ears. That this shaggy man could claim to have two hundred acres of land was fantastic. He turned with a look of such utter incredulity that Lafe Mitchell laughed.

"Kinda su'prises yo', don't it? Kinda sets yo' back on yo' heels t'think that a pore man like me kin have so much lan'." He shook his head. "Dawgone, sometime Ah can't believe it mahself. Ah've seen a lotta free lan'—yessir, Ah've seen a heap o' free lan' an' Ah ain't never seen none nowhar t' compare with this. Why, man, it's so rich that yo' gotta be keerful whar yo' put yo' gunstock or it'll take root." He roared with laughter.

Horatio looked at Lafe Mitchell closely. He remembered vaguely that he had heard of free land somewhere to the west. Somehow, though, it was associated in his mind with Indians and forest. The truth was that he knew almost nothing about this country to which he had come five years before. His entire world was bounded on one side by the cotton fields of Fair Haven and on the other side by the waterfront of Charleston.

"Where is your land?" he asked.

"In the Big Bend," Lafe Mitchell said. "Right smack in the middle o' the Big Bend."

"The Big Bend?"

Lafe smiled. "They call it that on 'count o' the Tennessee makes a big ole curve right thar." His eyes shone. "Man, it's the purtiest spot yo' ever seen. And game? Lordy! Ah ain't never seen the likes o' game, not even when Ah fit with Andy Jackson in the bottom-lands. Thar's deer an' turkey an' coon an' squirrel an' nigh onto every varmint Ah ever knowed of. An' fish? Friend, the river an' creeks is crowded with them. All yo' gotta do is drop a hook."

Horatio was fascinated. He looked at King and saw that he, too, was rapt with interest. "With all that game, it sounds as if the land isn't cleared," Horatio said.

Lafe Mitchell shrugged. "Wal, it is an' it ain't. Some of it's jes' plain woods, but most of it ain't kivered with nothin' worse'n cane." He laughed. " 'Course the cane thar grows like ever'thin' else. In some places it stan's twicet as high as a man's haid an' it's so thick yo' can stick in a knife t' the handle an' it'll stan' thar. 'Course a lotta lan' is cleared. Ah took me out a corn claim an' Ah reckon the patch Ah planted war nigh onto twenty acres. That corn war done two-three inches high when Ah got through throwin' mah li'l ole cabin together, but Ah reckon . . ."

Horatio broke in unbelievingly. "All you had to do was plant corn to make a claim?"

Lafe shook his head. "T'warn't really necessary," he said proudly. "Ah had mah warrants fer soldierin' so the Guvermint give me first pick, but Ah jes' didn't wanta take no chancet of thar bein' any mix-up. Ah could've made a tomahawk claim jes' as well."

Horatio didn't have the least idea what a tomahawk claim was, but Lafe's answer suggested another question. "What about the Indians?"

Lafe roared. "Man, thar ain't no Indians 'round those parts. Lordy! This heah is genuwine Guvermint lan' an' it's open t' settle-ment. People is rushin' in down thar like a fire a-eatin' through sage grass."

"You mean the land's open for anybody?" Horatio asked.

"Yessiree," Lafe said. "Anybody that's got enough git-up-an'-git t' make a claim. They stake them out a claim an' then when the Guvermint gits ready t' sell it, they jes' prove they's been a-sittin' thar an' they gits it fer a dollar an' two bits an acre."

Before Horatio could ask another question, he saw with regret that they were approaching James Talbot's wagon shop. Lafe Mitchell and his daughter climbed down from the gig and stood, hand in hand, while they made their thanks. "Ah ain't got no money t'speak of," Lafe said, "so Ah won't offer t'pay, but Ah'm plumb obleeged. If'n yo' ever git t' the Big Bend, Ah hope t' do you a favor."

Horatio felt that he had to talk to Lafe some more. "Look," he said, "we'll be passing back this way within the hour. If you wait, we'll be happy to have you ride with us."

Lafe beamed his appreciation. "That's mighty handsome, friend. We'll do it." He and his daughter stood waving as Horatio and King drove away.

After a while Horatio turned to King. "Have you ever heard of the . . . the Big Bend?"

King shook his head thoughtfully. "No, sir, but dat man sho' sounded like he war tellin' de trufe."

Horatio was mildly irritated. "Of course he was."

King smiled and shot Horatio a sly glance. "Yo' thinkin' 'bout saddlin' up yo' hawss an' goin' thar, Boss?"

Horatio looked at him sternly, then smiled and sighed. "B'fair, I'd like to."

King drove a while in silence. "Wal, better let me know when yo' go—yo' might need some help."

They laughed because they both knew they were only making conversation. Still, there were a lot of questions Horatio wanted to ask Lafe Mitchell, so he completed his shopping quicker than he might have ordinarily. But when they returned to the wagon shop, Lafe and his daughter were gone.

"Jes' so happened Ah had an ole wheel aroun' that suited him fine," James Talbot said. "He took it an' one of the Praeger niggers come along in a wagon an' give them a ride." He grinned. "That li'l girl musta be took with yo'. She wouldn't leave until she sat down an' writ yo' a note. She were a smart 'un."

He handed Horatio a piece of soiled paper. On it, in a careful child's hand, was written:

Dere sir,
    Me & Pa thanks you. We get a tote on a wagin,
                         yr. ob. serv. &c.
                         Ada Mitchell
                         Ae 6 yrs.

Horatio smiled and folded the note carefully and stored it in his purse.

CHAPTER XIV

GENERAL JAMESON threw back his handsome head and laughed delightedly. "Really, Tench! Really! Some backwoods clown has been having sport with you."

Horatio colored and looked down at his plate. For more than a week he had looked forward to telling General Jameson of his meeting with Lafe Mitchell. He had hoped to learn more of the fabulous region known as the Big Bend. Instead, halfway through his story, the General had burst into laughter. Horatio was torn between anger and embarrassment.

"But, sir," he said earnestly, "this man has been there. He says he's seen all these things. He's taking his family back with him."

The General took a sip of wine and wiped his lips carefully with a snowy white napkin. He seemed to be struggling to keep a straight face. "And what did you say this place is called?" he asked innocently.

Horatio's ears burned. The General knew quite well what the region was called. The mention of its name had provoked his laughter in the first place. Horatio looked at him steadily. "The Big Bend," he said defiantly.

The General shook with laughter again. "Bless me," he said, "bless me, I can't help it! It sounds like something one gets from drinking too much cherry brandy."

Clover broke in. "Now, Daddy, I think you're just being mean. Let Tench finish his story." Horatio looked at her quickly to see if she, too, was laughing. Apparently she wasn't. She was pouting prettily for her father, but her eyes were serious.

The General chuckled good-naturedly. "But, of course, my dear." He turned to Horatio. "I do apologize, Tench. Please go ahead with your story."

Horatio was mollified. "Well, I . . . well, I guess that's all there is to it. This man says he has claimed nearly two hundred acres of rich land just by planting corn on it. I . . . I didn't know things like that were possible."

The General's tone was bantering, but he looked at Horatio closely. "Are we to take it that you have been tempted, Tench?"

Horatio was shocked. "Why, certainly not, sir," he said quickly. "I was curious because I've never heard much about land being free for the taking."

"Nor has anybody else with intelligence, Tench," General Jameson said. "There are free lands—of course. There are areas open for settlement, but they have to be bought from the Government." He shrugged. "Of course, the land isn't much. It's either rocky or hilly or so thickly covered with forest that it would take years to clear."

He deftly carved a morsel from his turkey leg and chewed it carefully. "Don't you think that if there was worthwhile land lying bare that more enterprising, energetic persons would have found it sooner?"

"But, Daddy, there are free lands somewhere," Clover said. "I've heard of them myself."

The General chuckled. "Why, of course, my dear. We even have some land still unclaimed here in South Carolina." He lifted his brows. "Like most free land, it's no good for anything except watersnakes and marsh hens."

It pleased Horatio to see Clover taking such an interest in the conversation, and it warmed him because she seemed to be siding with him. He shook his head and sighed. "I just can't understand why this man—this Lafe Mitchell—seemed so sure of his claim."

The General made an airy gesture. "There are always people who are trying to get something free, Tench. They aren't willing to take their chances or try to make their way in organized society."

Horatio looked at the General's white, graceful hand, and for some strange reason he recalled Lafe Mitchell's weatherbeaten, callused paw. He blushed guiltily for his disloyalty.

The General was not finished. "Of course," he said with a smile, "I don't profess to know all about claims and such matters. When you are in town someday, why don't you drop by the Government land office? I think they can give you the facts. I believe you'll find that, basically, I am correct. Anyway, it might be interesting if you think it's worth the bother."

Horatio's voice was thoughtful. "Maybe I will someday."

Clover's reaction surprised him completely. When she slipped into his room later, she hugged him tightly. Her voice was excited. "Oh, you should do it, darling. You should do it right away."

"Do what?" he asked in bewilderment.

"Why, darling, go to . . . to that place and get you some land. I think you should go as soon as possible."

At first he thought she was joking. He held her at arms' length and looked at her serious face. He laughed.

She looked at him sadly. "You don't love me."

He was immediately contrite. "Of course I do, my dear. That's why I'd never leave you."

"But don't you see? This would be the answer to everything." Her voice was eager. "You could go to this place and get a nice, big farm and I could come and join you. Oh, my darling, think about that—we could be together always." She pressed tightly to him.

His voice was patient. "You don't understand, dear. The place this Mitchell told me about is nothing but wilderness. I couldn't take you there. Besides, I can't go off and leave your father now. I owe him too much. I'm free now and you've promised . . ."

She pulled away from him and sighed wearily. "Now don't go into that again."

"But you did promise," he said. "You said that we could go to your father when I finished my bond. Ever since then—"

"You don't understand!"

He looked at her steadily. "I think I do," he said sharply. "It's you that—"

She threw her arms around him. "Please, oh, please, let's don't fight again," she begged. "I've promised you that it won't be long now, darling. Can't you see that I'm looking forward to the time when we can be married just as much as you are." She gave him a long kiss and snuggled in his arms. After a long pause she looked up at him. "Darling, I'm staying overnight in town on Wednesday. . . . Can't . . . can't I go to that land place and . . . ?"

He released her. His voice was stern. "Why are you going to town again?"

She sighed. "Oh, it's another of those silly parties."

"You've been to town once a week for the past two months."

"But, of course, you know——"

"I know nothing," he flared. "I suppose that smirking Carter fellow is going to take you to the party."

She wrinkled her nose disdainfully. "I have to go with some-one and he does just exactly as I say."

Horatio knew this was probably true but he was seething. "I don't like it! Every time I look around, he's prancing at your heels."

"Now you're being cruel again."

He couldn't think of an answer so he sat silent.

After a while she snuggled up to him and began to stroke his cheek with her small, soft hand. "Darling."

"Yes?"

"Can't you . . . that is . . . won't you please see about the land? I know we could be . . ."

He sighed and shook his head. "I told you I have no interest in that place! B'fair, I'm sorry I mentioned it. I have work here. Your father will sell me land when I need it."

"But, dear . . ."

"No!"

She let the subject drop for the time being, but he knew he hadn't heard the last of it.

And maybe her idea was good? He lay in bed after she had left and thought about it. Maybe if he had land of his own—had a place to take her—she wouldn't be so hesitant about facing her father? He frowned. Sometimes it seemed as if she did not . . . But, no, he wouldn't think about that. Of course she loved him. He thought of her kisses and her tender little caresses—yes, she loved him and he was lucky. He sighed again and settled deeper in the bed. He had to be patient. Someday she would find the courage to go with him to her father.

But she kept him miserably unhappy all during that autumn. At least once a week some social engagement kept her overnight in Charleston. Almost always, when she returned to Fair Haven, one or more of her coquettish, showy little girl friends came with her. Young men, particularly the dashing Lieutenant Carter, came calling almost every afternoon. Horatio burned with anger when he heard them laughing gaily on the veranda, and he was disgusted at the way Clover and her girl friends squealed like helpless little children when they played croquet with the young men on the lawn.

If he protested, Clover looked martyred. "I didn't invite them. They asked me if they could visit with me for a few days."

"Why did you have to go to Charleston?"

She looked at him defiantly. "Because I wanted to go. Do you expect me to bury myself and give up all my friends just because you are jealous?"

Jealous. Jealous. Jealous. That was her answer to all his protests, and because he knew it was true, he could do nothing but fume.

She refused even to discuss going to her father and telling him that they were in love. She had a counterproposal now and she made it constantly. "You should go to that place and get some land of your own. I don't see why you don't do it. After you get land of your own, we could be married and . . ."

"No!"

He couldn't bring himself to tell her that he was a prisoner at Fair Haven.

If he had not been morose and short-tempered, probably he never would have done what he did one mid-October afternoon. It was late and he was riding his big bay back to the stable after a tour of the quarters when he came upon General Jameson behind a low stone wall around the garden patch, shooting doves alighting in the fields. It was the General's favorite sport during the fall months. He had baited the field with cracked corn and the gray birds fluttered in greedily, paying no attention to the report of his fowling piece.

When Horatio rode up, the General raised his head and smiled. His face was flushed with pleasure and excitement.

"They're thick today, Tench. Get your gun and join me." Horatio shook his head, but he reined up and watched. The General was an excellent shot and he liked to catch the doves while they were still in the air preparing to land. Every time he fired, one of the birds seemed to explode with a flurry of feathers, then fell limply to the ground.

Suddenly the birds swarming in to land veered sharply and went winging off. They were followed almost immediately by the birds feeding on the ground. The General looked up quickly and scowled with annoyance. A fat, lumbering old hog had wandered on the field and was nosing along noisily, feeding on the scattered corn.

The General's face was dark with anger. "Get that animal out of there, Tench!"

Horatio turned his horse toward the gate about a hundred yards away.

The General's voice was sharp. "No! No! Go over the fence, man."

Horatio stopped. He had picked his bay for its sturdiness. It was not much of a jumper, and although the fence was not very high, he felt that he should not take a chance. "I'd better not, sir. He doesn't jump very well," he said.

There were two bright spots of color on the General's cheeks. He smiled thinly. "The horse—or the master?"

Horatio stiffened. He was proud of his horsemanship. Without a word he wheeled his bay, dug in his heels, and headed for the fence. The horse should have made it easily, but at the last moment it hesitated and its back hoofs slid on the soft grass growing in front of the wall. Both front legs clipped the top of the wall and it fell on the other side on its knees. Horatio was thrown clear and he landed with a solid jolt. He arose burning with anger and embarrassment.

The General stepped over the wall and came forward anxiously. "Are you hurt, Tench? Are you hurt? I shouldn't have asked you to do it. It was . . ." He stopped.

Horatio brushed past him and went to the bay which was standing by the wall, its right front leg dangling limply. Even before he stooped for a closer examination, Horatio knew the leg was broken. He looked up at the General and all his bitterness and rage arose.

His face was white with fury. "Look what you've done! It's broken. It's all your fault!"

For a moment the General was taken aback; then he nodded slowly. "Yes, Tench, it is. I'm truly sorry."

Horatio did the only thing that could be done. His face was white and set as he removed the saddle and bridle from the bay. He stroked its nose gently for a while, then took the General's gun, reloaded it with a ball, and shot the animal between the eyes. He wouldn't look at General Jameson as he gathered up his equipment and started for the stable.

The General fell in with him and continued to apologize. "I understand how you feel, Tench. It was a good animal and I'm sorry that it was sacrificed because of my stupidity. I want you to take your pick of the horses. I want you to take the one you want." He talked all the way to the stable, but Horatio would not look at him.

When they entered the stable, King was in the tack room mending harness. His grin flickered out when he saw Horatio's face. He turned back to his work. Horatio hung up the saddle and bridle and started to leave. "Now, now, Tench," the General said. "Don't feel so badly. It was an accident and it was caused by me. Come, let's look around. You can have anything I own here in the stable."

Horatio never clearly understood what made him say what he did. Perhaps it was because of the way the General phrased his offer. Perhaps it was because he was so furious that he wanted to hurt or embarrass him any way he could. He turned and looked at the General levelly.

"In that case, I'll take King!"

The General started to smile at this sally, but when he saw Horatio's face, his lips froze in surprise. He stood shock-still for a moment, then licked his lips with the tip of his tongue. If he had not been so amazed, he could have laughed the matter off. But he hesitated until it was too late. He studied Horatio's stern face. There was a shadow of amusement in his voice. "What would you do with King?"

Horatio's expression did not change. "Set him free!"

General Jameson stood still for a long time. He turned slowly and looked at King, who had dropped the harness and was sitting stiffly. He looked back to Horatio. There was not a sound except for the drone of a horsefly against one of the windows. The General's eyes brightened with amusement, then his face crinkled in a slow smile. Suddenly he threw back his head and laughed delightedly. "Taken! Taken fairly, by God! I'll pay! I'll pay."

He insisted on making a ceremony of it. Still laughing merrily, he took Horatio and King to his study and drew up a bill of sale, then signed as a witness when Horatio turned it over to King. Even Horatio was beaming now. Only King did not smile. He sat calmly while the arrangements were made, and when he received the slip of paper making him free, he turned it over and over in his fingers and didn't say a word.

General Jameson chuckled. "You won't be leaving, King?"

King shook his head slowly.

"Fine! Fine!" The General laughed again. "We'll discuss your wages another time." He poured them all a glass of wine. King barely touched his lips to his.

It was growing dark when he and Horatio left the house. They stood in the courtyard a minute before they separated. King was still turning the paper in his fingers. Finally he spoke. "Boss, Ah . . . Ah thanks yo'." He walked away.

In his study the General sat smiling. What a story this would be to tell his cronies! Then he took down his journal, and chuckling all the time, wrote a full account of what had happened. He knew this would be another legend at Fair Haven, and it delighted him to think that years later his descendants would be telling the story with pride.

CHAPTER XV

HIS new suit was a work of art. Horatio squared his broad shoulders and beamed at himself in the dusty mirror. The velvet-faced waistcoat was the color of a summer sky and it buttoned snugly around his chest, and then fell away into a swallowtail that extended to the backs of his knees. The trousers were dove-gray and they seemed to be molded to his bulging calves and slim thighs. He pivoted slowly and examined his reflection from the rear, then grinned at Pierre Richer, the excitable little Huguenot tailor who clothed the gentlemen of Charleston. "It fits perfectly, sir."

But Monsieur Richer did not seem pleased. He eyed Horatio's right leg critically, then fell to one knee and pulled at the trousers near the ankle. He gave a little hiss of disgust. "It is too loose," he said. "It is too loose."

Horatio looked down in annoyance. He had waited more than a month for his new suit and had made a special trip to town to get it. "I see nothing wrong with it," he said. "I'll take it as it is."

Monsieur Richer lifted his eyebrows in surprise. "No! No!" He tugged impatiently at the trousers. "Like the skin they must fit. Like the skin! I cannot permit you to take them, M'sieu. I would be the laughing stock of Charleston!"

In spite of his annoyance Horatio had to smile. "But I've made a special trip to town," he said. "It will be another week before I can return."

Monsieur Richer was adamant. "Then I will work like the

wind, M'sieu, but I cannot permit these trousers to leave my shop. You must return in an hour or two."

Horatio was still smiling when he left Monsieur Richer's dark shop. He had already completed his other business in town so he had nothing to do. He wandered aimlessly toward The Battery, but at the foot of High Street he paused and snapped his fingers with remembrance, and turned back toward the center of town.

Five minutes later he was facing the bored young gentleman who was Federal Land Agent by grace of Congress and his family's fortune. He shook his head and looked blank at Horatio's question.

"There's no city by that name," he said.

"No, no, it's not a city," Horatio said. "It's the name of a region."

The agent delicately covered a yawn. "Never heard of it," he said.

Horatio tried to keep his voice even. "Don't you have a chart or map that might show it?"

The agent sighed and stood up slowly and slouched across the room to a battered cabinet. "Alabama, is it not?" he asked, taking down a dusty map.

"Aye." Horatio waited impatiently while the agent searched the map with his sleepy brown eyes. Finally he shook his head. "It isn't shown."

"But it must be," Horatio said. He spoke with an assurance he didn't feel.

The clerk looked again, then shook his head.

"It's . . . it's near a river," Horatio said.

"Which river?"

"Why . . . it's—the Tennessee River!"

The clerk sighed and patted another yawn. "It's not shown," he said. Horatio remembered General Jameson's laughter and he wondered if Lafe Mitchell had lied.

The clerk found his chair and slipped into it with a sigh. He waved a pale hand. "These old maps aren't much good. They still show Alabama as territory. If you're sure such a place exists, you might try Miss Willoughby's library at the head of Church Street."

"She has maps?"

The agent shook his head. "No, books—thousands of books. Miss Willoughby can find anything."

He nodded wearily at Horatio's thanks.

Miss Willoughby was a tall, angular woman with washed-out blue eyes. She sat at a low table in the center of the library and looked at Horatio coldly. "Are you a patron, Mr. Tench?" Her whole manner told that she knew he wasn't.

"I'm acting for General Randolph Jameson," Horatio said.

Miss Willoughby thawed. "In that case," she said, attempting a smile, "we'll be delighted to be of service."

She wrote down all the information Horatio could supply in a cramped, spidery hand, then tapped a bell on her desk and summoned a pale, pimply young man. She handed him her notes. "Please bring this information to Mr. Tench."

She nodded at Horatio's thanks and indicated a chair at a nearby table. "If you'll be seated, Mr. Tench, we'll have your information in a few minutes. The latest London and Washington newspapers are on the table if you care to read."

The London newspapers were in a neat pile. Horatio picked one up and looked at it curiously. He had read only a few newspapers in his life—never one that had come from so far away. But here were a half-dozen papers that had come all the way across the sea, from the land where he was born. He sat down and began to read, but as his eyes swept the fine print, he grew increasingly bored. There was nothing of interest in the paper at all—just column after column devoted to some dry speech in the House of Lords. He tried to follow its meaning but gave up after a few minutes. He turned the page slowly. A line of type leaped out at him. His pulse quickened.

FLAGSHIP AT YARMOUTH
His Britannic Majesty's Flagship, *NELSON,*
Was Sighted Off Yarmouth At Dawn, 25th Inst.

That was all. But it was enough to make him read it over and over again. And he thought of how he used to sit on the docks as a boy and watch the ships, and how Aber . . . Aber! He swallowed and sat staring into space for a moment. Did he dare? Was it possible?

He looked up with a start. The pimply young librarian stood at his elbow. "I was wondering, sir, if you . . ."

Horatio interrupted. He motioned to the paper. "Do you have any of these newspapers that go back several years?"

The librarian nodded. "Back as far as the war, sir."

Horatio's pulse quickened. He kept his voice calm. "Would it be possible for me to see the copies for . . . for 1816?"

The young man nodded. "It'll take only a minute, sir." He held out the paper in his hand. "I can't find anything relating to a Big Bend, sir. Can you suggest another name?"

Horatio shook his head. He had lost all interest in the Big Bend. "No," he said, "just bring me the papers."

The librarian was back in five minutes with a heavy bound volume. Horatio held it in his lap and plunged into it eagerly. He had forgotten the month he left England, but it was in the fall, that much he knew. September or October . . . aye, it was before December because his indenture was signed in September. He skipped the first part of the volume and started in August. He scarcely knew what to search for, but he swept his finger down column after column. Twice he stopped and read excitedly, once when he saw another ship sighting reported from Yarmouth and once when there was a report of a man's body being found. But it was in Bournemouth.

Up and down—up and down—turn page—up and down. It took a long time. After a half-hour he had lost his feeling of excitement. He began to flip the pages with less interest. Finally he reached the Christmas edition. Only a few pages were left in the volume. He knew then that he would not find what he was seeking. Discouragedly he leafed through the last few pages. He scarcely glanced at the last page. But a glance was all he needed. He sat bolt upright and the color drained from his face. He felt as if his heart had stopped.

CHAPTER XVI

I T WAS a short item, scarcely more than a dozen lines, but Horatio had to read it over and over again before he grasped its full meaning. It seemed that his mind would absorb only so much at a time, that it stopped stock-still with the horror of each new fact. He had to digest each line separately . . . slowly. The report was not at fault. It was plain enough—almost unbelievably plain for a newspaper which seemed to take pride in verbosity.

CRIME EXPIATED!

Evil Dwarf Hanged Before
Assemblage At Yarmouth

A vast crowd gathered before the gates to Yarmouth Gaol 24th Inst. when Aber Cheezum, a Notorious Dwarf, was hanged for the Foul & Brutal Murder of Saml. Tompkins, his Employer and an Honourable & Esteemed Shopkeeper. Cheezum began life auspiciously as the youngest son of John Cheezum, a Venerable Squire of Litchfield, but his Cruel Nature soon alienated him from his Family and Friends. In spite of this, his Forgiving Father left him a sizeable inheritance on his death several years ago. Cheezum had never claimed his bequest, choosing to live in a Mean & Miserly fashion, until, in an effort to Make Amends, he directed that the Full Bequest be paid to Horatio Tompkins, the Ward of the Man he so foully

Murdered. The crowd cheered loudly as Cheezum was led to the Gallows by the High Sheriff. He was still crippled and Blinded in one eye because of injuries inflicted by his Valiant Victim in the Throes of Death. Efforts are being made to locate the Younger Tompkins who is reported to be Sojourning in America.

He never knew how long he sat there. His face was white. His eyes were staring. His throat was dry because he had forgotten to swallow. Finally he realized that someone was shaking him gently by the shoulder. He looked up to see the anxious, curious face of the pimply librarian. "Eh? Yes?"

"I said, sir, are you all right?"

"Oh—all right. All right." Horatio stood up, dazedly, and looked about for a place to put the volume he held.

"Here, sir, I'll take that."

"Eh? What? . . . Oh!" He handed the book to the staring librarian. But Horatio was unaware of him. He turned stiffly and walked across the room and out the door and down the street. He did not see the people he passed or their startled glances at his set face. He had only one thought. It beat back and forth as persistent as a bell clapper. You killed Aber! You killed Aber! He walked up one street and down the other, and finally, almost automatically, he found his way to Angus Dowell's ordinary. He downed two glasses of whisky while a barmaid looked at him with concern. "If there's anything . . ." she began.

"Leave me alone!" he said sharply. She backed away, frightened.

After a while it seemed that his mind began to function. Then the weight of his grief and despair fell like an actual blow. He sat at a table with a bottle of whisky before him and held his head in his hands.

Aber was dead! He had killed Aber. He had as good as killed him with his own hands. Aber went to the gallows for him—Aber the kindly, the gentle friend. He saw the little man's smile, the way his face used to light up when . . . His face? My God! How could he have been such a fool? Why couldn't he have taken more time to examine Aber that night? Aber had been alive. The report said he had been blinded in one eye. But Aber was alive. He groaned. How could he have run off and left Aber there?

In his mind he could see what had taken place after he left Tompkins' shop—saw it as if he were there—and it tortured him. Aber had regained consciousness to find the shop darkened. He had groped his way around, seriously wounded and stumbling on his pitiful weak legs until he could strike a light. He must have seen that Tompkins was dead at once. Then had he stumbled out into the night, or had he shouted for help? Oh, God! But it didn't matter. Aber took the blame for him. Poor dear Aber, who talked of finding a use for his misshapen body. Why couldn't he have heard . . . ?

Heard? He straightened upright and his jaws tightened. The inquiries! General Jameson's inquiries! Surely . . . He sat with his mind racing. When he stood up, there was grim purpose on his face. His chair clattered to the floor. He strode out without heeding it.

Darkness had fallen when he reached Fair Haven. His horse was in a lather. His face was set and hard. He threw his reins to a wide-eyed stable boy and strode off toward the main house. A half-grown little Negro girl who worked as a scullery maid looked up in surprise when he swept through the kitchen. She caught one glimpse of his face and her mouth fell open. "Lawd, Gawd!" she said.

He entered the study without knocking. The General was at the desk writing. He looked up quickly. His frown of annoyance disappeared when he saw Horatio's face.

"What has happened, Tench?" he asked quickly.

Horatio crossed the room and stood before his desk before he answered. "You lied to me," he said. His voice was flat and cold.

The General raised his brows. "What on . . ."

Horatio's eyes never left his face. "You said they wanted me for the killing of Tompkins. They never did. They hanged Aber."

It seemed for a moment that the General had turned to stone. Not a muscle moved. Then the blood drained from his face. He licked at his lips and looked down at his desk. After a long time he sighed. "Please sit down, Tench."

Horatio didn't move. "You lied," he said.

For once the General seemed to be at a loss for words. Silence hung heavy before he spoke. He tried to manage a smile. "Now, Tench . . . it isn't . . . it isn't that bad. Sit down and let me explain."

Horatio's eyes bored into his. His voice was ragged with rage. "I want no more of your lies."

Sudden annoyance caused the General's face to regain its color. "Watch your language, Tench," he said sharply.

Horatio slapped his hand on the desk with a resounding bang. "I'll not watch my language! I came to get a full accounting of why you filled me with . . ."

The General had partially recovered his aplomb. "Now, now," he said soothingly. "Let's sit down and discuss this like gentlemen."

Horatio didn't move, but stood glaring at him.

General Jameson shrugged. "All right, Tench," he said calmly. "I'll admit I didn't give you the full truth of those reports from England. I thought there was no need to cause you worry about . . ."

"Not worry!" Horatio's voice was a whiplash. "Not worry when you . . ."

The General held up his hand. His voice was now remarkably calm and unruffled. "I read the reports on this . . . er, Cheezum's trip to the gallows and I decided that what was done was done. After all, the circumstances were so different from what I had been led to believe by your story that . . ." He shrugged and left the sentence hanging.

"Why didn't you tell me I wasn't wanted?"

The General hesitated and ran the tip of his tongue over his lips. "Why . . . I . . . But I did, Tench! I told you that you weren't to worry . . . and I thought you understood that . . ."

Horatio's laugh was mirthless. "You're lying."

General Jameson flushed. He realized that he was trapped. He had never considered the possibility that Horatio might discover his deception. He had not bothered to prepare a defense. He decided that his only hope was to assert his authority. He drew himself up with dignity. "Really, Tench, I must object to your tone. I've treated you fairly and I have nothing to hide."

Horatio was not fooled by this change in tactics. He had entered the General's study furious enough to pound the truth out of General Jameson, but the man had wilted so easily that his rage was turning to contempt. He looked at the General steadily. "No, you have nothing to hide now because it's all known. You would have kept me here forever. You had me in your pretty white hands like you have everything else at Fair Haven. I've sweated for you and I've fought for you, and I did it because I thought I was repaying you for what you were doing for me. But I know now that you've never done anything for anybody. You do it for yourself. Aye, for yourself! I've thought these things, but I never let myself believe them till now. All of you are alike—you and your fine friends who sit back and live off other men's sweat because they are black or because they are too poor to help themselves. You sit back and you talk about how you love your hands and how much you do for them. You do nothing. Nothing! D'you hear? You like to see them bow and scrape when you come riding by. You like to hear them say what a wonderful man you are. You say you treated me fairly. You think that because you gave me food and clothing, because you gave me some money and a fine gun. Aye, you gave me everything except what a man wants most —freedom! Oh, I know you said I was free because I finished my bond, but it's not a paper that keeps a man from being free. You kept me a lackey still because you had my price. You knew my price was fear. That's what you bought me with— fear! Well, you don't have my price now. You're not worth the little finger of the man who bought my freedom! I hope to God I live to see the day when the other people you own get their freedom! Aye! I hope to live to see the day!"

The General was pale with anger. "I've been fond of you, Tench, but I must warn . . ."

Horatio snorted and leaned forward. "You're fond of nothing except your blasted land and trying to be God. You are nothing but words and fine clothes. In your fashion you're worse than the scum that used to trounce me around when I was a lad. I'm not afraid of you! I'm leaving you—and the only thing you've got that I want I'm taking with me."

The General's face was a mask of rage, but he kept his voice controlled. "Very well, those are our terms. Take your possessions when you leave Fair Haven, but if you're on my land at sunup, by God, I'll have you shot!"

He threw back his shoulders and stood up. Horatio walked out of the room without a backward glance.

He found Jerusalem in the kitchen. "Tell Miss Clover I want to see her right away," he said.

Jerusalem's eyes popped in surprise. "Miss Clover's in her room."

Horatio repeated, "Tell Miss Clover I want to see her right away. Tell her if she isn't in my quarters in ten minutes, I'll come and fetch her."

Jerusalem looked at Horatio's face and backed away. "Yes, suh," he said.

She was furious when she entered his room. "Just what do you mean by . . . ?" She stopped when she saw his stern face and the signs of packing.

"Pack your clothes," he said levelly. "We're leaving at dawn."

She paled. "What do you mean?" she gasped.

"I'm leaving Fair Haven to find land," he said, "and I'm taking you with me."

She stared at him in utter bewilderment for what seemed a full minute. Then she squeezed her lips tightly and turned her head and put her hand to her mouth. Her shoulders shook. He heard something that sounded like a sob.

"Now, now," he said, and started forward to comfort her. He turned her around and drew her to him before he saw her face. He stopped dead. "You're . . . you're laughing," he blurted.

The humor left her face quickly. She curled her lips. "Of course, you fool! Whatever are you thinking of! What makes you think you can order me around like a nigger!"

He could feel the blood rushing to his face. He grasped her arm tightly. "Why are you laughing?"

She tried to wrench her arm away. "Let go of me! Let go of my arm, you fool! Let go—you're hurting me!" She struggled to free herself, but his grip was like iron.

"I'm leaving at dawn," he said.

Her pretty face was contorted with fury. Her eyes were flashing and her breasts heaving. "Go!" she spat. "Go then, d'ya hear! I'm glad you're going!"

Angry as he was, he suddenly realized that he had behaved both badly and foolishly. She knew nothing of his anger or his anguish. He let go her arm and she stepped back, rubbing it and glaring at him.

"I'm sorry I had to send Jerusalem for you," he said. "I . . . I had no other way of reaching you."

She looked at him coldly.

"You will come with me?" he asked gently.

"No! What makes you think I'll go dashing off with you? You've lost your mind completely!"

"You said you'd go."

She looked at him disgustedly. "Oh, you are a fool."

His anger was rising again. "You don't love me?"

Her voice was a snort. "Love you! No! I don't love you."

His voice was hoarse with rage. "Then you lied to me like your father."

She threw back her head and spoke between clenched teeth. "How dare you talk about my father like that, you . . . you nigger-driver!"

"You said you'd marry me."

Her full little lips curled. "I never intended to marry you, you fool!"

"Then why did you lead me on?"

Her laugh was almost a snarl. "Lead you on! Lead you on, indeed! I thought we could have fun together while I was cooped up here. But you ruined it. You and your fine ideas of marriage. . . . Why, I . . ."

He was trembling with anger. "Then you meant nothing you told me?"

She glared at him defiantly. "No! No, I meant nothing of it. I'm glad you're going. Thank God, you're going. I've been trying to get you to leave." She looked at him contemptuously. "If you must know, I'm going to marry someone else. Yes, I'm going to give Lieutenant Carter permission to speak to my father. What do you think of that, *Boss* Tench?"

He stepped back as if she had slapped him in the face. The anger on his face was replaced by disbelief. He looked at her blankly. Shock was written in every line of his body. Even while she raged, somewhere in the back of his mind he had set her words down as due to anger. But now he knew she was telling the truth. The look he gave her was so terrible that she licked her lips nervously and cursed the anger that tripped her tongue.

It was a long time before he spoke. His tone increased her uneasiness. "So you were having sport with me."

She shrugged and tried to make her voice brazen. "Call it that if you like."

He didn't seem to hear her answer. He took two stiff-legged steps forward. His voice had that same awesome note. His eyes never left her face. "You had sport. Aye, you had your sport." He took two more stiff, purposeful steps before she realized he was between her and the door.

"You must pay for your sport!"

Suddenly she was terribly afraid. She tried to keep her voice firm. "You're insane. Let me out of here!"

He smiled thinly, but his eyes were cold, piercing. "You'll go soon enough."

She shrank back and looked around nervously. He kept advancing slowly, ever so slowly. "I'll scream!" she breathed.

"Scream," he answered.

She took another step backward, than another. Her shoulders touched the wall. She pressed back against it. Her breasts were rising and falling with each quick breath. Her mouth was opened slightly. "Stop." It was almost a whisper.

His eyes never left her face.

The only sound in the room was her heavy breathing. She pressed back against the wall, bosom heaving, mouth agape, wide-eyed. He walked forward until he towered over her. His lips twisted in a snarl and he drew back his hand.

She cringed and trembled, then suddenly collapsed and slid down the wall to the floor. "Don't you hurt me! Don't you hurt me, oh, please, don't you hurt me," she whimpered.

He stood stock-still. Terror had robbed her of her beauty and for the first time he saw her as she really was. He looked at her white, stark, little face and he saw her cheapness and her vanity and her cowardice. He lowered his hand and his voice was thick with shame and disgust. "You're not worth the blow of a man."

He turned on his heel and went to the bed and picked up his saddlebags and left the room without another glance at where she sat whimpering.

His face was set and cold when he stood outside King's cabin. "I'm leaving to find land," he said. "Do you want to come?"

King was in his nightshirt. He stood looking at Horatio for a long time, then walked to the edge of the porch and looked up at the starry sky. "Ole stars sho' is low ternight," he said softly.

"Well?"

King turned slowly. His voice was almost a whisper. "Ah'll git mah clothes."

At the gate to Fair Haven Horatio didn't look back, but King halted and turned. He stood there a moment, then shook his head slowly. "Ole stars sho' is low." He turned and ran quickly to catch up with Horatio.

QUEST IN

THE BIG BEND

CHAPTER XVII

THE wind always lay before morning. All night long it moaned through the pines and whistled across the sandy fields and rattled the wintered stubble of Jimson weed. But shortly before the first glow appeared in the east, it eased off to a soft sigh and then a whisper and finally went away. There was nothing but chilled silence then. Folks on this sandy plateau in north Alabama called it "plumb-nigh" time—plumb past night and nigh to morning. It was an in-between time: too early for turkeys to flop down from their roosts in the sweet gums; too late for foxes and 'possums to be prowling the piny woods. It was the quiet hour when frost had a chance, and it was time for a man to be up if he aimed to make an early start.

Horatio opened his eyes when he heard the rattle of flint against steel. As always, he felt a moment's surprise to find himself lying on the ground with the star-splashed sky billowing out above as far as the eye could follow. He always felt this little nudge of surprise when he awakened. Somehow it seemed to be the only time he remembered that he had ever slept in a bed with a tight roof to hold back the wind and rain and frost. They had been on the trail so long that the days had faded into each other and he had lost all track of them. He lay sleepily looking at the graying sky and the dimming stars and feeling his own breath turn to frost and fall back on his face. He hunched deeper in his blanket and buffalo robe and turned his head sideways. In the frosty half-light he could see King down on all fours, his broad black face coming out red as he blew on the makings of a fire.

Horatio smiled and pulled his head under the edge of his covers, feeling warm and good and, somehow, safe. He could not have got along without King. Sometimes, lying this way and thinking, he almost shuddered to think what would have happened if King had not come with him. He had not had any idea of the distances and the heights and the freezing emptiness of this country. Looking back, it made him feel a little embarrassed and foolish to realize how ignorant he had been. He had not even known what supplies to buy, or how to roll them in a pack, or how to set a course. King had taught him those things. Without King he would have been lost in the first pine barren. He had not known that there were stretches of land where a man could travel for days without striking a road or trail. He had not known that there were so many hundreds of streams without bridges.

Aye, King had taken care of him. He had taught him how to bed down so he was warm in the coldest weather. He had taught him how to dry his clothes before a fire and how to find dry wood when rain had soaked the woods and made the ground squishy underfoot. King had cooked for him and kept him warm and guided him straight. And King had been understanding. Never once had he mentioned Fair Haven, not even in those first few days when Horatio knew he must have acted like a dazed man because of the aching lump in his throat and the feeling that a cold hand was tearing at his insides.

But King had done more than make the journey possible. King had saved his life. He would never forget those nightmarish, freezing days in the uplands of Georgia. Some marauding animal had stolen their supplies and it was two weeks before they reached a trading post. But King had fed them some way, though once they went for two days with nothing to eat except a hibernating ground squirrel which King dug out of the frozen ground. They had fed their animals on strips of bark cut from trees.

Horatio sighed deeply and again looked at the sky which was beginning to show a touch of gray. Well, it was over with now. The whole miserable trip was nearly over. Soon they would have their own land. They could forget Fair Haven and he could forget that she . . . He set his jaw. That was over, too. Gone and done with.

He looked up. The fire was crackling merrily now. He threw back his covers, grabbed his boots, and ran toward it.

King was patting out a hoecake between his broad palms. He looked up with a smile. "Gits cole in dis heah promised lan', don't it, Boss?"

Horatio grinned. "Aye." He stood with his back to the fire and let the heat creep up his legs, then sat down and began to pull on his boots. "Anybody pass during the night?"

King shook his head and placed the hoecake on the cooking rock beside the fire and began to quarter a rabbit he had shot and cleaned the evening before. "Not yit, but don't worry none. Dey'll be 'long directly." He dipped the pieces of rabbit in his meal sack and placed them on the stone next the hoecake. He sat back on his heels and brushed his hands slowly. "Yes, suh, dey'll sho' be stirrin' purty soon. Sometime Ah think dey's crazy ter be travelin' in dis kinda weather."

Horatio smiled. "We're traveling."

King grunted. "Wal, mebbe we's crazy too, but leastways, we ain't got no leetle biddy chillun erlong."

Horatio sat watching the pieces of rabbit draw in the heat. He knew how King felt. Ever since they had hit the Georgia State Road and crossed Sand Mountain into Alabama, they had been part of a caravan. It was not a migration, it was almost a stampede. They had seen whole families and whole communities traveling toward the Big Bend. And from the way they grinned and waved, a man would have thought they were on their way to a canebrake barbecue. At first it had been fun because he and King were hungry for company. They had always tried to camp down for the night with some of these folks. They had to stop that. They had only so much meal and flour and shortening and it was impossible not to share it when dozens of tangle-haired, runny-nosed children stood around and stared hungrily. Some of these children had not tasted bread in weeks. They lived on 'possum and rabbit and squirrel which their pas shot whenever possible.

Most of these people seemed to be poor. They rode miserable old horses which seemed to be held together with saddles of corn shucks or coon skins. Sometimes whole families walked, leading pack mules which huffed and sweated under the load of their possessions. Often they brought their goods crammed in a hogshead which had been fitted with shafts and transformed into a rude cart.

But occasionally King and Horatio had passed a settler who was traveling in style. They were the rich planters and their caravans would stretch for a mile or more. They had slaves and wagons and carriages and herds of fine horses. They brought everything with them—milch cows and steers, furniture and chandeliers, glassware and iron grillwork.

But they were all rollicking pioneers, and no matter how meanly they traveled, all of them had a few dollars. They had set out to buy land. They were bound for Arcadia—"Arcady" they called it, the town where the Government had established a land office, where an auction was held once a week and a man could get himself a piece of land if he were lucky.

King reached forward and broke off a piece of hoecake and picked up a rabbit leg. "Wal, le's eat, Boss, eff'n we's gonna git ter Arcady dis affernoon an' git us some lan'."

Horatio smiled. "Aye."

They broke camp just as the sun was beginning to peek over the horizon, and struck out westward along a deeply rutted road that wound in and out of pine thickets on a flat bluff overlooking the booming Tennessee. They traveled leisurely at first, but as the day wore on, they became impatient and began to push their horses. It was late afternoon, and both animals were blowing and sweating, when they mounted a slight rise and reined up in surprise.

They stood there for a long time, standing in their stirrups to get a better view, before King spoke. There was awe in his voice. "Ah ain't nebber seen nuthin' lak it, Boss."

Horatio could only shake his head. The ground fell away at their feet and sloped down gently to the river a quarter-mile away. Between them and the river there seemed to be all the wagons in creation. They were of all sizes and all descriptions. The most people he had ever seen in one place were swarming in and around them. It was a long time before his eyes could take it all in, and in the midst of all the wagons he saw a long row of barn-like buildings strung along a muddy gash that seemed to disappear in the boiling river. Arcadia.

They rode forward, picking their way between the clusters of wagons. It was like riding through a town where everybody lived on wheels. Worn, stoop-shouldered women bent over pots on open fires and lanky, weather-bitten men in greasy buckskins or faded homespun sat about whittling and spitting. Children were everywhere, running about chasing each other, ducking in and under the wagons. Except for an occasional, disinterested glance, nobody paid any attention to them as they rode past.

At the edge of one of the clearings, a gaunt young man with tousled hair and flashing eyes stood on the seat of a wagon haranguing a small crowd of men. Horatio caught only snatches— "Eff'n yo' ain't a-scarit . . . jine tergether . . . ain't got no right ter treat us like . . ."

As they neared the town, the wagons thinned out. When they reached Arcadia's single broad street, they were surprised to find it almost deserted. A few loafers lounged outside some of the buildings and three women, shovel-bonneted heads lowered, darted out of a small shack which had a tipsy sign proclaiming it a mercantile store, but otherwise the town seemed to be sleeping.

Despite the cold, the street was a mass of sticky mud, and their horses' hoofs made a sucking sound. There were not more than two dozen buildings in the town. Most of them were big and barny and seemed to clutch each other for support. Horatio had a confused impression of soupy mud and hitching posts and big lurid signs. "Bea's Rest," one said. "Dollar Bill's," "Honest Measure," "Faro," "Poker Evy Night," "Aunt Kate's."

Finally King spoke what was in both their minds. "Wut dem folks hang 'round heah fer? Why don't dey git dey lan' an' move on?"

Horatio shook his head glumly.

"Wut yo' gonna do, Boss?"

Horatio saw a sign at the end of the street. "Elite Hotel—rms. & bath." He smiled. "We'll get a place to stay and something to eat, and then decide."

The floor of the hotel was streaked with dried mud and shook under their feet. A short, fat little man with a round, pale face fringed with mutton whiskers was behind a scarred bar that ran the length of one side of the room. He wiped his hands on a meal sack. "What kin Ah do fer yo' mister?"

"I'd like to get lodging and a bath."

The man nodded. "Two dollars a day, hard money—vittles an'

bed." He looked at King. "Yo' nigger kin sleep in the stable—fo' bits extry."

Horatio flushed. "He's not my nigger. He's my friend. He'll stay with me."

The man lifted his brows. "Ain't but one bed."

"That's enough."

The man sucked a back tooth a moment, then shrugged; "Ever' man ter his likin', mister. Cost you double."

Without a word Horatio opened his purse and counted out four dollars.

"Got horses?"

"Aye, both of us."

"Fo' bits a day apiece."

Horatio placed another dollar on the bar. The man reached for the coins, hefted them in his hand, and looked at Horatio speculatively. "Nigger'll have ter eat in the kitchen."

King spoke quickly. "Thass fine, Boss."

The man smiled slightly. "Aimin' ter stay long?"

"Just until we can buy land at the sale on Thursday."

The man's smile broadened. "Monday, you mean, mister. Guvermint sale's on Thursday."

"That's what I mean."

"Nobody gits no lan' on Thursday."

Horatio felt his heart sink. "You mean all the land's been sold?"

The man grinned wisely. "Ain't that, mister. Plenty lan' left, but Asa Cole buys it all. He holds his sale on Monday." He chuckled at some secret joke. "You'll find out."

Horatio was confused. He wanted to know more, but he did not care for this man's smile and knowing manner. Besides, he was tired. He shrugged. "Well, we'll go to our room now."

The man reached on a shelf behind him and found a candle and handed it to Horatio. He nodded toward the stairs. "Third door on the right."

"Ah'll see ter our hawsses an' git our riggin', Boss," King said.

Horatio nodded and turned away, then remembered something. "We'll want baths."

The man smiled. "Cost yo' two bits apiece."

He stood with the same wise smile while Horatio dug in his purse and handed him two wedge-shaped quarters.

Horatio's body was tingling pleasantly under the one suit he had brought from Fair Haven when he came down to supper. A timid little Negro girl had brought two steaming pails of water to their room, and he and King had rubbed and splashed in it until they were glowing. The fat little hotel keeper was behind the bar serving a sprinkling of customers. He looked up with a smile and motioned toward a table in the far corner of the room. A tall, thin man with a limp mustache and the long, sad face of a coon hound was already seated, slicing away at a smoking roast of pork. He looked up with a smile when Horatio approached. "Sit down, friend. Sit down," he said affably. "Ned said Ah was gonna have company an' it's sho' a pleasure."

Horatio seated himself with a smile. Without asking if he wanted any, the man placed two slices of meat on his plate. "Jes' grab some o' them beans an' such-like an' eat hearty," he said. He served himself. "My name be Zachariah Cobb—most folks call me Zack. Ah'm the blacksmith in this heah dadburned town an' Ah reckon the only man that ain't lookin' fer lan'." He guffawed. "How do yo' sign, friend?"

Horatio told him his name. "Glad ter know yo', ole hoss," Zack said. "Reckon yo' come lookin' fer lan'?"

"Aye."

Zack forked meat into his mouth and began to chew vigorously. "Wal, jes' between me and yo' an' the other fellow, Ah don't hol' much with this heah runnin' 'round fer lan', but eff'n a man's bent that way, it's his own dadburned bizness."

He grinned at Horatio who was eating hungrily. "Good vittles, ain't they?"

Horatio nodded.

Zack licked his teeth thoughtfully and turned back to his dinner. "Ah ain't much fer givin' advice or followin' it neither, but lemme tell yo', it'll be easiest all 'round eff'n yo' don't try ter buck Asa Cole. Jes' go ter him an' git yo' lan'. It'll cost yo' more but it'll save yo' time." He snorted and waved his fork toward the outdoors. "Some o' them dadburned fools been sittin' out there all winter, jes' waitin'. Jes' waitin' an' hopin'."

Horatio frowned. "I don't understand. Who is Asa Cole?"

Zack sighed and shook his head. "Wal, it's kinda hard ter tell yo' 'bout Asa. Most folks 'low he's a skunk or a devil an' Ah reckon

they's right. But Ah don't think much 'bout Asa one way tother.
Eff'n it warn't him, Ah reckon it would be somebody else like him.
Ter really properly unnerstan' this heah bizness yo' gotta know all
the facts."

He hitched his chair closer to the table. " 'Bout twenty-odd year
ago, all this lan' 'round heah, somethin' like three an' a half million
acres, was part of Georgia. Wal, a bunch o' crooks called the Yazoo
Lan' Company got tergether an' greased some palms in the Georgia State House an' made a deal to buy it up fer something like a
penny an' a half a acre. Atter that, they set themselves up as the
Tennessee Lan' Company an' started sellin' lan' hand over fist at a
dollar an acre. Wal, they made a lotta money but nobody ever
found out where it went. It jes' disappeared, an', first thing yo'
know, there warn't even enough left ter pay Georgia all the money
that was still owin'.

"There was considerable yowlin' 'bout that, an' a new Georgia
legislature and the Guvermint stepped in an' said the whole deal
was illegal. That were all right far as the crooks were concerned,
but it jes' so happened that a lotta honest folks had bought lan'.
The Guvermint tried ter pertect them by givin' them some scrip
called Mississippi stock. Lotta folks used it ter reclaim their lan'. A
lot more jes' flung it away. Mississippi stock wouldn't fill a man's
belly or buy him a drink or buy him a stack o' chips, so first thing
you know, gamblers was gittin' it by the bale—an' course they got
it fer somethin' like a cent on the dollar."

Zack sighed. "Like as not, that's where Asa got his pile. Leastways most folks say he was a gambler. Ever' once in a while somebody pops up who says they remember seein' him in gamblin'
houses in New Awlins. They say he's a Creole. Other folks say he's
part Cherokee—an' he does look like one fer sartin. But anyhow,
no matter how Asa got his Mississippi stock, he sho' had a trunk
full of it when he turned up heah five, six years ago. An' he musta
knowed what was gonna happen 'cause right atter that the ole
Enterprise managed ter go all the way up the river an' folks went
wild. Before then, nobody had ever figgered that a boat could ever
git across the shoals.

"Wal, sir, when they foun' they could ship out cotton by water,
folks started rushin' in heah. They was crazy fer lan' an' Asa had it
ter sell. He calls his outfit the Tombigbee Land Company, an' at

first Asa was liked purty good. Ah remember seein' him buy a barrel o' likker at a sale an' knockin' the head in an' invitin' ever'body ter dip a horn. An' one time up Triana he shot a possum-faced bunco artist when he foun' him cheatin' some customers."

Horatio was so interested he forgot to eat. "But why can't a man outbid Asa Cole if . . . ?"

Zack smiled. "Ah'm comin' ter that, ole hoss. At first, folks did —all the time. Asa didn't like that—an' that's when he got his big idea. He went ter the other lan' companies an' sold them on the idea of stickin' together an' buying *all* the lan' when it was offered fer sale. He put up half the capital an' the other companies put up the other half." Zack's face was solemn. "There was jes' one man who wouldn't come erlong. Ole Colonel Floyd owned the Paint Rock Company an' he tole Asa ter go fry. Few days later some bushwhacker shot him in the back up near Bee Tree Shoals."

Zack sat for a moment sucking his teeth. "Lots o' folks been done in when they bothered Asa too much. He's kilt one o' two hisself. Man, he's cold as a copperhead. Nobody's never seen him change expression. Looks like he jes' ain't never learnt ter smile or frown." Zack smiled ruefully. "One night up in Decatur a likkered-up fool of a boatman said he'd make him change his look, by vum. He slipped up behind Asa's chair an' touched off a handful o' black powder. When Asa heered the hiss, he turned quick as a flash an' shot the durn fool smack-dab through the heart. He fell down daid with a grin still on his face."

Horatio frowned down at his plate. "If a man had enough money . . ."

Zack snorted. "Ain't enough money in tarnation ter buck Asa. Some big company might do it, but ain't no one man able ter. He'll bid any price fer one sartin section ter freeze a man out."

Horatio's voice was thoughtful. "How much does Cole charge for land?"

Zack shrugged. "Wal, mostly it depends on how much he had ter bid fer it. If he gits it at the minimum of a dollar two bits an acre, he usually charges five."

Horatio thought of the few hundred dollars he had and felt a surge of anger. "That's not right," he said grimly.

Zack nodded slowly. "It sho' ain't, ole hoss. That's why so many folks is a-sittin' out there on the slope ternight. They thought they had scraped up enough money ter git them forty or fifty acres. Now they's foun' out they can't git but eight or ten. Man can't make no cotton on that. He'd have to scratch hard ter even feed his family."

Horatio spoke slowly. "I wouldn't think Asa Cole would be safe."

Zack smiled. "Oh, he's safe enough. He's got six or seven big devils 'round him all the time an' they blow the life outta anybody who starts ter actin' up."

They sat silently a few moments, then Zack grinned and pushed back his chair. "Atter yo' eat, c'mon over ter Aunt Kate's an' jine me in a glass an' Ah'll p'int the gennelman out ter yo'."

When they reached the street, Horatio stood for a moment in amazement. It seemed impossible that this was the same town he had seen in the afternoon. The big barny buildings which had been so silent and empty were now ablaze with light. The long street was swarming with men sloshing through the mud or standing about in groups, talking loudly. From one end of town to the other there was the sound of music, the heavy thump of boots against wooden floors, the shrill laughter of women, shouts and an occasional tinkle of broken glass.

He and Zack picked their way across the street to a building directly opposite the hotel. Lanterns with silver reflectors lighted up the red sign which hung outside "Aunt Kate's." As they entered the swinging doors, Horatio could feel the whole building shake. They entered a huge smoky room and he saw the reason. In one corner a three-piece string band was playing merrily. A dozen or more men were stomping and whirling about with an assortment of women with heavily painted faces and bright dresses.

All about the room men sat at tables playing cards, and in one corner Horatio saw a dice game in progress. He and Zack crossed to the long bar. Zack slapped down a coin. "Couple glasses o' shinny."

They drank the fiery corn whisky and Zack leaned close. "Back there at the table in the corner—the man in the white clothes—that's Asa Cole."

Horatio turned slowly. He saw Asa Cole immediately. He was wearing a snow-white waistcoat and a wide-brimmed floppy white hat. He was a tall, slim man with swarthy skin, high cheekbones and black, fixed eyes. There was a stack of chips on the table before him but he did not seem to be playing cards. He was smoking a long, black cheroot and he rolled it back and forth in his mouth. He looked around the room slowly and for an instant his eyes met Horatio's. Horatio turned away.

Zack tapped his empty glass on the bar. "Yo' turn, ole hoss."

CHAPTER XVIII

"AN' TEW . . . an' tew . . . tewdollahtewdollah . . . tew . . . tew . . ."

The morning sun was bleak and the rocky field was pockmarked with frost, but the little bantam cock of a Government auctioneer was wet with sweat. He mopped his face and looked nervously toward the edge of the crowd while he chanted. "Tewdollah . . . tewdollah . . ."

The raw-boned old man who had bid two dollars an acre for a quarter-section of land stood tense and straight but his big knuckled hands shook and his Adam's apple bobbed with excitement. His frail, stoop-shouldered wife held tightly to his arm, her fingers dug in the faded sleeve of his homespun shirt. Horatio was close enough to see the hope in their eyes.

Suddenly the auctioneer's chant broke, then resumed on a new note. "An' a quarter . . . an' a quarter . . . tewaquarter . . . tewaquarter . . ."

The man's shoulders slumped wearily and his wife lowered her head. Horatio saw her lips tremble. He looked away and a cold anger gripped him. Even without turning he knew who had raised the old man's bid. There was a sullen murmur from the crowd. The auctioneer's chant was faster. "Tewaquarter . . . goin' oncet . . . goin' twicet . . . all done. . . ." He slapped his hands together. "Sold ter Asa Cole fer tew an' a quarter."

The crowd's angry drone became a roar. The auctioneer wiped his face and looked hastily at a chart. "Nex' township is . . ."

"Hole on thar!" A skinny young man, seemingly all jawbone and flashing eyes, pushed his way through the crowd and slapped the platform at the auctioneer's feet. Horatio recognized him as the man he had seen haranguing a crowd of settlers the day he arrived in Arcadia. He was shaking with anger now and glaring at the auctioneer. "Keep that scannel Asa Cole outta the biddin' an' give us honest folks a chancet!"

The auctioneer looked down in distress. "Friend, Ah'm jes' a-doin' m'dooty," he said plaintively. "Ah gotta sell ter the highest bidder."

"We'uns ain't got a chancet!" the young man shouted. "Asa Cole's a cheat—a dirty cheat!"

A dozen voices in the crowd took up the cry. "A cheat! A cheat! A cheat!"

Horatio turned and looked at Asa Cole. He was standing a little apart from the rest of the crowd, surrounded by four hulking men. His white shirt was immaculate and he was idly swinging a gold-headed cane. He seemed oblivious to the clamor. He reached inside his waistcoat and found a long, black cheroot. He sniffed it with satisfaction and rolled it back and forth in his mouth until it was moistened. Then he bit off about an inch of the cigar and tucked the fragment in his jaw. One of the men stepped forward with a lighted stick from a nearby fire and lit the remainder for him. Asa drew smoke deep in his lungs and let it escape slowly.

Horatio flushed with anger as he looked at the man. He turned to King. "B'fair, I've had enough. Let's go."

They started to push their way through the crowd when suddenly the chanting stopped. Horatio turned.

Asa was walking forward slowly. The crowd edged away to make a path for him. Asa's face was almost bored as he faced the young man. He took another pull from his cheroot and blew out a fine stream of smoke. The young man glared.

Asa's voice was lazy and soft. "Whuss er mattah with you, boy? If you want a lil' ole fo'ty acres er lan', come 'round an' Ah'll give it to you."

The young man's eyes flashed. "Ah don't want no hep from the likes o' yo', Asa Cole. Ah jes' want mah rights!"

Asa's black eyes never blinked. He studied the youth's flushed angry face, then shrugged slightly and flicked his cane. A lumbering, hairy man in greasy buckskins stepped from the crowd. "Shet yo' mouth!" He lashed out a heavy fist and caught the young man a solid blow on the back of the neck. The youth gave a retching gasp, clawed at the air, and fell forward on his face.

A frightened silence fell on the crowd. Those nearest Asa began to edge away. Asa Cole's face was expressionless as ever. He took another slow puff at his cheroot and poked the fallen youth with his cane. His soft voice was reproachful. "You mighta kilt this heah boy, mister. Nex' time why don't you jes' hit him in the ribs."

The hairy man was blowing on his knuckles. He looked surprised, then grinned wickedly. "Thass bes', Ah reckon." He drew back his foot and kicked the youth viciously. He looked at Asa as if expecting comment, but Asa was studying the ash on his cheroot. The man brought back his foot and aimed another kick.

It was never delivered. "Hold!" Still poised on one foot, the hairy man scowled over his shoulder. A fist smacked squarely in the center of his face. The blow twisted him around and lifted him in the air so that when he fell his shoulders hit the ground first. His legs twitched once, and then he lay still. Horatio drew back his fist again and stood over him, trembling with anger. He had not meant to mix in this fight. Even when the youth had been struck, he had not moved. But when he saw the frightened, sheepish way the crowd moved away and the cool, contemptuous way Asa disregarded it, he felt a deep shame. When he heard the sodden thud of the big man's boot against the youth's side, the anger that had been seething inside him all morning reached flood tide. He winced as if he had been kicked himself. When the man started to repeat the blow, he had been blinded with rage. He had stepped forward and struck without thinking. He stood above the man with fists clenched, chest heaving. He had not heard the crowd's startled gasp, and now he was only dimly aware of the half-cheer and murmur of approval.

Asa had not changed expression but some of his casualness was gone. He tossed his cheroot away and turned cold, black eyes on Horatio. He looked him up and down slowly, then flicked his cane. The tableau was broken. A half-dozen men moved forward determinedly. Someone shouted, "Watch yo'self, stranger."

Horatio already had sensed the movement. He planted his feet firmly and looked about challengingly. The converging men halted, then began to move forward more warily. There was not a sound except the distant thunder of the river across the shoals.

Suddenly a new voice rang out, calmly but loudly. "One at er time! Jes' one at er time—or Ah'll shoot!" King stepped to the edge of the circle with a long squirrel gun on ready. Earlier he had noticed the gun and smiled because it was almost as tall as the freckle-faced, tow-headed little boy who carried it. When Horatio first struck the hairy man, King had pushed into the crowd and snatched the gun away from the boy without a word. He held the gun loosely in his big hands and his black face was impassive, but his eyes swept the crowd watchfully.

Asa looked at King and spoke softly. "Bettah git yore nigger to put up that gun, stranger."

Horatio looked at him coldly. His voice was ragged. "We'll take no advice from you!"

Not a muscle moved in Asa's face, but his black eyes were shiny. His voice was almost a purr. "If it's shootin' you want . . ." His hand tightened on the cane. Horatio reached out and snatched it from his hand. "You'll do no more talking with this." With a back-handed toss he threw the cane over the heads of the crowd.

For the first time, something like anger darkened Asa's face. But only for an instant. Gently, he slipped another of his long cheroots from his pocket. He sniffed it with his eyes never leaving Horatio's face, then turned slowly and looked at the little auctioneer who was standing still and white-faced. "Ah ast this sale to be closed because of disorder."

The auctioneer gulped. "Sale closed," he shouted shrilly, and clambered down from the platform.

Asa turned and looked at Horatio. His voice was almost a whisper. "Nex' time we meet, friend, Ah'll deal the han'."

Horatio looked out the window gloomily while King packed their equipment. The street below was thronged with men and the saloons and gambling houses were going full blast, but he was unaware of the noise and confusion. His mind was on other things. He sighed heavily. "I shouldn't have done it."

King began to roll their blankets. His voice was gentle. "Yes, yo' should, Boss. It war right." He nodded. "Yo' war right aller way."

Horatio's voice was heavy. "It doesn't make me feel better to be running away like this."

King was reproachful. "Now, Boss, we done been all through dat. Quit sayin' things like dat. Yo' know yo'self dat we ain't got no bizness hangin' 'roun' dis heah place. We ain't leavin' 'cause yo's a-scarit. Sometime a man jes' ain't got no chancet." He shook his head vigorously and tied the bedroll. "Eff'n thar war any chancet of us a-gittin' lan', den it might make a diffurence. But thar ain't, Boss! We won't git no lan' 'roun' heah no mattah how long we stays. Nawsuh, de thing fer me an' you ter do is git outta heah an' be glad we had ernough sense ter go."

"I don't guess we'll ever get land," Horatio said.

King came and stood by him. "Course we will. We'll light out from heah an' go 'way west. Thar's plenty lan' thar. We'll git us a cotton crop yit."

Horatio forced a smile. King put his hand on his shoulder. "Ever'thin's packed. Ah'll go git de hawsses an' bring 'em 'roun'."

After King left, Horatio crossed the room and kicked disgustedly at the bedrolls. It was a humiliating business, this running away. No matter how they tried to change it around, that was what they were doing. But even while something within him rebelled, his common sense told him it was the thing to do. He knew he and King were marked. People edged away from them on the street, and when he went down for supper, the men at the bar took one glance at him and left the room. Zack Cobb hadn't even made an appearance. If he could get Asa Cole . . . He set his jaw. He would gladly tear the man limb from limb, but he knew he didn't have a chance. It would be suicide. One move and he knew Asa's men would cut him down. He and King had been lucky this afternoon . . . aye, lucky.

He lifted his head quickly. There was a clamor of boots on the stairs and he heard several men speaking excitedly.

The boots started scraping up the hall and he heard one man say, "Lift him up higher." He crossed to the corner and picked up his musket.

He was standing tense and waiting when the men reached the door. At first he thought they were carrying a heavy bundle. Then he saw it was King.

He stared a moment with his throat gone dry while the men

shuffled in and laid King on the bed. A short, squat little man with broken teeth began explaining rapidly. "It war me that run 'em away. Ah heered this scufflin' an' fightin' a-goin' on outside the stable an' Ah ran out thar 'cause Ah thought it war mah partner, Sam. Wal, thar war three men gun-beatin' this heah nigger, an' since Ah thought it war Sam, Ah hollered, 'Leave up or Ah'll shoot,' an' they run away."

Horatio heard only part of what he said. He was leaning over King, cold with horror. King's face was covered with blood which oozed from three long gashes in his forehead. His lips were torn and battered. He was lying still and quiet. "King!" Horatio said.

The little man kept jabbering. "Ah didn't know it war a nigger. Ah thought it war mah partner, Sam. Sam went 'round thataway. . . ."

Another of the men looked down at King. "He's purty far gone, Ah think."

Horatio heard that. He looked up, his face drawn and white. "Get a doctor."

"Thar ain't one near'n Florence, mister."

"Get a doctor!"

One of the men shrugged and left the room. Horatio looked at King again and, suddenly, his face became a mask of rage. His voice was tight. "Please take care of my friend." He stalked from the room.

It was almost as if they felt his presence. As soon as he stalked into Aunt Kate's, jaw set and face cold, the music came to a ragged halt. Everyone took one quick glance toward the door, then froze at whatever he was doing. Horatio did not look right or left. He had his eyes fixed on Asa Cole at the rear of the room. But he had not gone ten feet when the three men seated with Asa turned around bewilderedly. They saw Horatio and jumped to their feet. Two of them drew guns.

Horatio stopped, feet planted wide apart, and his voice was a snarl. "You're a yellow dog, Asa Cole. Come out from behind your men and fight!"

One of the men raised his pistol. Asa lifted a slender hand and snapped his fingers. The man lowered the weapon. Asa's voice was soft. "Ah don't need no men, Tench. Ah got you marked for mah own catfish bait."

"Come out and fight then!"

Asa stood up slowly. His black eyes seemed to glitter. "How will you have it, Tench?"

Someone shouted. "Take him down to the warehouse, Asa!" The crowd whooped with pleasure.

Asa waited a long time before he spoke. "Warehouse suit you all right, Tench?"

Horatio glared at him. "I'll fight you any way."

CHAPTER XIX

IT WAS amazing how quickly the word spread. Almost as soon as they emerged from the saloon, the muddy street was filled with a pushing, eager crowd. And the news was still traveling. Up one side of the street and down the other there were whoops and yells as men poured into the frosty night from saloons and dance halls and brothels. Horatio was still so angry that his breath came in short bursts of white vapor, but Asa Cole might have been planning a stroll in the moonlight. At the head of the steps he paused and went through the ritual of lighting a cheroot. He moistened it carefully and, after tucking a fragment in his cheek, lit the remainder. Then he stooped and carefully rolled up the legs of his white trousers to protect them from the thick mud.

By now it seemed that every man in town had gathered, and where they had run up laughing and yelling, unaccountably they grew quiet and solemn. The hush was almost unnatural. The only sound in the street that had been so boisterous a few minutes ago came from a tinny piano in a brothel at the end of the row. Then suddenly it stopped.

Torches appeared from somewhere. As if from a signal, the crowd parted in two lanes. Asa Cole and his men moved down one. Horatio still did not understand how he was to fight, but he was ready. Grim-faced and tense, he strode forward through his lane. At the edge of the crowd Horatio saw that the torches were carried by two frightened Negroes. After a wide-eyed glance around to be sure that Asa and his men and Horatio were on their heels, they began walking up the street toward the river. Except for the soft sucking of the mud underfoot, there was only one sound as the procession left town. Outside one of the buildings a half-dozen dance hall girls stood huddled around the doorway, staring into the street. As they passed, a skinny brunette in a sleazy red dress shouted shrilly, "Asa, honey, bring me back ez ears." No one answered. Asa didn't bother to turn.

They had left the lights of the deserted town before Horatio realized that a half-dozen men had fallen in step with him. He turned, ready for trickery, but he saw the man nearest him was Zack Cobb. Zack gave him a solemn wink and spoke quietly, almost in a whisper. "Me an' the boys jes' sorta wanta see that yo' git a clean deck, ole hoss." Horatio looked around at the other men. They all nodded.

Apparently the Negroes with the torches had been told where to go. At the edge of town they turned sharply and headed toward the river. Horatio knew that was the direction because now they reached the fog rolling in from the stream and he could hear the roar of the river across the shoals in the distance. The crowd heard the roar, too, and it seemed to break the spell. At the rear of the column someone shouted, "Ah gotta gold eagle that says Asa'll make catfish bait outta the stranger." Then a frenzy of betting broke out, accompanied by yells and laughter.

Suddenly it stopped as quickly as it had begun. The Negro guides had halted. Their torches threw flickering shadows on the side of a tremendous warehouse which sat on the edge of the river. Horatio looked up and for the first time that night he felt something besides anger. It was almost fear. For some strange reason just the sight of that warehouse looming so large in the half-darkness gave him a feeling of uneasiness, as if it were some giant animal waiting to devour him. "I'm going to die," he thought. "In a few minutes I'll be dead." He knew it and he couldn't tell why.

He could never be sure of just what happened after that. He remembered hearing Zack say something about his shirt. Suddenly he realized he had taken it off. "Gawd amighty," somebody whispered, "lookit them arms!" Another of the men had stooped and was tugging at his boots. In a moment they were off and he was standing in his stocking feet. Then awareness returned with a jolt. Something cold and grimy slapped him in the chest. "Hold!"

he said. He grabbed the hand at his chest and looked up to discover that it belonged to Zack. Zack looked surprised. "Take it easy, ole hoss," he said. "Look over yonder." Horatio looked in the direction he nodded. Asa Cole stood stripped to the waist, his slim arms held out while two of his henchmen slapped grease on his white chest and back. Zack now began to smear Horatio with grease in earnest. "Shucks, it ain't nothin' 'cept plain lard," he said. "Yo' most likely'll be mighty glad you've got it eff'n yo' grapple with that snake."

Horatio held still while Zack smeared him with the lard from the waist to the top of his head. He was beginning to understand how he and Asa were to fight and he was burning with the urge to get his hands on the man. Lard or no lard, he knew he could break Asa's slim torso over his knee. He wondered vaguely why Asa dared to face him in such a fight. Then he learned all the rules.

A short, pompous little man in a baggy suit and beaver hat clambered up on the warehouse platform. Despite the chill night air, he was sweating. He looked over the crowd and spoke deliberately. "This heah is gonna be a fair fight," he said, "an', by Gawd, ever' son Jack of yo' wanta keep that in mind. Whichever one of these heah gentlemen survives this fight is tole heah an' now to show up at mah court tomorrow an' surrender for a hearin' so a legal verdict can be handed down on the outcome. Seconds to whichever one of these gentlemen survives will kindly appear as witnesses. I want that clear."

He looked the crowd over again sternly before he continued. "I reckon yo' all know the rules in this heah type of contest, but I'll say them again. These heah gentlemen will be armed with a brace o' pistols an' a skinnin' knife. They'll enter this heah warehouse at opposite ends. The doors will be shut an' whichever one manages to come out alive will do so as soon as possible. This heah warehouse is empty all except for fifty-odd bales. I reckon that's as near empty as any we can find in town." He looked around. "Any questions?"

No one spoke. Horatio felt a sudden chill. He clenched his teeth lightly.

The pompous little man cleared his throat. "Aw right, see that the weapons are distributed an' yo' seconds hustle yore men aroun' to the right doors. Mr. Cole—" he made a short formal bow

toward Asa—"will take the south door an' Mr. . . . er, ah . . .
the challenger will take the north door." He made a bow in Horatio's direction. "Yo' seconds push yore men in when yo' hear
me fire this." He held up a derringer.

It was so quiet that Horatio thought he heard his own heart
beat. He realized that someone had handed him a knife. He started
to slip it into his waistband when Zack stopped him. "Hole it in
yore teeth, ole hoss," he said. "Ah'll keep it fer yo' till yore ready."
Somebody else thrust two pistols at him. They were the first hand
weapons he had ever held and he looked at them curiously. Zack
looked down. "Are they primed right?"

Horatio shook his head. "I don't know."

Zack looked at him in surprise. "Gawd amighty, ain't yo' never
shot a pistol?"

Horatio shook his head.

Zack groaned and inspected the pistols quickly. "They are all
right," he said, "but whatever yo' do, don't get the primin' greasy
against your belly. Jes' point 'em an' pull the trigger when yo' git
ready."

Horatio nodded.

The little man on the platform was bawling out again. "Aw
right, git the gentlemen to their doors."

"Le's go," Zack said. Horatio nodded. He had already taken
two steps when, for some unexplainable reason, he felt forced to
turn and look toward Asa Cole. Asa had also turned and was looking at him. His black Cherokee eyes glittered in the poor light.
Horatio took a deep breath and turned away.

At the door to the warehouse Zack slipped the skinning knife
in Horatio's teeth. The metal was cold and, involuntarily, he
shuddered. Zack was whispering advice, but Horatio scarcely
heard him. His heart was thumping heavily and it seemed he
couldn't breathe with the knife in his mouth. "Don't move 'round
too much . . . don't shoot till yore sure . . . let him come ter
yo', don't try ter find him. . . ." On and on went Zack. Horatio scarcely heard him. It seemed that he stood there a long time
. . . waiting . . . waiting. Then, seemingly from far away, he
heard a pop. The door at his face was pulled open and a hand pro-
pelled him into utter darkness. The door slammed behind him.
Then silence.

He had never known such complete darkness. It seemed to have substance, like smoke or heavy fog. He shut his eyes tightly and held them closed as long as he dared. It helped some. When he opened them again, it seemed he could find patches of blue in the blackness that enveloped him so completely. He lifted one foot cautiously and tried the floor. It didn't creak, so he stepped forward slowly. It was his first mistake. His ankle cracked. Almost simultaneously the darkness seemed to explode in his face. At the same time he was thrown back as if a horse had kicked him in the left shoulder. His whole left side was so numbed that the pistol in his left hand dropped to the floor. The shock caused his mouth to fly open and he lost the knife. He never knew how he escaped, but apparently when he hit the floor some instinct caused him to roll to one side. As it was, he didn't move quickly enough. There was another deafening explosion. Something slammed into his right thigh. It numbed his leg completely.

For a long time he wasn't able to move at all. It was several minutes before he realized what had happened. It wasn't until he felt his leg that he realized he had been shot. Somehow he had had the vague notion that a bullet would pierce and sting. But when he felt his leg, he found blood spurting from a small hole about five inches above his knee cap. He didn't dare let go of the pistol in his right hand to explore his shoulder, but he knew he would also find a hole there. After a while he shook off the surprise and shock and he realized that Asa must have run across the warehouse as soon as he entered. He had planned on taking him by surprise and he had succeeded.

But where was he now? Horatio smiled grimly in the darkness and held his pistol tightly. It was the only weapon he had left. He didn't dare miss. Asa still had a knife. He lay there, tense and waiting. His leg was still numb but his shoulder began to feel as if it were on fire. Then pains began to shoot from his armpit down his side. He fastened his teeth in his lips. He knew that Asa had heard him fall. Sooner or later, if he heard no movement, he might assume that his shots had finished him.

Finally that was what happened. But Asa waited a long time. The first sound was a low hiss, so soft that Horatio almost missed it. It seemed to come from the other side of the warehouse. Horatio lay still, scarcely daring to breathe. The hiss was repeated, a little closer this time. Horatio strained his ears. He couldn't hear the slightest movement, but Asa was moving he knew because his next sound was a low whistle to the right and closer from the position he had been before. Something came clattering across the floor. Horatio tightened his finger on the trigger, but caught himself just in time. It was one of Asa's pistols. There was almost a ten-minute wait before the second pistol came clattering across the floor. Even though Horatio was expecting it, he still almost fired. His shoulder and leg both were causing him pain now. He had to exert all his will power to keep from shifting position.

After a short silence there was another hiss, less than ten feet away. Horatio lay tense. His teeth had pierced his lips. His hand trembled weakly when he raised the pistol. There was another hiss, not more than five feet away. Horatio scarcely dared breathe. It was an agony of effort to hold the pistol outstretched. A short silence, then a slight creaking of the floor, and Asa suddenly spoke in an almost normal tone of voice. "Tench?"

Horatio could hold the gun no longer. He pulled the trigger. There was a blinding flash and a reverberating explosion. The pistol jumped in his hand and clattered to the floor.

He knew immediately that he had missed. Even though his ears were ringing from the explosion, he heard Asa's gasp of surprise plainly, then the patter of his feet as he dashed across the warehouse. Horatio fell back weakly. There was no need for silence now. He allowed himself the luxury of stretching his numbed leg. It was an effort just to move. He realized he had lost a lot of blood. He made an examination with his good hand but he could no longer feel the bullet hole above his knee. His whole leg was covered with a clammy jelly. He lay back again, feeling strangely sleepy. His eyes closed . . . the heavy darkness felt warm and comforting.

He never understood what happened next. Maybe some instinct for survival won over his weakness. Maybe the numbing shock of his injuries wore off. Whatever it was, he suddenly became alert. It was as if he had awakened after a long sleep. His heart began to pound frantically. His throat was dry. He had difficulty swallowing. He found himself panic-stricken because he was defenseless. He had to find a weapon. He had to!

His left shoulder was useless, so he rolled over to the right and began a wild search for the pistol or knife he had dropped when first shot. He had no idea where to search, but he threw his good arm out in wide sweeping motions against the floor. He could feel splinters from the rough boards ripping his flesh but he felt no pain.

He groped as far as he could from one position, then shifted his body painfully and made another wide sweep with his arm. His arm made a swishing sound against the floor. He tried to control his breath, but it came noisily, rasping. Every moment he expected Asa to pounce out of the darkness and plunge his knife in his back. It was good, this fear. It kept him scrambling and groping about in the darkness. And, eventually it brought him luck.

His probing hand struck something and a sharp pain stabbed him up to the wrist. It was the skinning knife. He didn't have to pick it up. The point was buried deep in his palm. Somehow he managed to work it out with his deadened left hand, then he grabbed the handle firmly in his right hand and smiled grimly. Painfully he raised himself to his feet. Standing on his one good leg, he roared defiance into the darkness. "I'm coming after ye, Asa. I'm coming after ye!"

Asa's voice was low and far away. "Come and be damned."

Horatio's right leg did not hurt. It was just useless, dead weight. It would not support him, but somehow it did balance him, allow him to rest on it briefly when he hopped and dragged himself toward the sound of Asa's voice. He held his knife before him. Strangely enough, he no longer felt any fear, only a fierce exultation that he was still alive. Hopping and sliding, he made his way forward. He knew that Asa could follow his movements, but he no longer cared. That was his second mistake. Suddenly he heard a swish behind him. He whirled awkwardly but quickly—just in time to catch a blow in his already numbed left shoulder. Just as he had been surprised at the force of a bullet, he was now amazed at the lack of force in a knife blow. At first he thought he had been merely pushed. It wasn't until he began falling backward and felt something tug then rip at his shoulder that he realized Asa had driven in his knife.

He struck the floor heavily and tried to shift his body to one side. It was a useless precaution. Asa did not follow up his advantage. Again stillness closed in. Horatio lay on his back. Through the heavy grease he could feel blood pouring from his shoulder. He had difficulty breathing. He felt too weary to try to listen for a sound from Asa. This is what it's like to die, he thought dully. This is what it's like to be shot, to be stabbed. He knew that he was doomed. Asa knew that he had no pistol. The thought infuriated him. He brought his knife up slowly and held the handle against his chest. He knew his only hope was to catch Asa if he moved in for the kill.

He knew Asa could hear his breathing and he no longer cared. He lay still, chest heaving, eyes wide, staring into the dark. Then suddenly he froze, stopped his heavy breathing. Asa was near. He knew it. Asa was moving in. It was a long moment before he realized how he knew. He almost smiled.

He could smell Asa. It was the thin, black cheroots, the sharp stale odor of tobacco he caught. He had never smoked himself, but was so used to the smell of tobacco that he almost never noticed it. Now the odor was heavy. There wasn't a sound in the warehouse. But he knew Asa was near. He was coming closer. The smell was stronger. He turned his head slowly and sniffed. It was strongest to his right. He lay rigid . . . waiting . . . waiting. The smell was strong . . . heavier and heavier. He tightened his muscles and waited. Another long wait—then, gathering all his strength, he lunged. He plunged his knife forward. It hit something solid and went in to the hilt. He had found Asa.

He pushed downward with all his strength. Asa floundered and almost wrenched the knife from his grasp, then he gave a strangled moan and went limp. Scarcely daring to move, Horatio drew the knife back and plunged it in to the hilt again. Asa gave a long sigh, a shudder, and lay still.

He never knew how long he lay there stretched across Asa's body. But, after a while, somehow he managed to stumble to his feet. He opened his mouth to shout but all he could force out was a feeble croak. "Open," he said to the blackness about him. "Open."

He was heard. Far in the distance, seemingly miles away down a long tunnel, he saw a patch of light. Stumbling, crawling, dragging himself, he started for it. A dozen arms were waiting for him. He heard gasps and shouts, and as he sank into total darkness he moaned, "King."

Zack laid him down gently and turned an awed face to the crowd. "God amighty," he said, "he said he was a king."

CHAPTER XX

THEY brought Asa and Horatio back to town in the same buckboard. Of the two, Asa seemed more alive. His smooth swarthy face was composed and serene and the only marks on him were two thin slits above his heart. For some reason they had scarcely bled and from all appearances they might have been mere scratches. Asa's body was laid out on a board between two sawhorses just inside the door of Aunt Kate's. As men walked past they shook their heads in wonder at those tiny wounds and marveled that Asa was dead. Then they walked back to where Horatio lay on a faro table, drenched in blood and breathing with difficulty, and they marveled that he was still alive.

Almost everyone who saw his wounds expected him to die. The gash made by Asa's knife alone seemed severe enough to have laid low most men. It stretched from below his left breast up to his shoulder, exposing the ribs and muscles. A hundred men watched in awe while old Doc Ware, who had been fetched from Florence across the river, sewed it up with a shoemaker's needle and thin linen thread. Old Doc, a rumpled, dusty man with a tobacco-stained mustache, philosophized as he worked. "Ah tell yo', boys," he said, "it don't make no difference how yo' stick 'em—it's all in whar you stick 'em." He paused to spit on the floor and motion to the front of the saloon. "Now yo' take them li'l ole holes up thar in Asa. They don't look like much but they went right t' the mark, an' Ah'll wager this heah man who made 'em don't know nothin' about knife fightin'. From the looks of the wounds, he chopped downward like an ole woman killin' a chicken. Now, lookit this, though—" he pointed to Horatio's wound—"Asa made this heah an' Ah reckon he knows as much about knife fightin' as anybody. He helt his knife point outward an' struck upward like he was supposed to—but what'd he do? Wal, he jes' miscalculated. He missed the belly an' the knife jes' bounced off'n the rib cage an' sliced through a lotta flesh till it hit the collarbone." He finished sewing the wound and took out his clasp knife and cut the loose ends of thread. He spat again and looked at the faces around him.

"But lemme tell yo' this—jes' in case yo' think it's an accident this fellah is still breathin' a little an' ole Asa is gittin' colder all the time. It took a lotta guts to take a slice like this an' not turn tail an' run. An' lemme tell yo' somethin' else—this fellah heah took a slug above the heart an' through the lungs that would of put six men like Asa outta commission."

He paused for another meditative spit. "An' Ah ain't mentionin' the fact that he lost enough blood t' float a flatboat from heah to Memphis."

"Is he gonna live, Doc?" somebody asked.

Doc Ware pursed his lips and looked down at the floor for a long time. "Wal, friend," he said finally, "Ah could say yes an' Ah could say no—but Ah ain't gonna do either. Ah aim t' sit heah till Ah find out."

Luckily King had not been as badly hurt as Horatio thought. His face was swollen and cut and he had a hundred aches, but apparently his assailants had been frightened off before they could do any serious damage. After Horatio left, one of the men who had brought King in had called the young Negro woman who was the chambermaid at the hotel. Together they had undressed King and bathed his cuts. He had lain awake for more than an hour, worrying about Horatio and begging them to bring his clothes so he could follow him, but eventually he had been overcome by weariness and weakness and he slept.

The Negro girl awakened him at dawn. Like nearly everyone else in town, black or white, she had been up to Aunt Kate's to gaze with awe at Asa's body and the barely living Horatio and she was still wide-eyed at the memory. "Yo' master done got hisself near kilt," she said.

Despite his soreness, King sprang out of bed immediately. "Bring mah clothes," he said.

"Yo' can't do him no good," the girl said.

King looked at her sternly. "Bring mah clothes!" he said.

Old Doc Ware and half the town were still keeping vigil over Horatio when he arrived at Aunt Kate's. Someone recognized him when he appeared in the doorway and shouted, "Heah's the Englishman's nigger—leave him through."

Obediently the crowd made a passage. Every eye followed King as he made his way forward. Just inside the door he shot a glance at Asa's stiff body, but there was not a flicker on his battered features. But when he reached Horatio, he looked down and stiffened. After a moment he put out his hand and gently pushed back hair that had fallen over Horatio's pale forehead. He looked around at the watching faces. "Ah gotta git him outta heah," he said.

Old Doc Ware spoke. His rough voice wasn't ungentle. "Yo' his boy, are yo'?"

"Yes, suh," King said.

A man in the crowd spoke up. "Thass the reason the Englishman jumped Asa, on accounta somebody beat up this nigger."

Doc Ware studied King carefully. "Whar would yo' take him, boy?"

King shook his head. "Ah don't know, suh. Back ter whar we is stayin' Ah reckon."

"Whar's that?"

"Down ter the hotel."

Old Doc sighed and shook his head. "This heah man needs a lotta sweet treatment, boy. Ain't yo' got no ole woman who could care for him an' cook for him?"

"No, suh," King said.

"Ain't yo' or him got no friends or kinfolks 'round heah somewhar?"

King shook his head and laid his hand on Horatio's forehead again. "No, suh, but yo' don't have ter worry none. Ah kin take . . ." He paused and looked at Doc Ware. His mind had been working desperately ever since he saw Horatio's bloodless lips and white face. He knew too well how difficult it would be to care for him in their cramped room without a stove, with no one to relieve him. "Ah . . . Ah do reckon thar's somebody who might hep us . . . mebbe if we could fin' him," he said.

"Who is it?" Doc Ware asked.

"His name is Mistah Mitchell—Mistah Lafe Mitchell, Ah think he's called. He usta be a soljer. He lives 'roun' heah somewhar."

A wizened little man stepped forward. "Ah know Lafe Mitchell," he said. "He's gotta place out near five-mile creek. Ain't too fur out thar, mebbe three mile."

Doc Ware looked at King sternly. "Now, yo' lissen t'me, boy. Ah done wukked hard over yore master an' Ah don't aim t' see all that wuk go t' waste. Now, yo' git right out thar an' see if Mistah Mitchell will take keer of this heah man. An', mind yo', he ain't gonna move an inch till Ah see this heah Mitchell an' tell him what t' do."

"Yes, suh," said King.

The wizened little man stepped forward. "Ah'll drive yo' out," he said. "Ah got mah rig down to the stable."

All the way out to Lafe Mitchell's, King was in a sweat of anxiety. He scarcely remembered the man, but he kept telling himself that he would surely help. The wizened man must have read his thoughts. He looked at King and smiled. "Yo' don't have to worry 'bout Lafe Mitchell. He wouldn't turn a sick dog away. Anyway," he added after a pause, "yore gonna find out yore master is gonna be a mighty popular man aroun' these heah parts 'fore long. Ah reckon he did folks a mighty big favor las' night. Most of them he helped the most ain't heard 'bout it yet 'cause they don't live in town. But they will hear an' yo' can bet yore bottom dollah they'll be grateful—mighty grateful."

He was right about Lafe Mitchell. He was in a field, about a quarter-mile from his house when they saw him. At first he didn't recognize King, which wasn't odd because of his battered face, but when King mentioned their last meeting, his face lighted. He grew serious as King told him what had happened and the help he needed. "Eff'n yo' hep us, Mistah Mitchell," King said earnestly, "we'll see dat yo' gits paid well an' Ah'll wuk fer yo'."

Lafe Mitchell snorted and threw back his head. "Man, don't start makin' me mad 'fore we even get acquainted good. Nobody pays me for a Christian duty. Besides—" his heavy beard split in a grin—"yo' folks got in all this trouble 'cause yo' listened t' mah braggin' in the first place. Come on, le's go git mah wagon."

While Lafe hitched up his mules, Mrs. Mitchell and little Ada spread cottonseed hulls over the bed of the wagon. Apparently neither of them had forgotten Horatio, but little Ada seemed to have spoken of him often. She had a name for him. "Is Mister Man hurt real bad?" she asked King.

King nodded slowly. "Yes, missy, Ah'm afeered he is."

Ada looked at her parents defiantly. "Then I'm aimin' to go back to town with you when you fetch him. He might need me to keer for him."

And she did go. When she saw Horatio, her face went white, but she listened carefully to Doc Ware's instructions, and because they had forgotten to bring a pillow, she held Horatio's head in her lap all the way home.

It was surprising that he even recovered. It was almost a miracle that he did it rapidly. His wounds did not become infected although it wasn't until he reached Lafe Mitchell's that all the lard was washed off his body. He was feverish and somewhat delirious for the three days before he recovered consciousness completely. After that he gained by leaps and bounds. A week after the fight Old Doc Ware made the trip all the way from Florence to find him propped up in bed, eating squirrel stew. Old Doc examined him and snorted disgustedly. "Man, Ah don't know whether Ah'm good or you've jes' got a carcass like an iron skillet. Whichever it is, yore sho' a good advertisement for me."

They were true words. Horatio had become the hero of the Big Bend. From Bear Creek to Decatur the word had spread that Asa Cole was dead. Every day dozens of people came to pay their respects to the St. George who had slain the dragon. These weren't the townspeople, the floaters and adventurers. They were poor people, people of the soil, men and women who couldn't pay Asa's exorbitant prices for land, or families who had and felt that their unfair burden had died with Asa. Apparently they were right. So far, no one had stepped forward to claim Asa's kingdom. Most of the cutthroats he had gathered around him disappeared the day after the fight. And because they left Asa's office ransacked and his iron safe empty, a hat had to be passed to pay old Doc Ware for embalming him. No one knew what would happen to his land holdings. No one cared. There was land enough for everybody—and now everybody had a fair chance.

One of those who came was the young man whose rescue at the land sale had led to all the trouble. He grinned embarrassedly and introduced himself as Sam Jackson. "Ah reckon yo' ain't thankin' me none fer the trouble Ah caused," he said.

Horatio smiled. "It wasn't your fault."

Sam still looked sheepish. "Wal, Ah don't know 'bout that, an', like the fellah says, Ah don't want folks messin' in mah bizness most times—but, man, how glad Ah was to see yo'." He held out a small jar. "Mah old woman sent these peaches—we'uns would be mighty happy if yo' would come an' stay with us when yore able t' be up."

Most of them brought some gift, a jar of preserves, a chicken, or, occasionally, a ham. The Mitchell storm cellar was bulging with their gifts. And most of them asked Horatio to come stay with them. They had heard how he lay on a faro table that first night, and they all hastened to explain how they had not heard about his injuries until the next day. Their offers to accommodate him and King were so obviously sincere that once Horatio said something about it to Lafe. He felt that he had been an unsought burden to the Mitchells. But Lafe snorted so indignantly at the idea of his going elsewhere, and little Ada cried so bitterly, that he never mentioned it again.

Actually the Mitchells had more than enough room. Their home was rude but weather-tight. Originally it had consisted of two large rooms, one on each side of a narrow passageway known as the dogtrot, but during the past winter Lafe had divided these rooms with partitions and added a front and back porch, so now it had four rooms. By comparison to other homes in the region it was large if not downright pretentious. Horatio and King had a room to themselves with a fireplace, and Horatio had the only bed in the house. Lafe and his wife had surrendered it.

As soon as Horatio became aware of this, he protested to Lafe. Lafe shook his great bearded head and gave that snort that Horatio was to learn so well. "Lookit," he said, "me an' mah wife slept on corn huskin' fer nigh on eight years 'fore we got that bed. Ah reckon we can give it up t' a sick man fer a few days."

Lafe was a roarer. He roared when he laughed. He roared when he talked, and he roared many times just for the joy of roaring. At first, particularly before his strength had begun to return, Horatio had not known quite how to take this robustness. King gave him a clue. Horatio noticed that whenever Lafe came near, King grinned. King was completely fascinated by Lafe and he respected him. And it was a respect that was returned. Almost every evening Horatio could hear Lafe and King, sitting together on the front veranda, Lafe roaring and King speaking quietly.

Perhaps the reason behind this immediate friendship was given by Lafe one day. He had stopped in to inquire how Horatio felt, and suddenly he looked at Horatio steadily. "How come a big, strapping man like yo' has t' buy another man t' take care of him?" he asked.

Horatio answered hotly. "I haven't bought any man. King's free—if that's what you mean."

Lafe grinned broadly. "Glad t' hear it," he said. "That was the only thing Ah had against yo'. We don't go much fer slave holdin' 'round heah."

Another time he came in and looked Horatio over wonderingly. "Fellah jes' told me you was an Englishman," he said.

Horatio smiled. "I was born in England."

Lafe shook his head at the wonder of it. "Wal, Ah'll be a broken-backed idjit," he said slowly. "Ah never knowed that. Ah never saw an Englishman before less'n it was over the sights of mah rifle." Then he roared with laughter. "Ain't sech bad people after all, is they?"

Lafe worshiped Andrew Jackson. He had served under him twice, once during the war of 1812 and later in Jackson's campaign against the Creek Indians. In any prolonged conversation he was almost sure to begin a sentence with, "Wal, when Ah was with ole Andy," or "Now me an' ole Andy . . ." He could sit for hours and spin stories about his fights with the Redsticks—"Worse dern critters that ever skinned a polecat"—and almost always he or "ole Andy" were the heroes. Horatio learned to admire and respect Lafe Mitchell.

Mrs. Mitchell bewildered him. He had never known anyone quite like her. She was so shy, so inconspicuous, that he had the odd feeling that she didn't exist at all. She almost never looked directly at anyone. Even though she entered his room a dozen times a day, he could not have shut his eyes and described her. Her quietness was uncanny. When she walked there wasn't the slightest sound. He never heard her make a sound while she was cooking. There was no clatter of pans, no rattle of dishes. Sometimes she passed a few words with him and her voice was pleasant, but it seemed to evaporate. Her expression was always the same—a shy little smile that barely lifted the corners of her mouth. She simply failed to register. He knew her ten years before he knew her first name was Lena. Lafe spoke of her, and to her, as "wife."

But little Ada—she was his constant companion, his devoted servant, his nurse. She was the first person he had seen when he regained consciousness. He had opened his eyes and she had been sitting there, looking at him solemnly. Oddly enough, he had remembered her, and he knew where he was almost immediately. She smiled and clapped her hands and ran from the room, curls flying, yelling, "Pa! Pa! Mister Man's awake. Mister Man's awake!"

That was her name for him—"Mister Man." She clung as closely as his shadow. Sometimes it was embarrassing. Once after she had sat regarding him gravely for an hour, he smiled. "Wouldn't you like to go outside in the sunshine?"

She shook her head slowly. "No, I got to sit heah an' wish for you to git well."

She treated him as if he were the child and she the grownup. "Now, Mister Man, I want you to drink all of your pot likker 'cause it's good for you an' it'll make you strong." Or, "I'm gonna be mad with you eff'n you don't eat all your food, Mister Man. You gotta git stout again."

Sometimes she amazed him. One day as she sat with her chin propped in one small hand, she said, "You know, Mister Man, I can tell things."

He smiled. "What things, Ada?"

"Oh, jes' all things," she said. "When my grandpa Gilbert died, I knew it 'fore we got the word. I knew it 'cause he come in mah room all dressed in a long, white robe an' he walked around real quiet." She frowned slightly. "An' you know, the very nex' day we'uns found that he had died over in Decatur." She sat a moment as if in deep thought. "You know, Mister Man, I think I got second sight like mah Ma."

"What is second sight, Ada?"

She looked surprised. "Why, don't you know? Second sight is when you see things 'fore they happen. It's like . . . well, it's like the way I knew you was comin' heah 'way 'fore you did. I usta sit up all the time an' wish you'd hurry—but I knowed you was comin'."

He laughed. "How could you have known that? I didn't know it myself."

She cut her eyes at him teasingly. "Oh, I know lots of things you don't know—an' there ain't no use a-askin' 'cause I won't tell." She leaned forward. "I will sing you my secret song, though, eff'n you want me to."

"I'd like to hear a song," he said.

Softly, in her thin child's voice, she sang:

> *"How should I your true love know*
> *From another one?*
> *By his cockle hat and staff,*
> *And his sandal shoon.*
>
> *He is dead and gone, lady,*
> *He is dead and gone:*
> *At his head a grass-green turf,*
> *At his heels a stone.*
>
> *White his shroud as the mountin snow,*
> *Larded with sweet flowers,*
> *Which bewept to the grave did go*
> *With true-love showers.*
>
> *And will he not come again?*
> *And will he not come again?*
> *No, no, he is dead:*
> *Go to thy death-bed:*
> *He will never come again.*
>
> *His beard was as white as snow,*
> *All flaxen was his poll:*
> *He is gone, he is gone,*
> *And we cast away moan:*
> *God ha' mercy on his soul!"*

He listened in amazement. "Why, Ada," he said, "I know that song. I've heard it—" he paused and frowned—"somewhere."

He looked at Ada and was surprised to see tears welling in her eyes. "No, you ain't heard it before either," she said fiercely. "It's mah song! Mah secret song! Mah Grandpa Gilbert taught it to me. He's dead now, so nobody else in the whole world knows it 'ceptin' me!" She fled from the room in tears.

It was a long time before he remembered where he had heard the song. Aber had read it to him long ago. It was mad Ophelia's song from Hamlet. He smiled as he remembered how Aber used to shake his head and sigh over the tragic Ophelia. "Ah, poor soul, Master Tench—her only crime was that she was doomed to love one man too much."

Ada did not return all afternoon, and when Lena Mitchell brought him supper, Horatio asked for her.

Lena did not lift her eyes. "Ada's put out 'bout somethin'," she said mildly.

"I'm sorry," Horatio said. "I'm afraid I hurt her feelings."

Lena clasped her hands in front of her and studied them carefully. "Ada's a funny young'un," she said finally. Horatio didn't say anything. Lena picked at her bony knuckles. "Sometimes Ada don't ack like a young 'un a-tall."

Lena still fumbled at her knuckles. Her little ghost of a smile didn't change. "Ada ain't never been a chile. She's been drug from one place t'other, an' she ain't never knowed no chillun her own age. All she's ever had's her Pa an' me, an' Ah reckon it didn't take long fer her t' cotch up with all we knowed." Then, after making what was probably the longest speech of her life, Lena glided from the room.

There was no doubt that Ada was advanced for her seven years. She refused to leave the room the day Lafe and King changed the dressing on Horatio's wounds. She looked alarmed when Horatio winced as they peeled the blood-hardened bandage from his shoulder. She paled when she saw the swollen, half-healed gash exposed, but when King dabbed at it with a damp cloth in his heavy fingers, she pushed him aside. "Now, you're goin' to hurt him," she said. "Give it to me." King surrendered the cloth. She set her small chin firmly and washed the wound with deft, gentle strokes.

But, for all her boasts about second sight, she wasn't infallible.

One afternoon she came in the room smiling and held out a handful of dry grass. Horatio smiled. "Why, you've brought me flowers, Ada. Thank you."

She looked at him scornfully. "They ain't flowers, an' you know it."

"Then what is it, Ada?"

She seemed puzzled. "Why, it's clover, that's what it is. All the time you was asleep when you first come heah, you kept groaning 'Clover, clover.' I tole King I was goin' to git you some jes' as soon as I could."

It was a long time before he could turn and manage a smile. "Thank you," he said.

As they prepared for bed that night, King slid the pillow from under his head to fluff it and the little cluster of clover fell to the floor. King picked it up with a grin. "Whass dis heah grass, Boss?"

Horatio looked at him levelly. "It's clover."

King's grin flickered out. Without a word he started to put the clover back under the pillow.

"Throw it in the fire," Horatio said.

King walked to the fireplace and threw the clover on the bed of hot coals. It smoldered a moment, then burst into flame. King stood watching it.

Horatio tried to put a touch of humor in his voice. "Was I too bad, King?"

King turned slowly. He smiled a little. "Yo' wasn't bad a-tall, Boss." He hesitated a moment and his voice was very gentle. "It's funny thing ter me—when a man loses his arm er his laig, folks gen'ally feel awf'ly sorry fer him. But when a man loses a woman, folks laugh lak it's a big joke." He sighed. "Dey can't seem ter unnerstan' dat losin' somebody yo' loves air the worst pain dere is."

Until that moment Horatio had not known that King had ever been in love.

It felt good to be back in a saddle again. It was a crisp, flat morning and the fields were still pock-marked with frost. King had brought his roan from town that morning tied to the buckboard of Lafe's wagon, and the three-mile walk had only whetted the horse's appetite for exercise. But now he wasn't so frisky. He was heaving and puffing and the jets of vapor from his nostrils were a foot long. Horatio laughed happily and slapped the winded horse on the neck and stood in his stirrups to look for King.

Less than ten minutes before, they had left the house together. At the top of the hill a covey of partridges had exploded from the ground. King's horse had balked indignantly, but the roan had laid his ears back and streaked off. Though he knew he should take it easy because of his wounds, the thrill of feeling his body respond to the movement of a fast horse was too much for Horatio. He had given the roan a slack rein until he began to slow down of his own accord. Apparently no damage had been done. Horatio slid a hand inside his shirt and ran his finger along the still tender scar on his shoulder. It had withstood its first test without trouble. Grinning, he pulled down his shirt and turned for his first good look at Lafe's land. He was disappointed at what he saw. He knew that the bleakness of the day and the pockets of frost helped create an illusion of lifelessness and barrenness, but it was something more than that. He couldn't help but compare the rolling, reddish land before him with the smooth, black acres of Fair Haven. The land he knew stretched unbroken for miles, except for an occasional marsh. But this land wasn't even cleared completely. From where he stood on a slight rise, he could see a half-dozen small wooded areas. And he could see a dozen reasons why this land would not be good for cotton. A heavy rain cutting away at the sides of these slopes could undermine and topple a heavily loaded cotton stock. Some of the dips in this land would shade cotton from day-long sun.

He dismounted and picked up a handful of soil. It wasn't anything like the clinging, chocolate-black soil at Fair Haven. It was reddish and rather coarse, more like a mixture of sand and clay. He was still examining the soil when King rode up. "What's wrong with this land, King?"

King grinned. He knew what Horatio had been thinking. "Yo can't think er nuthin' 'cept cotton, kin yo', Boss?"

Horatio knew that was true. Land to him meant cotton. It was actually the only crop he knew. At Fair Haven he had never concerned himself much with anything else. The corn and the wheat and the tobacco and vegetables had been important only because they supplied the needs and the luxuries for people who spent most of their time working for bigger yields of cotton. Cotton was money. When a man had cotton, he could buy other things that grew on the land. "What else should I think about?" he asked.

King slid from his horse and kicked at the hard earth with his heel. He was still smiling, but his voice was serious. "Lots er things," he said. "Lots er things dat dis heah lan' kin give. God didn't give dis kind er lan' fer a man ter git rich on. He give dis kind er lan' so as people could eat. Yo' kin grow near 'bout any kind er food on dis lan'—corn, wheat, taters, greens, an' peanuts. It's good an' it's rich. Ah reckon it air kinda plain—but it's an honest plain."

Horatio laughed. "It looks to me like a pretty hard-to-plow plain, too."

King cut his eyes shrewdly. "Man ain't gotta plow, air he? Man warn't born wif no plow handles in his han's, war he?"

"What the devil are you up to?" Horatio asked.

King laughed. "Climb up on dat crazy horse of yor'n an' foller me an' Ah'll show yo'."

Five minutes later he reined up at the top of a rise and pointed before him. "Look out dere," he said proudly.

Horatio was quite unprepared for the view. Less than three hundred yards away the Tennessee made a bend in a flat plateau that stretched for a square mile or more. But it was not the turbulent, rampaging river that passed Arcadia. It was calm and wide, and under the bleak sky it looked like a huge silver ribbon. Its color was all the more noticeable because there were almost no trees growing on its banks. Here and there a lone oak or a few pines dotted the fields on each side of the river, but otherwise they were as smooth as a well-kept lawn and they were the golden-brown color of ripe wheat. Horatio could see only one touch of green in the whole area. A small pine-covered island, diamond-shaped and scarcely bigger than an acre, sat in the bend of the river. He looked at the scene a long time. It was the biggest expanse of flat land he had seen since he left Fair Haven. He was delighted. "B'fair, a man could get his share of cotton on that land," he said.

King grunted. "No, suh," he said. "No, suh!"

"What will it grow then?"

"Grass," said King. "Nothin' 'cept plain grass." He swept his arm in a wide arc. "Ah rid' ovah near dat whole section on Mistah

Lafe's mule t'other day. Unnerneath dat grass, de soil's either too sandy er too rocky ter grow anythin' 'cept grass—but a man could grow aller grass he wanted." He pointed to the stretch of land in front of them on the near side of the river. "Dat passel dere kivers 'bout forty acres. It belongs ter Mistah Lafe. It's fer sale. Mistah Lafe say he thinks ever'body else who got a stretch dere would sell, too."

"I don't wonder," said Horatio.

King turned to look directly at Horatio. His voice was serious. "Boss, wut air it dat ever'body has ter have? Wut is it dat ever'-body needs dese days?"

"Why . . . why—food, I suppose," Horatio said.

King nodded. "Food's part er it, all right." He paused a moment. "Now Ah'll tell yo' 'bout it. Boss, me an' yo' ain't got no call ter try ter raise ourself no cotton. All de good lan' 'roun' heah done been took up. It take a heap er men ter wuk cotton. How much cotton yo' think me an' yo' gonna raise by ourself? We'd sweat an' we'd sweat an' we couldn't git enough." His voice was earnest. "It take a lot er men ter raise cotton. But wut's it ever'-body needs, Boss?" He held up one big hand with fingers outstretched. As he spoke, he began to tick off each finger. "Dey gotta have meat, Boss. Dey gotta have ham an' beef an' lamb. An' dey gotta have hawsses, Boss. Dey gotta have hawsses ter ride, an' dey gotta have big, fine stallions ter service dere mares. Dey gotta have big bulls ter service dere cows. Dey gotta have milk an' dey gotta have all kinds o' stock when they fin'lly stop dis heah bizness er chasin' 'roun' lak crazy men affer lan'.

"We could gib dem all those things, Boss—jes' me'n yo'. We could wuk an' we could sweat, an' dat down dere—" he pointed to the grass-covered plateau—"dat would do de rest. Dere's water down dere, Boss, an' dere's all de grass in de world. More things dan jes' cotton comes outta de groun', Boss!"

Horatio looked at King's shining eyes and he knew that King had had a vision and that vision was good. But almost immediately he knew why it could not come true. He spoke quietly, almost gently.

"How much would we have to pay for that land, King?"

King broke into a grin. "Eight dollahs a acre, Mistah Lafe say, Boss."

"How many acres would we need?"

" 'Bout a hundred, Ah reckon."

Horatio sighed and looked down at his saddle. He hated to say it, partly because of himself, but mostly because of King. "I couldn't even buy that much land, King," he said finally, "much less buy stock to put on it." He smiled gently. "It's a fine idea, though."

King looked bewildered. The light died in his eyes. After a long time he spoke heavily. "Ah nebber even thought er dat."

It was the truth, unbelievable as it was. King, the former slave, the man who had lived all his life without the need for money, had simply for a while forgotten that Horatio was not a General Jameson who could buy anything he wanted.

They rode back to the house silently. Horatio was so glum all evening that Ada and Lafe chided him for taxing his strength too much on his first day out.

He was lying in bed the next morning, still half-asleep, when he found a solution. He jumped up and dressed quickly, thinking all the while that King was not the only one who had forgotten the importance of money.

It was noon when he walked into the office of the lawyer in Florence that old Doc Ware had recommended. "My name is Horatio Tompkins," he said. "I want to get a sum of money that is being held for me in England."

CASTLE

BY THE RIVER

CHAPTER XXI

IF OLD Marius Henshaw had been poor, folks might have called him lazy. But since his sprawling saddlebags store at Taylor's Ford was bulging with everything from beeswax to watered silk, they had to accept old Marius' explanation that he was only patient. "Ah'll tell yo', boys," Marius would chuckle, settling his great bulk comfortably in a split cane chair on the front porch of his store, "eff'n a fellah jes' squats in one place long enough, near 'bout anythin' wuth seein' will trot pas'." Then, with the river roaring past his back door and the afternoon sun warming his moon face, like as not old Marius would fall asleep.

Through the years Marius seemed to have forgotten that an accident, not judgment, caused him to establish a store at Taylor's Ford when the nearest white family was two days away and a man had to stand on a horse to see over the canebrakes. One summer day in 1790 he and a partner had been poling a flatboat loaded with supplies up the river to do a bit of trading with the Indians when somehow they had been pulled into the Big Suck. Marius had managed to reach shore, but the boat and his partner disappeared forever.

A less patient man might have bowed to fate. Not Marius. He spent nearly a month salvaging his goods. When he wasn't diving for the heavier articles like a box of trade hatchets and a keg of nails, he was walking the banks recovering bolts of calico and boxes of raisins that had been caught on the snags.

Marius said it was simple after that. "Wal, by an' by Ah got t'gether a few things under an ole tree, an' Ah war standin' thar, lookin' at 'em an' feelin' purty sick when the bushes parted an' this big greasy buck come walkin' out. Wal, Ah jumped an' he jumped. Ah looked at him an' he looked at me. Fin'lly he looked down at mah goods an' said, 'Me trade.'

" 'Brothah.' Ah said, 'jes' make me an offer.' Wal, he went off an' purty soon he come back with two prime beaver skins. Ah give him a handful of raisins an' a couple nails an' he went off happy as a pig in the sunshine. Atter that, Ah jes' sat down an' waited fer the rest o' the Injuns, an' atter a few years 'long come yo' folks."

Marius could be patient about humor, too. Each spring he carefully placed a duck egg in the nest of each of the scrawny hens that scratched in the yard or wandered in and out of his store, leaving their droppings everywhere. As each clutch of eggs hatched, Marius would sit watching carefully until the duckling waddled into the river. While a startled hen dashed frantically up and down, clucking hysterically to her foster child, Marius would hold his great belly and laugh until the tears streamed down his cheeks. "Gets 'em ever' time," he would wheeze. "Skeered the tail feather plum' outta her!"

Best of all, Marius loved to see strangers come down the river road from the North. For the past nine years a stranger coming from that direction always meant more fun than his ducks and chickens. So one sunny August afternoon when he saw an unfamiliar wagon approaching, he chuckled and settled back expectantly.

The wagon was a ramshackle, lumbering affair which seemed to be held together by wire and rope. It was piled high with household goods and pulled by two skinny, harness-scarred mules. A lanky, bearded man in greasy, tattered buckskins was driving. Beside him sat a woman who was equally as dirty and greasy, but who must have weighed two hundred pounds.

Marius knew immediately that they were squatters, shiftless, nomadic no-goods who refused to farm but settled on other people's land until they had killed all the game or had been run off. Marius had been known to refuse to do business with squatters, but for purposes of his joke he found them admirable, so he smiled pleasantly when the man brought his weary mules to a stop.

"Howdy," said the man.

"How-do," said Marius.

It was the woman who asked. Marius had discovered that they usually did. "That thar place back up the road, mistah," she said, "that thar big place made outta rocks—who do it belong to?"

Marius smiled and settled back. "Wal, ma'am, 'round these heah parts we call that place Tench's Castle."

The woman's suety face broke into a smile. She nudged her husband excitedly. "Thass wut it is, Jim—thass wut Ah was a-tryin' ter say. It's a castle! Ah've seen pic-chers of 'em. A castle! Land sakes." She turned back to Marius. "Who do yo' say it belong ter, mistah?"

Marius chuckled inwardly. "Wal, ma'am, it belongs ter an Englishman an' a nigger."

The couple exchanged glances. "An Englishman an' his nigger, you say, mistah?" the woman asked.

"No, ma'am," said Marius innocently, but wiggling his toes with enjoyment. "Not *his* nigger—*a* nigger!"

The woman seemed bewildered. "Land sakes, yo' hear that, Jim! A nigger an' an Englishman!"

Jim scowled. "Wut's a nigger doin' ownin' somethin' like a-that?"

Marius kept a straight face. "Why, him an' this heah Englishman is partners," he said.

Jim's scowl grew blacker. "Looks like yo' folks 'round heah would take keer o' somethin' like that."

Marius nodded solemnly. "Sho' do, stranger, but Ah reckon they's afeered ter do it." He studied the man's scowling face a moment. "Ah reckon folks would be mighty grateful eff'n *yo'* could find yo' way clear ter do somethin' 'bout it while yo' air passin' through." Then he could no longer suppress his chuckle. "Ah think Ah oughta warn yo', though," he said, shaking with laughter, "that this heah Englishman is 'bout ten feet tall an' he could use yo' fer a toothpick."

Jim lowered his eyes sullenly. "Eff'n Ah lived aroun' heah Ah'd do somethin' about it."

His wife tightened her mouth and nodded. Then she asked Marius, "How did that Englishman an' that nigger git all the money ter build that castle?"

"It war easy, ma'am," Marius said through his laughter. "All they did was git a few romantical-inclined hawsses an' cows an' pigs an' then let nature take her course."

It had not been quite so simple, but they had been amazingly successful. On the day after his return from Florence, Horatio had bought the forty acres of land that Lafe had on the plateau by the river. Lafe had refused steadfastly to take more than five dollars an acre for it, though he had mentioned eight dollars in his earlier conversation with King. "Shucks, take it an' be sorry, man," he roared. "Ah ain't got no need fer that lan' an, jes' 'cause Ah felt pitiful fer takin' advantage of yo', Ah'm gonna let yo' cut all the timber yo' want outta mah woods an' no questions asked!"

Lafe was a rock. One afternoon while Horatio and King were splitting rails for fences, he appeared. "Saddle up that hawss of your'n an' go into Arcady an' git ten gallons o' shinny," he told Horatio. "Me an' the boys air comin' 'round tomorrow ter do a leetle log-rolling." Horatio got the whisky, and the next day Lafe and fifteen of his neighbors roared and sawed and got drunk and somehow managed to throw up a sturdy one-room cabin. It was a godsend because that winter was cold and dreary. There were many days when the river froze over completely. But even on the coldest days they managed to get some work done, and before the next spring they put the last rail in place and stood back and grinned at each other. That afternoon they took little Ada fishing.

Now there was nothing to do except sit back and wait. Horatio had no idea how much money he would receive, but he knew it wouldn't be much. He had already looked over the stock that was available and he felt that with five hundred dollars he and King could make a good start. He still had most of the three hundred dollars that remained after he had paid Lafe for his land. It had cost them almost no money to live that winter and spring. The nearby woods kept them supplied with game and the fish in the river were theirs for the dropping of a hook. After the spring thaw King had planted a vegetable garden and it flourished. They bought meal from Lafe for twenty-five cents a peck.

Finally a letter of credit came from a Lichfield bank. It was an hour before Horatio could realize that he was a rich man.

His legacy came to twenty thousand dollars. And there was a note from Aber.

> Build your castle, Master Tench, and remember
> Your affectionate,
> Aber

He stood whitefaced, reading and rereading the few words until they blurred before his eyes. Then he set his jaw and walked to the nearest saloon and ordered whisky.

King found him there at noon the next day, slumped forward on a table in the rear of the room, his clothes wilted and whisky-stained. King nudged him gently. "Boss. Boss. Come on, Boss, we best go home now." Horatio fell back and looked up with bloodshot eyes. He tried to rise but the effort was too much. King slipped an arm around him and helped him gain his feet. As they passed the bar, a half-dozen early drinkers eyed them curiously. Already the tall Englishman and the powerful Negro were a legend along the river. At the door Horatio halted and made an effort to pull himself together. He stood straight and shut his eyes against the glare of sunlight. "I want to build a castle, King," he said thickly. "Ye must help me build a castle."

Two days later Giuseppe Cavagnari appeared. He rode a fat, heavy-footed old white mare, but when he reached their cabin he reined it up with a flourish. He was a beautifully dressed, swarthy little man with sad eyes. He had a slight accent. "Could you direct me to the estate of Signor Tench?" he asked.

Horatio smiled. "My name is Tench."

Giuseppe's polite smile faded. He stared at Horatio and King and then turned to gaze slowly around at the small cabin. Finally he sighed and shrugged and slipped down from his patient old nag. "Ah, forgive me, signor; with me I fear someone has been having a joke. My name is Giuseppe Cavagnari, a builder. I rode half the morning because I was informed that you, signor, wanted a castle."

Horatio flushed but continued to smile. "I want no castle— only a house."

Giuseppe smiled sympathetically. "Ah, signor, I do not work with the logs. I am the artist. I am the pupil of the master Ferdinand Sannoner, who give you the beautiful Florence, signor." He drew himself up proudly. "I stay here after my patron go back to Italy. I give you many beautiful homes and garden, signor."

Until Giuseppe Cavagnari's arrival, Horatio had given no thought to a home, but now he looked at the Italian with interest. "Could you build me a home," he said, "—a home of wood?"

Giuseppe shrugged. "The houses of wood, they cost money, signor."

"I have money."

Giuseppe's eyes lighted with interest. He looked at Horatio closely. "A small house perhaps?"

Horatio smiled. "A house—a strong house." He paused a moment. "With windows—many windows—and a veranda, a big veranda."

Giuseppe cocked his head shrewdly. "No castle?"

"No castle."

Giuseppe sighed and shook his head. "Ah, signor, it is too sad." He made a sweeping gesture at the landscape. "There are stones here, beautiful stones of many colors. They lie on the ground and you Americans, how you swear and curse them because God placed them in the way of your plows. In my country, signor, a man can see the beauty in stone. Even the peasants have homes of stone, signor. God placed stone here for men to use, signor. Even a small house can be of stone." His eyes were shining. "Here, I show you," he said, springing forward and grabbing a wooden shovel leaning against the side of the cabin. He took a crayon from his pocket and began to sketch swiftly on the smooth blade while Horatio and King looked over his shoulder. "So—and so— and here—and now here," he muttered as he worked. Within a matter of minutes he had drawn a castle of stone which was stately but somehow not bleak. "The windows do it, signor," he explained. "They are wide windows, good for sunshine, not like the archer's scuppers in the old castles in my country."

Horatio and King looked at each other delightedly. Then Horatio remembered something. "The veranda? It does not have a veranda."

Giuseppe tapped the drawing with his crayon. "In here, signor, behind these walls. Not a veranda. A courtyard—a courtyard where a man can smell the sweet flowers and look up and see the stars above his head. A bit of peace and quiet, signor. A place where the bambinos can play."

"And the cost?"

Giuseppe shrugged. "As much or as little as a man has to spend, signor. It can be large or it can be reasonable. In such a home as this goes the knowledge of centuries, signor. In such a home as this, I, Giuseppe Cavagnari, could put my heart."

It was no idle boast. Giuseppe demanded perfection. He walked over every inch of Horatio's land and shook his head. "It is too flat," he said. "A castle was not made to be held by the land—it must be held by the sky." He pointed to a small hill down the river, on adjoining land. "We must build there."

Horatio bought the site and the hundred acres that surrounded it. Later he bought another forty acres across the river, giving him one hundred and eighty acres in all.

Giuseppe was everywhere during the building. Stamping his foot and screaming at the masons one moment, scowling ferociously at the day laborers the next. He had not been too happy about the day laborers, but Horatio had refused to allow him to lease slaves for the work. Giuseppe had a sensitive appreciation of Horatio's humanitarian rule, but, still and all, his thrifty Latin soul cringed every time he remembered that these lazy fellows were getting fifty cents a day. Apiece!

There was stone everywhere for the asking and the hauling away. But Giuseppe was not satisfied with just any stone. They had to be of a certain size, of a certain shade, and woe to the poor mason who tried to remedy a clumsy fitting with a too lavish use of mortar. After a few weeks even the dimmest-witted laborer had learned a few words of Italian—none of them nice.

News of this strange house spread fast. Every day more and more people passed along the river road to stare at the slowly rising walls. It was inevitable that people should begin to refer to it as "Tench's Folly," but the name never stuck. As the walls got higher, the wise grins and the snickers disappeared. It was too impressive for that. It would have been an oddity anywhere, but in this raw, new country which was to wait another thirty years before huts became cabins and cabins became houses and houses became mansions, it was—well, it was a castle.

Of course, it wasn't a castle in the truest sense. It had only fifteen rooms and, except that it was built of rough field stones, it had a startling resemblance to the farm villas in Giuseppe's native land. It was built in the form of a square around a courtyard. Three of its sides were long, hollow, box-like ("Like three durn covered bridges slapped together," Lafe said). The other side was a wall with room left for a gate. It was two stories tall and perhaps it would have been bleak and forbidding looking if it had not been for the windows. The windows were amazing. They were of all sizes and there were so many of them that Horatio wondered how they could ever be filled with glass. But, of course, Giuseppe had the answer to that. He filled them with mosaic panes, sprinkled with bits of red and green glass here and there to satisfy his flamboyant soul.

The castle was not nearly as large as it appeared to the gawking throngs who passed by on the river road. There were already larger houses in Decatur and Athens and Florence, and here and there a planter had a dwelling almost as large. But they were cold, unimaginative. Sitting in the bare fields without lawns or gardens, they seemed half-finished. And they were. It was to be years before they received their immense pillars and rambling wings and box-wood borders and became a part of what later generations called the "Old South."

This house Giuseppe Cavagnari built demanded nothing of the land. It stood alone. As Horatio watched it rise, he shook his head in wonder at Giuseppe's artistry. The watch tower at one end of the two-story building was really nothing except a place to put wide bay windows, one for each floor. A barbican at the other end of the building served the same purpose. And Giuseppe had built a gateway leading to the courtyard that would have accommodated a carriage and four. Finally, when he saw the waist-high parapet laid completely around the roof, Horatio felt as awestruck as Ada, who had been scrambling around for weeks in a daze of happiness and amazement.

But Giuseppe was not finished yet. After the masons had finished, the carpenters arrived. They laid floors of pine and covered the walls inside the house to the height of a man's head with thick, unfinished boards of oak. Horatio protested when he saw this rough paneling put in place, but Giuseppe waved his hands wildly. "It is fitting," he said. "This house, it is strong, powerful. It is the house of a man. Anything except the strong hewed oak would make it look foolish, like a man in woman's dress."

Horatio shook his head doubtfully, but let Giuseppe have his way.

He had not spent all his time watching his home grow. He and King had scoured the countryside for animals. Horses were not difficult to find and he had bought twenty brood mares and two stallions. Hogs were also plentiful. A man could have a hog for going into the bush and taking a chance on losing his leg. But such hogs—lean and sharp-backed, fleet and stringy. Horatio remembered the round, placid porkers at Fair Haven and snorted with disgust. King wasn't disturbed at all. "These heah is good hogs," he said. "Wut's good in one place ain't allus good in another. These heah hogs belongs on dis lan' an' all we gotta do is git us some good boars an' dey'll be happy an' so will dere chillun."

There were only a few sheep and no cattle. It was five years before he managed to build up a sizable herd of English short horns, and by that time he had abandoned the idea of raising sheep altogether.

It was a hectic time of work and planning. In later years Horatio had difficulty recalling all that had happened in those busy, exciting days. It was as if he had awakened to find all his dreams come true. So very much happened in so little time.

But, of course, he never forgot the day his home was finished. He and King and the Mitchells and Giuseppe Cavagnari and the workmen stood grinning at each other and admiring it from all angles. Then they went inside, and while Lena slipped around quietly preparing a supper, Horatio and Lafe and the workmen drank each other's health. Giuseppe got quite drunk on happiness and shinny. He stood in the middle of the great bare parlor and lifted his glass. "To this house and to my friends I wish all life's pleasure—and many bambinos!"

"What's they?" little Ada asked.

"Babies, my cherub," Giuseppe said, "many fat babies!"

Ada grinned. "I hope they's all boys," she said.

Everyone laughed and drank and sang until midnight. That night Horatio and King slept side by side on a pile of skins on the parlor floor because, naturally, Tench's castle still had no furniture.

The amazing Giuseppe took care of that, too. He threw up his hands in exasperation at Horatio's plans to furnish the castle with furniture sent up the river from New Orleans. Giuseppe puckered his mouth and minced about the room. "Look, what do you see? Do you see a signorina? No, you see the foolish man, and this house—this house, it looks foolish, too, with the furniture of France. I will get your furniture, signor. I will get the furniture it begs."

He did. He scoured the countryside, and every day he came back with a wagon piled high with chests and beds and tables, rough, crude furniture. It was furniture that the early settlers had hacked and hewed themselves. It bore the marks of their axes and adzes. It was unfinished and darkened with age and stained with use. When he first saw it, Horatio's heart sank. But after Giuseppe had arranged it and had altered some pieces and added deft touches to others, he realized that Giuseppe was right. The heavy, rough-hewed furniture belonged.

Only when the house was furnished completely would Giuseppe accompany Horatio to Florence to buy the rugs and curtains and other household goods. Here, too, he was astounding. He turned up his nose at the few truly fine Persian rugs and brocaded hangings which were available. He smiled and clasped his hands over the varicolored wool rugs, heavy and coarse-textured, which slaves wove in their spare time for pocket money. He bought yards of heavy goods, coarse as bagging, for curtains. He even frowned when a beautiful set of china caught Horatio's eyes. He ordered pewter instead.

There was no accounting for Giuseppe's taste, but when the last rug had been laid and the last curtain hung, Horatio stood numb with pleasure. "B'fair, it's wonderful," he said. Giuseppe smiled. He had one last surprise. He untied a heavy package and unfurled a long tapestry and spread it along one wall of the huge parlor. It was a medieval hunting scene, the work of some master of the loom in Giuseppe's country. It was as colorful as a rainbow and the tiny figures were worked so skillfully that they seemed to be painted. Giuseppe looked at the tapestry critically, then threw up his hands. "It is finished," he said. "This gift of mine, it is the last touch." He beamed like a child.

That night Horatio made a final totaling of the cost of his

castle. It came to a little more than six thousand dollars. It was a shocking figure, he knew, but after he had climbed into his big, four-posted bed and listened to the sounds of the night outside his wide window, he decided it was worth it.

Old Marius Henshaw exaggerated when he said Horatio was ten feet tall. But he was as close to it as most normal men get. In his thirty-second year he stood six feet six inches tall and weighed two hundred and forty pounds. He was not fat, there was not an ounce of fat on him. He had merely lost the slimness of youth and reached his full growth. Wherever he went, people turned to follow him with their eyes. It was not his size alone. Every schoolboy in the Big Bend had heard the story of how he fought the fabulous Asa Cole in a darkened warehouse and somehow survived wounds that would have killed an ordinary man. But he was not the high-booted Boss Tench of Fair Haven. No longer did he find his pleasure in cheap dives. No longer did he drink alone. He was the Tench of Tench's Castle. He could take a quiet glass of wine at the finest clubs in Florence and Decatur. He rubbed shoulders and did business and held the notes of the most aristocratic gentlemen in the Big Bend. He had always been vain about his appearance. Prosperity had made him more so. His waistcoats and trousers came up the river from New Orleans, his vests were hand embroidered, and his high, light-colored hats and his soft sleek shoes came from England. He drove the best span of horses on the river, although sometimes they were bays, sometimes chestnuts, and sometimes dapple grays. It was no wonder. He had the finest horse farm south of Virginia.

There were women now, too. Many women. Women found him fascinating, and for a while, at least, he had returned the compliment to a dozen or so. But they never seemed to last a long time, and however else they may have differed, they had two things in common. They were beautiful and gay, and if not shady —well, at least they never shone with virtue. These laughing ladies were not his companions through necessity. More than one deep-bosomed dowager had virtually hurled her dewy-eyed, dove-sweet daughter at him only to discover that the very substantial Tench was as elusive as light. Most people could not understand this because a bachelor, particularly a bachelor who could make a successful marriage, was an oddity in the Bend.

There were other things about this tall, handsome man that bewildered his neighbors. He never gambled. Other men gambled as naturally as they ate. They gambled on everything from horse races to cock fights. They lost and won plantations on the flick of a card. They flipped coins and threw dice the year around. Horatio Tench never joined them. Most of all, they could not understand his attitude toward Negroes. They were used to a man being jovial and paternal or sharp and severe where Negroes were concerned. They could not fathom a man who behaved otherwise. This Tench never made the little black boys who held his horses scramble for a coin. He never berated or joshed the slaves who served him at his clubs. And it annoyed his neighbors because the Negroes treated him differently. They could talk to him quietly. They never rolled their eyes and whinnied with laughter. They never acted the clown. Why, damn it all, you would have thought they were human.

Most people knew of Horatio's association with King, and they had heard rumors, all sorts of rumors, but somehow they could not comprehend them. And, one thing certain, this Tench was not one of those stupid, wild-eyed people who called themselves Abolitionists. It was true he didn't hold slaves, but no one had ever heard him stand up and say that it was wrong. It was a mystery.

It was and it wasn't. The truth was that Horatio was a man of his times. He was no visionary. He thought slavery was wrong and he refused to have slaves. There he let the matter drop.

Essentially, he had not changed at all. He could still sweat and labor from daylight to dusk. Most days he did. The horses were his special love. From January, when the barren mares were separated from those in foal, until September, when the early foals had to be weaned and wormed, he was busy. There was the breeding to supervise, feet to be trimmed, feed had to be mixed, and more than one night he sweated over a heaving, suffering mare who was having a difficult delivery. He refused to send his yearlings to market. It was a luxury he could afford. People flocked to his farm to buy. And he refused to strap and curry and polish and rub his yearlings. He let them run right up until the time they were sold. If a buyer preferred a too-fat, worked-over colt to his thin, rugged, sunburned stock, he shrugged and let him go elsewhere. But few professional buyers went farther than his farm. They bought all the horses he had to offer and wanted more.

He took almost no interest in his other stock. That was King's responsibility, and even though half the year around it brought in most of the revenue, he almost never knew the price of beef or pork. There were always half a dozen hands around the farm. They came and went, sometimes after a few months, sometimes after a few years. Horatio paid them well and fed them well. All he required was that they work and that they obey King's orders implicitly. There had never been any trouble on that score. When employees left it was usually because they were drifters in the first place or because they had saved enough money to buy land of their own. Lafe was the only one who had remained year in and year out.

It was more or less of an accident that he went to work for Horatio. During that first eventful year he had established his farm, Horatio learned that a school for girls was being established in Athens. He had thought of little Ada immediately and went to Lafe and offered to send her. Lafe looked at him in amazement. "God amighty, man," he roared, "a girl ain't got no use gittin' no book larnin'! Her ma'll learn her all she needs ter know."

That was that. Horatio did not press the issue. But the next morning Lafe presented himself sheepishly. Sometime during the night—Horatio suspected the meek Lena's hand—Lafe had changed his mind. "Ah'll let her go," he said, "but Ah aim ter wuk fer yo' ter pay her way."

"If you work, I'll pay you, too," Horatio said. They finally had reached an agreement. Ada had been bundled off to Mrs. Cleo Jackson's School in Athens. She had remained there for nine winters, coming home only in the summers, until she had graduated when she was sixteen.

School had made quite a change in Ada. Where once she had always been tagging at Horatio's heels, she now seemed almost to avoid him. Even though Horatio had given her the job of keeping his books, she never approached him unless it was absolutely necessary. And somewhere through the years she had stopped calling him "Mistah Man."

She now called him Mister Tench, and while her manner toward him may have been due to shyness, he also had the impression that she was cool and distant. It was annoying at times. She was too quiet, too soft-footed. Her books were a marvel of neatness and it was evident that she had done well at Mrs. Jackson's. Yet when he remembered how fond she had been of him once and how much he had enjoyed her company when she was a child, Horatio was almost sorry that she had ever gone off to school.

At the same time he had to admit with almost a blush that his own attitude may have had something to do with the change in her. Ever since the summer Ada was fourteen—almost three years ago—he had found himself a little embarrassed and self-conscious when he was around her. Looking back, he could see that her own attitude seemed to have changed about that time. He supposed it was because that was the summer she had turned from an awkward child into a young woman.

Horatio knew she had been a young woman that summer. It was that knowledge that brought his blush. During that hot summer it had been his custom to rise at dawn and take a plunge in the river. He liked to swim naked, floating and splashing in the cool water which was covered with a cloudy fog until the sun came up. Usually he would swim to the little wooded island in the middle of the river and stretch out on a grassy knoll about ten feet back from the river's edge and watch the sun rise.

He was lying there one still dawn, reveling in the coolness of the morning and the feel of grass against his body, when he heard a small splash in the river. He raised his head slightly. Then, for an instant, he thought his heart had stopped.

A woman arose dripping from the misty river and stood on the bank of the island. In the soft light of the dawn her naked body was almost whitely luminous. She stretched elaborately, throwing her arms back in a glad, extravagant gesture. It was a beautiful body, and against the river in the background it was as detailed as a fine cameo.

It was several seconds before Horatio could catch his breath. Then it was too late. He dared not give a warning now. He lay still, not moving a muscle. The woman leaned forward and let her long hair hang before her while she began to wring the water from it. After a moment she threw back her head and shook her hair down her shoulders and looked directly at Horatio. It wasn't until then that he saw this exciting vision was Ada. He had not known that she was home from school. And never, never had he realized before that she was no longer a child. She was not only a woman, but a breath-taking woman.

When first she looked up, he thought she had seen him, but she hadn't. She stood there, brushing at her hair with her hands a little longer, then turned and waded back into the river. He waited a long time before he dared to swim back to the house.

Later in the day Lafe came in grinning to report that Ada was home and to invite Horatio and King to dinner. He had been a little nervous about meeting Ada that night, but he had no reason to be. In the familiar setting of Lafe's house she still seemed to be very much of a child. He looked at her as closely as he dared and it was as if he were seeing her for the first time. He realized that Ada had become an extremely pretty girl. No, pretty wasn't the word, Ada almost had beauty. There was strength in her face. Her lips were neither too full nor too thin. Her chin was firm and her brow was level and calm. Looking at her slight figure with her long blonde hair gathered in a strand down her back, he found it difficult, however, to visualize her as the nymph he had seen in the dawn's light.

He was strangely relieved to find that the past year had made a change in her behavior toward him. She no longer clung to him or tagged at his heels. He realized for the first time that she was calling him Mister Tench. He saw very little of her that summer and somehow he was glad when she went back to school.

That had been two—almost three—years ago, but now that Ada was sixteen and was home permanently, he still was slightly ill at ease around her. There was no doubt that Ada bothered him. Soon she was to shock him to his toes.

CHAPTER XXII

NO ONE understood why the bull considered Lafe his special enemy. It was a mean, evil-tempered brute at any time, but at the sight or smell of Lafe it went berserk. Even King, who was wise in the ways of animals, shook his head in bewilderment. "He ack jes' lak yo' done stole his chew er terbaccy, Mistah Lafe."

Lafe would roar with laughter. "He's the meanest consarn crittur Ah ever saw. He's half tornado an' half houn' dawg an' he's sho' got it in fer me. Ain't yo', yo' ole black devil!" he would shout, grabbing the top rail of the fence and shaking it in the bull's enraged face. The bull would fix its red-rimmed eyes on Lafe and bow its sleek, powerful back. Saliva would run down its chin. Its throat would begin to swell. It would snort and blow and paw the ground, then lunge against the stout fence with enough force to knock the breath from its huge body.

Lafe would howl with delight. "Come an' git me, yo' hind end o' Satan! Come an' git me!"

It was uncanny. It seemed impossible for Lafe to come near without the bull's realizing it. Horatio was down at the pens one crisp fall day when he saw a demonstration of this strange awareness. The bull was standing quietly in its pen, gazing longingly at his harem grazing in the distance, when Lafe walked from behind the stable, a good thirty yards away. Without looking around, the bull began to swell with rage. It stood with its head away from Lafe for fully a minute, heaving and pawing and blowing, before it turned with a roar and began running back and forth in the pen, its eyes never leaving Lafe.

There was something so awesome about this display of ferocity that Horatio warned Lafe, "We're going to turn him out in the fields next week, Lafe. When we do, I think you'd better use the river road when you come to work."

Lafe laughed. "Shecks, that ole Devil's gonna have mor'n me on his mind when he gits loose with those heifers. Anyway, Ah allus make sure he's in one end er the fiel' 'fore Ah cross the other." He picked up a chunk of soil and threw it at the bellowing bull. "Don't Ah, yo' ole fool!" he yelled. "Don't Ah, yo' hunk o' wuthless devilment!" The bull went mad with rage.

It was the sort of thing a man would have forgotten if nothing had happened. But something did happen—a week later. It was early morning. Horatio was in the stables filling one of the stalls with a mixture of fresh earth and lime when he heard the bull roar. He halted and listened, and then he heard Lafe shout. He had dropped the shovel and started toward the door when he heard the scream. He knew it was Ada. The sound chilled him. The first thought that came into his mind was that he had forgotten to tell Ada that the bull had been turned out in the field. Oh, God, if . . .

When he ran from the stable, he saw Ada climbing through the pasture fence less than a hundred feet away. He was so relieved that he stopped and stood there. Then he looked beyond her into the field and began running again. At first he had the impression that Lafe was clutching the bull's horns and that it was trying to toss him free. Ada screamed again and started to climb back through the fence before he realized that Lafe was limp as a straw man and was impaled on the bull's horns. He reached Ada before she was halfway through the bars of the fence and dragged her out. He pushed her aside roughly. "No! No!" he said. He vaulted the fence and ran toward the bull. It saw him coming and lowered its head. Lafe dangled limply from its horns. After eying Horatio an instant, it bellowed and tossed its head again and charged. Horatio moved quickly. He stepped aside, and as the animal went past, he caught Lafe around the waist. He never knew how he managed to get him free. It took all of his strength. He strained and tugged while the bull bellowed and snorted and tossed its head. It was a confusion of sounds and images. He was only conscious of how difficult it was to get a grip on Lafe's clothes, of how every time he pulled at Lafe's limp body the bull's head seemed to lift, too. But some way, somehow, he finally had Lafe free.

He eased him to the ground and the bull was gone and he was surrounded by the stable hands and King and Ada. He was still breathless from the exertion and his hands trembled. It was King who examined the limp Lafe. It wasn't difficult to find the wound. The bull's sharp horn had passed completely through Lafe's left groin. The ragged wound was the size of a silver dollar, blue-edged and ugly. There was only a trace of blood oozing from it. When Horatio saw that, he felt relieved but King knew what it meant. He pulled Lafe's torn, bloody trousers back around the wound and looked at Horatio and shook his head. "But he can't—" Horatio began. Then he looked at Lafe's stark white, blue-lipped face, and he knew it was true. He fell back on his heels with the shock of it. King spoke softly. "He's bled to death, Boss." That was what had happened. The sharp horn had pierced the femoral artery. Lafe's blood had drained from him as quickly as water can be poured from a pitcher.

It was a long time before Horatio looked up at Ada. She had heard. She knew. Her face was set and white. She was staring unbelievingly at Lafe's body. "He said for me to run an' he'd hold the bull," she said. "He said for me to run. He said for me to run." King stood up and took one of her hands gently. "Now, Missy," he said. "Now, Missy."

It was then that Horatio noticed one of the stable hands had snatched up a musket when he ran to answer the screams. He stood up and without a word held out his hand. The man surrendered the gun and Horatio looked to see that it was primed properly and turned toward the pasture. The bull was about twenty feet away, snorting and pawing as if debating whether to attack so many humans. Lafe's blood glistened on its head and shoulders and ran from the end of its nose. Horatio felt rage boil within him. He moved forward. He had not taken more than two steps when he heard Ada's voice. "No!" She walked forward, white-faced and cold-eyed, and took the gun from his hand. Before he could recover from his surprise, she was walking toward the snorting bull. She looked so small and frail with that huge black beast in the background that Horatio felt a tug of panic. He heard King call out, "Missy Ada. No, Missy." He fought down his own desire to shout, to overtake her and snatch the gun away. Instead, he followed her slowly. If she wanted to do this thing, he felt that he had no right to stop her.

It must have been surprise that kept the bull from charging. Or maybe it was disdain for this slight, white-faced creature. At any rate, it stood huffing and blowing and pawing at the ground, but making no other move. Ada walked to within three feet of where it stood. Her shoulders were straight and stiff. She raised the heavy musket slowly and pointed it directly at that huge, bloodstained head. There was a sharp crack. Black smoke poured from the barrel. For a long, tense moment Horatio thought she had missed. The bull shook its head slowly, but stood there with an evil gleam in its red-rimmed eyes. Then a bloody froth came cascading from its mouth. It bellowed and shuddered and fell to the ground. It kicked convulsively, trembled, and lay still.

Ada stood there as if in a trance. Then suddenly she threw the gun at the dead animal. Her voice was sharp. "You hellish beastie! You hellish beastie!" She put her hands to her face and began to sob. "Oh, Pa! Oh, Pa! Oh, poor Pa!"

Lafe's death left a void in all their lives, a void they couldn't fill. They missed his strong, willing hands when they worked. They missed his roaring enthusiasm. But most of all they missed his laughter. Horatio thought many times that long winter just how dull and spiritless so many things had become simply because Lafe was not there to throw back his great bearded head and laugh. Without him laughter seemed to have left Tench's Castle.

Ada still came every day to keep their records in her small, neat hand, but he saw very little of her. After the funeral he had asked her and her mother to come and live at the Castle. He had the feeling while he spoke that it was a useless request and he was making it rather clumsily. Both women had sat quietly until he finished, looking strangely alike in their long, black dresses, then, without looking at each other, they shook their heads. "We'uns ain't got no cause t' leave heah," the quiet Lena said.

"But you'll still come and keep the records, won't you, Ada?"

She had hesitated for a long time, and he felt something strangely like fear, but finally she nodded. "I'll come as long's you need me."

He had wanted to offer them money, but he knew that they would refuse. He had to be content with giving Lena the receipts for a wagonload of hogs after convincing them that Lafe had owned them personally.

He knew that life must be empty in their big, barny cabin, and Ada seemed to bring that emptiness to work with her. He went to nearby towns for pleasure many times that winter. It seemed that every time he returned, he read reprimand in her blue eyes. Once when she came upon him reading a scented note from a laughing young widow he had met in Decatur, he found himself blushing as furiously as a schoolboy. He folded the note quickly and held it in his hand while he answered some inquiry she made, but all the while she stood there he was conscious that the gay widow sprinkled her writing paper with a disgustingly lavish hand. He knew Ada could smell the perfume, too, but she gave no sign. She looked at him steadily, and suddenly he realized that she seemed unusually wan these days. There were light blue shadows around her eyes. "You're well, aren't you, Ada?" he asked.

"Yes," she said. She picked up her ledger and left the room without another word. He looked after her a moment, then shrugged in bewilderment, and turned back to the laughing lady's note. He saw the widow often that winter, but when spring came, like all the rest, she disappeared as quietly and completely as the ice floes in the river.

March was always his busiest month. For days at a time he worked the clock around. This was the month when the big, over-ripe brood mares turned their backs on the wind-swept fields and plodded into the stables to await their foaling time. They almost always foaled at night. A normal foaling was over in a few minutes, but a wrong presentation or a prolonged labor was always a serious matter. Many nights, while the cold March wind whistled around the stables, he bedded down beside a sweating, panting mare to be on hand when he was needed, or worked frantically in the light of a lantern to save a weak, long-legged foal or its dam after a difficult delivery.

It took patience and willingness and good temper. King assisted him whenever possible, but sometimes he was busy with his own stock and he had to depend on one of the heavy-handed, slow-footed workmen. Most of all, he liked to have Ada help him. The first time she assisted him had been an accident. Near dusk one afternoon he had come upon a mare in one of the stalls laboring before it was due. After ten minutes he realized he needed help. He began shouting for King. Ada was on her way home when she heard him. She came quickly, and after one swift glance was at his side, working competently and quickly. After that, he called on her often. He was astonished at how quickly she learned. She seemed to do instinctively what it had taken him years to learn.

He mentioned it to her one night while they were washing up after a particularly difficult delivery. She paused a moment, then smiled slightly. "Maybe it's because I'm a female beastie, too," she said.

His flush warmed his ears. He had forgotten what an intimate, lusty, peculiarly sensual thing birth could be. Through the years he had begun to think of his work in the foaling season as just another task like tipping yearlings or worming foals. It was different after that night, though. She helped him many more times, and he was glad to have her, but labor and birth became almost embarrassingly significant.

The same thing happened when the breeding began. Sometimes, when the men laughed and shouted, he flushed and shot a glance toward the Castle and wondered if she had heard.

By the beginning of May most of his work was finished. The mares and the foals had been turned out to the green pastures and there was nothing important at hand to claim his attention. He put aside his heavy, worn work clothes and brushed off his fancy waistcoats and dove-gray trousers that strapped under the instep of his English boots. He spent a week in Florence and another week in Athens. He drank champagne at Mademoiselle Renaud's gilt- and mirror-filled gentlemen's rest. His beautifully matched bays were often seen hitched outside Harriet Segall's quietly run house of repose. It was his only vacation of the year and he played as hard as he had worked. He was a handsome, prosperous man and there were many pleasures available. He grabbed at them all.

He returned to the Castle feeling quite at peace with the world. There was only one thing to bother him. Ada looked positively ill. The last dim spark of gaiety, which he had glimpsed now and then when they worked during foaling season, was gone. She was almost like a shadow around the Castle—shyer and more elusive than her mother even. She seemed to have lost weight. Her eyes were deepset and dark with shadows. Her appearance worried him, and he wanted to talk to her, to ask her if she was ill or worried, but her whole manner prevented it. Anyway, he saw her even less than usual. Sometimes for days at a time she wouldn't come near the Castle, but got all the information she needed from King at the pens and returned home to enter it in her ledger. At first he had not known this. When she didn't appear for several days, he saddled up and rode over to her home because he felt sure she was ill.

Lena was sitting on the veranda of the cabin. She shot Horatio one quick, shy glance and looked down at her hands folded in her lap.

"Ah don't know whar she's got ter—lef' heah 'bout an hour ago," she said in answer to Horatio's question.

"Is she well?" he asked.

Lena studied her hands. "Tol'ble, Ah reckon."

Horatio felt that he had to have some information about Ada's strange behavior. "I've noticed that she seems to be worried, Mrs. Mitchell. I almost never see her any more. Do you suppose there is something I could do or . . . ?" he faltered.

Lena sat so long without answering that he thought she was going to ignore his question. Finally, though, she spoke. "Eff'n yo' ain't knowed Ada long ernough ter know what's a-ailin' her, Ah reckon Ah can't holp yo'."

He didn't know what to say to such an answer, so after a short pause he told Lena good-by and turned his horse. Lena spoke again, more quickly. "She's roun' sommers—Why don't yo' ride up by that hick'ry grove on the hill?"

He found Ada there, sitting quietly under a huge scaly-bark hickory tree. She turned her head when he rode up, but he caught enough of a glimpse of her face to see that it was tear-stained. He felt a flood of tenderness toward her. He tried to keep his voice casual so as not to embarrass her. "I've been worried about you," he said.

She didn't look up. "I got all last week's figgers from King. The book's at the house if you want to see it."

"Oh, I wasn't worried about the books. I just wanted to make sure you were all right."

"I feel fine," she said without raising her eyes.

He made some small talk and then rode off, leaving her there. But all the way back to the Castle he was worried. Ada gave him the strangest feeling.

A week later he was seated at his desk when she entered quietly. As always, she had her ledger. "I didn't understand," she said. "Is William Kinsey takin' two fillies or three?"

"Three," Horatio said. "I'm going up to Florence on Saturday. I'll tell him they're ready."

Ada stiffened. "This Saturday?"

"Saturday morning."

Ada raised her head slowly and looked at him. Her lips began to tremble. She turned away quickly.

Horatio was alarmed. He stood up. "Why, Ada, what's wrong?"

She stopped, but kept her back turned. Looking at those straight, slight shoulders, he wanted to go up and put his arm around her. Instead he spoke gently, "Ada, what is it? Can you tell me what's bothering you? I'll do anything—you know that, Ada?"

She stood there for a long time, then turned slowly. Her head wasn't down now. She looked up in his face. Her own face was white.

"Anything?" she asked quietly.

"Why, of course, Ada—anything at all."

Her eyes never left his face. She swallowed. "You're a man of honor—of your word, aren't you, Mister Tench?"

He was surprised. What awful thing did she have to tell him? His first thought was that it had something to do with a man—she was in trouble because of a man. The thought of it infuriated him. "You know I'll keep my word to you, Ada."

Her eyes were still on his face. "You'll do what I ask you to do?"

"Yes," he said slowly, waiting with dread to hear her secret.

She hesitated for a long time; it seemed as if she couldn't speak, but then she threw back her shoulders and looked him straight in the eye. "Then, Mister Tench, I want you to marry up with me!"

For a moment Horatio was numb with surprise. He could only look at her blankly. Finally he began to recover. He even managed a weak laugh. "Why, Ada, you shouldn't . . ."

She was still looking straight into his eyes. Her face was pale and drawn. She spoke quickly, loudly. "I'm tired of waitin' an' sufferin'

an' standin' around an' hopin' you'll take some notice of me! I'm
tired of lovin' you an' havin' you look right past me! I've been
dyin' of the love for you ever since I was a little girl! I love you an'
I don't care who knows it! I'm tired of you goin' off week after
week, month after month, an' runnin' around with fancy women
an' never once lookin' at me an' knowin' mah heart is about to
break! I love you an' don't care who knows it! You said you'd
marry up with me an' now you have to do it! You said it! You
said it! You must do it! You just must!" Tears began to run from
her eyes and down her cheeks. She brushed them aside angrily.

Horatio stood transfixed before this outburst. He couldn't find
his voice until Ada turned her back and began to cry, with big
racking sobs. Even then he stammered. "Now, Ada . . ."

She had lost her heat but not her determination. "You're goin'
to marry with me," she sobbed. "You said you would an' you must
do it!"

He stood by helplessly until she stopped sobbing. He spoke
gently. "But, Ada, you're just a child. You're barely eighteen,
Ada."

She wheeled quickly. Her face was swollen and tear-stained but
her gaze was level. "I'm eighteen all right, but what gives you the
right to think I'm not a full-grown woman? I'm a full-grown
woman an' I think like a full-grown woman!"

"But, Ada, I'm thirty-three. I was a man when you were a little
girl!"

"That don't make no never mind! Lots of people get married up
with each other when there's more difference than that!"

"Now, Ada . . ."

She shook her head slowly. "I know you don't love me, Mister
Tench. I know you've never taken notice of me. But you need a
woman. You do. You do! I can cook an' I can mend clothes an' I
can keep books an' I can help you in the stables. I'll not bother
you." She looked determined again. "But you did promise to marry
with me! You promised it an' I aim to hold you to it!"

He didn't know what to say, so he only shook his head. It was
bewilderment. She thought it was refusal.

"You won't do it?"

He looked up slowly. He looked at her blue eyes, reddened from
weeping now but still beautiful. He looked at her straight little

nose. He noticed how firm her chin was even though it trembled a little. He looked at her straight shoulders. He knew what he must do. "Yes," he said quietly. "I think it would be an honor."

He had at last discovered why Ada bothered him.

They were married quietly three days later. Horatio had thought she would like to have a large wedding, but she refused because she said it would cause too long a delay. So, when they stood in the front room of the Castle, there was no one there except Lena and King and the stable hands and the old Methodist preacher from Arcadia. Lena was her usual shy, smiling self and the hands were a bit awkward and ill at ease. But King's broad grin split his face. He hadn't stopped smiling since the first night Horatio had embarrassedly stammered the news.

There wasn't much to remember about his wedding day. Through the years the details blurred and were forgotten. But one thing he remembered vividly until he died.

When at last they were alone and it was time to go to bed, he suddenly found himself once again feeling as if he were an adult and she was a child. He choked out something about her going on upstairs and he would follow her later. She started to go, but turned and came and stood before him. She smiled wisely and looked up into his face.

"I reckon it doesn't make much difference if you come on now," she said. "We don't have no secrets. I saw you that day on the island, too."

CHAPTER XXIII

SHE brought more than happiness to the Castle. She brought order. After years of indifferent housekeeping, the many corners and crannies of the big house were overflowing with boxes of worm medicines and liniments, crates of halters and surcingles and hundreds of masculine odds and ends which Horatio and King could not bring themselves to discard. She piled her blonde curls atop her head, armed herself with mop and broom, and attacked the rooms ferociously. She sent the medicines and the tack to the stable. She let Horatio and King paw over the broken boots and worn breeches and battered hats and rescue those they wanted, then she burned the rest. She polished furniture, washed drapes and curtains, and beat rugs. She flailed at cobwebs and mopped floors and scoured dishes. Horatio and King watched these labors with both dismay and embarrassment.

She grinned at them. "I do declare—you're nothin' but pack rats, both of you! This house hasn't had a good cleanin' since it was built."

She worked wonders. Within two weeks she had the Castle glistening from the ground floor to the parapet. King looked at the clean rooms and empty corners and shook his head and grunted. "A wife sho' do make er heap er differunce in er house."

Horatio grinned. "A house sho' do need a wife."

She came to him and put her hand on his arm lightly. "A wife sho' is glad!"

But if she worked wonders in the house, she stopped little short of a miracle in the kitchen. Their food had been noted more for its abundance than for its excellence. It was their custom to keep the heavy oaken table in the kitchen piled high with hams and roasts and preserves and relishes. Every morning King checked the three iron pots on the stove to see that they were filled with vegetables and sowbelly. After they began to simmer, they were pushed back on the stove where they stayed hot until the workmen found an opportunity to eat. King baked the meats and made the breads once a week.

She refuse to continue this haphazard method of feeding the hands. She served dinner at the Castle at noon-sharp, and the hands sat at the table and had huge fluffy biscuits and crumbly hot cornbread. They ate vegetables which did not have the life cooked out of them. And she baked cakes and pies and made gingerbread. She served piping hot coffee and cool buttermilk. The men smacked their lips over her cooking and treated her with a shy reverence.

It seemed impossible that she had any spare time, but she did. She couldn't bear to let Horatio out of her sight for more than an hour or two. If he couldn't return to the Castle from time to time during the day, she came out to find him. King would chuckle when he saw her coming across the fields or walking toward the stable. "Heah comes leetle boss a-huntin' big boss again." She just wanted to say hello and grin at Horatio or pat his arm lightly and look at him with adoration.

She went hunting with Horatio and King that fall, and they laughed heartily at her because she was gun shy and she always shut her eyes when she fired one of the muskets. In spite of this she managed to kill a dove one afternoon, and she ran forward to retrieve it with all the eagerness of a child. But when she picked it up, she took one look and her face melted and her eyes filled with tears. Horatio chided her gently. "Why, Ada, you've eaten doves all your life. They were Lafe's favorite game."

She held the bird in her hand and stroked its feathers. "I know, but I reckon I never knew they were so soft an' warm before. I always thought they were cold, stiff little beasties."

She was a source of never-ending wonder and delight. He was the center of her universe and sometimes it was almost frightening. Her words were as trite as the words of love usually are, but there was something fiercely intense about the way she said them. "I love you, Mister Tench, I love you more than anything." She meant it. She loved him more than anything. Not more than she loved anything else. Just more than anything. She was passionate, ardently, excessively—in the truest sense of the word which indiscriminate usage has somehow cheapened.

And what of his love? He loved her dearly, but it was a pale imitation of the emotion she had for him. He was not aware of this because, quite unconsciously, he compared his love for her with the spine-tingling emotion he had felt for Clover. It was years before he loved her as much as she loved him. And, lucky man, as a result he was able to love her more each year.

That first winter they went to Florence for a week of gaiety, but both of them were bored. He took her to the finest restaurants and he tried to shower her with new clothes, but she really wasn't interested and she sighed with relief and hugged him tight when, finally, they drove up the river road and saw the Castle in the distance. "We don't need anybody else, Mister Tench—just you an' me's enough."

He smiled. "Don't you want anybody else?"

She shook her head. "Nobody exceptin' King an' Ma when she comes to sit every day—an' the boys when they come."

He looked at her quickly. "Ada, you're not . . ."

She wrinkled her nose and shot him a teasing smile. "No, Mister Tench—but I'm goin' to set my mind to it, an' I reckon it won't be long."

Ada's first child, a boy, was born eleven months later. He was a husky, bawling baby with incredibly long legs and arms. A grizzled old horse trader who called at the farm a week after his birth watched those long limbs flailing the air with a grin. "Ah vum, ma'am," he said, "he's as leggy an' as rambunctious as a foal."

Ada grinned shyly. "I reckon he oughta be. He was born in a stall!"

It was the truth. She had been alone that quiet, bright day in May. The hands were at work in the fields making fences, and Horatio and King had gone to the neighboring farm to look over some shoats which were for sale. Horatio had hated to go, but Ada had scoffed at his worry. "It's near onto two weeks before I'm due," she said, adding with a teasing smile, "Anyway, what could you do?"

Horatio smiled. "You may be all right, but what about Nellie?"

Ada giggled. "Any mare that can jump an eight-foot fence don't need no help from you."

Nellie had furnished much of their amusement that spring. She was a docile old gray mare and one of the first horses Horatio had bought. She had been a placid matron even then. Twelve years of sunshine and rain, numerous breedings, and almost constant motherhood had wrung the strength from her old withers and swayed her back. When the teaser stallion had been brought near that spring, Nellie shot one contemptuous glance at his bold, bright eyes, snorted disgustedly, and waddled away. She did the same thing on several other occasions and she looked disdainfully at her tittering, excited younger sisters. Finally they decided that old age had claimed Nellie and they turned her out to pasture.

But sometime in the early summer the warm sunshine and the greening grass wrought a miracle in old Nellie. Her dull eyes lighted and the blood hummed through her worn veins and her tired heart began to beat in the two-step of the "Song of Spring." No one had known about this until one early morning when they found Nellie in the stable yard with the boldest, sleekest stallion on the farm. The fence was fully eight feet high and no one could understand how creaking, aged old Nellie had been able to surmount it. She probably wouldn't have told if she were able. There was a shrewd gleam in her eye when they turned her back to pasture.

Ada had a great fondness for Nellie. After Horatio left, she scraped and washed the breakfast dishes and put aside the scraps of bread to carry to Nellie later. She moved about deftly and lightly despite her advanced pregnancy. She carried her child high, and although her slight figure bulged enormously, she had felt almost no discomfort. Her well-being always astonished Lena when she came to the Castle on her daily visits. "Ah jes' don't know how yo' do it," she said. "Ah war a-moanin' an' a-wrenchin' right up to the day yo' was bawn. Ah reckon yo' was meant to be a ma."

This pleased Ada. The very thought of motherhood pleased her. Next to Horatio, she already loved the constantly stirring burden she carried more than anything. She talked as she moved about in the big empty house. "Now, stop your kickin' an' be a good boy, your ma's got work to do. Stop it, sir! Stop it, I say." She giggled.

Suddenly, astonishingly enough, the kicking had stopped. And the baby was quiet all the rest of that morning.

She thought about that when she left the Castle shortly after noon to walk down to give old Nellie the scraps. It was perplexing, but since she felt as well as usual, she decided it was only another of the unexplainable mysteries of pregnancy, and she put it from her mind. It was such a clear, sunshiny day that she decided that she would turn Nellie out into the yard for an hour or so.

But she found Nellie in no mood for either sunshine or exercise. She was in the first stages of labor and enduring it with the stolidness of experience. It was a normal birth and there was very little that Ada could do. However, she did stay with the old mare and, forgetful of her condition, made a half-dozen hurried trips to a trough in the yard to soak an old saddle blanket with which to rub down Nellie's sweating sides.

It was all over in an amazingly short time. While Nellie cleaned her wobbly-legged, trembling offspring, Ada filled the manger with cut feed from a nearby bin. "Now, you eat it every bit," she said, smiling, "I reckon you earned it this day." She had scarcely spoken when the first pain struck. It was a searing, jolting pain that rocked her from head to foot. Her first thought was that her labor had started, but then she knew this couldn't be true. Everyone had said that her first pains would be light, more like a pressure than a pain.

The thought had hardly crossed her mind when the pain struck again. It left her gasping and weak-kneed. She held to the side of the stall. She was panic-stricken. How was she ever to get to the fields to shout for the workmen to call the doctor or her mother?

She started toward the door. Another pain racked her, left her momentarily blinded and staggering. Then another pain. She knew she couldn't get help now. There was a stall three feet away, a soft stall, piled high with hay. She reached it just as another pain struck. Her knees gave way. She lay back panting, her head whirling with pain and panic. Another pain. She set her chin firmly. "If ole Nellie can do it, I reckon I can," she thought.

She could and she did. After it was over, she wrapped her howling pink son in her petticoat and carried him to the Castle. When Horatio and King returned late in the afternoon, he was sleeping peacefully in the deep oaken cradle King had made. And Ada, the smiling Ada, had a hot supper waiting on the back of the stove.

They named their son Aber. Horatio had never thought of him as anything else, for Ada would not let him consider the thought that she might have a girl. He had been hesitant, almost apologetic when he first mentioned the name. "I know you would like to name him after your father, Ada, but . . ."

She looked at him solemnly. "He's your young'un, Mister Tench, an' you name him what you want. We'll call him Aber—little Aber."

Horatio smiled thoughtfully. "No, dear, he'll be Big Aber."

She looked at him curiously a moment, then shot him one of her teasing, sidelong grins. "All right—Big Aber—an' don't worry, we'll get a baby for Pa. We'll get lots of babies. There's plenty more where this one comes from."

Ada. How could he tell her how much he loved her?

Big Aber was a laughing child. He had his mother's hair and coloring, but he was built like Horatio. His long arms and legs became chubby, then slimmed again. It seemed no time at all before he could run squealing about the Castle, before he was clambering all over King and riding piggie-back on a tour of the stables and barns, before he rode in the saddle with Horatio. The neighbors smiled when the pair came by, the huge, handsome man and his handsome little son. "That young'un forked a hawss afore he could walk," they said. It was King who first started calling him Big Ab, and finally this became something that sounded like "Bigab."

Bigab was three when his flame-haired brother was born. This was Lafe. And after Lafe came Horatio. This was Hoe. And after Hoe came Young King. Tongues clacked about this, evil, mean tongues, but never where they could be heard by the happy family that lived in the Castle.

Where did the years go? How could time crawl for part of a man's life, then suddenly roar past, each year trampling on the heels of the next until it seemed he could only snatch a memory here and there? How could one year, two years, three years—a dozen years pass and leave nothing in their wake except a handful of memories that weren't memories at all, only a few bright colors against a background of peace and deep and abiding happiness?

Horatio couldn't understand until . . .

CHAPTER XXIV

THEY climbed the hill slowly, Horatio and King. It was early spring and somewhere in the woods behind them a mockingbird was warbling for a mate. Below them stretched the bright green fields, crisscrossed with white fences and dotted thickly with heavy mares and fat, placid cattle. In one of the fields the boys were clustered around a yearling, and very faintly they could hear their squeals and yells as they dared each other to try to ride it. In the distance, against the backdrop of the silver river and the blue sky, the Castle stood like a watchful sentinel.

King stood looking at the scene a long time before he spoke. His voice was thoughtful. "Ah don't know jes' how ter figger dat, Boss. Ah've studied on it a long time mahself. Ah reckon it's jes' de way things is. Ah do know dis, though. Ah know lots er folks nevah learns dat time passes by a heap quicker eff'n dey fines demself somethin' ter do an' den does it. Ah means do somethin' simple-like, like plowin' dem some groun' er raisin' dem some chillun.

"It ain't de troublesome times dat goes by fast. Dey jes' drag an' drag an' seem lak dey nevah ain't gonna git pas'. It's lak Ah 'members wut ole Zeke usta tell us when we was chillun. Ole Zeke war a wise man, Ah reckon. He learnt hisself ter read an' ever' night we usta sit 'round while he read us a chapter outta de Good Book. Sometime ole Zeke usta turn some pages wifout readin' 'em an' he'd allus say, 'Ain't no use tellin' yo' chil'lun dis part 'cause all dey's a-doin' now is begattin'. Dis 'un air begattin' dat 'un, an' dat 'un air begattin' dis 'un an' ernuther 'un is begattin' ernuther 'un.

We ain't got no mind ter 'member dese folks 'cause dey didn't do nuthin' 'cept begat.'

"Ah reckon ole Zeke knowed wut he war a-doin' an' Ah reckon der man who put it down 'bout dose folks knowed wut he was a-doin', too. Mos' likely dey war like ever'body else 'cept dat nuthin' much ever happened ter 'em. Mos' likely dere Pa give 'em some groun' an' dey plowed it an' built 'em a house an' jes' set back an' begat. Dey didn't have a lotta troubles ter speak 'bout, so when de man come erlong ter write 'em down, he couldn't fine nuthin' ter say.

"Ah reckon de same thing is happen' ter yo', Boss. Dere was a lot ter say 'bout yo' ter begin wif. Mebbe dey will be a lot ter say 'bout yo' later on. But right now ever'thin' is jes' easy an' smooth, an' eff'n a man come erlong ter say somethin' 'bout yo', mos' likely all he could say war dat yo' war begattin'.

"It's jes' a short chapter, Boss. It's jes' a short chapter."

THE PATRIARCH

CHAPTER XXV

EVERY morning, rain or shine, summer or winter, he walked in his courtyard. He could not understand people who stayed indoors while the sun was rising. It was the best time of day for him. He liked to stand with his strong long legs wide apart and draw the freshness of morning deep in his lungs. He liked the nip of frost against his bearded face and the taste of dawn mist on his lips. He liked the smell of his land while dew was still on it.

He threw back his head and breathed deeply. It was a heady odor and, familiar as it was, it always gave him a feeling of pleasure. He could smell the damp earth in the unplanted fields and the sourish odor of stacked fodder and, strongest of all, the pungent, caustic scent of horses and stables.

He was sixty-one, but age had scarcely marked him. He was straight of back and flat of belly. His happy years had dimmed the fierce light in his eyes, but they had etched his face with lines of vigor and force. He had a strong face. It was a summing-up of the man. No longer did men look at him and wonder what personality went with his massive frame and thews. They knew at a glance.

It was good he lived in a castle. He had become the kind of a man who needed a castle. An ordinary house would have imprisoned him. And he was too rugged and weather-cured for the polished floors and brocades of a plantation manor. He needed a house of stone—a strong, solid home without fripperies. There was no weakness about him, unless, perhaps, his beard showed his vanity. He had always followed fashion. When men began to grow hair on their faces, he not only joined them but outdid most of them. He had a great beard, a curly, fiery mane. He was proud of it. He trimmed it himself and anointed it with rose oil and burnished it with daily brushings.

This morning as he stood in his courtyard, he was vaguely troubled. For the past few mornings he had awakened with a nagging little feeling of unrest, almost uneasiness. It was hard to define. It was almost the way he had felt when he was a boy and began a new day in Samuel Tompkins' shop.

He took a deep breath and walked slowly. But that was foolish. What did he have to worry about? Maybe it was all this talk of war . . . this business of setting up a new government. He snorted. Nonsense! There was always something like this. Once it was "Fifty-Four-Forty or Fight," then a lot of fools shouting "Remember the Alamo." He snorted again. Let them fight. He wasn't a slaveholder and he didn't—He stopped and fingered a slender branch of the small plum tree that grew next the wall. It was covered with half-opened buds. He smiled. Spring was definitely on the way. He would be glad to see it. Everything was always better in the spring.

Maybe it was age that made him feel this way? He took another deep breath and slapped his flat stomach. No, that wasn't it. He smiled. He had thought of that because spring had reminded him of King. All winter long King had been saying that his rheumatism would disappear with spring. No, he wasn't getting old. King was —my God!—he paused for the little grunt that was habitual when he realized King was within a few years of eighty. Eighty! He shook his head and grunted again.

Well, sixty-one wasn't exactly young. Everybody called John Brown *old* John Brown. He called him that himself although they were almost the same age. Maybe that was one reason that crazy old man's death had affected him so strangely. The account of how that old man had shuffled to the gallows in his baggy suit and carpet slippers made—But leave those things to the politicians. He took another deep breath and sighed.

It could be that he was beginning to feel his age after all. Maybe it crept up so gradually that a man didn't realize it? Something like—well . . . like this courtyard had changed. He looked around at the hard, smooth ground and smiled. That first year he and Ada married, it was green with grass and thick with flowers. The boys had attended to that. They had trampled the flowers and worn down the grass so gradually that almost nobody remembered them. He chuckled. That reminded him of the day Judge Davis and his wife had come out to buy a colt. Plump Mrs. Davis had taken one look at the courtyard and thrown up her hands. "Why, my dear," she told Ada, "you should plant grass in here. It would be lovely."

And what had Ada said? The memory of it made him laugh. Ada said, "Well, I tell you, Mrs. Davis, we're growin' boys—not grass."

B'fair, they had grown boys too. Man to man, he'd put his boys up against . . .

"Mister Tench, what's makin' you so pokey this mornin'?"

It was Ada. She had walked up behind him. She was still as slim as a girl, but her blonde hair had darkened and was streaked with gray. He turned and smiled at her.

"Come here, Ada."

Ada looked at him severely. "Now, Mister Tench, ever'thin's gettin' cold on the table."

"I know, Ada. I know. Come here a minute."

Ada approached slowly, looking at him suspiciously. Horatio grinned. Raising four boys had taught Ada to be on guard against pranks. He looked at her trim figure and her unlined face and he was filled with a great tenderness. Ada hadn't changed one . . . but, yes, she had. Ada grew more beautiful every year. Or was it because he loved her more each year? He waited until she stood before him.

"Ada, look at me. Do I look like an old man to you?"

She smiled slowly, then cocked her head. "Turn 'round."

He turned slowly. Ada giggled. "I knew it! I knew it! When I heard that rain crow this mornin', I knew the sap was a-risin' in all the ole trees."

He grabbed her in a bear hug and she squealed with laughter. They went in to breakfast, still laughing, and arm in arm.

Bigab and Lafe were already at the table when Ada and Horatio entered. They looked up and smiled. Bigab raised an eyebrow. "Who's that filly the ole man's got, Lafe?"

Lafe shook his head slowly. "Beats me. Looks like a Memphis woman."

They arose grinning while Horatio took his seat at the head of the table. It was something Ada had taught them when they were children. Horatio smiled at them. He was proud of these two. Any stranger could have told they were brothers and that he was their father. They were both big men, about the same size, and only an inch or so shorter than Horatio. Lafe was red-headed and Bigab was a blond, but they had the same build, the same open, handsome faces. Between them they actually ran the farm.

"Haying today?" he asked.

Bigab nodded. "Looks like it."

Horatio looked at the two empty chairs at the table. "Where are the other boys?"

Ada bustled in from the kitchen and placed a plate of eggs and ham and grits in front of him. "Hoe's with King. I fixed up a double tray an' they're eatin' together."

"Where's Young King?"

There was a short silence. The boys exchanged glances with Ada. Finally Lafe smiled slowly. "Where would yo' guess, Pa?"

Horatio frowned with annoyance. "Still in bed?"

Ada spoke quickly. "He was readin' till real late las' night, Mister Tench."

Horatio's voice was stern. "That makes no difference." He looked at Bigab and Lafe. "You're the ones who'll be short-handed. What do you let him get away with it for?"

Lafe looked down at his plate and rubbed his cheek thoughtfully. "Well, Ah reckon it's mah fault, Pa. Ah looked in that new book of his las' night an' Ah figgered—well, Ah reckon Ah figgered any durn fool can pitch hay but a man's gotta have a lotta brains to understan' that book."

Horatio looked sternly at all their sober faces, then shrugged and sighed. "Well, hustle him up if you need him. Let Hoe keep King company for a while, though. King gets pretty lonesome and his rheumatism isn't any better."

An hour later he was in his room dressing for his weekly trip to the store to get supplies when he heard Young King clumping downstairs to breakfast. He shook his head and sighed. Young King puzzled him—and yet he also gave him a feeling of pride. He couldn't understand that. He felt he understood Lafe and Bigab perfectly. They were like he was. But Young King—he sighed again and smoothed his beard down against the bosom of his starched white shirt.

It wasn't that Young King was merely lazy. Hoe—now he was the lazy one. He ducked work every chance he found. But labor, any hard, sweaty labor actually seemed to pain Young King. Once when they were cutting oats, Young King worked with such evident misery that he had tried to draw him out. Young King hadn't been able to make him understand. All he could say was, "It's such a foolish way to earn a living. I don't like to do this kind of work."

It was a mystery. If Young King did nothing but spend time with his books, perhaps he could understand. But he wasn't a moody, retiring boy at all. And he was handsome, even if he was the smallest of the boys and the only one who wasn't a blond. He had brown hair like Lafe Mitchell, and he also had some of Lafe's exuberance. He was the only one of the boys who seemed to be interested in girls and social activities. He was a good shot, too, and he loved hunting. That was something else about Young King. When he became interested in something, he didn't rest until he was an expert. He was the first one of the boys to order one of the new breech-loading rifles from Pittsburgh. And he knew everything about calibers and cartridges and powder weights.

Horatio grunted and put his heavy gold watch in his pocket and looped the chain across the front of his vest. At first he had thought Young King might be a professional man, maybe a doctor or lawyer or even an Army officer. But he showed no interest. He finished Haynes' Seminary like his brothers, then showed no more interest in school. Well, he was young yet—only . . . only nineteen. Why, that made Bigab twenty-six . . . and Lafe twenty-three . . . and Hoe twenty. He grunted. Time *was* passing.

Still, he felt very fit as he crossed the courtyard to pay King a visit before he left the house. He had the stride of a man of twenty. And, definitely, King did not look as if he was in the shadow of eighty. He was seated in the sunshine by the window. Hoe was with him. A checkerboard was spread over their knees. Horatio smiled. They were inseparable, these two. King had been a second father to all the boys, but he and Hoe seemed to have a special understanding. It had always been that way. From the time he was a toddler until he was about fourteen, Hoe had slept with King. He was twenty now and a six-footer. A flush covered his handsome, freckled face when he saw Horatio. "Ah'm goin' to hep the boys with the hayin' right after this game, Pa."

King snorted. "Wut yo' tellin' yo' Pa dat lie fer? Yo' ain't fixin' ter go near dat barn less'n Ah jes' won't play yo' no mo'."

Hoe grinned sheepishly while Horatio and King laughed.

King's hair and bushy brows were snow white and age had weighed his broad shoulders a little, but otherwise he was the same alert, smiling man. Up until that winter he had never missed a day's work. Around Christmas a severe attack of rheumatism had forced him to go to bed for two weeks and since then he had hobbled around with a cane. For the past two weeks he had stayed close to his room because of the dampness of the weather. But as he sat laughing in the sunlight streaming through the window, it seemed to Horatio that he was greatly improved. Apparently he was. He grinned and pointed to the window. "Ah tole yo' all Ah needed was a little sunshine. Ah ain't had er ache all mawnin'. Dis heah weather keeps up an' me'n Hoe go git us a mess o' fish down at de ribber."

Hoe looked at him scoffingly. "What about that pain in yo' side. Tell Pa about that."

King looked indignant. "Dat war a cotch in mah side. Ain't yo' nebber had no cotch in yo' side when yo' stood up too quick."

Horatio smiled at him fondly and shook his head. "Just the same, as soon as it gets warmer I'm driving you in to Florence to let the doctor look you over again."

King grinned. "Ah don't need no doctor. Dis heah sunshine's all de doctor Ah need. Two or three more days liks dis an' Ah'll be chuckin' dis ole stick away."

The sunshine was wonderful. As Horatio drove down the river road in the buggy, he could feel its heat against the back of his neck. He clucked his roan along at a trot, but when he reached Lafe Mitchell's old cabin site, he reined up and passed by slowly. There was only a chimney of Lafe's old cabin standing. It had burned sixteen years before. That was two winters after Lena died. Up until the last, she refused to come live with them. Horatio never got to know Lena. He shook his head and looked puzzled when he thought of her now. She had died of pneumonia as quietly and as calmly as she had lived.

Horatio clucked his horse back into a trot. The sight of that old chimney standing so forlornly in the bare field always gave him a feeling of sadness. He had always been sorry that he had allowed Ada to sell Lafe's farm to Squire Allison. Still, he had to admit it was a good price and he didn't have any use for the land. Besides, Allison already had bought out nearly everybody else and had already started building his big house. Actually, Allison hadn't been a bad neighbor. He had never bothered them and there was nothing he could complain about. All the same, he didn't care too much for the man. He was too soft-spoken, too ready to smile—too much like General Jameson. He was like General Jameson in many ways. He had the same elegance and he had built a big rambling old manor which was called Brierwood. Then, too, he had slaves— nearly a hundred of them. They were thick around his grounds, and during the planting and picking season they could be heard singing as far away as the Castle.

Maybe he didn't care for Allison because he was a slaveholder? He thought about that a while and shook his head. No, that wasn't it. Apparently he treated his Negroes well—he had never heard anything to the contrary. He frowned. He wasn't so sure about Jeb Allison. No, he definitely didn't like the squire's son. His hair was just a little too long and curly. He smiled just a little too recklessly. His hand was just a little too heavy and brutal when he rode his spirited horses. That reminded him he hadn't seen Jeb in some time. He seemed to have a vague recollection that one of the boys said he was raising militia for this new government. He grunted. It was just the sort of thing the man would do. Well, he'd be home soon . . . soon as old Jeff Davis and this new man Lincoln stopped glaring at each other and made an agreement.

It made him almost angry. It was people like the Allisons and the Jamesons who were causing all this bickering. He was sorry that Allison had ever moved in. He liked it much better when all this territory had been broken up into small farms, all good, honest people working their own ground. He wished—he stopped and grinned. By God, he was getting old. What was it King said? "When a man keeps sayin' things ain't as good as dey usta be—he jes' means he ain't."

Old Marius Henshaw was nearing ninety and almost too feeble and flabby to navigate, but he still kept a watchful eye on his store. He was sitting on the front porch, soaking up the sunshine and dozing, when Horatio drove up. Horatio grinned and tied his horse at the crowded hitching post. He mounted the steps before old Marius saw him. "Glad yo' fin'lly come erlong, Mistah Tench. Been sittin' heah all day, hopin' a smart man'd come erlong." He waved disgustedly at the door of his store. "Lissen ter all that carnsarn bellerin' a-goin' on in thar. Eff'n Ah warn't a poor man an' needed yore money, Ah'd tell yo' ter go somewhar else."

Horatio smiled. He could hear a man speaking loudly in the store. "Sounds like a regular Saturday afternoon to me, Marius."

Old Marius grunted. "Secesh! Secesh! Ain't heered nothin' else all day long! Go on in, Mistah Tench. Charlie'll hustle up yo' order. Mebbe they'll hesh up that noise when they see yo'."

There was the usual Saturday crowd in the store. More than a dozen men were lounging around on boxes and barrels, spitting and whittling. A tall man stood in the center of the floor, speaking hotly. Horatio was well in the doorway before he saw it was Jeb Allison. But such a Jeb! His tall, raw-boned figure was resplendent in a uniform of gray and gold. A gleaming sword hung from a gold sash around his waist. He wore a wide-brimmed hat and he had grown fluffy side whiskers. He was pointing an angry finger at the faces around him. "An' what'll we do? Ah'll tell yo' what we'll do —we'll run ever' dam' one of 'em right back up there where they belong! They don't stand a chancet once we—" He stopped when his eyes fell on Horatio. He lowered his finger and smiled. His voice was half-jeering. "This heah's Confederate territory, Mistah Tench. Be sure yo' got the password."

There was a chuckle from the men around the store. Horatio smiled and nodded to them as he made his way to the counter. He didn't look at Jeb Allison.

Jeb was not to be ignored. His voice still had that jeering note. "Yo' boys joined up yet, Mistah Tench?"

Horatio turned and eyed him levelly. "Joined what?"

Jeb colored. "Why, the Army, man. What'd yo' reckon?"

Horatio's voice was calm. "No, the boys are at home."

"They aim to join, don't they?"

Horatio said, "I haven't heard them speak of it." He smiled at the clerk and handed him a list Ada had made out. "I'll be looking around while you fill this," he said. Without looking at Jeb Allison, he walked to the back of the store and began scanning the shelves.

He liked to rummage around old Marius' big store, and within a few minutes he had forgotten Jeb Allison and the heated discussion in the front of the store. He found a new well rope, a half-dozen heavy staples for the south pasture gate, and he picked up four heavy spikes to nail an overhead beam in the stable. By the time the clerk called to him that his order was ready, he had found a half-dozen other small items, including a heavy wooden milk pail.

He returned to the counter and put his purchases with his other supplies. Jeb Allison folded his long arms across his chest and leaned back against the counter a few feet away. He wore the same half-jeering smile. "Ah'm sorry to hear yo' boys aren't goin' to the war, Mistah Tench."

Horatio looked at him with annoyance. "What war?"

Jeb feigned amazement. "My God, man, we'll be fightin' any minute now." He eyed Horatio closely. "Ah take it yo' don't hol' with fightin' the dam' Yankees, Mistah Tench."

"No." Horatio turned his back.

Jeb's voice was derisive. "Then yo' want the dam Yanks to tell yo' what to do!"

Horatio hesitated a moment, as if making up his mind about something, then he turned slowly. His voice was calm. "Young man, I don't want anybody to tell me what to do. This trouble doesn't concern me. I don't own slaves and I don't intend to buy any. I'm against slavery."

Jeb's smile was thinner. "Yo' don't aim to John Brown us, do yo', Mistah Tench?"

Horatio looked at him sternly. "What do ye mean by that? I've lived near your father for years now and I've never interfered with the way he runs his farm. What he does is his business. I have work enough to keep me busy on my own place."

One of the men spoke up. "What about State's Rights, Mistah Tench?"

Horatio faced the men in the store. He spoke slowly. "I don't know everything about this trouble. I've tried to follow it as well as I could, but there are some points I may have missed. As I see it, nobody is trying to take away any of your rights. Even slaveholders haven't been asked to free their people. From what I've read, it seems that every guarantee has been made that they won't take away a man's rights to own slaves in the states where slavery is now in force." He scowled. "But why does that concern us? Not a man in this store except Allison here owns slaves." His eyes swept their faces. "I've known most of you for years, and I know that you don't intend to buy slaves—so why does this cause you trouble? It's nonsense!"

Jeb Allison drew himself up stiffly. His voice was sharp. "Yo' have a right to yore opinion, Mistah Tench, but Ah'd advise you to use discretion."

Horatio snorted. "I'm glad, young man, that you think there's somebody left who still has discretion." He turned back to the counter.

The men in the store roared with laughter. Jeb's face was pale with rage. "That's the kind o' talk yo'd expect from a man who lets a black nigger sit at his table and ack like one of the family! He even named one of his kids after that black nigger!"

Horatio's shoulders stiffened, but he didn't turn. One of the men put a hand on Jeb's arm. He shook it off angrily. "Leave me alone. Ah oughta teach the ole booger a lesson." He snarled, "Yo' gotta notion niggers are as good as we are, haven't yo', Mistah Tench?"

Horatio eyed him contemptuously. "I know one who's better than some people I can name."

Jeb trembled with rage. "Yo' hear the old booger! Yo' hear him! He lives with a nigger an' sits at the table with him! Ah don't see how he's sure he's the pappy of all them children he's got!"

The wooden milk pail was on the counter right in front of Horatio, but it was incredible that he could pick it up so quickly. It was a blur as it flashed through the air and struck Jeb directly in the face. Jeb fell backward over a sack of dried beans and hit the floor as if poleaxed. Horatio stepped forward and swung his arm again before he realized the handle had broken from the bucket. He doubled his fist, but two men stepped between him and Jeb. "Now, now, Mistah Tench," one of them said. Horatio's face was white and his chest was heaving. It took all of their strength to push him back.

Jeb lay on the floor a moment, then sat up and shook his head dazedly. There was a dull, red spot in the center of his forehead and blood was trickling from his nose. He lifted a hand slowly and felt his face before his eyes began to clear. He arose trembling with anger. His voice was shrill. "Why, yo' ole booger, Ah'm goin' to . . ."

Horatio pushed the men aside and raised his right fist. Jeb took a step forward, then halted and pulled at the handle of his sword.

"No, yo' don't, yo' young scannel!" Old Marius stood in the doorway, his flabby frame quivering with indignation. He had grabbed a long hay fork from a nearby rack and he waved it menacingly. "Git outta mah store or Ah'll drain the meanness outta yo' wuthless hide!"

Jeb stopped and looked at Horatio with blazing eyes. "Ah'll git yo' for this. We'll hang folks like yo' before long." He stooped and retrieved his wide-brimmed gray hat and brushed at his uniform.

"Git outta heah!" Marius commanded.

Jeb eyed him coldly and walked toward the door. "An' yo'll be sorry for this, too. Hell will freeze ovah before another Allison ever comes in heah to trade."

Old Marius snorted and made a jabbing motion with the fork. "Git! Yo' ain't no customer o' mine. Yo' wouldn't be in heah now eff'n yo' warn't killin' time while yo' hawss war bein' shod."

CHAPTER XXVI

OUTSIDE the April day was coming to a close. From his desk near the study window, Horatio could lift his head and see shadows creeping across the courtyard. A couple of robins were settling down noisily among the pink blossoms in the peach tree, and far off he could hear the lowing of a cow.

He looked up when Ada entered the room. Her face was worried. "Have you seen King, Mister Tench?"

Horatio shook his head. "Why, no, Ada—not since he left to go fishing."

Ada crossed to the window and looked out toward the gate. "Well, he hasn't come back yet, Mister Tench, an' he shouldn't be out in the cool air."

Horatio smiled at her and closed his ledger. "Don't fret, Ada. Maybe he's down with the boys. I'll go take a look."

Ada sighed exasperatedly. "If he is, Mister Tench, yo' tell him I'm goin' to get him good. He knows he's not well enough to be runnin' 'round like this."

Horatio chuckled. "I'll tell him you said so, Ada, but I don't think he'll believe it."

He was still smiling as he walked toward the barn in the gathering dusk. The past week had been warm and sunny and King had recovered rapidly. He still shuffled a little because of stiffness in his joints but he had laid his cane aside. It had taken all Horatio's persuasion to keep him from helping the boys with the work. But neither he nor Ada could convince him that he should stay off the damp river bank. King snorted indignantly. "Ain't wet whar Ah go. Ain't wet a-tall! Does mah bones good ter git out." Every afternoon he took his cane pole and a box of worms and shuffled off fishing.

At the barn the boys had knocked off work and were washing up in one of the troughs. They had not seen King. Hoe grinned and slipped on his shirt. "Ah know where he goes, Pa. Ah'll go down there an' fetch him on."

It was dark and the lamps had been lit when Hoe returned. Horatio and the boys were in the sitting room and Ada was in the kitchen preparing supper. Hoe entered with a grin. "Where's that ole scamp? Lawdy, after all he's told me, he went off an' left his pole jes' a-hangin' . . ." His grin flickered out when he saw their faces. "Ain't he heah?" he asked quickly.

For the first time Horatio felt a stab of uneasiness. He stood up slowly. Ada had come to the door when she heard Hoe enter. She spoke quietly. "You mean you didn't find him, son?"

Hoe shook his head bewilderedly. "No'm. His pole was stuck in the bank an' Ah thought it was funny he didn't have it pegged down like he aimed to leave it there. He always . . ."

"Go see if he's in his room, son," Horatio said.

Hoe was back in less than a minute. His face was pale under his freckles. "He ain't there, Pa."

Ada's little gasp was almost a moan. "Oh, Mister Tench."

Horatio spoke with an assurance he didn't feel. "Now, now, Ada, there's nothing to worry about. Just put supper in the oven and keep it hot." He spoke to Young King. "Son, go to the barn and fetch us some lanterns."

A chilly, gray mist was rising from the river bank. In the yellow glow cast by their lanterns, Hoe kneeled and pointed to a small round hole in the clay. "Right heah's where his pole was stuck, Pa."

Horatio held his lantern high and stepped back. His foot struck something and he looked down. It was King's worm box. "This is the place all right, son," he said. He tried to keep his voice calm, but ever since they had left the castle, shouting for King as they walked, he had been tight with worry. He swung his lantern so the light swept the sparse growth of cocklebur weeds and buckeye bushes on the bank. He knew this place well and he felt relieved. At least there was no danger that King had toppled into the river and been swept away. To check his memory he walked a few feet and looked down. He was right. The banks sloped gently here and the river moved past sluggishly. His voice was thoughtful. "Maybe King had another pole and went off somewhere. . . ."

Hoe shook his head emphatically. "No, he didn't, Pa. He always came heah 'cause he could follow the road most of the way. It hurt his rheumatiz to walk over rough ground."

Horatio felt a new surge of relief. The road passed within fifty yards of where they stood and was separated from the river by a small, rocky field. There was mild reprimand in his voice. "You should have looked on the road first thing, son. You and Young King go do it now. The rest of us will look around here. Holler as you go."

As Hoe and Young King moved off shouting, he turned to Lafe and Bigab. "Now, let's scatter out and search the bank good. He may have crawled in the bushes somewhere and gone to sleep or . . ." He swallowed and left the sentence hanging.

For a half-hour they crossed and recrossed every inch of the area along the bank. They trampled a small blackberry bramble flat and circled the small field between the road and the bank, swinging their lanterns in wide arcs and shouting as they went. In the distance, Young King and Hoe echoed them. "King! Yea, King! King!"

Horatio was in a far corner of the field, trampling through a thicket of slender wild plum, when he noticed the lanterns Hoe and Young King carried bobbing back down the road. At the edge of the field they halted for a long time, moved forward slowly, stopped again. Horatio was about to call to them when Young King shouted, "Come heah, Pa!"

Bigab and Lafe also heard the shout. They all gathered quickly. Young King pointed to the ground. "They's fresh hoof marks leading through heah, Pa. We noticed them first up where they left the road." He swung his lantern and pointed a few feet away. "Over there's where they came out again."

Horatio knelt and examined the horseshoe prints. There was no doubt that they were made recently. "Looks like several horses," he said.

Hoe nodded. "We make out three."

Horatio straightened up. "Well, let's see where they went."

They followed the trail across the field easily. It led to within three feet of where King's pole had been sticking in the bank. Up to that point the U-shaped marks were clear and distinct, but then they widened out in a welter of churned earth. Hoe looked up slowly, his young face tense. "They was heah all right. They saw King."

Lafe examined the marks closely and shook his head. "Can't tell much by these—nothin' 'cept one of the hawsses has jes' been shod."

Horatio felt a tightness in his throat. He dropped to one knee quickly. "Are you sure, son."

Lafe shrugged. "Look for yo'self."

Horatio looked at the mark Lafe outlined with his finger. There was no doubt about it. It was clear and distinct and the shoe that made it had sharp, unworn edges.

He set his jaw and his voice had a ragged edge. "Hoe, I want you to run down to Squire Allison's. See if marks like these come from his place."

The boys exchanged glances and Hoe stood up. His nostrils flared. "All right, Pa."

They sat on the bank, silent and grim-faced, while Hoe was gone. He was back in a surprisingly short time, breathless and wet with sweat. His face was pale. "You're right, Pa. They came outta the Squire's gate."

Horatio's great bearded face was set and cold in the yellowish light from the lanterns. "We'll go up to the Castle first. I want to get something before we go to the Squire's."

Squire Allison was a slender, elegant man with a small tufted beard under his bottom lip. He was frigidly polite when he received them in his book-lined study. "What can I do for you, gentlemen?"

Horatio held his rifle in the crook of his arm. His voice was cold. "Our business was with Jeb, Squire, but I understand he isn't at home."

The Squire nodded curtly. "Mah son left early this afternoon to rejoin his regiment. They march at midnight."

"Was he alone."

The Squire lifted his brows slightly. "Why, no. Two of his men joined him heah and they left together. May I ask why you are interested?"

Horatio's gaze was level. "My friend, King, has disappeared, and we have reason to believe that Jeb saw him last. He may have taken him with him but, anyway, he knows what happened to King."

The Squire's lips curled slightly. "Surely you are mistaken, sir. Why would my son want to be delayed by an old nigrah man?"

Hoe stepped forward and spoke hotly. "There ain't no mistake! Jeb saw King an' if he did anything to him, I'm goin' to kill him! I'm goin' to kill him!"

Squire Allison stiffened and drew himself erect. "My son is not at home to speak for himself, young man. When he returns, I know he'll give you any kind of satisfaction you demand." He looked at Horatio. "If there's nothing else, I'll ask you to excuse me."

Horatio's voice was tight. "There's nothing else—at this time."

They left the house silently and were almost to the gate before Hoe spoke. He was on the verge of tears. "Ah think he's right 'bout one thing. Ah don't think Jeb took King with him. Ah think he did something to him. Ah believe King's 'round heah somewhere an' Ah'm goin' to find him. Ah'm goin' to find him if Ah have to look all night. Ah am! Ah'm goin' to look for him some more!"

Horatio placed his arm around Hoe's shoulders. "We all are, son."

They searched through most of the night, walking the river bank and scouring pine thickets and tramping through brier patches and shouting themselves hoarse. And it was just before morning when Hoe finally found King. He was in the river after all, within five feet of where they had found his pole. His head and shoulders were resting in a small gulley in the bank and the rest of his body was submerged in the cold, yellow river.

They came running when they heard Hoe's frantic shouts. When Horatio first saw King, stretched out cold and stiff with his calm black face gone gray, he was trembly with fear. He stripped back his wet clothing and put his hand on his icy chest and almost cried when he caught the faint beat of his heart.

They took off his wet clothes and wrapped him in their coats and carried him back to the Castle and massaged his cold limbs, and, gradually, some heat came back into his body. But they could not revive him.

It wasn't until Ada washed the mud from his face that they saw the livid welt that extended from one cheek to the other across his broad nose. They knew what it was immediately. They had been around horses too long not to recognize the mark a braided leather quirt left on flesh.

When Hoe saw it, he seemed to go mad. He straightened up with a sob and his eyes were blazing. "What are yo' waitin' for? Are yo' cowards? We'll git our guns an' kill him. Ah'll kill him! Ah'll shoot him like a yellow dawg!"

Horatio stood up and caught Hoe's arm tightly and his face was terrible to see, but his voice was almost gentle. "Steady, son. We can't overtake him—but we'll be waiting when he comes back."

It was nearly noon, and bright sunshine was streaming under the half-drawn curtains when King regained consciousness. Horatio was sitting beside his bed, slumped forward wearily with his head in his hands. He had sent Young King to Florence for the doctor. The other boys and Ada were napping in their rooms.

"Ain't nuthin' but trouble, is Ah, Boss?"

For a moment, Horatio thought he imagined the hoarse whisper. He raised his head slowly. King was looking at him and smiling weakly.

Horatio felt numb with relief. He stared unbelievingly for a long time, then put out his hand and laid it gently on King's shoulder. "How are you feeling, old fellow?"

King's smile faded. He rolled his head from side to side. "Trouble, trouble, trouble," he said.

Horatio's throat tightened and he felt tears brim in his eyes. "Why did he do it, King? Why did he bother you?"

"He . . ." King stopped and closed his eyes. "Ah fell, Boss. Ah'm too ole—Ah jes' fell." His voice was very low.

Horatio shook his head slowly and stroked King's shoulder. "No, we know, old fellow," he said softly. "We'll see that he—"

He paused. "I'll call Ada and she'll fix you some broth." He started to rise.

King opened his eyes. "No, wait, Boss. Wait. Ah wanta tell yo'," he said weakly. He shut his eyes and lay quietly for a moment before he spoke again. "Yo' gotta lissen. He didn't know he had hurt me. Ah's jes' too ole. Dey was laughin' when dey rid off. Dey didn't know Ah was hurt. Dey was laughin'."

His voice was a whisper. "He war jes' a-showin' off. He didn't mean no real harm. Atter he fuss at me an' talk big 'bout yo', he say Ah sass him. He slap me across de face an' knock me off'n de bank. Dey didn't know Ah was hurt. Ah's jes' gittin' ole. Dey was laughin' when dey rid off. Ah heerd dem laughin'."

He paused again and lay quietly. After a while he shook his head weakly and there was wonder in his low whisper. "Dat watter jes' seem ter freeze mah laigs. Dey felt like ice. Ah couldn't git 'em under me. Ah tried, hard's Ah knowed how, but Ah jes' couldn't move mah laigs. Ah hollered. Ah hollered a lot, but nobody come. Nobody come an' Ah went ter sleep." His little sigh was very faint. "Ah jes' gittin' ole." He opened his eyes and looked at Horatio pleadingly. "Don't git in trouble 'counta me, Boss. Ah ain't neber caused yo' nuthin' 'cept trouble." He shook his head slowly and his low voice was almost a moan. "Trouble, trouble, trouble."

Horatio's throat was too tight to speak and his anger was long since spent. He could only look at him with tears falling down his cheeks.

The doctor was a quiet young man with wise, sad brown eyes. When he came from King's room and looked at their grave faces, he shook his head. "He's an old man, a very old man, and his heart is tired." He sighed. "There's nothing I can do right now. So far there are no signs of congestion but—" He shrugged.

Horatio's face was drawn. "Do you think he . . . ?"

The doctor shook his head slowly. "I don't know, Mister Tench." His voice was gentle. "You need rest yourself. Why don't you try to sleep?"

After the doctor left, Horatio stumbled up the hall and removed his boots and fell across his bed. He must have gone to sleep immediately.

It was mid-afternoon when he heard Ada awaken him. He raised his head quickly and when he saw her white face and trembling lips he knew what had happened. "Is he . . . ?"

Ada nodded and the tears in her eyes spilled down her cheeks. "Hoe was with him." She threw herself on the bed and buried her face in his shoulder. She shook with sobs. "Oh, Mister Tench, what can we do? What can we do!"

CHAPTER XXVII

KING dead! It was unbelievable. Horatio moved in a daze. He had to go to King's room and stand over that big figure stretched out so unnaturally quiet and still; he had to put out his hand and feel the chill on that familiar, beloved black face before he could grasp the truth.

He sat with his great bearded face in his hands and had the sobbing Hoe tell over and over again what had happened. He wanted every detail, an account of every moment. He tried to probe every last thought of this dear friend who had at last taken a journey without him.

There wasn't much to tell. Hoe had been sitting beside the bed and King was sleeping quietly. Suddenly he opened his eyes and tried to sit upright. Hoe leaned over him and put his hands on his shoulders and called his name. King seemed to relax then. He lay back and after a minute his face twisted with pain. He lay gasping for a while and the spasm seemed to pass. He sighed deeply and turned his head and smiled at Hoe. "Tell yo' Pa, Ah said not ter . . ." That was as far as he got. He sighed again and his tired old heart stopped.

"He . . . he didn't say anything else, son?"

"No, Pa."

"Didn't he . . . ?" Horatio stopped. He had asked that before. What was he trying to find out? What did he want to know? It was foolish. What could King possibly have said that would have added to forty-five years of loyalty and affection? King was his friend, his brother. He was lost without him. He held his head and great sobs wracked him.

He laid King out himself. He bathed and dressed him in his stiff, black town suit. He would allow no one to help. He had Bigab and Lafe take the wagon and go to Florence for a casket. He showed Young King and Hoe where to dig a grave in the little wooded vale near the Castle. It was the spot he wanted to be buried in himself. Ada was as dazed and crushed by grief as he was, but she set about to make arrangements for the funeral. She took the buggy and drove to Taylor's Chapel to ask young Parson Hicks to conduct services.

They all went away and left him in the silent Castle with his friend. How peaceful King looked. All his years, all the lines and marks of time seemed to have left his serene face. Except for the snow-white hair, he might have been the King he had met in General Jameson's warehouse so many years ago. No, there was a difference. For the first time in years he noticed the long, thin scar on King's cheek. He remembered a morning long ago when he sat in his study. The window was open and in the courtyard the boys were gathered about King while he carved them wooden guns. He heard Hoe's childish voice. "How did yo' get hurted on the face, King?"

He had smiled and lifted his head to hear better. There was a long pause, then King chuckled. "A young rooster gimme dat."

There was a chorus of amazement from the boys. Bigab asked, "How did he do it, King?"

"Wal, Ah'll tell yo' how it war," King said. "Dis heah rooster war purty young an' he didn't know who war his frens an' who warn't. Ah kinda made er mistake er tryin' ter clip his wings an', man o' man!—we went 'roun' an' 'roun' ever' which way fer a few minutes." He chuckled. "Yes, suh, we sho' did."

"Did yo' wring his neck, King?"

"Wring his neck? Lawd, no, chile!" King chuckled again. "Ah fin'lly got outside dat fence an' Ah said, 'Looky heah, big boy, yo' mind yo' bizness an' Ah'll mind mine.' Yes, suh! Ah say, 'Yo' stay on yo' side er de fence an' Ah'll stay on mine.' Atter dat, me'n dat rooster git erlong purty good—yes, suh, me'n dat rooster git ter be purty good frens."

Horatio gently touched the scar on that still face, then lowered his head and wept.

People from miles around came to King's funeral. Their buggies and wagons and saddle horses filled the courtyard. Some of them came out of curiosity. For years they had heard of the relationship between Old Man Tench and his nigger, and this was their chance to find out if the rumors were true. Some came because they wanted to see the old man who had knocked Captain Jeb Allison flat with a wooden milk pail. But many of them came because through the years they had come to admire the smiling King. Old Marius Henshaw was one of these. A buggy or a wagon seat would not accommodate his great bulk, so he had made the three-mile trip sitting in his split cane chair in the bed of a wagon. He looked at King's quiet face for a long time and shook his head sadly. "He war a good man. Not many come erlong like him, no matter wut color they is."

The parlor was already filled when Parson Hicks arrived. He was a slender little man with scraggly chin whiskers. His women parishioners said Parson Hicks was a sweet man, and it was a good description. He had a sweet, toothy smile. He almost never looked at anyone directly, but kept his eyes averted heavenward, as if in constant communication with the angels.

Horatio, Ada, and the boys were seated in the first row near the casket. Clucking sympathetically, he made his way to them and gave them each a damp handclasp. His sweet little smile was sad as he looked at Horatio. "Ah'm regretful, Brothah Tench, that Ah have to visit your home the first time undah such tragic circumstances. Ah pray, God willing, that ouah sorrow this day may vanish, but ouah friendship may be lasting."

Horatio said nothing. All night long he had sat beside King's casket and he was weary from lack of sleep and grief. Ada was clasping his arm tightly and she spoke for him. "We thank you for comin', Parson."

Parson Hicks moved to the casket and stood looking down, shaking his head sadly, then he turned and lifted his eyes. "Let us pray."

They recited the Lord's Prayer and Parson Hicks read a short passage from the Scriptures in his mild, sweet voice. He closed his Bible softly and looked about the room with a tender little smile. "Dearly Beloved," he said softly, "it does mah heart good to see so many of yo' heah today. It warms me to know so many of yo' have dropped yo' duties an' come heah to pay a last tribute to this white-headed ole nigrah daddy who has laid down his worldly burden of care an' toil." He shook his head sadly. "How it saddens us all to know that he died because of a thoughtless prank, but by yo' presence heah today yo' have shown that the actions of a few boys cannot brand a community. Yes, when Ah received the call to come an' conduct these sad services, Ah thought how very much it typifies the position of ouah glorious Southland today. Ah felt that Ah had received a sign—" he drew himself up proudly—"for tomorrah Ah will don the uniform of mah Southland an' join the Fo'th Alabamians as their chaplain. That is mah answer to the No'th—an' this gathering today is ouah answer to the No'th. Thoughtless we may sometimes be, but cruel nevah! This memory Ah shall carry with me. This is how we treat our nigrahs! This is ouah answer to charges that we mistreat ouah nigrahs!"

He gestured toward the casket and there was pride in his soft little smile. "This ole faithful servitor—this good ole white-headed nigrah daddy, how he could have answered them. Would that the breath could return to his faithful, toil-worn ole body. Would that he could rise an' say to them, 'Ah served mah massa well an' mah massa buried me from his own parlor.' Ah, what truths this white-headed ole daddy could tell if—"

"Hold!" Horatio's voice was as sharp and loud as a pistol shot. He had risen, trembling with rage. Parson Hicks took one look at his face and paled and licked his lips nervously. There was hate and disgust in Horatio's voice. "You came here to bury a man! This is no mule who fell in the traces in the barnyard! This is my dearest friend. You'll not stand over him and mouth your lies! You'll not stand there with a smile on your face and act lordly over a man who was worth six of you." Parson Hicks looked shocked. He swallowed hard and lowered his eyes. Horatio's lips curled with contempt. "You hypocrite! You soft little milksop! You stand there and read your religion and pray one moment, then turn with a smirk and deny it the next. You pray to your Lord to make it on earth as it is in Heaven. You read His words that He has gone to prepare mansions for us—Then you turn—aye, you turn, you hypocrite—and act superior to the murdered man who lies there because your skin is white and his skin is black. You call him a servant, you who've never done a day's work. Do you think he'll

be a servant to the likes of you in Heaven? Do you think your Lord
has one place for men whose skin is black and another for men
who are white! Answer me if you can! Tell me, you who know all
about the Lord and Heaven! If your Lord answers your prayers
and makes earth like Heaven, will black men be slaves? Are there
slaves in Heaven?" He was thundering in his fury. He walked
toward the casket. Parson Hicks shot him an alarmed glance and
shrank back, but Horatio ignored him. He put one hand on the
edge of the casket and turned to face the stilled crowd. His voice
was tight. "I'll tell you about this man—He was good and kind
and I loved him dearly. He was my brother and he was killed because he dared defend me. We worked together and sweated together and everything I have I owe to him. He was part of my
family and I thank God for it! You call him black—" he threw
back his head and glared at them—"aye, you call him black, but
he was as white as any of you because his whiteness was in his heart
and mind where it counted. Think of that—remember that, those
of you who hide your blackness under the skin you wear as if you
earned it instead of being born with it. Who gave you the right
to look down on him? Who gave you the right to judge a man by
his color? How could you know what went on in his heart and
mind? He was good! Aye, he was good—as good as any of you! I
loved him dearly. I . . . I will be lost without him." His voice
was ragged. He clenched his jaw and looked down at the floor a
moment, then lifted his head and glared at the white-faced Parson
Hicks. There was hate in his voice. "Get out! Get out of my house!
We have no need for the likes of you, you hypocrite!"

Parson Hicks drew himself up with all the dignity he could
muster and walked away. There was the sound of scraping feet.
Horatio turned. Some of the mourners had risen and were follow-
ing the Parson. Horatio snarled. "Leave! Get out! No one asked
you here! Get off my land!" Ada and the boys came and stood
by his side while most of the crowd marched from the room with
cold faces, leaving only old Marius Henshaw and a half-dozen
others. Horatio stood stiff and erect until the last person walked
from the room. He looked at those who remained, and his voice
was gentle. "Now we'll bury my friend."

CHAPTER XXVIII

IT SEEMED he also buried a part of himself. For days after King's funeral he was crushed. His great shoulders were bowed and his face was white and drawn. It was as if all his years had fallen on him at one time. He sat in his study for hours at a time, huge head slumped forward, staring into space. A half-dozen times a day he walked to the fresh mound in the little vale by the river and stood there with bowed head. His life had been surprisingly free of grief. It was no wonder that when it came, it found him defenseless.

Even more than King's death, his despondency brought gloom to the Castle. The boys walked quietly and talked in half-whispers. Ada tried to carry on as usual, but she was pale and her eyes were reddened from weeping. She tried to comfort him.

"King was old, Mister Tench. He had a full life. We got to remember that—We got to remember all of us have to go some-day."

He said nothing. He only looked at her. His eyes were full of pain. She lowered her head and pressed her lips tight and hurried from the room.

But his grief had not quenched his hate. It was still there—fierce, unreasoning. When he went to old Marius' store on the Saturday after King's funeral, the usual crowd was there, discussing secession. Horatio's face was set and cold when he entered. He ignored all his neighbors, even the few who nodded hesitantly.

One man tried to break the embarrassed lull. "Think thar's gonna be wah, Mistah Tench?" he asked affably.

Horatio looked at him steadily and his lips curled with contempt. "It's a matter that only interests fools." The man swallowed hard and his weak smile died. Silence hung heavy in the store until Horatio left.

Late that afternoon he was walking back to the Castle after visiting King's grave when he saw three horsemen, wearing stiff new Confederate gray uniforms, near the fence to the south pasture, looking over his yearlings. While he stood watching them with angry eyes, one of the men left his companions and rode up the lane toward the Castle. Horatio met them halfway. "Get off my land," he said. His eyes were blazing.

The soldier, a blond young man, reined up in surprise. His smile of greeting faded. "Ah jes' wanted to ast if them yearlin's are for sale, mistah," he said.

Horatio's chest was heaving with anger. "Not to the likes of you, they're not! Get off my land!"

The soldier flushed. "Yo' got no call to talk to me thataway." He looked at Horatio's angry face a moment, then shrugged and turned his horse.

Horatio stood in the middle of the lane, stiff with anger, until the soldier passed through the gate and rejoined his companions on the road.

Only one thing seemed to help him forget his grief and his bitterness. That was work. For the first time since the boys were grown, he put on his heavy work clothes and gave them a hand with the chores. And, as always when he was troubled, he did the work of three men.

He and the boys were building a new corral fence that bright day in mid-April when the news came. Little Sammy Dowd, whose father ran the cotton gin at Shoal's Bluff, came galloping up the lane on a heavy old plow horse which was flecked with lather and heaving from exertion. Sammy's eyes were bright with excitement. "It's war!" he shouted. "They's done started fightin' at Fort Sumter!"

Horatio's face hardened, but when he spoke his voice was calm. "How do you know, son?"

Sammy wheeled his horse importantly. "Pa jes' got the news from Florence. We'uns took Fort Sumter away from 'em."

The boys exchanged glances and Bigab drawled. "Where's that at, Sammy?"

"Caroliny," Sammy said. He was a little abashed at the calmness of these big men. Everywhere else along the river road people had whooped and grinned at his announcement.

"Well . . . well, Ah gotta spread the news aroun'," he said. He thumped his puffing old horse in the ribs with his bare heels and galloped off.

Lafe spoke slowly. "If Sammy ain't careful, that durn ole hawss will be the first thing to die in this heah war." No one smiled. Their faces were thoughtful as they turned back to the fence.

They worked in silence for a few minutes before Young King spoke. "What do yo' reckon we ought to do, Pa?"

Horatio straightened slowly. His voice was stern. "Do? We'll do nothing. I'm no slaveholder."

Young King's voice was calm. "Maybe that's all the more reason we should do something, Pa."

Horatio looked at him coldly. "What do you mean?"

Young King held a post-hole digger. He leaned on it and rubbed the smooth handle against his cheek thoughtfully. "Well, if we don't hold with slavery, Ah reckon this puts us on the side of the No'th. Maybe we ought to figure on . . ."

Horatio interrupted him. His voice was thick with anger. "What makes you think we have a side in this! Because fools fight, do we have to mix in?"

Young King flushed but his voice was still calm. "This thing is bigger'n that, Pa. Maybe they'll make . . ."

"Make you! Make you!" Horatio's voice was sharp with contempt. "You are a free man and nobody can force you to fight for anything. No one! Do you hear me? You're no lackey who has to go running off to fight for a lot of lily-handed men who've never done an honest day's work in their lives. They brought this war on! Let them fight for themselves!"

Young King lowered his eyes before Horatio's glare. "Maybe we can't stay out of it as easy as all that," he said quietly. "When it rains everywhere, you're bound to get wet."

Lafe snorted. "Not if yo' stay in the house where yo' belong."

Young King ignored him. He looked at Horatio's angry face for a moment, then shrugged and turned back to the fence. Horatio continued to glare at him. "All your life," he said harshly, "I've taught you that you don't have to jump to the bidding of any man. You're free! You don't have to fight on anybody's orders." He turned on the other boys. "I've taught all of you that."

Lafe grimaced. "Yo' know how Ah feel about this, Pa."

Hoe spoke slowly. "There ain't but one soldier Ah aim to shoot an' he ain't around yet."

Young King had not turned. He was digging a post hole but the back of his neck and his ears were a deep red. Bigab looked at him and his face was troubled. Then he sighed and picked up a hammer and turned to the fence. His short laugh was almost a snort. "It ain't even worth talkin' about. Those durn fools ain't goin' to fight to amount to nothin'. They'll be home afore we git this fence whitewashed."

But they didn't come home. All through that summer and fall and long winter, more and more men rode away. Men who sweated over a few rocky acres for a bare living went as quickly as planters whose fortunes and way of life were at stake. Horatio could not understand these men. They rode up the river road on bony, harness-galled old nags and laughed and slapped their lean thighs and called it a rich man's war and a poor man's fight. But still they came. They passed day after day, night after night, all that year. Maybe it was as old Marius had said one afternoon when they stood on the porch of his store watching a long column straggle past. "Look at 'em, jes' look at the pore fools! They don't know nothin' 'cept thar's a fight an' somebody tole them they oughta git in it." He settled back in his chair. "Don't let folks tell yo' that menfolks don't like war, Mistah Tench. If they didn't like it, we'uns wouldn't have no more. Wars give 'em a chancet ter quit sweatin' in the fields or stop clerkin' in some big ole dark store. They gits ter leave aller their troubles at home an' strut aroun' in purty uniforms an' bust up things an' feel the manhood arisin' in their bones. They likes it an' that's a fack. Atter they git a bellyful of it, they yowl aroun' 'bout how they hate war—but jes' leave 'em alone for a few years an' off they'll go agin."

A horseman left the column and rode up to the porch. He was

a youth, not more than sixteen. The soft down on his cheeks had never been touched by a razor. He grinned at them. "Got any terbaccy fer sale?"

Old Marius grunted. "Might. Whar yo' headin' fer, son?"

The youth threw back his shoulders. "Up to Decatur to jine up."

Old Marius' voice was mild. "Wha'cha wanta fight fer, son?"

The boy looked surprised, then grinned wisely to show he could understand a joke.

"No, Ah means it," Marius said. "Wha'cha really gonna fight fer?"

The boy scowled. "God amighty, mistah, yo' think Ah'm gonna let ole Abe put niggers to lordin' ovah me?"

Horatio turned away, cold with anger and disgust.

He thought of that youth many times that year, as more and more men rode or walked up the dusty river road past the Castle. He wondered about him and the hundreds like him who moved toward the battlefields in a steady stream, laughing and spitting tobacco juice, damning the Yankees and the government that had been given them by Washington and Franklin and Jefferson.

He tried to ignore them, but their shouts and their laughter and the tramp of their feet awakened him during the night. He tried to forget the war and live on his land in peace. It was impossible. He was reminded of it constantly, in a hundred different ways. He received top prices for his hogs and cattle that fall, but he was paid in crisp new currency which had been printed by the new government in Richmond. He had a strong box stacked with it, but it would buy nothing. Partly it was because people—even those who loudly proclaimed their loyalty to the Confederacy—distrusted it, but mostly because nobody seemed to have anything left to sell. In the spring of 1862 he and the boys scoured the countryside but could not find any stock to buy and fatten for the fall market, so he was left with only his horses. It was just as well. He had a great supply of fodder and a new crop on the way, but corn was too scarce to feed to cattle and hogs. They ate cornbread with all their meals. Flour had disappeared even though it brought five hundred dollars a barrel. Tea was five dollars a pound and boots sold at twenty-five dollars a pair. Shoes were selling at a hundred and fifty dollars a pair and beef was three dollars a pound.

The high prices infuriated Horatio, but he realized that he was fortunate to have the money to pay them. Poor people along the river road were grinding corncobs to get the last particle of corn. They grubbed for sassafras roots to boil for tea and they made coffee from a mixture of roasted acorns and chicory.

Bigab's remark about the corral fence took on a new meaning. It had been whitewashed once, but they all knew that the men would come marching home before it received another coat. Old Marius and other storekeepers not only had run out of lime for whitewash, they were out of nails and wire and needles and thread and cloth and everything else which had come down the river from the North. There was no need for Horatio or his family to leave their land to go to the store or to town. So they lived completely apart.

CHAPTER XXIX

BULL RUN. Fort Henry. Fort Donelson. The Peninsula Campaign. The *Virginia* and the *Monitor*. Men were straggling up the river road from the other direction now. They plodded along wearily. They were gaunt and hollow-eyed and their filthy gray uniforms hung in rags and stank. Some wore dirty, blood-crusted bandages, and occasionally one had an empty sleeve or a flapping trousers leg.

They were beggars. Ada could not bring herself to turn them away. Horatio's eyes would grow cold when he saw them coming up the lane, but Ada set her shoulders defiantly and gave them a bite of food or old clothing. They were grateful for anything— a piece of cold cornbread, a plate of boiled cabbage, or a pinch of powdered charcoal for the dysentery which racked them. After a while they learned that not all these men had been discharged or were returning home because they were wounded. Many were deserters. They learned to spot these fugitives almost at a glance. They whined just a little too much and spoke a little too vividly of the horrors they had seen. And, almost always, they came on horseback because they were fleeing and not marching home.

Horatio was filled with contempt for these men. He thought all of those who passed were fools, but despite his stern face, he was too much of a fighter himself not to give those who had fought with honor a grudging respect. But he could not feel charitable toward a man who came begging on horseback. He nailed a sign on the front gate: "Horsemen Pass By."

It failed to stop the two men who came in May. Horatio was in the stable filling the foaling stalls with fresh straw when he heard Bigab call. He walked out into the sunlight to find the boys gathered around two men on horseback. One of the men was fat and bearded. The other was a thin, mild-looking little man with a receding chin. Both wore dust-stained blue suits. They had silver badges pinned on their lapels and heavy cavalry pistols strapped about their waists.

There was sarcasm in Bigab's voice. "These heah men come to take us to war, Pa."

The fat man leaned back and bounced with laughter. "Ain't that bad, Mistah Tench. Ain't that bad a'tall." His voice was affable. "Ah'm Jere Mackay, Confederate marshal for this heah district, an' this air mah deputy, Hiram Turner."

Horatio nodded slightly but did not speak.

Marshal Mackay shifted sideways in his saddle. "Bein' out in the country an' all, Ah know yo' folks jes' ain't heard 'bout the conscription law that was passed las' month. Jes' a pure oversight, Ah know. Lots er folks ain't heard 'bout it. Wal, me'n Hiram was ridin' pas' this mawnin' an' Ah thought Ah'd jes' drop by an' save yo' boys a trip to town."

Horatio felt a little chill inside him. His voice was stern. "What do you mean—conscription?"

Marshal Mackay laughed jovially. "Wal, ole Jeff Davis an' the boys up thar decided they warn't gittin' enough men, Ah reckon. We gotta git a record of aller men 'tween eighteen and fo'ty-five an' some of 'em air gonna haf to start soldierin'."

For a moment Horatio stared at him unbelievingly, then his face became hard and grim. "How can you expect men to fight for something they don't believe in? How can anyone be made to fight?"

Marshal Mackay shifted uneasily and stroked his beard. His voice was conciliatory. "Wal, yo' got a p'int thar, Mistah Tench, an' that's a fack. But Ah don't make the laws, Mistah Tench. Ah jes' try to carry 'em out the bes' way Ah know how." He chuckled. "But, pshaw, ain't nothin' to it—ain't much chancet yo' boys'll haf to go. Yo' got enough good work to keep 'em busy heah. Thar's exemptions fer overseers an' sech, an' if they'll jes' sign up, Ah reckon—"

Horatio's voice was ragged with anger. "They'll sign nothing!"

There was a long silence. Marshal Mackay looked down at his saddle and Deputy Turner blinked nervously. Finally Marshal Mackay spoke. His voice was soothing. "Now, Mistah Tench, ain't no use of yo' actin' this way. Ain't nobody bein' conscripted. We jes' want to git a record. Why, it ain't even wuth talkin' 'bout." He looked at the boys and made his voice hearty. "Air it, boys? Yo'll sign up an' save an ole man a lotta fuss an' bother, won't yo'?"

There was another silence. The boys exchanged glances, then looked at Horatio. His eyes were fixed on Marshal Mackay. It was Bigab who spoke. "If you wanta get mah name, Ah'll write it down for yo'—but yo' can set down beside it that Ah don't aim to go to war. An' yo' can send it straight to Jeff Davis!"

Marshal Mackay chuckled and pulled a sheaf of papers from his breast pocket. "Ah thinks that's fair enough. Ah reckon ole Jeff won't be pleased none, but—" he chuckled again—"Ah done mah dooty anyhow."

Hoe looked at Horatio. "Should we do it, Pa?"

Horatio's face was cold. "You are men. Do as you like." He turned and walked back into the stable.

Only Ada seemed upset over the incident. When she heard what had happened, she looked at Horatio anxiously. "But what will they do, Mister Tench?"

He smiled and patted her shoulder. "What can they do, Ada? They can't force a man to fight. The boys will just refuse to go."

"But what if they try to make them, Mister Tench?"

Horatio sighed and shook his head. "But what good would it do for them to take men who don't want to fight, Ada? There are enough fools who are willing to go. They can't be bothered about four boys out of so many."

He was wrong. It was less than a month later when Marshal Mackay and Deputy Turner appeared. Horatio was in the courtyard when they rode up. He flushed with anger when he saw them. "What do you want?"

Marshal Mackay kept his voice jovial. "Wal, Mistah Tench, Ah jes' . . ."

"What do you want!"

Marshal Mackay's grin flickered out. He fumbled in his saddle-bags and withdrew four envelopes. His voice was apologetic. "Ah'm a-feered yo' boys done been called, Mistah Tench. Ah reckon thar ain't much . . ."

Horatio snatched the envelopes and glared at him. "Get off my land! Get off and don't ever come back!"

"Now, looky heah, Mistah . . ."

"Get off!"

Deputy Turner had already turned his horse and was anxious to be off. Marshal Mackay turned slowly and blustered. "Yo' bettah take heed to those orders—or thar'll be trouble." Horatio walked toward him and he put his horse in motion. He called over his shoulder. "Yo' can git in trouble fer this."

Ada and the boys had heard the voices in the courtyard. They were standing at the sitting room door when Horatio strode inside. Without a word he handed the boys the envelopes. They ripped them open without a change in expression. Hoe handed his induction notice to Horatio. It ordered him to report to Decatur in three days for mobilization. Horatio threw it aside. His face was a mask of rage. "Well, do you intend to go?"

Bigab wadded his induction notice in his big hands. His voice was harsh. "No, we ain't goin'. Thar ain't nobody in Alabama big enough to make us. If it's a fight they want, they won't have to go up No'th to find it!"

Lafe and Hoe nodded grimly, but Young King stood quietly. Horatio looked at him levelly. "Well?"

Young King began to fold his induction notice very carefully. His voice was thoughtful. "We don't have no choice. We're bound to fight."

"No!" Ada stepped forward quickly. Her face was pale. "You'll not fight. You'll not mix in trouble that don't concern us."

Young King put his arm around her shoulders. "But it does concern us, Ma." He looked defiantly at his brothers and Horatio. "We got to fight. Ah knew we would all the time. The only question all along has just been what we'd fight for."

"Ah'm goin' to fight for mah rights," Bigab said hotly.

Young King's voice was edged with scorn. "Yo' don't have no rights in this."

Horatio's voice was sharp. "What gave you that idea?"

Young King faced him calmly. "You did," he said. "You an' King gave me that idea."

Hoe spoke angrily. "He never did! Pa never said no such thing and neither did King!"

Young King's eyes flashed. "They didn't have to say nothin'! We knew. From the time we were children we knew. We knew Pa had scars on him he got fightin' for King. An' we fought for him, too—every day of our lives we fought! Ah fought a hundred times because mah name was King an' the rest of you fought because the boys at school snickered an' said dirty things because King sat at our table an' was one of us." He paused and looked at their set faces. "Almost the first thing Ah remember was Bigab fightin' Tom Isbell down by the river one day because he called us nigger-lovers. Ah couldn't been more'n four or five at the time but Ah still remember how proud Ah was of Bigab. And later on when Ah fought mahself, Ah was proud ever'time Ah did it. Ah was proud ever'time any of us fought—right up to the day Pa stood over King's coffin an' told off the neighbors." He turned on Bigab. "You didn't yell about your rights when it came time to fight for King. How come you're doin' it now?"

Bigab didn't answer, but Hoe spoke sullenly. "It's not the same. King was different."

Young King's lips curled. "If that's what you thought, it proves you never struck an honest blow in your life!"

Hoe's freckled face paled with anger. "Yo' can't talk to me thataway! Ah'll show yo' who . . ."

"Stop it!" Horatio glared at them. "There'll be none of that!" He turned on Young King. "Hold your tongue! You have no right to sit in judgment over your brothers."

Young King flushed under Horatio's gaze but his voice was even. "Ah'm not tryin' to sit in judgment, Pa. Ah'm tryin' to tell the truth. Sayin' King was different makes it sound like he was a pet hound. He wasn't different at all. He was a man an' we fought because he deserved to be treated like a man. We couldn't be honest an' do nothin' else. The minute we were born men instead of hawgs we lost all right to lay in a corner and think of nobody 'cept ourselves."

Some of the anger had gone from Horatio's voice. "This doesn't have anything to do with our feeling for King, son. This is war."

Young King's face was intense. "But it does have to do with King, Pa! It has everythin' to do with him. An Ah know it's war. It's our war!"

"That ain't the way Ah see it," Lafe said.

Young King turned on him. "Ah know you don't. None of you see it that way, an' that's where you're wrong. All of you! You seem to think that all of a sudden we're bein' made to take sides in this thing. That's not the way it is at all. We don't have to join in with nobody. We picked our side a long time ago. What's happened now is that folks have joined in with us." He hesitated. "Ah'm ashamed of mahself. Ah'm ashamed of all of us! Ah'm ashamed we waited until we got our backs pushed up against a wall before we got stirred up enough to talk about fightin'. The way we've been actin' reminds me of the fox cub we caught up on the hill when we were little. When we used to stake him out he would dig a hole an' bury the chain we put around his neck. Ever'time he covered that chain with dirt he thought he was shet of it. But when he tried to run away, the chain used to snap tight an' throw him a-windin'. He couldn't run away—he couldn't run away no more'n we can run away. Ever since we toted King out of this house an' buried him we been actin' like we didn't have no more need to stand up an' fight for what we knew was right. We been actin' like when we covered King that we'd thrown dirt on all that we had been taught was good an' proper—all the things we used to be proud to fight for.

"Well, we're findin' out it's not as easy as all that. We've been pulled up with a jerk. We deserve to have the stuffin's knocked out of us!" He looked at Horatio. "You're to blame as much as anybody, Pa. That day you jumped me out in the corral, Ah couldn't answer you. But Ah can now because Ah've studied on it an' Ah know where you've been wrong. You said we were free an' could do as we pleased. Well, that wasn't right! You was offerin' us somethin' you couldn't give. You forgot that nobody's free to run away when it comes time to fight for what's right. Bein' free means a man's got to fight! He's got to look his duties an' his responsibilities an' his future right square in the face. An' even if you could make us a gift of the things you wanted—how do you know we would be satisfied with them? Maybe we want somethin' more'n what you've got! Maybe we want somethin' better, just like you had to go out an' find somethin' better than what was offered you!"

He turned to his brothers. "You got to fight now! One way or the other, you got to make up your minds. You got to load your guns an' stand out there in the courtyard an' shoot it out with the men who come to take you off—or you got to run away to the hills an' dig a hole an' hide until this thing is over. Would you call that bein' free? Would you be any freer if they shot you down in the courtyard an' you didn't die for nobody but yourself? Well, Ah'm not goin' to do that! When Ah fight, Ah'm goin' to fight for something worthwhile an' if Ah dies, Ah want to die for something worthwhile!

"Ah'm goin' to fight for the things Ah was raised to believe in. Ah'm goin' to fight just like Ah used to fight for King—except that this time Ah'm goin' to help tear the cause of our trouble out by the roots. There won't ever have to be another King when Ah get done fightin'! You better thank God that it's still not too late for you to get in on the same fight! You better thank God that we all still got a chance. Ah'm not sure we deserve it!"

He stood looking at them, two bright splotches of color high on his cheeks, then he spoke slowly. "There was a man named Wendell Phillips who made a speech right after they hanged old John Brown. Ah never have forgotten it. Ah cut it out of the paper an' carried it in mah pocket until it fell apart. Ah know every word of what he said. He said it wasn't true that old John Brown was a traitor. It was Virginia, the state that hanged him, that was a traitor. It was a traitor because it claimed to be a government an' that was a lie. Virginia wasn't a government because it didn't speak for all the people. It didn't give every man who lived in it the same chance to earn a livin' or the same chance to live a decent life.

"Phillips said Virginia wasn't nothin' except a pirate ship because it had the laws of a pirate ship. He said that John Brown was sailin' God's seas and he had a right to sink every pirate he met. It didn't make no difference that John Brown was just one man because in God's world there's no such thing as majorities. There's no such thing as minorities. Just one man on God's side is a majority.

"Well, there's ten other states joined in with Virginia now an'

that's the government that says we have to fight for it. Ah'd rather
die first! Ah will die first—but if Ah do they won't have the satisfaction of writin' me down as a coward. They'll have to call me
an enemy . . . an' they'll have to remember me the same way
they do old John Brown."

He drew himself up and looked at his brothers. "Ah'm goin' to
Decatur—but Ah'm goin' to keep goin' until Ah get up No'th.
You can do as you like—but if you want, we'll ride together."

There was a long silence. Nobody moved. Young King stood
facing them, feet planted wide apart, face flushed and jaw set
challengingly. After a long time Bigab spoke softly. "Ah'll ride
with yo', Ah reckon."

Lafe nodded slowly. "Ah'll go."

Hoe's eyes had never left Young King's face. Now he bit at
his bottom lip and looked down at the floor. Something almost
like bewilderment shadowed his freckled face. "Ah . . . Ah don't
. . ." He shuffled his feet and raised his head. "Would . . . would
yo' do it, Pa?"

Horatio had not moved. He was still looking at Young King,
and on his bearded face and in his eyes there was a look of great
emptiness.

"Would yo', Pa?"

Slowly, very slowly, Horatio turned and looked at Ada. She
was still and tense with one small hand at her breast. Her face
was white and drawn. Their eyes met and held for a long time.

Finally Horatio looked down. His voice was heavy. "Yes, son,
I would go."

Ada's face seemed to melt. Tears came to her eyes and her lips
trembled, but she lifted her head and thrust out her firm little
chin. Her voice was almost fierce. "Ah would be proud to go!"
she said.

They left at the first light of dawn. Ada kissed them and wept
softly, and for the first time since they were children, Horatio
embraced each one and held him close. And to each he whispered,
"I'm sorry, son—I'm sorry."

He and Ada stood waving while they rode from the courtyard,
then turned silently and, arm in arm, climbed the stairs to the
roof and watched their sons ride down the lane. It was a long

time before Horatio spoke. His voice was sad. "I failed them, Ada."

Ada held his arm tight. "No, you didn't, Mister Tench. You didn't. You raised them free to fight—an' you taught them to fight for what's right. Nobody could do no more." She clutched his arm tighter. "Look, Mister Tench—look—Young King is leadin' them. He's the baby an' he's leadin' them." She lifted her head and there was pride in her voice. "Young King will look after them."

At that moment the morning sun peeked over the horizon like a great fiery ball, and with startling suddenness the last lingering gloom of night disappeared from the land. The river became a sparkling silver ribbon and sunlight danced on the green and brown fields. From far off they heard the cooing of a dove and a mockingbird began to trill in the little vale near the river.

Suddenly Horatio realized tears stood in his eyes. He put his arm around Ada's slim shoulders and pulled her close. "Yes, Ada," he said softly, "King will watch over them."

THE END